The Bermuda Covenant

VJ Nash

Thank You

To my family for their support; to Heather and Rob, whose feedback was invaluable and inspiring; to Indie author Mark Daydy for his time, generosity and wisdom; to David Gaughran and Tammi Labrecque for steering my way; and to my dogs, Dinky and Popcorn, for regularly coming to check on my progress.

ABOUT ME

As someone who is Canadian by birth, Hungarian/Yorkshire by blood and brought up in the south of England, it's fair to say I've never quite fitted in. I didn't help my already slim chances of fitting in by becoming a DeadHead in 1983. Nobody knew who the Grateful Dead were in rural Surrey in the 1980s, so I had to follow that obsession all alone. I have always had a love of horror and spent much of my childhood terrifying myself by reading books and watching films that I really shouldn't have. It probably didn't help that my grandparents' ancient house (it pre-dates the founding of the United States by 200 years) was undoubtedly haunted. Neither did the fact that all the sensible adults in my life had stories to tell of bizarre, unexplained happenings they'd experienced. One of my Hungarian aunts – a reasonable and intelligent person – was even convinced that werewolves and vampires actually existed back in 'the old country'. So, it's hardly surprising I'm writing horror. And there's a lot more where this came from.

Contents

Chapter One

So Much To Do...

"And so little time..."

That must be what's going through the head of the ageing man bustling out of the back door of the large mock Tudor country house. He's in such a hurry that he hasn't noticed the back door hasn't shut properly behind him. Too late! He's already halfway down the gravel path to the double garage. His hair is starting to ditch the grey and turn white, but he's not carrying any extra weight, looks fit and moves easily for his seventy years on the planet. But his face tells a different story. It looks old. No, more than that, it looks haggard. Once it was undoubtedly handsome, with quick brown eyes, an intelligent brow, a well-defined, clean jaw and aquiline nose. Now the cheeks are hollow and mottled with four days of stubble, the hair is a mess, and his eyes are sunken and surrounded by dark brown circles of exhaustion. He looks like he hasn't slept in a week and yet his determined movements show that he's either a superman, able to ride sleep deprivation easily, or that he's got a final burst of energy before the inevitable collapse.

Whatever the truth, he's not dressed for the weather. The light chinos and polo shirt are not sensible choices in the gathering gloom of a late afternoon at the end of January - even in the south of England. And that's where he is, deep in the wooded heart of Surrey. The house, with its vast, perfectly manicured back lawn, is nestled amidst a forest of high trees. Their bare branches are clattering in the chill breeze as the man hurries on. His name is David Kidd and he's a retired nuclear engineer. A clever man, but clearly not clever enough to have avoided something bad. He is distracted and muttering to himself,

"Got to hurry! No time, no time... they could be here any minute."

He's well spoken, but is clearly at the end of his rope. As he approaches the garage, he produces a key fob from his pocket and presses a button. The garage door starts to rise and he times it so that he can enter without breaking stride. Another press of the button and the door begins to lower with a metallic clatter, amplified by the concrete floor and breeze block walls. Before the door is down, he's crossed the garage to the light switch and two sets of bright, overhead strip lights blink into action.

As is so often the case, it's clear that this garage is not for storing cars – the fact that David's black Citroen C6 is on the driveway being decorated by birds is proof of that – no, this is a serious workshop. The entire back wall is hung with tools. Everything has its place in this meticulously neat display. Beneath them is a long, solid workbench and this too is the full width of the garage. The work surface is two-inch-thick solid oak and has clearly defined workstations. At one end there is a lathe, at the other there is a large wooden vice. There are two metal vices set about four feet either side of the centre of the bench. Other tools for working wood, metal and electronics have their own places around the garage. Only two things seem out of place in this well-ordered world. The first is a diesel generator, which has been placed under one of the two high, narrow windows so that an exhaust pipe can be run up to the window and out. Unlike almost everything else, this looks improvised and hurried. In this neat little world, a window left open for a pipe to run out of it is sloppy. Very sloppy. The other thing is the heavy, metal chair that has been bolted into the floor about six feet from the generator. It has solid-looking arms and legs, but the seat has been replaced with nothing more than canvas strapping in a sort of rough mesh. A switch has been fitted to the right arm of the chair and a set of wires runs down the outside of the chair leg and across the floor to a box on the workbench. It is in the electronic section of the bench, next to the soldering iron stand. Wires connect the box to the generator. Under the chair and also bolted to the floor are two small metal stands. These curious features aside, this is a place of serious work and from the way David is moving, it is clear that some more serious work is about to be done.

David is working quickly, but methodically to set something up. He turns on the generator, which starts chugging away and, even with the exhaust piped out the window, the acrid smell of diesel fumes spreads throughout the space. He goes to the box on the bench, fiddles with something, seems satisfied and leaves it. Now he picks up a curious looking contraption from the top of the generator. It looks like an athletic cup or cricket box with leather straps to step through and attach it to the body. But it's what's inside that's strange – two mini crocodile clips have been set inside and their wires run out of a hole in the front of the cup and into the box of tricks on the workbench. David takes the contraption across to the chair, carefully laying out the wires behind him. He leaves it on the ground next to the chair and hurries back to the workbench.

"Come on, David! Keep moving. It's been six weeks – they're bound to realise what's happened. Got to do this before they get here," he says to himself. He's worried and keeps glancing at his watch. He must get this done!

He leans down, opens a drawer and takes out... a sawn-off shotgun. And then another one. In rural Surrey, these are not normal things to be found in a garage. He cracks one open, confirms that the shells are inside, closes it and places it on the workbench, then goes through the same process with the other. Satisfied, he takes them to the chair, where he kneels down and fixes one to each stand under the chair. The barrels are just inside the chair legs, pointing up at about a seventy-five-degree angle. He moves quickly back to the bench and takes two lengths of thick fishing line, which he runs to the chair. Kneeling, he carefully attaches the looped end of one line around the trigger, then runs the line around the back of the trigger guard. He does the same for the other shotgun. Once done, David hurries back to the bench, takes the other end of each line and attaches them to a weighted contraption on the edge of the workbench, which is also wired into the electrical box. There are two weights, one for each line, and it's clear that when the weights drop, the attached lines will pull the triggers and things will end very badly for whoever is sitting in the chair.

"Yes, yes!" the words come out like a snake hissing and David runs a hand through his dripping hair. He is sweating in spite of the cold and his unseasonal clothing choice. This is tension sweat – sour and unpalatable.

David stops and looks at the setup. He's running through the process in his head. Yes, that goes to that, then that, yes that's in place, then that, then finally... yes. That's it. All done except... he opens another drawer in the workbench and takes out four cable ties, a thick leather belt and a tube of superglue. He takes them over to the chair and sets them carefully on the seat. He straightens up and takes one last moment to look around him. He has some fond memories in here, but then his face clouds and crumples at other thoughts - hundreds of them, thousands – horrible, dreadful thoughts, memories that he can never erase. He starts to take off his shirt, then stops.

"Idiot!" he says angrily, "You'd forget your own head if it wasn't stuck on..." and he goes back to the bench, takes a pencil from the neat cup of pencils on the surface, pulls over a pad of post-it notes and writes on the top one,

"I deserve this", then signs it.

Now the time has come, he hurries towards it. At the chair, he first kneels to take the safety catches off the shotguns, then strips himself naked, throwing his clothes away across the room as fast as he can. He takes up the athletic support and carefully puts his legs through the leather straps. He holds the athletic cup with its crocodile clips in front of his balls. He hasn't been looking forward to this bit. He knows that it will be simultaneously painful and fiddley. The process doesn't disappoint. He opens up the jaws of the first clip and sets them next to his scrotum. Damned thing's retracted in the cold.

"Bollocks!" he curses, not registering the irony, then he gives his balls a good rub to warm them up. That's better – a bit more play now. Again, he positions the sharp, metal jaws of the clip and pinches some loose scrotum between his other fingers. He takes a deep breath and slowly clamps the clip onto his skin. His breath hisses out of him.

"Jeeesus!"

Oh yes, that hurt. That's brought a tear to the old eye, but it doesn't stop him. He reaches for the second clip, pinches a section skin and slowly releases the sharp little teeth to bite into the wrinkles of his scrotum. The problem is, it's tricky in the athletic cup. The skin around the first clip is already oozing small drops of blood, and sweat is breaking out across his body. His fingers slip and the crocodile clip snaps shut.

"Fuck! Jesus, fucking... shit!"

The teeth of the clip have torn across the delicate skin and now it's bleeding. Worse, the clip itself isn't attached and he knows he's got to try it again. His fingers are shaking now, but he sets his jaw and delicately clamps the crocodile clip to a good scruff of scrotum. His face reveals exactly how sharp and unpleasant this is. He takes a couple of long, deep breaths. Phase one complete.

He reaches back onto the seat of the chair and grabs the tube of super-glue, carefully opens the lid and squeezes a generous amount all over his shaved crotch. He adds a load to the rim of the athletic cup and pushes it onto his groin. He holds it for far longer than the ten seconds the adverts always said it needed. And now it's stuck fast. He throws the tube of glue away and gingerly takes the cable ties and the belt off the chair and eases onto it. Every move is causing sharp twinges, but he knows that he isn't even in the foothills of pain yet. He runs the belt around the back of the chair and loosely fastens it across his waist. Then he slowly attaches cable ties around each ankle and the chair legs, so that his legs are on the inside of them.

"Jeees!"

Yes, that's tweaking those crocodile clips! But as he straightens up, that takes the pressure off. Now he attaches his legs to the chair with the remaining cable ties at the point just below his knees, which are a couple of inches in front of the barrels of the two shotguns.

Once he's done it, he tries to move his legs – stuck solid and in a perfect position for the guns. That's good. He tightens the leather belt holding him to the back of the chair until it's uncomfortable. He tries to move his body. No play. That's good, too. Now comes the clever bit. Around each of the arms of the chair, two cable ties have already been loosely attached.

He slips his right hand through two of them, positions one at his wrist and one at his elbow and draws them tight with his left hand. He repeats the process for his left arm. Without the use of his right hand, he struggles to get the upper tie all the way back to the elbow. He can only edge it halfway up his forearm. He looks at it with annoyance. At least the one at the left wrist is exactly where he wants it. He heaves a sigh and decides that he can't let the perfect be the enemy of the good and leans down painfully to pull the cable ties tight with his teeth. The wrist one is great – he'll never get out of that. He sits and lets out a long breath, and stares at the electrical box on the workbench. Has he done everything right? Will it work, or will he be found in this humiliating position? Only one way to find out. He looks down at the switch next to his right index finger. He knows that once he flicks that switch, there's no going back. Once engaged, the machine can't be turned off. At least, not from the chair. His eyes, so deeply sunk into his face by exhaustion and a host of hideous emotions, are staring straight ahead. They aren't seeing the neatly laid out garage with this ingenious little set up that's a bit like a very dark Heath Robinson contraption. No, those hollow eyes are staring into the screaming abyss of vicious acts and abhorrent behaviour that have been the last thirty years of his life. Tears come. Not for him, but for those he has harmed. He wishes more than anything that he could take it all back, wishes he could do something to make it all right... wait! What's that? A car? Dammit! Time to act. He flicks the switch.

The result is instantaneous and quite spectacular. David Kidd is convulsed by a burst of electricity that has him pulling at his bonds and trying to arch away from the pain, but he is held fast. The burst lasts for ten seconds and then stops. His head drops and the sweat is beading all over his slender body. He is puffing.

"Fuck!"

That was more painful than he'd expected. Seconds tick by and he knows that just when he's got his breath back...

Bam!

The electricity has him writhing again, this time he's groaning through it. Then it stops after ten seconds and he flops again. Twenty seconds later and it starts again. And again, and again.

Before the torture continues, a little background...

David Kidd has been a keen sportsman – mostly racquet sports, but also running. He knows that for him, the first five minutes of a run are always the worst and that after that, he can more or less block out the pain unless he has to really exert himself. He has run a few marathons, so he has an intimate knowledge of his pain threshold. Therefore, when he designed his little box of tricks, he had to be sure that he couldn't get used to the pain. His solution was to randomise the duration and level of current after the first five minutes. The current would never be enough to kill him, but it would cause him unspeakable pain and after the amuse-bouche of those first five minutes, he would never know what would come next or when. And that would be when the real fun started.

That fun is about to start...

Sure enough, the first five minutes have been regular and he has clearly got used to it to some extent. Those first five minutes are now up. David Kidd wonders when the next burst of electricity will come. How powerful will it be? How much pain will it...

The force of the shock jolts his whole body at once and the high-pitched scream lasts for the full twenty seconds of the current. When the electricity releases its grip, he falls limp. He is sweating heavily now, but before he can even gather himself, he's convulsed again. This is only a short one and not as bad. There is stillness in the garage, save for the sweating figure on the chair. God, he'd forgotten how bloody weird electricity feels when it's running through you. But there was more to this. His placement of the electrical clips is making the pain very personal and horribly intimate. It's like...

His long, single syllable cry of pain is drawn out over fifteen seconds as the burst of enveloping agony surges through him and just keeps going and going and going, then stops.

"Fuck!" and now he's laughing and crying at the same time. He has a moment of clear thought where he pats himself on the back for taking a large dose of laxatives yesterday, not eating today and then flushing out whatever might be left up there with a hose ten minutes before leaving the house. Otherwise, he'd've shat himself and he doesn't want that humiliation. Likewise, he hasn't drunk anything all day and he relieved himself prior to kick off, so there should be no chance of pissing himself. He is happy that at least those things won't happen. The happy moment shatters in another jolting, jerking pulse of pain.

As the minutes tick by he is weakening. Every new charge saps more of his strength. He's like a rag doll crushed in the hand of an invisible giant. He no longer has it in him to keep his head up until the electricity surges through him again. When it does, his head snaps up, sinews straining in his neck as the veins stand out. It looks like his neck could tear open at any moment. Then there's a crack. When the current finally stops, his head lolls and he spits. Bits of tooth and blood. He's bitten down so hard that he's split a tooth. He breathes in and instantly regrets it. He makes a sound like someone who's trodden on an upturned plug in bare feet. The cold air on the exposed nerve of the broken tooth gives him a new kind of pain. It's a solid, searing explosion of white that stabs right up into his eye socket, then slowly recedes back down the nerve pathway to leave a throbbing memory of agony in the stump of his tooth.

"Fu-aaaaaaah!"

He can't even complete the four-letter word as he's gripped again in the effervescent pain of the electricity. It causes his teeth to clash so that the stump of his right molar super-novas in his head again. When the charge stops, he starts mumbling incoherent swear words. Not in his wildest nightmares did he expect this level of...

And he's writhing and grinding his teeth again. For a full minute. Tears are streaming down his cheeks. Then it stops. His chest is heaving, but he manages to choke out,

"I deserve this."

Later, when the medical examiner comes, he will find four broken teeth in the man's mouth and bits of them in his stomach. Today is his day off. In fact, he's barely a mile away, rushing to finish his round of golf at Hankley Common before the darkness sets in. Three days from now, he'll be here sorting out the mess, but for now he's taking a one wood for the par 4 eighteenth, while David tortures himself to death. David is better at this than the medical examiner is at golf (he's currently shanking his tee shot into the rough). Yes, David has done this perfectly and, in between the electric shocks, random, disjointed thoughts appear. They're all bad. Acts of cruelty, broken commandments, intimate horrors – all bubble up and play out before his exhausted eyes. His double life – the perfect professional at work, successful, respected, liked by the more sociopathic greasy-pole climbers, and then there was his life outside work. Where most people come home from work and watch TV or go to the pub, he would plunge into a pool of depravity and merrily sink to the bottom. Good Christ! What had he done with his precious, precious life? How did Boris Johnson phrase that thing? Yes, 'spaffed it up the wall'. David had spaffed half his life up the wall engaging in dreadful activities.

And now the electric shocks have stopped. There hasn't been one for at least three minutes. Slumped in the chair, a mess of sweat and blood and drool, David Kidd is swimming back to some level of regular consciousness. His breathing is laboured, but there is a flicker of something and now he gathers all his strength,

"I deserve this," he lisps through bloody, chewed lips and snapped teeth,

"I deserve this," he knows what's coming, he planned it meticulously

"I deserve this," it's his mantra and he'll keep saying it until

"I deserve..." he stops short as the weighted mechanism on the edge of the workbench clicks and one weight drops off the side. There is a split second in which he is able to comprehend that it is all over and to see the fishing line tighten.

The barrel of the shotgun behind his left knee explodes and the sound in the enclosed space is unbearable. It is closely followed by the shriek. It's inhuman – like a fox caught in a steel trap and screaming. David's knee is nothing more than a vapourised red mist slowly settling towards the floor. He is writhing and screaming as blood gushes from the gaping hole that was his knee. His lower leg is only being held in place by the cable tie around his ankle and a thin bit of skin and sinew on the far-left side. And now, as he gasps and chokes, his eyes fix on the other weight. How long did he space them? Was it a full minute? He's teetering on the edge, but his will keeps him conscious, desperate for every last ounce of the punishment the law could never give him. He sees the second weight drop and again the room becomes noise and screaming. This time, the leg is completely severed and as blood spouts from the stump of his thigh, his lower right leg tilts and droops forward. It would be comical, but for the display of shattered bone and ripped flesh. David is jerking in the chair in agony, spouting blood in an arc in front of him. Now his movements are slowing. He's bleeding out. Paling visibly. Eking out the last moments of agony. Slowing, slowing, slowing,

"I deserve this,"

Stop.

Chapter Two

You've Got Mail

"Well, that's the end of that..."

The words themselves were bland, but the odd mix of light-heartedness and resignation in the man's voice caused his wife to look up from her phone.

"What's up?"

Jack Kidd, still in the shorts and T-shirt he wore in bed, dropped the letter onto the marble top of the breakfast bar.

"Dad's dead."

He might just have said 'The kettle's boiled' for all the emotion he put into it.

Annie Ingels, sitting on a bar stool next to him in the sunny kitchen of their open-plan apartment, reached over and took his hand.

"I'm sorry, Kiddo. I know you weren't close, but all the same..." she left the rest unsaid as she looked into his grey, steady eyes.

"Thanks," he said, holding her gaze. Annie had an outdoorsy beauty with copper-coloured hair tumbling to her shoulders, an open face, freckled from sun exposure, and glittering blue eyes. But what made Jack's heart sing was the way she looked at him. It was a look reserved for him alone. It was a look that said, 'You're my man and I love you to forever and back'.

Annie took the letter and scanned it. It was from a law firm in London, England. Now it was here in New York, New York.

"Distant to the end. I'd love to be able to say 'I can't believe your family didn't pick up the phone and call you to tell you your dad died', but..."

"My family are a bunch of wankers?" Jack suggested.

"Yeah, in your glorious British vernacular, yeah all the evidence points to them being a bunch of wankers."

Jack laughed. There was something about Annie saying 'wankers' in her Upper East Side Manhattan accent that tickled him.

"Good to see you're over it already," Annie smiled, but still looked at him closely. Was he hurting somewhere deep inside at yet another slight? Or had thirty plus years of familial brickbats toughened his skin so much that whatever pain he felt from losing his father was gone as quickly as that of a stubbed toe?

"There's nothing to do, so why get down about it?" Jack shrugged.

As ever, Annie could glean nothing about his feelings from what he said. You had to give those English boarding schools credit – they were still able to churn out stiff-upper-lipped men to run the British Empire, even after it had been consigned to the trashcan of history.

"Sure you're ok about this, Kiddo?" Annie pressed, trying to read his boyish, almost chubby features.

"Yeah, well, y'know *obviously* there's a lot of things I'd've loved to say to the old sod before he went, but maybe it's all better left unsaid anyway? What good would it've done? It wouldn't've changed anything. It wouldn't've changed him. And if I'd been looking for closure, or reassurance, or... well, anything... I wouldn't've got it."

Incredibly, Annie thought, there wasn't even a hint of bitterness in what Jack said. He was just stating facts. From what he'd told her about his old man, he'd been closed off and had nothing to give to his only son. Clearly this had gone on so long that there was nothing between them anymore. And she'd always thought her family was screwed up! On that front, Jack's lot knocked hers into a cocked hat. But that got her thinking,

"Hey, does this mean I finally get to meet your sisters at the funeral?"

Jack's head went back with a dry, mirthless laugh, and when he looked over at his wife, his face was set and his eyes were fierce.

"Those two haven't let him out of their sight for over thirty years - they're not going to stop now. They'll be watching him until the last shovel of earth covers him up. So," he said, with brightening features,

"You'll undoubtedly get to meet my darling sisters."

"I almost feel like I know them."

"Bad luck!"

"No, really," Annie said earnestly, "They're always appearing in the gossip columns..."

"Usually being cited in other people's divorces."

"They're everywhere – Vogue, the Washington Post, the National Enquirer. I know what they eat, who they date, how they stay fit and young looking..."

"They've finally admitted to witchcraft, then?"

Annie playfully punched Jack on one of his large biceps,

"I'm serious – this is a big thing for me. Your sisters've been part of my world since before I met you and now I get to see them in the flesh. It's kinda exciting."

"Yeah, like being thrown into a pit of wolverines!"

"Oh c'mon! They can't be *that* bad."

Jack shook his head mockingly,

"Ah, dear, sweet, innocent Annie! Always seeing the good in people. Well, you'd better take your microscope, because you're going to need it to find any good in my sisters."

Annie stuck her tongue out at him.

"This is how the introduction will go:

Oh, hi Rosalind, hi Veronica, I want you to meet my wife, Annie...

And then they'll look at you like I'd just pointed out a dog turd on the lawn,"

"Eww! Don't be gross," Annie cried with feigned disgust.

"Then they'll say:

Really? You found someone imbecilic enough to marry you? Well done, you!

And I'll say, Annie's a photographer..."

"Action Sports Photographer of the Year 2022, thank you!" Annie interjected.

"And they'll say:

Oh, well it's nice to have a hobby - something to keep you busy... especially if you don't have the talent to *actually* be creative. No, we won't shake hands, thank you, we're lunching with the King of Sweden and don't want to pass anything on. Anyway, we've met you now and we must be orf, so ta-ta and go fuck yourselves."

"They're not going to be that stuck up – anyway, I come from a good family," Annie protested.

"Rosalind is *literally* a princess now she's married that Stahlberg bloke. Unless you're titled Antoinette Von Ikea or Lady Anne of Valhalla Smorgasbord she's going to treat you like crap."

"And Veronica?"

"As the muse of the world's most famous Avant Garde artist, she'll put your achievements on a par with what you'd get if you gave a chimp a Polaroid camera."

"Oh," Annie said glumly and looked down at the floor.

Jack gently took her chin in his hand and raised her face so he could look into her eyes.

"It's like I told you... they - are - wankers."

Annie gazed at him, feeling a familiar heat building in her chest.

"You say the most romantic things," she said archly and then kissed him. She felt his slight surprise and then he started kissing her back. She reached her left arm around his broad shoulders and slipped nimbly from her stool so that she was straddling his lap. She kissed him more deeply and wrapped her legs around him as he ran one hand down to stroke her buttocks through her lycra leggings. The heat between them rose as they pressed into each other, and she slid a hand down towards the waistband of his shorts. Her clever fingers pushed beneath it and sought

"Mommy, I pooped!"

The voice of the little boy with strawberry blonde hair was full of pride and, of course, it shattered the moment.

Lips that had been instruments of passion suddenly disengaged and the clever hand used its quick wits to slip out of the shorts and onto the breakfast bar.

"Honey, that's great," Annie gushed, starting to move from Jack's lap, but he held her firmly in place.

"Just give me a second or two to compose myself, babe," he said, shifting uncomfortably in his seat, "What are you up to, Harry?"

"Pooping!" cried the toddler proudly as he ambled towards his parents, feet slapping on the polished wooden floor.

"Can I get off now?" Annie whispered and Jack gave her the nod, "Okay, amigo, let's get you cleaned up!" she declared, gracefully dismounting and sweeping Harry into her arms in one movement. It was something she instantly regretted.

"Ugh! That is stinky!" and she held the boy out at arm's length. He laughed and kicked his legs.

"Maybe daddy should change you?"

"What? No, you know the rules – whoever picks him up cleans him up!" Jack protested.

"Want mummy!" Harry chimed in.

"You see? Truth from the mouths of babes, babe."

"Okay, but the next one's on you," Annie said, taking Harry towards the bathroom.

"No stuffing him with cauliflower just to make it nastier for me!"

"Like I would," Annie called back over her shoulder, before leaning in to Harry and whispering, "Do you want cauliflower for lunch?"

The pair disappeared up the stairs to Harry's room, leaving Jack alone on the bar stool. He looked around the apartment at the little world he and Annie had created and smiled. The main floor was pretty much one big room. The kitchen was divided from the main area by the breakfast bar, then the rest was an airy double-height living/dining room. Stairs on the far side led up to 2 bedrooms, a bathroom and a mezzanine where Jack and Annie had their workstations. Big, south facing windows looked across 108th Street to a small forest of trees that had been planted within a phalanx of tower blocks. Since they were up in the roof, 3 skylights added to the sunny feel. To balance all this light, the previous owners had taken the walls around three sides of the room back to the original brickwork. The dark red bricks, treated with some kind of sealant, came alive at night, creating a cosy feel in spite of the size of the space. Naturally, the walls were also home to some of Annie's best photographs, blown up and framed. Feats of rock climbing, surfing, skiing and other action sports lent a dynamic feel to the space. It was welcoming, warm and a great place for a party – although since Harry's arrival, such events had been more tilted towards jelly and ice cream than shots and hard rock.

The neighbourhood was great, they had some good friends and they'd had a ton of fun enjoying all the delights of New York nightlife before Harry had turned their duo into a trio. Now Jack was discovering a new side to New York and that was fun, too. There was a lot to do in Central Park and there was always the excitement of a trip to Pop Pop's over on Central Park West. Pop Pop was Annie's father. Jack and Annie had encouraged Harry to call her dad this because he was the least Pop Poppy person you could imagine. Nathaniel Ingels was a serious man of finance, who favoured tailored suits, hand-made shoes and nights at the opera to the plaid shirts, dusty boots and country music that the name 'Pop Pop' conjured in Jack's mind. But to his credit, Pop Pop unbuttoned for his only grandson and the visits to his luxury pad were usually fairly riotous. And with Annie's mother (divorced and remarried to a friendly doctor) living out on Long Island, the family had a town and country support network that made them all happy.

Jack looked back at the letter. Yes, this life of light and laughter and love that he and Annie had built for themselves was a world away from what that letter represented. For ten years since he'd left England, he hadn't known whether his dad was alive or dead. And that had suited him just fine. If he didn't know, that meant that there wasn't any contact. If there wasn't any contact, then he wasn't thinking about the old man. If he wasn't thinking about the old man, then the likelihood of thinking about the rest of what had happened was low. And that had suited him just fine, too. But now here was this letter. Here was the definitive answer to the question he hadn't been asking for the last ten years. Now he knew and the knowledge had awakened memories that he had so carefully stowed away in wooden boxes in the corners of his mind. He could feel the boxes shaking, the memories within knocking dust from their rough-hewn sides as they tried to escape so they might run helter-skelter through his head.

Jack's features set hard as he tightened his jaw, trying to keep the memories in place. His face, usually so friendly and boyish with its hint at a double chin, now looked older than his thirty-three years. Without touching it, he read the letter again. It was a grappling hook, fired across the Atlantic to drag him back to the darkness. The language was sparse, written by lawyers to state the case and no more. It struck Jack that it was all in keeping with his relationship with his father. There was no feeling, no condolences, just details of the funeral and the where and when of the reading of his father's will. Jack laughed out loud. The laugh was dry and cynical. His father had given him nothing in his life – why should he start now he was dead? But wait, had it really been nothing? The old man had paid for his expensive education, although boarding school was really a way of getting Jack out of sight and out of mind. And his dad had given him other things: ritual humiliations when he was home for the holidays; a constant stream of snide remarks; a mountain of guilt; and more than enough damned good hidings before Jack got too big to hit. Yes, David Joseph Kidd had given his only son plenty of crap to last his lifetime.

And now those boxes, so carefully constructed, so carefully stored began to split and the memories inevitably scrambled out. The beating with the curtain pole! Yes! There it was, as fresh as if it had happened yesterday. The terrified nine-year-old watching in horror as his raving father jumped onto a chair to reach up and take the four-foot pole out of the bedroom curtains. The look of blind rage on his father's face as he'd come at him, pounding his arms and legs as the boy balled himself on the floor. The beating that seemed to go on forever, even though it was probably only half a minute before his father smashed the lightbulb on an upswing. Maybe the noise of the bulb shattering, or the shower of glass brought the man to his senses? Whatever, the lightbulb had stopped the attack. His father had thrown the curtain pole onto him and screamed,

"That's your fault! Clean up this mess and put your curtains back up!" before storming out of the room. Jack had lain there sobbing, covered in broken glass and bruises, for a full half hour before he gingerly got up and set the room straight.

It was like watching a film of someone else's life. A surreal picture show in a cinema with just one seat, to be enjoyed with a flat Coke and stale popcorn. Parts of it were almost comical – really, who goes to the trouble of taking down a curtain pole to beat their child? It was a Tom and Jerry move – fiendish yet ridiculous. The odd thing was, he could remember clearing up, ensuring that no bits of glass were left in the carpet, but he couldn't remember how it had all started. He couldn't remember – scratch that, he couldn't imagine - what he'd done to deserve a beating like that. Somehow *that* memory had escaped completely. It seemed funny that he should forget the cause, yet be able to recall so completely the small details of the effect. The smell of the carpet as he lay on the floor, or the way his father's comb-over was standing straight up in the air as he put all his strength into the beating.

"Fuck!"

The memory had soured the day. Even the sunbeams pouring through the skylights had lost their warmth. He hated the feeling, that first pull on the hook to drag him back to England and the pain of the barbs lodged in his flesh. And he knew that this wasn't even one of the darker memories. No, he'd stacked those away deep within him. Their terrors made that little beating look like a doll's tea party. Jack sighed and looked at the floor. That memory was just an opening. Pawn to C4.

Jack shook his head, hopped down from the stool and dropped to the floor to crank out fifty press-ups. He needed to move, to do anything to keep busy, to stop his mind from idling and allowing the memories to run wild. Movement had always been his coping mechanism. Fortunately, just as he was pressing out the last rep, the world's greatest distraction device arrived on the scene,

"Dada play!" Harry squealed, holding out his arms towards his dad as Annie carried him down the stairs.

"Yes!" Jack smiled, "Let's play!"

By the time Annie was down to the last couple of steps, Harry was a thrashing bundle, desperate to run to his dad. When she put him down, he was off like a shot and climbing all over Jack before he could even get up.

"Woah! What did you do up there – put in new batteries?"

"No, he's just three pounds lighter. That was a record-breaking diaper."

"Aww, and I missed it!" Jack smiled up at Annie, who grimaced back at him.

"You owe me! What you owe me I haven't figured out yet, but you owe me," Annie warned.

Jack started crawling towards the sofa, Harry's chubby arms wrapped around his neck.

"Coffee?" Annie asked.

"Oh God, yes!" Jack replied as he disappeared behind the sofa and into the living area which had now been strewn with wooden blocks and toys for 63 days straight.

Once the initial boost of a poop-free diaper had worn off and Harry had decided that none of the wooden blocks fitted into dada's ears, he set to building, while Jack sat on the floor, leaning against the sofa sipping his coffee. Annie slid down next to him.

"So, the funeral's Thursday – you good to go?" she asked.

"Yeah. The deadline for the first designs on the website is Tuesday and the client isn't due to feedback for a couple of weeks, so I'm free as a bird."

"Freelancers!" Annie exclaimed, rolling her eyes, "You got it too easy!"

"Yup!" Jack nodded happily, "That's why I do it. And anyway, your magazine pays you to sit around when you're not dangling off some mountain taking pictures of adrenaline junkies."

"It's not sitting around it's…"

"Loafing?"

"No…"

"Lollygagging?"

"No! It's admin. That's what you've gotta do when you have a real job."

"Oh," said Jack, finally understanding, "You mean you get paid for trying to look busy while you're really doing sweet FA?"

"You got it!"

"Maybe I should rethink my career choices," Jack mused.

"Point is, I can come with. If we leave Wednesday and return Sunday, that gives us two whole days after the funeral to enjoy seeing the sights of your childhood home."

"Well, that should take us to about ten a.m. on Friday."

"C'mon! I want to see where you grew up, where you hung out, where you had your first kiss," said Annie, nudging him in the ribs.

"Oh God!" Jack leant his head back on the sofa seat and studied the ceiling.

"I want to see it all – see what made this big, strong man who won my heart," Annie's tone was light, but she was quite serious. Even though they'd met and fallen in love in London, he'd never once invited her to meet his family or go back 'home', even though it was barely fifty miles away. It hadn't really mattered, because they'd been madly in lust and barely made it out of the bedroom, but now she had the chance to see it, she was desperately curious.

"Anyway, it'll be great for Harry to see the land of his fathers..." Annie began, but stopped. It was like all the air got sucked out the room.

Jack's head snapped back from looking at the ceiling and his entire body stiffened.

"No. No, no, no. Absolutely not!" Jack was staring straight ahead now and seemed to be talking only to himself.

"No way. No. Never happening."

Annie felt his, what was it – disquiet? Fear? No... terror. Christ, he was terrified! He was running through every possible scenario in his head and what he saw terrified him. She examined his face and could see tears welling. What the fuck?

"I'm sorry..." she began, but he shook his head. Like a dog with something in its ear. Suddenly he was back in the room with them.

"It's okay," he said, in between taking gulps of breath. God, he was sweating like he'd run a hundred in ten flat!

"But Harry stays here. His safety is..."

"His *safety*?" Annie was shocked, "Why wouldn't he be safe?"

Silence.

"Why wouldn't he be safe?"

"Because of them!" Jack was looking into some other world again.

"Who, Jack?"

Jack stared into a possible future so bleak that he thought he might vomit.

"Who, Jack?" Annie shook his shoulder, "Who would make it unsafe for Harry?"

Again, Jack came back to her with a shake of the head and now he turned to look Annie full in the face and it was the most unsettling thing she'd ever seen.

"My sisters," he said simply, and now the tears came. He wasn't crying, it was more like the tears were being forced from his eyes alone.

Annie couldn't understand. Did he *really* think that his sisters were a danger to their son? How? Why? Why, for God's sake? She was confused and found herself stupidly saying,

"Your sisters?"

"You don't know them."

"But they're your family, what could they possibly...?"

"Don't even think it!" he said fiercely, "Don't think about what they could possibly do, because once you start..." and now his breath hitched in his throat at some unspeakable vision, "Once you think about what they *could* do, you can't unthink it. And then it's with you. And you do not want that."

Annie was struggling. None of this made sense! Yes, Jack had often referred to his sisters as jackals or something equally derogatory, but always with a wry smile or a wink. There'd been nothing to suggest that it was anything more than sibling bullshit. But this, this was something deep. Something that he'd buried so well that she'd never, in over ten years, had the slightest inkling about it. Now the truth was bubbling up and it was hideous.

"I don't know what to say," she admitted and, remarkably, she was finding her own tears coming. She never cried, and yet seeing Jack like this choked her like nothing she'd ever experienced.

"There's nothing to say. You and the rest of the world see what *they* want you to see. Larger than life, comic-book characters. Okay, so they wreck a few marriages and people gossip about them. All a bit of fun. They're rich and beautiful and that's what rich, beautiful people do. But if anyone knew them like I know them, they'd fucking run."

"You mean that, don't you," Annie believed it. His look made her believe it, but something in her wanted him to say it out loud.

"My sisters are wicked."

"Wicked?" Annie would have laughed at such a dramatic description, but Jack looked so very serious that she could only take him seriously.

"Wicked, vicious, cruel, vindictive, malicious. Like dirty cops. There's something rotten inside them. Everything they touch gets contaminated. And the only way I can keep Harry safe is by making sure he's three thousand miles away from them."

Annie remained silent as this sank in. What he said must be the truth. But it was so fantastic! What was she supposed to do with it? Then her professional side kicked in and she became business-like.

"Okay, then he stays. Mom can take him for the weekend – she's always complaining she doesn't see enough of him."

"Yeah, yeah... but maybe you should stay..."

"No," now it was Annie's turn to be firm and she took his face in her hands, "I've never seen you like this – shit, I've never seen anyone like this – so what sort of a woman would I be if I let my man face whatever this is alone? No. I took a vow when we got married. For better, for worse."

"I told you you'd regret that one day," Jack sniffed with a half sob, half laugh.

"Come here," she said, putting her arms around him and holding him tight.

"Hug!" Henry shouted, looking up from the blocks which had so absorbed him.

They turned as Harry got up and lumbered clumsily over to them and into their open arms. Jack pulled him up so that all three of their faces could touch as they hugged and kissed each other.

"Wet!" Harry said, pulling away from his parents' tear-streaked faces and grimacing. His look caused Jack and Annie to laugh.

They broke apart and Harry went back to his blocks, wiping his face on his arm. Annie and Jack sat on the floor and looked at each other. In the silence, they appraised each other honestly. They had shared this moment, this truly bizarre moment and now they had to gauge where they were and how they felt. Finally, Annie spoke.

"Are you totally fucked up, Jack?"

He looked sheepish.

"Maybe?"

"Shit!" Annie said it with mock venom, but she was concerned. Jack had totally hidden this side of him from her. And they'd been together for over ten years. What else could he be hiding?

Chapter Three

Offloading

Tuesday arrived, cloudy and cold with half-hearted flurries of snow. By ten, Annie had wrapped up her work and was able to start gathering the mountain of equipment her mom would need to look after Harry. Like every parent, she wondered whether they really needed it all, but she wanted Harry to have fun and the experience to be easy for her mom, so she packed every possible soft toy, book and plaything she could find.

"Is Harry off to scale the Matterhorn?" Jack asked, looking down from his workstation eyrie at the seemingly endless array of bags and equipment Annie had piled up by the front door.

"I wish!" Annie sighed, standing in the midst of the mess, "When I went up the Matterhorn, I had one pack. This is more like the prep for an assault on Everest."

"Ooh, have you climbed Everest?" Jack asked in mock ignorance.

"This finger certainly has," Annie smiled, raising her middle finger to her husband. The spectacular framed photograph of Annie standing on the roof of the world, which adorned the wall by the bottom of the stairs, proved that the rest of her had done it, too.

"Need a hand down to the car?" Jack offered.

"Nah, I got this. You go back to creating your pretty web designs."

"I'll be finished in a couple of hours, then I can start our packing."

"Works for me. And if you could fix dinner and bleach the johns while I'm out, that would be wonderful," Annie smiled sweetly.

"Love you, too, babe!"

Half an hour later, Annie eased her slightly battered Storyteller Overland Beast onto Grand Central Parkway and headed for Southampton. It was still grey and miserable, but inside the warm and comfortable 4x4 campervan, Harry was already starting to nod in his child seat in the back. That was good, because it would let Annie process what had happened over the last couple of days. After his unexpected outburst of emotion, Jack had done the very British thing of apologising. Ridiculous, but kind of cute. And then he'd gone back to his normal laid-back, humorous self. They'd done the weekend parent things – the park, playing, watching cartoons, endless diaper changing - but there was clearly a cloud hanging over him. Annie had noticed it in the moments between conversations or activities. The troubled lines on his usually smooth forehead. The 'looking moodily into the middle distance' when he thought he wasn't being observed. His random bursts of push-ups, pull-ups or sit-ups. Although these weren't totally out of character – he loved the gym and had the strength of a bull – their sudden frequency showed something was awry. Annie hadn't wanted to press him, because she didn't want to trigger him again, but this British stiff-upper-lip nonsense wasn't helping her understand the situation. Once they'd got through the next few days, Annie would have to work on making him think like an American. He was an American citizen now, so he'd better stop apologising and ditch the diffidence, otherwise the people at Homeland Security might start asking questions.

Maybe his desire to become a citizen indicated something deeper? It had taken very little persuading to get him to quit Britain and come to America to marry her. Obviously, she was his Love Goddess and he'd go wherever she was, but there had been no question of him trying to lure her to Britain. In the end he'd made the move without a single backwards glance. When they'd met back in 2012, he hadn't seemed unhappy to be in Britain. Of course, that was when the country had been riding high. The Olympics were in London and the world could see what a successful, multi-cultural, welcoming country looked like. Annie had been there to cover the Games – fresh out of the Rhode Island School of Design and keen to make her mark in sports photography. They'd met at a party and just clicked. The whole thing had been so simple that Annie suspected there was some chemical connection between them, which had bonded them the second they'd met. And even though she'd left three weeks later to go back Stateside, their bond had remained rock solid. She had thrown herself into the midst of the surfing scene, surrounded by fit, fuckable men, but none of them tempted her. Same with the extreme skiers and climbers she'd spent the winter with. However many times she'd been asked out – and that had been a *lot* – she'd only wanted Jack. Their long-distance relationship had taken some diarising, but every time they'd got together, it had been incredible. They got married just over a year after they first met – even though they'd really only spent about ten weeks together. Thinking about it now, she realised how little she'd known about him when they'd tied the knot.

To be honest, in some ways she still didn't know that much about him. Their relationship was always so in the 'now', that the past seemed irrelevant, plus Annie was the type of person who took people as she found them. And she found Jack amazing. One thing she did know was that his mom had died when he was seven. She drowned in a river while he watched from the bank. Annie couldn't begin to imagine how traumatising that must've been and just thinking about the little Jack helplessly watching his mother die kind of choked her up. The most obvious effect of the tragedy was that Jack wouldn't go near open water. No rivers, no lakes, no beach holidays – he wouldn't even get in a bath! Seriously, the first time she'd drawn a romantic, candlelit bath for them to share, he'd turned it down flat. Even the promise of slow, intimate massage beneath the bubbles was met with

"Sorry, babe, I just can't do it."

Thankfully, he was very happy to shower, otherwise their relationship would've been short-lived. Apart from that, he seemed totally grounded, so Annie had never pushed him on it. It was more of a foible than a problem. It wasn't like it affected their day-to-day. And when it came to holidays, they would snowboard or go hiking and biking. This was fine, because Annie spent about half the year on beaches or in the water.

As she swept the Beast around to join the Long Island Expressway, a bump caused Harry to wake up for a moment. Annie looked in the rear-view to see if he was ok. He made a bleary survey of his surroundings, seemed assured that all was well and went right back to sleep. As Annie drove onwards, she couldn't help feeling some disquiet prickling inside her. She was realising that the past of the man she loved was pretty blank. Sure, he'd shared tales of his days at boarding school, which were hilarious, anachronistic and kind of tragic in equal measure, but his home life was a fog to her. She knew that he didn't like his father - so far, so Freudian. After his mother had died, his dad had barely spoken to Jack before finally packing him off to boarding school. In some ways it was the best thing he could have done, because he sounded like a cold, distant man. She knew that David Kidd was a very successful engineer, who had worked in nuclear energy in Britain and across Europe. And beyond that? Nothing. Jack simply didn't talk about him. Annie didn't think this was to hide anything, but because Jack didn't give his father a moment's thought. What did concern her was his honesty about his sisters.

Rosalind and Veronica Kidd were famous, and yet it took three years before Jack mentioned that they were his sisters. Annie remembered her dumbfounded amazement as they sat having brunch in a bustling Italian bistro in the Village:

"Get out of here!" she exclaimed so loudly that other diners turned to look at her.

"No, it's true," he said with an embarrassed smile.

"What? Nah! You're fucking with me," she said, pointing an accusing forkful of clam linguine at him.

"Well, I'd certainly like to do that later, but right now I'm being honest."

Annie's fierce blue eyes bored into his with a photographer's critical gaze.

"I think the boy *is* being honest," she exclaimed, "I can't believe you're related to Rosalind Lockwood, soon to be married to Billy Payton, the King of Nascar."

"Yes, I believe she's somehow hooked him, poor bugger."

"AND, as if one isn't enough, you're related to Veronica Fowler, wife and muse of Andy Fowler the lead guitarist of heavy metal monsters Conch."

"Yes, that would be my middle sister. Such a delicate flower, such a pure soul..."

"Such a revealing spread in Playboy!" Annie grinned wickedly.

"Congratulations!" Jack said, laying down his fork, "You've put me right off my squid ink risotto."

"You've seen it, then?"

"No!" Jack was appalled. "She's my sister for goodness' sake! Of course I haven't looked at her naked pictures in Playboy."

"Yeah, that would be kinda sick," Annie conceded, but then she lowered her voice conspiratorially, "But I've gotta say, she is HOT! I mean scorching! Almost made me want to give up cock and start carpet munching."

"Please! You're going to make me hurl."

Annie loved the way Jack was squirming – it was the best entertainment she'd had in ages. And anyway, he deserved the discomfort for holding back such a secret from her.

"I can't believe you didn't tell me!"

"I honestly try not to think about them."

"But they could've come to our wedding!" Annie cried in the golden light of revelation.

"They wouldn't have come."

"And Veronica was still married to that fashion designer..." Annie looked to Jack for help remembering the name, but he looked blank. Then it came to her, "Mazzoni! Luca Mazzoni! Jesus, Jack, I could've got a discount on a designer wedding dress!"

"No, you couldn't, because she hates me. Both of them do, but that's okay, because I can't stand them, either."

"What? Why?"

And then Jack had told a lie – maybe his first lie to her – as he brushed it off.

"Oh, you know, brother and sister stuff. We just don't get on. It happens in families all the time. Now..." he said, taking one of her hands in his and looking at her deeply, "Why don't we stop talking about my screwy sisters, get the bill, stroll home and have some fun?"

"But..." Annie wanted to know more.

"We can do that thing..."

"Which thing?"

"That new thing."

"Oh..." Annie felt her pulse speed up. Yes, they had discovered something new and mind-blowing.

"In that case," she said, pushing her plate away and turning towards the nearest waiter, "Cheque, please!"

And that, Annie thought as she muscled the Beast through the Expressway traffic, was what Jack always did when his family came up. He made light of it, deflected and distracted until the questions went away. The problem was that his family past was clearly a problem. Grown men don't suddenly go into cold sweats for no reason, so whatever had happened must've been real bad. And somehow his sisters were at the heart of it. They were still famous – or infamous, depending on which gossip columns you read. Only their surnames had changed. Rosalind's Nascar driver had ended his career in a ball of flames at Darlington, leaving her with a cool fifty million. Not that she needed the money, as she'd taken her first husband to the cleaners for treble that. Now she was married to a billionaire industrialist and sported the title Princess Rosalind Stahlberg of somewhere unpronounceable. It was one of those titles that had long since lost whatever land and power went with it, but it sure gave her a ton of snob value. And then there was Veronica, the Queen of Chaos. Like so many other rockstars, a speedball had done for her axe-wielding hubby and she – looking drop-dead sexy in her skin-tight mourning dress - had quietly pocketed his twenty mill' fortune. Again, this was small change, because she'd already inherited the entire five hundred-million-dollar estate and business empire of her first husband, Luca Mazzoni (drowned in a boating accident on Lake Como). Husband number three was the Dutch artistic bad-boy Brego Matser, whose 'shocking' artworks delved into the darkest depths of human depravity. Yes, Veronica fitted right in there. Idly, Annie thought about that Playboy spread and shook her head in mild bewilderment – she was about to meet her sister-in-law for the first time, but already knew exactly what her vulva looked like. How fucked up was that?

Annie blinked hard and looked around in the vague hope that she could erase that last image from her head. They were somewhere around

Brentwood, although you couldn't guess it from their surroundings. The Expressway was mostly lined with trees so that even with the Beast's high driving position it was hard to see much of the countryside beyond. She could catch glimpses of buildings through the bare trees where wet snow clung to the branches, but little more. It was a monochrome day – perfect for the sort of moody photography she'd made fun of at university. No, she'd take vibrant colour, life and action over that stuff any day. And that was part of what was bothering her. Her life with Jack had always been lived in glorious technicolour, but since the arrival of that letter the colour had started to fade. They were slipping into a world of shadow and fog, black and white. She had the feeling she was going to have to fight to keep the light in her life, but she didn't know why. She had a lot of questions and she needed answers. She needed wise counsel. In short, she needed her mom. Annie stepped on the gas and the Beast gave a satisfying growl in response as it ate up the miles.

Forty-five minutes later, they were crossing the Shinnecock canal and Annie glanced left to where it led straight into the brooding grey mass of Great Peconic Bay. Jack hated this bit of the journey. The canal and the expanse of water beyond always made him shiver. Literally. A six foot, two-hundred-and-twenty-pound mass of muscle actually shivered at the sight of all that water. Given his mini breakdown the other day, Annie wondered whether she should have tried to get to the bottom of it instead of making fun of him. Every time they visited her mom, she poked at him, threatened him with a dunking and laughed at a man afraid of water, who lived on an island. His response was always the same,

"It's only an island when you look out to sea. Otherwise, it's just dry land."

Now, what had seemed like fun and something to laugh about, had developed a menace like that of the bay – dark, massive and lurking.

"C'mon, Annie!" she said to herself. It wasn't like her to focus on the negative and she didn't like it. Fortunately, her mom was a gloriously positive person and her step-dad, Doctor Bob, was cut from the same cloth. Thinking about the pair of them cheered her up and it wasn't long before she was turning off Hills Station Road and down their driveway.

The house, like so many on the road, was hidden from view by trees, giving it the feel of a secluded hideaway. It was imposing, with wooden steps up to a white-columned front porch, which stuck out from the rest of the building like the prow of a ship. It was clad in weather-mottled wooden shingles and patchy snow lay on the grey slate roof. Inevitably, the act of pulling up and switching off the engine woke Harry, who wanted out of his seat before Annie could take off her belt. As things were about to get out of hand, the cavalry arrived in the shape of Annie's mom, hurrying down the steps and calling out,

"Where's my big boy?"

"Gamma!" Harry squealed, kicking his legs and squirming to get out.

"Ok, hold on, stop kicking you little horror..." Annie demanded as she dodged the flailing legs to unbuckle the restraints. Then, with a loud click, Harry was free and sliding down to the floor, to be gathered into his Gamma's arms and smothered with kisses.

Nancy Harrington, flame-haired, sprightly and lithe looked about ten years less than her sixty as she held her giggling grandson in the air.

"And how are you, my little cutie? How are you?" she cooed, before bringing him in for more kisses.

Annie smiled and wondered whether having the love of a good (and younger!) man was keeping her mom young.

"Hi mom," she said, muscling in on the hug.

"Hi Sweetie, how are ya?" and then she put on her serious face,

"And how's Jack? I was so sorry to hear about his dad."

"He's bearing up," Annie nodded, flawlessly using the coverall phrase to avoid the truth that she wasn't sure how screwed up he was.

"It must be hard... okay, let's continue this conversation in the warm – it's freezing out here!" and Nancy made a brrrrrr sound as she jiggled Harry in her arms, much to his delight.

"You get him in and I'll unload," said Annie.

Nancy started for the house, calling over her shoulder,

"Coffee?"

"Please!"

Once all the clobber was in the house, Harry changed and provided a bottle, Annie was able to sit back at the big oak kitchen table and relax. She sipped her coffee and glanced around the large country-style kitchen with its solid wood surfaces and enormous range cooker.

"New curtains?" she asked, noticing the neatly bunched golden material framing the window looking out onto the garden.

"Yes! Thank God someone noticed. It took Doctor Bob three weeks."

"Let's hope he saves his eagle eyes for his patients," Annie said, "And how is Doctor Bob when he isn't overlooking seismic shifts in his home life?"

"Oh, you know, busy. There are plenty of old, rich malingerers in Southampton to keep him out of trouble."

Annie smiled, but must have appeared distracted, because her mother cocked an eye at her.

"Mmm," Nancy 'mmm-ed' as she looked at her daughter.

"What?"

"Come on, spill it," Nancy said.

Annie tried to look like she didn't know what her mother was talking about but failed.

"I know when things aren't right – and I don't mean the fact that Jack's lost his dad."

One reason Annie was glad she'd left home was her mother's unerring ability to read her feelings.

"You don't wanna hear about it. And anyway, I don't even know what's wrong."

Nancy sat back, sipping at her coffee and looking at her daughter over the rim of the mug that had "This is what an awesome Grandma looks like" written across it. Annie tried to ignore her mother's direct, ice-blue stare, but could feel herself weakening and finally cried,

"Okay! I'll talk! You missed your calling in life – you should've been an interrogator for the CIA."

"Who says I wasn't?" Nancy smiled.

Annie took a deep breath and started talking.

They say that a trouble shared is a trouble halved, but judging from the look of concern on Nancy's face after listening to her daughter for fifteen minutes, 'they' are clearly wrong. This was a trouble doubled.

"He's so closed. How can I get him to open up?"

"That's a question for the ages," said Nancy, "Women always want men to open up to them, but half of them regret it if they finally do... sorry, that's not very helpful, is it?"

Annie waved away the apology,

"Should I have pried more? Thing is, everything's been so wonderful – he's so wonderful. There didn't seem any need to push for details."

"You sure got yourself a keeper. Good looking, rugged, artistic, sensitive, helpful, lets you go galivanting off round the world and doesn't wreck the place while you're away..."

"Maybe he's too good to be true?" Annie worried.

"No, I think he's good, but something from his past might not be."

"Which brings us right back to how do I get him to talk about it?"

Nancy leant her elbows on the table and rested her chin on her intertwined fingers as she pondered the problem.

"Maybe I'm not the best person to ask," she sighed after a pause,

"You know better than anyone how unsuccessful I was with getting your father to communicate."

Annie nodded, somehow suppressing the urge to say, 'No shit!'. Watching her parents' break up was like watching people resigned to the fact they were drowning in quicksand. There wasn't much of a struggle, just a slow, suffocating inevitability.

"But Jack's never struck me as being like your father."

"Thank God," Annie exclaimed.

"He's always so chatty... and he's sensitive. Christ! By the time your father and I got divorced I'd may as well have been married to this table," Nancy rapped on it for effect, "We didn't talk and if we did, he didn't listen, and as for feelings – forget it."

"No, Jack's nothing like that," Annie said, looking out of the window at the gloom in the garden.

"So that's good. Think about it – the person he is, has been shaped by whatever happened in his past, right?"

"Yeah," Annie said slowly, wondering where this was heading.

"And he is a wonderful person,"

"Yeah..."

"So, whatever happened, however bad it might have been, he has come through it to be the wonderful person we know. Which means that in his core, he's strong enough to handle the past and whatever the future might bring," Nancy was looking directly into her daughter's eyes as she spoke.

Annie wanted to believe her, but she still had that sense of disquiet. She dropped her eyes and made an investigation of the grain of the table as she said,

"But what if he barely survived his past? What if he spent all his courage in fighting to get through it? Courage isn't a bottomless well and now, if he has to face all that again, what if he just breaks?"

Nancy took a breath to speak, but Annie ran on,

"You didn't see him the other night - he was a mess! Sweating, shaking... he was terrified. What if he totally breaks down?"

"Do you love him?"

"Yeah," Annie restrained herself from the knee-jerk 'Duuuh!' that she wanted to say.

"Then if he breaks, you help put him back together. That's what love is," and now Nancy leaned across the table and clasped her daughter's hand in hers,

"But I don't think it will come to that."

"Really?" Annie couldn't get past the fact that Jack had looked broken that night.

"He'd had a shock. A wave of emotions must've crashed over him and in that moment, of course he went under. But you say he was pretty much okay after?"

"Yeah... a little distracted, maybe..."

"So there you go. It was a thing that happened, but it hasn't wiped him out."

"No."

"And you two are honest in your relationship, right?" Nancy looked keenly at her daughter.

"Yeah. We are," Annie answered, meeting her gaze.

"Then just tell him how you're feeling. Tell him that you don't want to make this about you, but you're worried and you want to know what happened."

"Is that what you did with dad?"

"No. By the time I'd realized I should be direct, it was too late. I didn't love him anymore and I wanted to change my life. Don't make that mistake," Nancy said firmly.

"Okay," said Annie, leaning back and slipping her hands from her mother's,

"I'll make my own mistakes."

Chapter Four

A Glass Or Three Of Malbec

W hen Annie arrived back at their apartment building, it was already getting dark. She'd stayed longer than intended with her mom, but it had been worth it, because she now had a clear view of what she wanted to do and how to do it. Standing in the elevator heading to the top floor, the only slight snag was that her stomach was knotted with trepidation. It was weird – give her a monster wave to ride or a mountain to conquer and sure, she'd have a bit of tension, but nothing too bad. This, however, this feeling was almost unbearable – and the only thing causing it was the prospect of a conversation with her husband! The elevator jolted to a halt and the doors opened. She stepped out into the thickly carpeted hall and turned left towards their apartment. As she walked, she was struck by the solid silence in the hall. The walls of the building were thick and the doors of each apartment were so heavy that there was no way for her to guess what might be going on behind them. It had been a selling point when they'd first viewed the place:

"And the sound proofing!" the realtor had exclaimed in her thick Brooklyn accent,

"You could have a Foo Fighters concert in here and none of your neighbours would know!" she flashed a mouthful of very shiny teeth, which seemed in keeping with her shiny trouser suit,

"God forbid, but you could take a sledgehammer to that marble work top and the baby in the apartment below would sleep through it!"

Now, all that soundproofing, which had helped them create their own little world in their apartment, was working against her. The hallway was oppressive. The only sound was the swish of her Helly Hanson waterproof jacket against her jeans as she walked. Even her footsteps were lost in the deep, maroon carpet which, when coupled with the beige walls and ceiling, gave an added sense of solidity. The jingle of her keys seemed to be instantly sucked into silence as she took them out of her pocket. She paused with the key just touching the lock.

"Nothing to worry about. It's only a conversation. You have them all the time, remember?" Annie thought to herself.

Seconds passed. This was weird and she didn't like it. She was all about action, but here she was, frozen outside her own front door. She'd seen it in other people – even experienced mountaineers could get stuck on part of a climb – but it had never happened to her.

"Come on!" she hissed and then suddenly the key was turning in the lock and she was through the door.

"Aha! The wanderer returns!" Jack cried, turning from the meatball sauce he was tending on the stove.

"Smells good!" Annie said, hanging her coat on a hook by the door.

"How's your mum?"

"Thrilled to have Harry for a few days," she said, walking over to deliver her husband a lingering kiss.

"Thank you," said Jack, who always felt that good manners should be observed even in affairs of the heart,

"And Harry, was he thrilled? No traumas when you left?"

"Nah! He's used to seeing me go. And anyway, Gamma has a big garden with snow in it, so I'd've caused more of a fuss by trying to take him away."

"Well, here in the big city, I ran through your list. The lavatories," (Annie was always tickled by the way he said that), "Are not only bleached, but properly cleaned; I am packed; your bags are ready to be filled; the dinner is ready bar the pasta; and *I* am ready for a relaxing evening before our four-a.m. cab ride to the airport tomorrow. Wine?"

Jack proffered the bottle of Argentinian Malbec, from which he'd already siphoned off about a quarter.

"Yes please," said Annie gratefully. That's what she needed – something to stiffen the sinews.

Jack poured her a glass and gave it to her, then picked up his own and clinked hers,

"Here's to happy trails," he said and their eyes met as they both drank.

Even a casual observer would have noticed the crackle of something special in that moment. It was clear that these two were still very much in love – and lust.

Then Annie's eyes slid away. She took a breath and decided, this was it – now or never.

"Before we go, I think we need a serious talk," she began.

An alarm bell started ringing in Jack's head and his kneejerk reaction was to deflect,

"Absolutely! Spaghetti or penne? It's a big question."

"Nice try," Annie was having none of it,

"But I need to know what I'm walking into. I need to know about you and your sisters."

Jack puffed his cheeks and blew out like a tired pony.

"Well, it might ruin my appetite, but you're right, you should know… although it comes at a price," he finished darkly.

"What price?" Annie was already wishing she'd kept her mouth shut.

"I get to choose the pasta."

Annie sighed,

"Do you know how much effort it took me to broach this subject?" she said with a touch of anger, "Since the letter came and you went weird, I've been worried, Jack. And even worse than that, I haven't known what to do. I hate that. I don't know how to handle it."

"Sorry, sorry," Jack took her shoulders, kissed her gently, then gave her a hug. The scent of her coconut shampoo comforted him and as he held her, he knew that he shouldn't have left her to ask him. He pulled back and looked her in the eyes.

"Okay, here goes – and don't worry, I won't go all PTSD on you. So..." Jack paused as he thought, while absent-mindedly reaching for the jar of penne,

"I don't have a relationship with my sisters for a whole bunch of reasons, so I'm going to distil it down to the top five..." and then he began.

Chapter Five

Stings And Things

I t's a bright day in late July of 1994 and another Great British summer is in full swing. The garden of Forest House, nestled in woodland near the Surrey village of Elstead, is extensive and boasts a lawn large enough for two grass tennis courts (if the owners were inclined to mark them out). Three children are playing in the sunshine on the part of the lawn furthest from the house. Two girls – aged fifteen and thirteen respectively - are playing piggy-in-the-middle with a little, blonde pudding of a boy. He can't be more than four and is running to and fro in nothing but his sandals and y-fronts, trying to catch the ball the girls are throwing over his head. They're all having fun, but especially the girls, who are enjoying the little boy's pratfalls and total inability to catch the ball. These are the Kidd children. Rosalind, the eldest, Veronica, the middle one and Jasper, the youngest. It will be another six years before his school friends realise that Jasper Algernon Charles Kidd's initials spell 'Jack' and dub him that for ever after. He, still so young, is somewhat clumsy, but his sisters move with a preternatural grace like nymphs or dryads. For them, throwing the ball close to, but just out of reach of their brother is easy and their catching is fluid and flawless. When they jump, they seem to defy gravity, and when they land, they barely seem to dent the soft grass beneath their bare feet. How they laugh! And yet... and yet there is something sharp in the laughter of the girls, something dissonant.

Now a look passes from Rosalind to Veronica. The older one has had an idea and the younger picks it up and agrees in an instant. Could they be telepathic? A moment later, their plan is put into action. Veronica throws the ball and it sails high over Rosalind's head and lands in a large patch of mature nettles standing three feet high.

"Bad throw, sister!" cries Rosalind in a flawlessly posh, but somehow metallic English accent.

"Sorry, sister," Veronica replies. Her voice is brittle, like frozen glass.

But it's not simply their voices that jar, it's what they say. 'Sister'? It's the nineteen-nineties, not the seventeen-nineties. Sisters haven't referred to each other in such a way since Jane Austen. And yet, it seems in keeping with their ethereal nature.

"I know," says Rosalind, with a glint in her aquamarine eyes, "Whoever finds it won't have to be piggy-in-the-middle again."

"Yay!" shouts Jasper, who loves playing with his sisters, but hates being piggy all the time.

"Wait!" calls Veronica before he can set off, "We've got to do this properly! All of us have to stand in a line, and when I say 'go', we can run in and get it. Yes?"

"Yes!" Jasper nods eagerly as he lines up with his sisters. Being a little boy, he's sure he can win because he's the fastest and cleverest person in the world. Unfortunately, standing there in only his pants, he is totally ignorant of the fact that nettles sting. This is something his sisters are fully aware of and, as they look at each other over their little brother's head, they exchange another look. There is delicious triumph in Veronica's deep, sea green eyes.

"Wait..." she commands, "Waaait... go!"

In a split second, the little boy is running, his pudgy arms pumping as his short, fat legs go twenty to the dozen. He can feel his sisters running just behind him and he tries harder. Just before they get to the nettles, the sisters stop and watch as the boy crashes wildly into the midst of the sharp, stinging nightmare. The forward motion into the nettles stops. There is a pause. And now a wail goes up from the midst of the nettles, which sway violently as Jasper thrashes about in blind pain and panic. At the edge of the nettle patch, his sisters screech with laughter. It's hard to tell which is worse – their cruel, high-pitched laughing or the screaming of their brother. Finally, he stumbles out, fat arms flailing as he runs around desperately trying to escape the pain. The soft skin of his back, belly, arms, legs and face is now a deepening red and you can see the dimpled centres where the prickles of the plants have delivered their poison. Somehow, seeing the tormented boy makes it all the funnier as he runs in moronic circles around the lawn.

"What the hell?" a woman's voice bellows from the house, closely followed by its owner.

Sylvia Kidd sprints across the lawn to her son and tries to calm him, but even though she is fit and strong, she struggles to control the thrashing, squealing ball of agony.

"What happened?" she yells at her daughters who have stopped laughing and donned masks of sisterly concern.

"He ran into the nettles," calls Rosalind.

"Goodness knows why!" Veronica adds.

"Fetch me the hose!" Sylvia demands and when that is met with no response, she shrieks, "Now!"

The girls hop to it and within a few moments, Jasper is being doused with cold water and calming down as the nettles' defensive chemicals are washed from his skin.

"What happened, Jasper?" Sylvia asks, kneeling down in front of her beloved son. The truth should be simple, but comes out a garbled mess from the confused little boy, who just wants to be held by his mummy. She takes his hand and leads him back to the house for a cup of tea and his favourite biscuits. As he looks up at her, she is framed by the sun and her golden hair with its sparse flecks of grey shines around her beautiful face like sacred fire. He could not love his mother more if he tried. Behind them, the girls look at each other and smile – that was brilliant! And it isn't over yet...

It's a week later and the bright glare of July is starting to tip into the baking gold of August. The scene is similar – there are the three children playing with a ball on the lawn. The boy is wearing shorts this time, but otherwise all seems the same. The big difference is that this time the mother is out shopping and the only person in the house is their father. Again, a look flashes between Rosalind and Veronica. Again, the ball ends up in the nettles, and again, Rosalind suggests

"Let's race to get the ball."

"No," says Jasper firmly. It has taken most of the week for his soft skin to recover from the last stinging and he won't go through that again!

"The winner gets a... chocolate ice cream!" says Veronica with a winning smile. She knows how much her little brother loves chocolate ice cream.

"Don't want to," says Jasper, who loves not getting stung much more than ice cream.

He doesn't see the twisting look of fury that sweeps across Veronica's face at his response. The little brat is ruining their fun – how dare he! She glances at Rosalind, who nods and now the two girls walk up to the boy and tower over him, their shadows darkening his world.

"Go and get the ball, Jasper," says Rosalind and her eyes are mesmeric.

"No."

"Go and get the ball, Jasper," both girls say, and their commanding tone and beguiling eyes are uncannily persuasive. But it doesn't work on the boy.

"NO!" Jasper is defiant and sticks his bottom lip out.

"Go and get the ball, Jasper!" and this time there is threat wrapped up in the persuading tone. They are clearly used to getting their own way.

"I'm going inside," says Jasper and he turns to go.

"Oh no you don't, you little brat!" Veronica hisses, grasping his arms.

"Leggo!" he yells, squirming.

"Come on!" says Rosalind, and before Jasper even knows what's happening, she's taken his ankles and his sisters are carrying him across the lawn.

"This is what happens to little brothers who don't do as they're told!" Veronica spits.

And now they're at the nettle patch with the little boy held fast by wrists and ankles. They start to swing him back and forth.

"One!" they call as he swoops towards the nettle patch, then back and away with the sun in his eyes.

"Two!" and he's swung further out over the nettles – if he squirms now, they'll drop him in, so he stays still and hopes that they wouldn't dare.

"Three!" and now he's flying, high and wide over the first few feet of the nettles, and then down he goes.

The 'whump' as he lands must surely wind him. And as if that wasn't enough, he's crushed a bunch of nettles on landing, which are pumping poison into all that soft, exposed skin. And here again, the shrieks of laughter. This time it's even funnier! And again the wail rises from the nettles as the boy thrashes his way out of them and runs around the lawn. But this time, no cavalry arrives. It's a full two minutes (of delicious hilarity for the girls) before the hullaballoo in the garden draws the attention of their father. David Kidd saunters out of the house. He's tall and fit looking – probably plays tennis – and quite dashing in his blue polo shirt and white linen trousers. With his salt and pepper hair he's just the sort of man that could attract younger women with a daddy fixation. He enters the scene with an academic curiosity.

"What's going on? Wasp sting?" he asks his daughters calmly.

"He ran into the nettles," Rosalind lies.

"Stupid boy! You'd think he'd have learned after last week." And the father turns, get the hose and douses his son.

As the water washes away the irritants, the boy starts to shout between gulps of air and sobs,

"No, daddy! Rosalind and Veronica threw me in!"

"No, father!" Veronica sounds cut to the quick by such an outrageous slander.

"They did, daddy!

"We didn't, father," Rosalind's liquid, aquamarine eyes hold her father's.

"They're mean and they threw me in!"

"We would *never* do that, father," the two girls say together and you can almost feel the pulse of their mesmeric aura.

"Don't be ridiculous, Jasper. Your sisters love you. They would never do something like that to you."

"But daddy…"

"No!" David Kidd shouts with a flash of fury that silences the little boy.

"You mustn't lie to get your sisters in trouble. You tripped and fell in, and if you ever want to be a man, you will have to admit to your mistakes. It is the only way to learn."

Jasper looks up at his father with tears of pain and injustice streaming down his face. He wants to say more, but he controls himself. He understands that complaining will lead to more trouble. More pain. Another afternoon kneeling on a log by the woodshed with the bark cutting into his knees.

"Yes, daddy," he whispers.

"Good. Now, I'll hear no more of this and we certainly don't need to bother your mother with it. Get dried off and go to your room."

And so, the bedraggled little boy trudges away, leaving the father with his two beautiful daughters. Beyond what has just happened, there is something very wrong about the way the three of them look at each other.

Like all dramas, the story of the nettles has a third act. It's a Saturday afternoon – the last of the summer holiday. It's hot, with that baked, late August dustiness. The sun-browned lawn is empty. Rosalind has a couple of friends over and she and Veronica have gone for a walk with them in the woods at the back of the garden. The friends are boys. To Jasper, they are giants! Big boys from the big school. While they are all out in the woods, Jasper is in the kitchen with his mum, helping her cook lunch. He loves helping his mum and she loves having such a cute little helper. But now the roast is almost ready and she says,

"Could you go and fetch the girls, please?"

"Yes, mummy!" says Jasper happily, taking off his little pinny and heading into the garden in his shorts and T-shirt.

He's not worried about going into the woods. He's been in there loads of times with his mum. Since the first incident with the nettles, she's been teaching him about all the trees and plants and mushrooms in the woods. Which you can touch and which you should avoid. So, he knows the woods pretty well now and has even been in there on his own a few times.

The woods, which are predominantly a mixture of scots pine, beech and oak, are cooler and hum with the insects of late summer. Jasper has guessed where his sisters and their friends are likely to be. There's a clearing with a couple of fallen trees to sit on, just before the big hill down to the public footpath. That will be the place. Jasper trots along happily. Even though he is a bit fat, he does like to move and is already learning badminton – even though he keeps calling it 'badmington'. Now he's coming up to the clearing and he can hear noises ahead. There, he was right! This is where the girls... and now he stops. The sight of what's ahead is so curious that he can only stand and look at it. He is just outside the clearing, half-hidden from the view of the four teenagers by a holly bush. The two boys are standing next to each other with their trousers down. Rosalind and Veronica are kneeling in front of them, sucking their pee-pees! Jasper is utterly bewildered by the sight. Why would they do that? And why are the boys making those funny grunting noises? It is very strange. But, whatever their reasons for doing it, he has a mission – to tell them that lunch is ready.

Jasper steps out into the clearing and has barely said

"Rosalind..." before all hell breaks loose.

His sisters are off their knees and over to him in a flash, screaming at him, shaking him, pushing him to the ground. The boys are swearing and pulling up their trousers and now they come over too and Jasper is surrounded by giants!

"What the fuck are you doing, you little shit?" Veronica's rage has created a hideous mask for her face. She comes in close as she heaves him up off the ground.

"Are you spying on us?" Rosalind yells, pushing him.

"Is that it, you little fucker?"

Push.

"You like watching us, do you?"

Push.

"No, I..."

"Shut up!" screams Veronica and shakes him so ferociously that he sees stars.

"What if he tells?" asks one of the boys, clearly terrified. This wasn't supposed to happen. Not at all.

"Oh, he won't tell, will you Jasper?" Rosalind's voice is calm and dangerous.

"No," Jasper shakes his head.

"If you do, we'll strangle you in your sleep!" Veronica's threat is so very real that Jasper believes it totally.

"I won't tell. I won't tell," he says, shaking his head.

"Maybe we should go?" says one of the boys, but the girls round on them and fix them with their bewitching eyes.

"No, you can't go. We haven't finished," says Rosalind, stroking the hair of her boy, "And besides, we need you to do something first."

"What?" the boy says in a daze. She smells so good and is so beautiful that it hurts. Her face, framed by her long, blonde hair and with those uncanny aquamarine eyes, is other worldly – like some sort of angel.

"We need you to punish him for interrupting us," Veronica purrs with a tone that wraps itself like silk sashes round her boy, binding him to her will. Her lustrous dark hair and deep, sea green eyes entrance him completely.

"And then we can finish what we started," Veronica winks.

The boys are hooked and take Jasper's arms and legs.

"Take him to the slope," Rosalind commands and, despite Jasper's kicking and wriggling, the boys carry him to the steep slope that falls to the footpath thirty feet below. The slope is hard and dusty, with only a few scraggy shrubs here and there. It would be taxing to climb down it, but doable for a fit adult or teenager. Jasper is yelling now, begging them to let him go and that he'll be good and won't tell. Rosalind comes in close and says,

"This is what happens to nosy parkers... You tell mother and father that you fell down the slope looking for us and we won't get angry," then to the boys, "Throw him down!"

Some sense of right and wrong fights within the boys as they stand, holding the screaming child. Then each of the girls fixes her boy with a look so full of lust, so full of the promise of transcendent ecstasy that right and wrong are forgotten. Holding the boys' gaze, Rosalind and Veronica then speak as one,

"We'll swallow."

And the boy is gone. Now he's rolling, falling, scraping, grazing, flashing past ground, sky, ground, sky, a bump, a crack, a roll, then nettles, then pain, then darkness.

Up above, two zips are pulled down and the girls are as good as their word.

Ten minutes later, the girls come in for lunch. Sorry, the boys had to go home... No, we haven't seen Jasper... He came looking for us? When? No, we weren't in the woods, we were off down the lane... Yes, we can help find him... He's probably got lost – you know Jasper...

Chapter Six

WTF?

Annie stared at Jack in utter disbelief and bewilderment. Surely that couldn't be true? She took a slug of her wine.

"Broken arm and a concussion. That's why I can't fully extend my left," Jack said, pulling his shirt sleeve up and demonstrating.

"My mother was beside herself with guilt. Thought it was all her fault."

Annie said nothing. Her brain was furiously processing. Jack turned and pulled the bubbling pasta off the stove and drained it before adding it to the pan of meatballs and sauce.

"You all right?" Jack asked. Annie's silence was beginning to worry him. Part of the reason he'd never shared was because, looking back, he himself found it unbelievable. He had come so far and made such a different life from that of his childhood, that some of his memories seemed utterly bizarre and disconnected from reality. Also, he didn't want Annie to think he was some sort of closet psycho.

"Fucking bitches!" Annie said with feeling. She'd gone from disbelief to anger.

"And you never told your parents?"

"No. I was terrified of what my sisters would do to me. But I had coping strategies. After that, I only ever went into the garden when my mother was out there."

"I'm surprised you ever went out at all. That shit's just..." Annie fished hopelessly for words of sufficient weight and ended up with nothing more than "...wrong."

"Families! What can you do? Come on, let's eat – if you've still got an appetite."

"Always!"

Horrible story or not, Annie was starving.

They took their plates and sat at the dining table.

"Do you want to hear the rest of the top five, or has that story given you enough to make a decision about my darling sisters and their delightful ways?"

"I don't know. Was that the worst one?"

"No, of course not. Who does a top five and starts at the top? No, that story's just the taster. The rest are much more nasty," Jack said with a winning smile. He was full of bravado – he was going to end up reliving it all anyway, so why not on his terms?

"Yeah, I wanna hear them," Annie said after a moment's thought,

"But do any of them involve your sisters giving blowjobs – we're eating now."

"I can promise all the other stories are blowjob free."

Annie took a deep breath,

"Okay, go for it."

Chapter Seven

Brush Carefully

Forest House, tucked away in the woods of Surrey, was built during the 1930's craze for mock Tudor mansions. The outside is all dark wooden beams and white walls in between. The leadlight windows (set in a traditional diamond pattern) add that dash of Olde Worlde charm that foreigners love about England. It's a generous 5-bedroom house, with a large extension on one side - it's a ballroom, which the family calls 'the big room'. It's early evening and Jasper is in the family bathroom, brushing his teeth under the watchful gaze of his beloved older sisters. Jasper's arm has recovered from his fall and everything is good in the world. Or is it? Rosalind and Veronica seem to be taking an unnaturally close interest as Jasper measures out the toothpaste onto the brush. It's almost as if they are waiting for something to happen.

Jasper puts the brush against his teeth and starts brushing away. Veronica gives Rosalind a glance that says "Phooey!" and leaves without a word. Rosalind waits it out just in case something happens, but in the end everything's fine. Jasper slooshes his mouth out, says "Finished!" and heads for bed. Although he doesn't trust his sisters since the nettle incident, he is still glad that they are there. The house is big and has lots of dark corners, and when he's brushing his teeth, he can't hear if the monsters are coming. What monsters? Well, the ones that his sisters have told him about – vampires, werewolves, headless ghosts, sea monsters that eat ships whole, and many more. Every night when it's time for bed, the monsters crowd around his imagination, ready to spring out and drag him into the night. His mummy, tired of the way he was dragging out bedtime and teeth brushing, has recently said that neither she nor daddy will come up with him, and that he has to be a big boy and do it himself. The snag is, that it's not possible to turn on the light in the upstairs hall from the downstairs switches. This means that if it's dark when he comes up to bed, then there is a moment at the top of the shadowy stairs when he has to gather his courage and rush to the light switch across the landing before the monsters can leap out of the dark and get him. Now it's late October, this is a nightly problem. It is complicated by the fact that so many doors open onto the landing at the top of the stairs. There's Rosalind's room, just to the left; his room next to that; then straight ahead the door leading up to the loft; then just to the right of that, the door to his parents' room. So many hiding places for monsters!

Now that his sisters are coming up with him to oversee his tooth brushing activities, things are much easier. And thus the scene is played out night after night. Mummy and daddy sitting in their easy chairs in the drawing room, kissing their little boy goodnight and watching him march off with his sisters; his father remarking on how devoted they are to their baby brother; his mother nodding, but not looking quite so convinced; the trio mounting the stairs with Jasper in the vanguard, feeling brave with his sisters behind him; the monsters vanquished by the hall light; the quick change into PJs and then into the bathroom; the girls waiting until after he's had a pee – that's the last thing they want to see the dirty little brat do; and then the brushing of the teeth. This has gone on for seven nights and with each passing evening, the tension of the girls has ramped up for some reason best known to themselves. And now they have come to night number 8.

"Lucky number eight?" Veronica asks Rosalind with a wink.

"Fingers crossed!" the older girl replies. And they crane forward to watch as the toothpaste is squeezed onto the brush and the brush goes into the mouth.

Jasper always brushes with gusto and tonight's no different... but it is! Suddenly his mouth is on fire and he can't breathe! As his whole body stiffens in shock, twisted delight breaks across his sisters' faces. He starts choking. His mouth! His nose! They're melting and he can't think. He's spluttering and falls off the low stool he uses to see himself in the mirror. He's scrabbling at his mouth, pulling out the toothpaste, spitting and choking all at the same time. His head is exploding! This is the end of the world! It's also hilarious – at least for his sisters. They are laughing silently, because they know that their parents might suspect them if they hear laughter. Jasper is jogging up and down on the spot as he starts a long wail. However, wailing and spluttering and choking, while fine separately or even in combinations of two, do not make a good trio. His chest heaves. He can't breathe. He lurches forward, hunches over the bath and projectile vomits, redecorating the tiles in spaghetti hoop red. This is too much for his sisters, who are barely containing themselves! They'd hoped the result of injecting strong English mustard into his toothpaste would be funny, but this is spectacular!

"Are you all right up there?" Sylvia Kidd calls up the stairs.

Quick as a flash, Veronica exchanges the mustard-filled tube of ToyTown Strawberry flavour toothpaste (for sensitive children) with a regular tube of it and pockets the evidence of their perfidy.

"Jasper's being sick in the bath!" Rosalind calls back.

"Shit!" Sylvia comes up the stairs at a canter and arrives to see the last of Jasper's dinner cascade from his mouth and down his pyjama top.

"He suddenly started puking," says Veronica with a perfect performance of wide-eyed innocence.

"Right, bring me the rubber gloves and the kitchen roll," Sylvia says as she strips her son.

"Are you all right?"

"My mouth went all hot and burny," is the only intelligible thing that Jasper can manage. Three minutes ago, he was the happy master of his world, but now he is a mangled mess of tears, toothpaste and vomit. Looking at the scene as she re-enters with the kitchen roll and rubber gloves, Veronica struggles not to burst out laughing. This is perfect! Just perfect!

Chapter Eight

The Messy Pranksters

"You mean they injected the mustard into the toothpaste and then bided their time every night until you finally got to it?" Annie marvelled at the cruel patience of their plan.

"Yup," said Jack, sipping at his wine, "And they did it again three weeks later, only that time I didn't puke."

"Mother-fuck-ers!" Annie lingered on the word in her smouldering anger.

"Yup."

Annie didn't really know what to say. The whole thing showed a high degree of cunning and malice, but was it really worse than being thrown into nettles via an embankment? She said as much and Jack didn't even have to think about his reply,

"No, the toothpaste was much worse, because it meant I never trusted it again. I didn't know what the problem was or why it was happening. It was only when I came home from boarding school one summer when I was about fifteen that Veronica taunted me with it. By that time the damage was done – literally."

Jack opened his mouth and pointed to his molars with their large fillings.

"After those incidents, I faked brushing my teeth for years. That, plus drinking buckets of Coca Cola and taking three sugars in my tea landed me in the dentist's chair for a lot of painful procedures. Yeah, those so-called pranks had long-lasting effects."

"Pranks? No, that's not a prank, that's mental torture!" Annie said angrily, "It's child abuse, for Christ's sake! Who called it a 'prank'?"

"Veronica and Rosalind. Everything they've ever done to me, they've laughed off and then taken the piss out of me for not being a big enough man to get over it."

"And have you got over it?" Annie looked at him frankly and for once he didn't look away or deflect. Instead he smiled at her,

"I brush my teeth twice a day, floss and use dental sticks to keep my gums healthy. So, yeah, I think I got over it."

"Well, you do have a lovely smile," said Annie with a twinkle, "Although you could have warned me you were going to tell a story about throwing up pasta while we're eating frickin' pasta," she added.

"Fair point... and, spoiler alert: we are eating beef meatballs and this next story involves cows," Jack warned.

"Duly noted," said Annie, "Okay, hit me with it."

Chapter Nine

Cows!

It is two years later - the summer of 1996. The Kidd family have been spending Sunday afternoon visiting their mum's parents. Nanna and Grandad are very well to do and live in a massive house in the country just a few miles from Elstead. The village is called Frensham and the picturesque river Wey flows through it. The Wey is a tributary of the Thames and just before it arrives in Frensham village, it glides lazily in textbook meanders through beautiful water meadows full of lush grass and wild flowers. Rosalind, Veronica and Jasper are walking down a very steep path towards a quaint wooden bridge over the river. Their grandparents' house is somewhere at the top of the slope, but the children have left the old folks to talk their boring nonsense while they have a walk. The two girls are hardly children anymore. Rosalind is seventeen but carries herself with the confidence of a high-powered lawyer. Her straight, blonde hair falls halfway down her back and when it catches the sun, it is like spun gold. Veronica does not look fifteen. She has the curves of a woman, but it's her attitude that makes her look older. There is something distinctly adult and unsettlingly predatory about her – something that her sister also shares. Gossip is rife about what they get up to with boys from some of the private schools in the area. Jasper, meanwhile, looks like a bog-standard six-year-old boy with scuffed knees and his shirt only half tucked into his shorts.

They get down to the bottom of the slope and wander onto the bridge. Each of them has a stick in hand to play the classic game of Pooh sticks.

"Look! There's Eeyore!" laughs Jasper, pointing at a lonely donkey munching on grass in the field on the bank of the river they've just come from.

The donkey looks up at them and brays harshly, then turns, kicks out its back legs and trots out of sight behind some willows clinging to the bend in the river.

"Stupid donkey!" says Veronica. She hates animals and animals hate her – even Nanna and Grandad's super-waggy spaniel Mollie growls at Veronica. Every time they visit, the dog must be locked in a bedroom for the duration.

"Shall we play?" asks Rosalind.

"Okay," says Jack, "But this time I'm going to win!"

"You never win," Veronica says, shoving him.

"Gerrof!" Jack complains and it takes his mind off the fact that he has never won at this game. He's not even come close, and they must've played it upwards of thirty times.

They line up, sticks at the ready with the two girls flanking him.

"One, two... three... Go!" Rosalind cries and the three of them drop their sticks into the clear, sparkling water.

Jasper's stick hits the water first, but instead of being instantly carried off downstream, it holds its position. It's not snagged on anything. Although there are clumps of river grasses waving their tresses in the clear, flowing stream, none of them are nearby. It's as if the stick is being held there by an invisible hand. And now Rosalind and Veronica's sticks have hit the water and boy, do they shift! They zip off under the bridge as Jasper's stick finally starts to move. The children rush to the other side of the bridge to see whose comes out first.

"Dead heat!" says Rosalind.

"Rubbish! Mine won by a nose," says Veronica, and the two girls start to bicker. Only one thing is certain – Jasper lost. He looks sadly at his stick as it glides away over the sandy riverbed, interspersed with waving grasses. One day he'll win! He sighs and looks across the fields on the other side of the river. Black and white Friesian cows are grazing dreamily in the late afternoon heat and beyond the fields, the old church stands on top of the ground that rises up from the floodplain. It is a perfect postcard of old English bucolic harmony.

"Let's take a look at those cows," says Rosalind.

"Yes, sister, what a good idea!" Veronica smiles, but there is something in the smile that shouldn't be there. If Jasper had seen it, he might have changed his mind about going with them, but he doesn't see it and readily agrees to the plan.

The two girls trit-trot across the bridge like the billy goats gruff, with Jasper keeping pace with them at the rear. He's been worried about crossing bridges ever since he was told the story about the billy goats and the troll under the bridge. They walk along the footpath in the dappled shade of the river willows until they get to a turn where the path goes up the hill to the church. On their left are the fields, with the cows about two hundred yards away. On their right is the churchyard where, in just three short years, they will gather to bury their mother and where they will later lay their father to rest. Today is sunny and warm and even the proximity of the graveyard isn't worrying Jasper.

"Follow me!" says Rosalind as she easily vaults the five-bar gate into the field.

"Last one in's a rotten egg!" says Veronica and before Jasper can even reach the gate, she's hopped over it with uncanny grace.

"Hey, that's not fair – you had a head start!" Jasper protests, climbing heavily over the gate.

"Ugh! What's that smell?" asks Rosalind.

"Oh, that's Jasper," Veronica replies, "He's a rotten egg and he stinks."

"Must be why everybody hates him," Rosalind laughs harshly.

"Heee-ey!" Jasper pouts, but he can't make any more of it, because his sisters are already striding towards the cows and he doesn't want to get left behind. He's still little and he knows that cows are big, so he wants to be in relative safety with his sisters.

Like most fields where large animals graze, the ground is uneven, with plenty of foot-sized indentations to twist an ankle. There's the odd thistle to avoid and plenty of cow pats, buzzing with flies in the summer heat.

Jasper, who is still a chubster, is already sweating and puffing to keep pace with his long-legged sisters. Suddenly, a thought strikes him

"There isn't a bull, is there?"

"Don't worry, these are only cows. They're harmless. The bull is in the field on the other side of the river," Rosalind replies, causing Jasper to cast a worried glance to his left.

Yes, there it is! Even from over three hundred yards away it looks enormous.

"It can't get over here, can it?" he asks.

"Don't be stinky AND stupid," says Veronica, "It's got to get through two fences, across the river and over that hedge."

Jasper sighs, but part of him is still worried. What if the fences are flimsy? And it's a big bull – the river wouldn't stop it. And it could come around the hedge and then they'd be trapped between the bull and the cows!

"I want to go back," he says in a small voice.

"Why have we got a stinky, stupid cowardy custard for a brother?" Veronica complains.

"Just bad luck," says Rosalind and she slows her pace as they approach the cows.

The two girls step silently as they get to within thirty yards of the cows. Jasper is feeling very small and looking very scared. The cows are ginormous to him – at least double his height – and there are millions of them (although in reality, it's more like fifty). He reaches out to take Rosalind's hand for reassurance, but she bats him off. She and Veronica are concentrating hard as they approach, trying to get as close as they can before the cows properly notice them. They finally stop about 20 yards away. Jasper stops a couple of yards behind his sisters. This is plenty close enough! He looks at the cows with trepidation, but they all seem placid enough chewing away in the sun. Then his sisters turn to him.

"Now we're going to have a race back to the gate," Rosalind whispers.

"That's not fair – you've got longer legs than me!" Jasper whispers back.

"You've got a head start," whispers Veronica, "And anyway, we're going to give you a reason to run fast."

Veronica's sea green eyes darken wickedly and suddenly Jasper knows that something terrible is about to happen.

Rosalind and Veronica turn back towards the cows and let out the most unearthly shriek that Jasper, the cows, the bull across the river or even the 12th century church has ever heard. In a second, the sleepy pastoral scene explodes into a frenzy of panicking cows. They scream in terror and turn towards the children en masse.

"Run!" Rosalind yells and, before Jasper's turned and taken a step, his sisters are past him and racing across the field. Jasper is also in flight-mode. Where some children might freeze, or cry, or shout in the hopes that the others might come back to get him, Jasper's instincts have him sprinting in a heartbeat. Deep down on an unconscious level he must know that if he stops, or turns, or falls or slows down, he's dead. He's seen the size of the cows. If they run over him he'll be squished. That's why he's running like a madman. And at the same time, his brain is sprinting, too. Unlike his sisters, he's not going for the gate, which is in the corner of the field. He's cutting off the angle and heading for the barbed wire fence along the side of the footpath. All he can hear is the screeching of the cows and the pounding of their feet, like a landslide hurtling after him. Everything's a blur except for what his brain is looking to avoid – the cowpat that'll slow him down, the divot that'll trip him, the thistles that'll catch his clothes. It's a wonder of nature that this fat little boy is able to make all these calculations and ignore the pain in his legs and lungs as he bursts every muscle fibre to survive. His entire being is focussed on one thing – running to that fence.

The cows are a black and white wave of fury, catching him up by the second. They are rising like a breaker driven by a hurricane and any moment they will crash down upon the boy and he will be lost in the crush of hooves. He's already been overtaken by the smell of them - that animal mix of beef, piss, shit and leather – and in the midst of the maelstrom of noise, he can feel their bulk bearing down on him. His sisters hop the gate and immediately turn to watch the spectacle, but their smiles turn to grimaces. What the hell's he doing over there? Why didn't he follow them? Why hasn't he fallen? But wait! Oh, this is going to be close! From their almost side-on point of view, they can see the gap between the stampeding cows and the boy closing. Ten feet, nine feet, eight feet – with every passing second, oblivion is gaining. But Jasper isn't slowing. If anything, his legs are pumping faster.

Inside the nightmare, Jasper's unconscious mind is already calculating the final leap. There is no deliberate thought involved. Jasper, the well-spoken, chubby little boy who loves eclairs and Tintin books, is not in charge. His genetic need to survive is driving him forward and, just as the spume from the first of the cows flecks across his brown hair, he puts on an extra burst of speed. At the same time, the cows begin to slow and split to left and right as they see the fence. Jasper leaps. His head, shoulders and torso fly easily through the gap between the first and second wires of the fence, but his legs catch on the barbs, and he is gouged as he sprawls through the fence and across the footpath.

"Shit!" Veronica spits, "Now we're going to get in trouble!"

"No. We can say that we told him to stay at the gate and we didn't realise he'd followed us in," Rosalind says calmly.

"But we *are* going to have to help him get back," Veronica says morosely as she thinks about the steep hill up from the river to the house.

"No, we'll make him walk," says Rosalind and the two saunter easily to where their little brother is lying with blood running down his legs. The cows are leaning over the fence, chewing at him. They are calm again and are giving him a "what was all that about?" look. Incredibly, Jasper is so full of adrenalin that he isn't even crying.

"Come on!" Rosalind grabs him under his armpits and heaves him to his feet, then pushes him back towards the bridge.

Chapter Ten

Sisters Aren't Gentlemen

"That day taught me two things," said Jack as he placed his plate into the dishwasher,

"Never trust my sisters and never trust cows."

Annie looked at him in silence, then handed him her plate.

"Did they ever try anything like that again?"

"I didn't give them the opportunity. I never went anywhere alone with my sisters again. I might look it, but I'm not stupid!"

"You're too cute to look stupid," Annie smiled.

"And you're not half bad yourself," said Jack, sharing out the last of the bottle of wine,

"Shall I open another?"

Annie thought for a moment. It was already seven thirty and she still needed to pack, but then maybe after these stories she'd need more wine to get her to sleep.

"Yeah, bring it up and I can drink and pack and listen."

"You mean you want to hear more? I didn't know you were so ghoulish."

"I want to hear exactly what made you, you," Annie said, moving around the breakfast bar and cuddling up close. Then she looked up into his face,

"But I don't know how you're going to top attempted murder by cows."

"It sounds so dramatic when you put it like that."

"How else can you put it?"

"I didn't think they were trying to harm me. I thought it was a race that got a bit out of hand," Jack said as he followed Annie to the stairs.

"And you're sure you're not stupid?" Annie asked.

"I was six."

"Not much of a defence," said Annie as she opened the suitcase on the bed, "Get on with the story, Forrest Gump – we've got a plane to catch."

Chapter Eleven

The Panetiere

The clock has turned back two years. It's Christmas time and the entrance hall of Forest House is adorned with holly, ivy and a large sprig of mistletoe over the heavy oak front door studded with iron nail heads. It's a large, welcoming hall, which offers easy access to the dining room, drawing room, kitchen and study. The staircase is directly opposite the front door, but side-on to it, so that the last two steps turn through ninety degrees to give access to the hall. Nestled beneath the stairs with their intricately twisted wrought iron bannisters stands a panetiere. This is a wooden piece of furniture about two feet high, three feet long and just over a foot deep. It's a box with vertical wooden spindles like bars across the front and sides. There's also a door set in the middle of the front, which has a heavy brass lock. Historically, panetieres were hung on the walls of French farmhouses where they were used as bread safes – high enough to escape mice and rats, and with a locked door to keep out peckish family members. This particular panetiere is made of dark walnut, dates from the late eighteenth century and is beautifully carved with designs of leaves and flowers. It is adorned with fine finials at each corner and one set in the middle above the door. The family uses it for storing linen rather than crusty loaves. It's also a talking point.

Rosalind, Veronica and Jasper troop down the stairs and into the hall, where they stand together in front of the panetiere.

"Right, who's going to count?" demands Rosalind.

"I'll count!" cries Veronica, beating her brother to it.

"Where?" asks Rosalind.

"Not in the big room," says Jasper. The big room is well named. It is a ballroom accessed either from the dining room or the drawing room. It is about double the size of those rooms put together and Jasper is scared to go in there on his own.

"Okay, not in the big room," Rosalind says with an uncharacteristically kindly smile. Jasper feels reassured. He likes his older sister more, because she's a little bit nicer to him.

"I'll go to the kitchen and count to a hundred," Veronica says in a business-like tone.

"We'll hide. If you find both of us in ten minutes, then you win a point. If you don't find one of us in ten minutes, then that person gets a point. First person to three points wins an extra big slice of chocolate cake," says Rosalind.

"Agreed!" Veronica's eyes shine at the thought of cake.

"What if she finds me first?" asks Jasper.

"Then you're out and you don't get any points at all for that round. And you have to stand in the corner on your own until the ten minutes are up," says Veronica, delighting in the look of worry on Jasper's face.

"Okay, off you go," says Rosalind.

Veronica goes into the kitchen and announces,

"I'm starting... now! One, two..."

And Rosalind is already haring up the stairs before Jasper can even move. She will probably hide in her den in the loft. Jasper stands and waits. He doesn't need to move, because he's already in the perfect place. All he needs is for Rosalind to get out of sight and then he can hide. He listens very carefully. Even though Rosalind has done it quietly, he can hear that she has opened the door to the loft staircase.

"Fifteen, sixteen, seventeen..." Veronica has found a droning rhythm for counting.

Now Jasper makes his move. With infinite care – a surprising amount for such a young boy – he silently opens the door of the panetiere. He takes out an armful of folded tablecloths and stores them under the panetiere so that they can't be seen. Satisfied that there's enough room for him inside, he squeezes in. This isn't easy. He has to go in headfirst and get himself right into the furthest corner, jack-knife his body and pull his legs in through the door. Once they're in, he ever-so-gently closes the door. He's now in a semi-foetal position. The smell of wood and fresh linen envelopes him. He likes the smell. He's done this many times before – usually to keep away from the cleaning woman, who scares him. This is his safe place, even though it's getting ever more difficult to get into. One day he'll be too big to fit inside and that will make him sad.

"Thirty-eight, thirty-nine, forty..."

Now for phase two. He takes his time and hides himself under the remaining linen. He does this very effectively. By the time he's finished, it's impossible to tell that he's in there. In the past, he has escaped notice even when the cleaner has opened the door to look in.

"Eighty-three, eighty-four, eighty-five..." Veronica drones on, but in that way children have when they're bored of counting, she suddenly puts her foot on the gas. She gabbles her way through the last fifteen numbers, ending with

"...ahundredcomingreadyornot!"

Veronica runs straight into the hall and looks directly at the panetiere. That's where her little brother is bound to be. She swaggers up to the door with the arrogance of a mean-spirited victor.

"Are you in there, you little brat?" She clearly loathes her younger brother. She flings the door of the panetiere open and looks in. Nothing but linen. She cocks her head and listens for breathing. Nothing. Jasper is holding his breath.

"Oh... Shit! Little bastard could be anywhere!" Veronica curses as she slams the little door shut. The noise must hurt Jasper's ears, but he doesn't flinch. Veronica moves around checking other parts of the hall. Then she stops and there is slyness in her voice,

"I know where one of you is!" she announces loudly, "You're in the loft, aren't you, sister," Veronica calls, before thundering up the stairs, crashing open the door to the loft stairs and then thundering up those, too.

Jasper is alone. Bundled up in his clever, safe hideaway. The muffled sounds of a distant, noisy search filter down to the hall. The panetiere is still. There is no evidence that a little life is hidden inside. The hall is a static picture of middle-class taste and solidity. Until...

What's that at the top of the stairs? The sisters are creeping silently down. Both are concentrating hard on not making a sound. Their faces are set with conspiracy. Their brother, tucked under the linen and cocooned in the wooden box won't see or hear them until it's too late. But too late for what? What plan have the girls cooked up? Are they going to give their little brother a fright? Get right up to the door of his hiding place and then shout 'Boo!' to make him start and maybe hit his head? No. Looking at their faces, reading their expressions, there's something more going on here. There's a disconcerting glint of cruelty in their eyes. They have something specific in mind. Something they cooked up long before this game of hide-and-seek. It's clear that they've got a plan. But what?

The girls have now got down to the point where the stairs make a ninety degree turn towards the front of the house. They know exactly what they're doing and they're executing it with perfect, ruthless precision. Now they're off the stairs. They are closing in. Slowly. Not breathing. They need total surprise to make their plan work. They stop in front of the panetiere and exchange a conspiratorial glance. This is going to be delicious! And now Rosalind reveals what she's been holding in her fist – an ornate brass key. The bow of the key has a design that is mirrored by the pattern of the heavy brass lock on the panetiere's door. So, that's the plan. The girls grin at each other.

The heavy silence, the slowness, the stillness – smashed in an explosion of noise and movement. Rosalind strikes, locking the door. She and Veronica both roar. It's primal, hate-filled. Horrible to witness. And the looks on their faces! Snarling, visceral... then the scream from within. The involuntary start. The inevitably bumped head.

"Gotcha, ya little brat!" Veronica is gleeful.

"Aw, diddums bumped his lickle head," Rosalind ladles on the sarcasm.

Inside, the wriggling boy uncovers himself from the linen. He pushes at the door, but it is firmly locked. He pushes and pulls at the bars, but they are more than a match for a four-year-old.

"Let me out!"

"No. You're staying right there," says Rosalind.

"I'll tell mum and dad!" Jasper shouts. He's angry.

The girls laugh. Shrill and unpleasant.

"Mum and dad *know!*" says Veronica triumphantly.

"*They're* already at the airport. *We're* all going to Bermuda and we're leaving you right here," Rosalind says happily.

"We're going to be a happy family again, like we were before you turned up and ruined it," says Veronica with venom. That's not sibling taunting - she means it.

"No, that's not true!" Jasper bleats. The tears are starting to come.

"Oh, it's true all right," says Rosalind.

"They said they were going out and you had to look after me. I heard," the boy insists. He is lying on his side looking up at them through the bars.

"Yeah, but while you were playing, they told us the real plan. We're going to Bermuda and we're leaving you here in this box, because we all hate you," says Veronica.

"How long do you think he will last?" asks Rosalind.

"Only a few days without water. Then he'll die and then he'll rot and he'll smell bad and all the flesh will fall off his bones," Veronica is enjoying herself.

"And no matter how loud you shout, no one will hear and no one will come. You know why? Because nobody cares," Rosalind is brutal and Veronica smiles at her.

"Mum cares!" Jasper shouts.

"No, she doesn't. In fact, all this was her idea. Anyway, we don't have time to talk. We've got a plane to catch. Come on, Veronica!"

And with that, the girls get up and go to the front door. Rosalind opens it and they stand silhouetted in the light to deliver their final, killer line.

"See ya! Wouldn't wanna be ya!" they chorus, then turn off the lights and slam the door. Jasper hears their feet on the gravel as they run away, laughing, then the distant sound of car doors slamming and the rev of an engine as it pulls away.

"No!" he screams, a desperate, trapped little animal, scrabbling at the bars.

"No, come back! Please! Come back! I'll be good," he is crying and kicking to no avail.

And now there is nothing but the abandoned little boy, crying and fighting to get out until he has no more tears and no more fight left in him. He cries and he screams and he pulls at the bars, and kicks at them and pushes on the door for a full hour. Sixty minutes of shouting for his mum, shouting for his sisters, he even shouts for his terrifying dad. The tears, the snot which he wipes on his sleeve, the look of terror on his face as he realizes that he's trapped in a tiny cage and there's nothing he can do. His chest visibly tightens and his breathing fails as a full-on panic attack grips him. That's it. He's going to die. He feels it. It's there in his face. He is powerless. He can't get out and now he's going to die and rot and smell bad. His world has fallen in on him. He knows Veronica hates him. She says it often enough. He knows his dad doesn't like him. He's always shouting at him. But he thought Rosalind liked him a little bit. And surely mum loves him? She sings him songs before bed. But she can't love him. They said this was her idea. Maybe she's been pretending all this time?

Just after an hour has passed, the little boy's spirit breaks. His physical strength has dissipated and he becomes lost in his own thoughts. His family hates him and now they've gone. He knows there is nothing he can do. He knows there is no way out. All he can do is lie there. Then he will die and become a ghost or something. He's not sure how death works, but he knows it's going to happen and that there's nothing he can do about it. There he is, a little boy in his little prison thinking about his death. The next hour is silent as the four-year-old gives up on life. He looks exhausted and resigned as the hour drags by. He's too tired to be terrified. He just lies there as his grey eyes become dull. He is changing. His hope is draining away. The third hour stretches out as dusk rises up from the earth and engulfs the house in shadow. By the end of the fourth hour, the boy is in total darkness.

The effect of this experience isn't going to be some catastrophic, violent change in character. The effect will be insidious. Will he ever really trust anyone again? His family? No. His friends? Maybe. His wife? Well, he hasn't mentioned this in ten years of marriage, so that's a 'no', too. Will he even trust himself? Maybe he will always know deep down that he isn't fully engaging in life, because to fully engage, you need to give your trust. The central transaction of life, love and everything that stirs the soul is the giving and receiving of trust. After the panetiere, will he simply go through the motions of life, but always feel removed from it – removed from himself? Will there be an empty space in the core of his being, which over the years will slowly fill with regret at a life not quite lived? And it all started here with the broken little boy, hunched up in his wooden prison.

But what's that? He hears a car pull up in the drive. Doors open and close. There is a bit of muffled talk, then the car moves away. Footsteps approach the door. Jasper doesn't even look excited - he is just staring, lost in his own world. The front door opens.

"Hey brat – you still here?" Veronica greets her brother with her usual cordiality.

Jasper says nothing. The girls approach the panetiere, get down on their haunches and look at their brother. He looks back at them. They smell funny. Like beer and boys.

"Okay, we're going to let you out," says Rosalind, her voice thick after a couple of hours of drinking and fucking. She and Veronica have surpassed themselves with a couple of sixth formers from a very well-known public school, taking them simultaneously in the Bentley Continental one of them had borrowed from his papa.

"But you can't attack us. You've got to be good," Rosalind adds.

"And if you're not good, we'll put you in the bomb shelter, lock you in and bury you alive!" Veronica is very good at threats. She knows her brother is terrified of the relic of the Second World War, half buried near the woods at the bottom of the garden.

"I'll be good," he mumbles.

"And you mustn't tell mum and dad, or we'll put snakes in your bed when you least expect it," Rosalind adds.

"All right."

They don't have to worry. He's not telling anyone. He's not telling anyone, because he can't trust anyone. He won't share this experience with another human being for twenty-nine years.

Rosalind unlocks the panetiere and Jasper squeezes himself out. He will never go in there again.

"We did this to keep you safe. Mum and dad are out until very late and we wanted to go out for a drink. We couldn't take you with us and we can't trust you not to do something stupid, so we put you in here for safety," Rosalind explains.

"You should be thanking us, you ungrateful brat," adds Veronica.

"Okay, go to your room and keep your mouth shut," says Rosalind.

And, both physically and psychologically, that's exactly what Jasper does.

Chapter Twelve

What's 'Normal' Anyway?

As Jack finished speaking, Annie ran across the bedroom to him and clasped him in her arms. As she held her man tightly, she tried to transfer all the love, all the feeling she had into him. Suddenly, she was crying. She couldn't help it. It was a mixture of horror, sadness and anger, which were all so great and so muddled that the only way of expressing them was through tears. Jack hugged her back. In the darkest hours of so many nights, he had already cried a well of tears over what had happened. He had no more tears for young Jasper, but as he held Annie, he felt her love and it warmed him. They remained clinging to each other for two full minutes. Finally, Annie let go and wiped the tears from her eyes,

"Sorry," she said, trying to regain control of herself.

"That's okay."

"Fuck!" Annie said, shaking her head in disbelief. Then in acceptance of the truth, "*Fuck!*"

A pause. The silence of the sound-proofed apartment crowding in on them.

"I don't even know where to begin..." she said, and then backtracked,

"Yes, I do – how come you're so normal?"

Jack shrugged and held up his hands to heaven,

"God knows – maybe it's because I'm good at compartmentalising?"

"Maybe," but as Annie looked at Jack - this strong, apparently 'together' guy who'd built a regular life and held down a good job - she realized that he wasn't 'normal' at all. If that crap had happened to a 'normal' person, they'd probably be a basket case.

"Fuck, Jack! That is insane! I... that's pure torture. I'm just... I don't know what to say."

"What is there to say? It happened. It isn't happening now and it won't happen again, so I don't let it interfere with my life. Don't get me wrong," he said quickly, sensing her doubt, "I'm sure it affects me every day in subtle ways I probably don't even realize, but I don't consciously dwell on it. Obviously, I'll never go potholing or cave diving, but I honestly haven't thought about this stuff for years. It just stays locked away in boxes somewhere at the back of my mind. It's part of me, but it doesn't define me."

Again, the silence squeezed them. Annie couldn't think of anything to say, so she broke the stillness by adding one more sweater to her suitcase and closing it.

"I'm done," she said, snapping the locks. She took the case off the bed and wheeled it to the bedroom door. Both of them found a strange comfort in the mundanity of the action. Sometimes that's what the brain needs, something to do that's brainless, just so it can catch up. They spent the next twenty minutes piling their bags by the front door and checking that they had everything ready to go. They hardly spoke to each other, but it wasn't a difficult silence. Doing things – any things – filled the void. However, they were fast running out of things to do and a pressure started building up inside Annie. She knew that there was one more item on Jack's list of things that had made him sever all ties with his sisters. And whatever it was, it was worse than putting a four-year-old into a cage, telling him that everyone hates him and then apparently leaving him alone to starve to death. Whatever was worse than that had to be pretty bleak, and Annie wasn't sure she wanted to know anymore.

She'd asked Jack to open these boxes and show her the contents, but she'd not dreamed it was anything like this! Maybe this had all been a big mistake? Did any of this knowledge help her relate to him? Not really, because it seemed so totally divorced from the man he had become, from the man she knew and had fallen in love with. If anything, it might negatively impact their relationship, because she might think about these things and try to reverse psychoanalyze his actions in everyday life. Worse than that, a few hours ago she had thought she was his truest friend and only confidant, but now she knew that he had always been holding back. And not only that, but the mask he'd been wearing all the time she'd known him, had fooled her into thinking that she did truly know him. But the reality was that all she had known was what he had *allowed* her to know. In the last couple of hours – at her request – he had torn down the stage set of their relationship. What had looked so solid, so real, was nothing more than painted wood and coloured cloth. She had asked for this and now she was regretting it.

Then she remembered how she'd felt before he'd started talking. She had been uncomfortable because she'd been walking blindly into a fog of uncertainty. And that had been worse. Yes, this knowledge was painful, but the not knowing had been hellish! At least now she had some inkling of what she was getting into and who her enemies were. That fed her determination to help Jack get through this, and this knowledge would help her do that. Besides which, who is ever totally honest with their partner? Is it really healthy to share every thought and feeling bubbling up from our subconscious? How many people in happy, stable relationships tell their partners that they've had more adventurous times in bed with previous lovers? Who would tell their partner that a previous lover was funnier, but a bit crazy, so they decided to settle with someone more stable? How would total honesty help their relationship? Isn't it more honest – more human – to acknowledge that total honesty isn't healthy? That we all have skeletons in the closet, but that picking over their bones in public can do more harm than good? Annie had always lived in the moment with Jack and almost all their moments had been great. So why get hung up on something that hadn't mattered in any material way before seven days ago?

"We're ready," Annie said finally as she laid her travelling coat over her suitcase.

"But?" Jack sensed a 'but' on the way.

Annie led him over to the sofas, pushed him onto the three-seater and then settled onto the two-seater, which was at right-angles to it. The darkness outside the window, the low lights in the apartment and the warm, glimmering red brick walls made the perfect setting for what she wanted,

"But... you've got one more story to tell – and I'm all ears."

Chapter Thirteen

Wet Work

I t's six in the evening and Forest House is already enveloped in the winter darkness. From the outside, golden light twinkles in the windows, promising a warm welcome inside, where the glorious smell of roasting chicken is filling the house. Sylvia Kidd is in the kitchen and busily preparing potatoes and parsnips for roasting. She's humming to herself, happy with the world. David Kidd is sitting in his recliner in the drawing room, reading a report on the effects of tritiated water on marine life. In the generously proportioned bathroom with its tasteful cream tiling, Rosalind and Veronica are supervising Jack in the bath. He is having fun in his own little world with a toy submarine and a toy destroyer hunting each other through the islands of bubbles. This sort of scene has been regularly played out since Jasper was about two, when Sylvia finally caved in to his sisters' requests to bathe him - although recently, the girls have seemed less keen. Sylvia has put it down to their growing up and that normal teenage desire to have done with the boring bits of home life.

Right now, Rosalind is paying little attention. She is standing by the window thinking about Rupert, a very handsome, very rich boy who boards at a school nearby. She has been regularly sneaking into the school at night, climbing the drainpipe to his dormitory window and slipping in to have sex with him. He is seventeen and captain of the rowing team. She thinks about his slender, tightly muscled body and wishes she was with him. He thinks she's seventeen, too, and would do anything for her. He doesn't know that she's only just fifteen and that he's breaking the law. Meanwhile, Veronica *is* paying attention to bath time. She is sitting on a low stool by the bath, watching her brother in disgusted fascination as he plays with his toys. Her eyes sneer and her lip curls as she looks at the rolls of puppy fat on his belly. Sitting in the bath, he has four rolls of unsightly blubber, which shift in a sickening way when he moves. His chubby arms wobble with fat and even his fingers are thick. And down below, half-hidden by bubbles is his ridiculous little winky. It's pathetic! Veronica wonders if all men are like this when they're young. Since Easter, she has had a range of encounters with teenage boys, but they have all been sexually mature. Their equipment has been nothing like this. She gazes at Jasper, taking him in all at once. How can mother possibly love this disgusting ball of blubber and stupidity? Veronica despairs at the pair of them. Thank God father can see through this nonsense!

"Don't forget to wash his hair," Sylvia calls up the stairs.

"We won't!" Rosalind calls back, turning from the window and looking at Jasper. He looks slightly worried. He hates washing his hair, because he once got shampoo in his eyes and it stung. He prefers it when his mum washes his hair, because she is careful. When she rinses his hair, she rests his head gently in one hand and uses a cup to pour water right along his hairline. With his head tilted back, none of it ever goes into his eyes. That was the way that Rosalind and Veronica were taught to do it, but recently they've changed. They're rougher and don't care if he gets water in his face or even soap in his eyes.

"Right, come on, let's get this over with," says Rosalind approaching.

Veronica sighs, gets off the stool and moves it away.

"Turn around or we can't do it," she says harshly.

"I want mummy to," says Jasper in a small voice. Since the nettles and the panetiere, he knows what happens when he annoys his sisters.

"Nyah, nyah, nyah nyah nyah!" Veronica mimics his tone and delivery with babyish nonsense, then leans in close and hisses, "Well mummy isn't here, because mummy can't be bothered, so turn round and shut up, or there'll be trouble!"

Jasper does as he's told and pushes his toys down the bath to get them out of the way. Rosalind leans down and puts her hand under his head. Jasper tentatively leans back and allows Rosalind to get his hair wet. With his head tipped back he feels the warm water rise up the sides of his face and cover his ears. Just his mouth, nose and eyes are out of the water. The bubbles have parted from around his body and Veronica is sickened by the sight of his blubbery, white flesh with its maggoty little appendage sticking up. Suddenly, Veronica's eyes light up with the spark of an idea. It's a moment that will change the course of Jasper's life. She leans over and whispers something to Rosalind which Jasper can't hear, because his ears are under water. Veronica moves across and closes the bathroom door. She returns, plucking the bottle of 'No More Tears' shampoo from the shelf as she does. Rosalind roughly pulls Jasper up into a sitting position and both girls put shampoo in their hands and lather up Jasper's head. There are a few knots in his fine brown hair, but the girls don't care and work vigorously.

"Ouch!" Jasper cries as his head is jerked to the side. Veronica has caught a knot.

"Oh shut up, you little brat," she growls.

"But... ow!"

This time Rosalind has caught a knot.

"Stop being a baby! You're always whining," she taunts.

"Am not! Owwww!" this time his head is jerked back hard and it really hurts.

"Right, that's good enough. Time to rinse!" declares Veronica, and with that, the real fun starts.

There is no gentle hand behind the head. No careful ladling of water. Suddenly, Jasper's head is pushed down under the water by Rosalind, while Veronica holds down his body to stop him squirming free. The whole thing happens so fast, that Jasper doesn't even have time to take a breath. Bang! He's under. He's instantly thrashing like a game fish, but they hold him down. His legs are kicking, so Veronica takes them in a firm grip and pins him with her full weight. He's screaming for his mummy, but under the water only he can hear it. The whole room has been transformed in an instant into a splashing frenzy of struggle. After a few moments, Rosalind lets him back up and he surfaces coughing and spluttering, hardly seeing and in total panic. While he is unable to orientate himself, Veronica says,

"My turn!"

And the girls switch places. Veronica is a picture of cruel delight as she grabs two handfuls of Jasper's hair and yanks him down under the water. Again, he splashes and thrashes, but again he's no match for the two girls, who are laughing. This is pure, unalloyed joy for them! They are laughing, but the sound bouncing off the hard tiles is hideous.

Jasper is terrified and struggling for his life. This time he was able to take a breath before going under, but already his lungs are starting to scream and he's fighting the urge to gulp for air. Something deep within him is forcing him not to do it. His eyes are open and the soapy water stings, but that's the least of his worries. He's trying to pull his head up, but Veronica's grip on his hair is unbreakable and every time he moves, it feels like all his hair is going to be pulled out at the roots. He is squirming his legs and suddenly gets a foot free from Rosalind's grasp. He kicks out and catches a glancing blow on her shoulder, but she replies by grabbing the offending foot and twisting it. Jasper screams in pain, but again, only he can hear it. And that's the end of his breath. He's got nothing left in his lungs and now he's fighting with all his might to deny the urge to gulp in air. His limbs have stopped thrashing and he enters a strange place of calm. Through the water, he can see his sisters talking, but their voices are muffled by the water and he can't hear them.

"Don't hold him under too long, sister," says Rosalind.

"Why not?" Veronica grunts, pulling Jasper's head down more firmly. Her face is right over the boy's and it is pure, demonic hate.

"You know little boys die if you hold them under water too long."

"So?" Veronica has bunched her lips between her teeth and is biting down in sadistic delight.

"So, mother and father would know that we did it, and not even father would be able to protect us from the law. We can't do it. Not like this."

"Fuck!"

Fury twists the demonic look on Veronica's face. From Jasper's perspective – upside-down and through the water – it is terrifying.

"But that doesn't mean we can't have a lot of fun," the smile that crowbars open Rosalind's face would give hyenas nightmares.

Under the water, the lack of oxygen which had delivered Jasper into a calm space has now reduced to a level where a final animal instinct for self-preservation explodes within him. His entire body convulses violently, catching the two girls unawares and for a split second, his face strains out of the water and takes a breath, but then Veronica regains control and he's under again.

"Do I let him up?" she asks.

Rosalind considers. The boy definitely caught a breath and now he's gone back to struggling again.

"Keep him under a bit longer and see what happens."

And they do. Not as long this time, because Jasper is visibly tiring. When they let him up, he's a confused shambles of coughing, spluttering, gagging and crying. Concerned that their mother might hear, Veronica pulls Jasper to her and claps a hand firmly across his mouth.

"Make another sound and we'll dunk you a third time, but we won't let you up," she hisses into his ear. Jasper's energy is spent and he nods feebly.

"You really are rubbish," Rosalind sneers. She hates his weakness. There is nothing she can take from him. Not like Rupert. He has strength in abundance and even though she drains it from him whenever she sees him, he always has more to give the next time.

"Maybe we should drown him?" Veronica says with a sneaky wink to her sister.

"I'm sure mother and father would thank us for getting rid of such a weak, useless, fat little stain like him," Rosalind replies. Then he's under again.

They half-drown the little boy for another ten minutes until his lack of fight takes away the pleasure of it. They finally stop, but make it crystal clear that if he should breathe a word of any of this to their parents, then they will kill him. In his miserable, stupefied state he is sure that they would. They pull him out of the bath and start roughly towelling him down. Veronica dries his hair and deliberately raps his skull with her knuckles as she does it. When he is dry and standing naked before them, Veronica makes one last threat,

"And when mother says it's bath time and we offer to give you a bath, you'd better look happy about it, or I'll take some scissors and cut off your willy!" and she lunges forward with scissoring fingers towards the nubbin between his legs. He shies away. He'll do anything to avoid that!

"Hurry up and put your PJs on," Rosalind says, shoving him towards the pyjamas hanging on the towel rail.

"Yes, hurry up," says Veronica, "I'm sick of looking at you. You disgust me."

Chapter Fourteen

An Honest Conversation

"And they did that to me every bath time for about four months, until the day mum walked in and caught them in the act. I genuinely thought she was going to kill them. Secretly, I hoped she would. She dragged me out of the tub and then laid into them – punched Veronica in the face and damn near took her eye out with her engagement ring. And my sisters started screaming for dad, and the next thing was he arrived and dragged mum off them, and then they had a huge row, because he didn't believe her. It's funny," Jack said, looking into Annie's face for the first time since he'd started the story, "But I felt guilty about causing my parents to argue."

Annie couldn't speak. She merely nodded as Jack continued,

"Like it was all my fault. I believed all that crap my sisters told me – and they never fucking let up. Every time either of them was alone with me, they'd start in with the whole 'you're shit, everybody hates you,' routine. So, yeah, I thought that if only I was better, my parents wouldn't have been yelling at each other and my sisters wouldn't have been mean to me."

Silence flowed over them and filled up the room. Sitting opposite this big, happy-go-lucky, successful man, Annie was having trouble believing that he had been so badly abused. Could he have misremembered or embellished some less evil pranking and turned it into the horror show he'd just described? Our memories from when we are young tend to be a mishmash of images - could he have misinterpreted the garbled film of his early life? Annie's gaze took him in as he slumped back into the sofa and bowed his head to look at the floor. No, he hadn't embellished or misremembered, or made things up. If anything, he'd probably softened the reality of his brutal treatment. Now he looked wrung out, like he'd aged a couple of years. And suddenly, in the way he was sitting, Annie caught a glimpse of the little boy who'd been bullied into thinking that he was worth nothing. Then Jack stretched his arms and legs in a nervous yawn, and the boy was hidden from view once more. Jack looked over to her warily – had he gone too far? Had he been too honest? Would she want to run for the exit? She wasn't saying anything and wasn't meeting his eye. The low lighting and the way it cast shadows made it even harder to read her. This was why he'd never told anyone before. He'd always known it wouldn't be fair on them. Finding out that a person you like has been abused isn't easy. How do you reply to it? And now, having avoided putting any of his girlfriends into that position, he'd done it to the one person in the world that he didn't want to lose. Christ! Why hadn't he just kept his shit together and his trap shut? If he hadn't lost control when the letter arrived, he could've got through the funeral and come back without Annie being any the wiser, and then they could've gone on living as normal. Stupid, stupid, stupid, Jack!

"I know what you mean about feeling guilty," Annie said at last,

"That's how I felt when my parents divorced. I felt like if only I'd been better – got better grades, been captain of a team, or somehow made them get on better – then they wouldn't have split up. And I was seventeen when that happened, so you'd think I'd've seen that it wasn't my fault or my brother's fault, but just parental bullshit. But no... so a four-year-old being told everything is his fault, no wonder you felt guilty."

More silence.

Jack looked at the coffee table, which for once wasn't strewn with the mass of plastic tat that are a toddler's chattels. At this point, silence was his friend. He wasn't tight-lipped because he was re-living all those happy times with his darling sisters, he was keeping schtum because he didn't want Annie to ask about his mother and father. If he had to talk about that on top of the happy tales of sibling bullying, he might break down. And he didn't want to do that. He felt a wave of emotion rise up at the general thought of his parents. He held on tight and let it break over him. It wasn't easy to keep it together. If a specific memory appeared, he'd fall apart.

Annie stared out of the window at the New York city lights defying the February darkness. She could see snowflakes falling, and part of her mind idly wondered whether their flight would even get off the ground tomorrow. Meanwhile, the rest of her mind was struggling. She didn't know what to say and it was killing her. Even though she'd been through the trauma of her parents' divorce and the suffocating silences, broken only by bickering and recriminations, none of it had left her wanting to talk about it. It was more like a sports injury. Yes, it had been painful, but she'd got through it and then she'd got on with the rest of her life. She'd never been one to cosy up with girlfriends and console over bad boyfriends or open up about her feelings. Yuk! Pure schmaltz! She was a problem solver, not a sharer. She glanced across to the picture of her on top of Everest. It looked great. The glittering sun on the snow, the vast blue of the sky, the pose of triumph and elation. But it didn't capture the hell of the climb, the pain and oxygen starvation, the howling wind trying to blow her off the top of the mountain, or the loss of one of their team. But in this moment, she'd rather be back on the South Col than trying to talk this through. She lived in the moment, showed her feelings in the moment – this delving into the emotional past wasn't in her wheelhouse. What was she supposed to say?

She drew her gaze from the window and focused on Jack. This man had chosen to spend his life with her. He'd known that she wasn't a 'tell me your thoughts and emotions so we can hold hands and be all empathetic and shit' type of girl. He loved her and he'd married her because she was a 'straightforward, take you as I find you' type, so maybe she didn't need to suddenly change now? Instead of trying to articulate some psychobabble which wouldn't help either of them, she should be honest and be herself. Annie looked at him seriously and said,

"You'll have to forgive me when you introduce me to your sisters and I punch them both in the fucking mouth."

Jack's laugh was forced out by all the built-up tension.

"What a pair of grade-A psycho bitches!" she continued, "Why aren't they locked up? I'm serious – why aren't they locked up?"

Jack was laughing partly because, after all the silence, Annie's reaction was hilarious, and partly in relief that she clearly wasn't going to delve deeper,

"I don't know," he said, shaking his head.

"And now I know why you don't go near the bath. Wow! I mean – that is crazy shit, Jack!"

"It is, isn't it?" Jack laughed, "And saying it out loud makes it seem even crazier."

"I'm sorry, but I can't think of anything to say to make that better. They are fucked up!" said Annie vehemently.

"Yup!"

"And they fucked you up."

"Good and proper!"

"And there's nothing you can do about it."

"Nope!"

"So, you're fucked."

"Yup!"

Annie and Jack caught each-other's gaze and laughed.

This release of all the built-up tension was glorious! There had been times in his life when Jack had wondered whether he'd dreamt the whole thing, but now he'd said it out loud to another human being, it all became simultaneously real and yet somehow less impactful. It was the difference between worrying about what slimy creatures might be lurking in a dark cellar, and turning the lights on and seeing them in the glare. The memories lost some of their power. And now the woman he loved was in on the secret and she hadn't run away. He had an ally – and in Annie, he had an ally he could trust with his life. It was incredible! Meanwhile, Annie was equally relieved. Her husband wasn't a broken wreck because of her prying questions. Now they could go to England, get the funeral over with, maybe hospitalize the bitches he called sisters and live happily ever after. This was great. Unbelievably, after the horrific stories she'd just heard, *she* felt great. And suddenly she had one overwhelming urge.

She moved with the speed and lightness of a pro climber and was straddling Jack in a second, kissing him, loving the feel of his powerful body beneath her. And he took her in an inescapable grip, fiery in his desire to devour her. Then they were pulling each-other's clothes off, and she was running her hands over his heavily muscled shoulders and chest, before he began kissing her throat and running his tongue down her lightly freckled breasts to take one of her pink nipples in his mouth. Her right hand reached down and this time, without Harry to interrupt, it found what it was looking for and deftly positioned it so that she could case it inside her.

"Thank Christ Veronica didn't cut it off!" Annie sighed as a deliciously full feeling radiated through her.

Their eyes locked in a moment of fierce desire, and then their bodies had a more honest conversation than their minds could ever hope to.

Chapter Fifteen

Merry Olde England

Even waking in a comfy bed in an elegant, ivy-covered, historic hotel in Farnham cannot change the grim reality of a grey English morning in mid-February. As Jack stood looking out at the hotel garden – so neatly laid out, so easy on the eye – he found the scene somewhat bleak. Much of this was caused by the fact that he was there for a funeral and the baggage he brought with him – the grind of a four-a.m. start, the long flight, the hell of getting into fortress Britain, the bureaucracy of car hire and then the drive through the dark to the hotel. But the good old British weather just had to add to it. He looked up at the severe, grey clouds. If ever there was a day for getting back into bed, pulling the duvet over your head and sleeping through, this was it. No such luck. He pulled the curtain closed and turned the bedside light on. It gave the room a warming feel and provided more light than the day outside.

Thankfully, he wasn't able to wallow in morose thoughts, as Annie emerged from the bathroom, wearing a ridiculously fluffy hotel bathrobe and vigorously rubbing her hair with a small towel.

"Great shower!" she said brightly and she came over to plant a dainty kiss on the end of Jack's nose. He looked bleary.

"Hop in – it'll do you the world of good. Smell!" she ordered, opening the top of the robe and offering him the valley between her breasts. Jack did as he was told. She smelled heavenly.

"Patchouli, lemon and rosemary," she said, modestly closing the robe, walking round to her side of the bed and looking into her suitcase that was open on the floor.

"I think I'll go casual to breakfast and save the mourning clothes for later," she mused, "Or would that break some unwritten law of the English countryside?"

"No, you'll be fine. And anyway, I want to show you the sights after breakfast. Can't do that looking like an undertaker."

"Are there many sights?" Annie clearly thought there weren't.

"I'll have you know that this is a historic town with a number of places of interest," Jack said with mock pomposity.

"Is that why we're here, not in Elstead?" Annie's question caused a momentary flicker of disquiet in Jack's demeanour, which she noted. His nerves were more raw than he was letting on.

"No," Jack replied, "Elstead's just a bit small and I've always wanted to stay in this hotel. When I was little, we'd come here for afternoon tea if my dad was feeling generous. They're famous locally for their afternoon tea, you know."

Annie nodded along with a mischievous look that said 'I ain't buying this flim-flam, mister'.

"Besides, the funeral's in Frensham, so this is closer. And we wouldn't've got dinner last night if we'd been in Elstead – that I can guarantee you."

"Hey, I'm not knocking it – it's quintessentially English," then Annie put on a nasal New York twang,

"And you know how much we Americans love the history in Brit-land with your Queen and Princess Di and York-shy-er puddings and Worces-ter-shy-er sauce!"

Jack laughed,

"Not to burst your bubble, but the Queen and Princess Di are no longer with us and we're hundreds of miles from Yorkshire or Worcestershire."

"Oh, whatever, it's all so quaint!" Annie added in her put-on voice, while picking up the plain, green coaster from the bedside table as if it was some antique curio.

"I think I'll have that shower," Jack said, crossing the room. As he got to the bathroom door, he turned to make a quip, just as Annie slipped her bathrobe to the floor. She was facing away from him and the vision of her made him totally forget whatever he was going to say. He gazed on her perfectly toned physique and felt a wave of desire.

"Down, boy! We're here for a funeral," he muttered.

"What's that, Kiddo?" Annie asked, turning to reveal her equally stunning front.

"Nothing," he gulped, "Just, y'know, shower and stuff."

After a hearty breakfast, they set out to see the sights and Annie had to admit that despite the gloom of the day, the town was quaint and quite pretty. Most of the buildings were in the local Farnham brick, with its subtle tones of peach and burnt orange, so the town itself was a cheery balance to the overcast weather. Jack showed her where they had craft and food markets on the street leading up to the castle overlooking the town.

"And you won't believe what they named the street," he said.

"What?"

"Castle Street."

"Wow!" Annie exclaimed, "That is so imaginative! Mind blown!"

They walked on a few hundred yards looking at the shops and then got to Downing Street.

"No, this isn't the one where the Prime Minister lives," Jack pointed out helpfully, "Although it does literally have a butcher, a baker and a candlestick maker on it."

"You're shitting me!"

"Nope."

"Are we going to be smothered by 'quaint'?" Annie asked. Jack said nothing, but led her further along West Street to an ancient looking building with a herring bone pattern of bricks between dark vertical wooden beams. In the middle of the building, a great entrance large enough for a stagecoach opened into a cobbled street beyond. As they walked through the entrance, past the huge oak doors, Annie nudged Jack in the ribs,

"Have you brought me to Diagon Alley? Are we in Harry Potter now?"

Jack laughed. He'd never thought of it that way, but it had all the hallmarks – the cobbled street and the ancient Tudor-style shops that seemed all higgledy-piggledy.

"Quaint enough for you?"

"I might be about to overdose... let's have a nose around!" said Annie eagerly and they dived into the nearest shop.

As they went from shop to shop, Jack was struck by how small it all seemed. Hardly surprising after living in New York for ten years, but there was also that sense of smallness you get when you return to a rural hometown. Smalltown lives, smalltown dreams, smalltown problems. Having said that, of the places he could remember from his childhood, this one was a happy place. His mum had liked to come shopping in Farnham and every trip included coffee and cake in the Lion and Lamb yard. Usually, it was just her and Jack, and she seemed more relaxed than she was at home. Home was always full of tension. His sisters were constantly on the verge of arguing with their mum and seemed to get a kick out of seeing how far they could push her before she'd snap. Then, inevitably, dad would weigh in – always on the side of his daughters. At home his mum seemed on edge, but out and about, he remembered her as bright and breezy. Those times had been full of laughter and, as Jack showed Annie around, he held those golden memories close, because he knew that in the shadows there were other memories, which he would soon have to face whether he liked it or not.

By the time they had returned to the hotel and changed, Jack had a knot in his stomach. It had been building over the previous hour and, as he squeezed himself into the Abarth 595 they'd hired, he regretted not getting a bigger car.

"Still think this is going to be fun on the country roads?" Annie asked in response to Jack's grunt of discomfort.

"Just you wait," Jack replied as he finally settled into the driver's seat.

Annie turned and looked around the tiny car that had barely taken their suitcases and cabin bags.

"I could fit two of these into my Beast."

"Yes, but the Beast would get stuck halfway down the road to my dad's house, so...!" and he finished the sentence by blowing a raspberry.

He fired up the Abarth and, as he pumped the accelerator, it made a frenzied growl like a Yorkshire terrier on steroids.

"Aw, it's so cute when it's angry!" Annie laughed while Jack made a show of ignoring her and concentrating on easing into the surprisingly busy traffic. Even though it was tiny, Annie could feel that the car hated going slowly and was desperate to escape the confines of the town and cut loose. She couldn't help but laugh and added,

"Is it safe to leave it parked on its own, or will it try to hump the legs of passers-by?"

"You can laugh..."

"I am!"

"But it'll be worth it."

Ten minutes later, when they were barrelling up the Tilford Road with woodland blurring past them and the Abarth barking happily, Annie had to admit it,

"All right, yes, this is fun, but you could slow down – I want to enjoy the countryside."

"All right, grandma," Jack smiled and reigned the car in, much to its disappointment, "I've taken the scenic route to give you a bit more of a taste of the countryside – the other road to Frensham's more built up."

"Cool," Annie replied, though the scenery was distinctly muted by the dreary day. The thick, low-slung clouds gave a feel of late afternoon and all the trees looked damp and sad. They passed a swathe of pines that loomed black along the side of the road. It made her shiver and she turned the heat up a notch. Then they were out of the woods and cutting through fields that were partially hidden behind brown, leafless hedges. Boy, was it drab! And in the tiny car, she felt small and vulnerable.

They took a right turn up a hill and now she could see why Jack had chosen this micro-car. The road was pretty much a single track between ten-foot-high hedges into which sporadic passing places had been gouged.

"It's like driving around near Newquay," she said, and Jack nodded. Annie had covered a few surfing competitions down in the Cornish town and had got hopelessly lost on the inscrutable roads through the hinterland on numerous occasions,

"Why do they let the hedges grow so high – are they afraid people are gonna spy on their crops?"

"Dunno," Jack mused as he eased the car through some bends, one of which was there to avoid a huge tree.

"You'd think they'd cut the tree down instead of bending the road round it," Annie said.

"Some of these are ancient trees. They were here before the road, so they take priority."

"You English and your tree hugging!"

"I say, don't bring me into this madness, I'm as American as apple pie, don't you know," Jack replied in his most English accent.

As they crested the hill, the trees thinned and the road widened to two lanes and straightened, arrowing straight down the other side of the hill and onto a long flat. The road ahead was empty. Jack grinned,

"Here we go! Death from above!" and he gunned the engine. The Abarth roared and slapped them back into their seats as it swept them to 70 mph in a matter of moments. The knot in Jack's stomach was forgotten in the thrill of speed, and Annie's eyes sparkled as the car flashed through the open countryside. They briefly touched eighty, then Jack had to brake and go down through the gears as the straight ran out and they were into a narrower section with earth banks and more trees crowding into the road.

"And that's The Reeds Road," Jack proclaimed.

"Fun," said Annie.

"A friend of mine drove her mini into that tree - clipped it, skidded across the road, up that bank and then the car rolled 360 and back onto its wheels. She drove it home, but it was a write off."

"She?" Annie was intrigued.

"Don't get excited, she was just a friend. And even if we had been a thing, I wouldn't kiss and tell."

"Spoilsport!" Annie pouted.

The road, overhung with evergreen trees dived downhill, so that it looked like they were going down a rabbit hole. It became darker as they plunged down the steep slope,

"Creepy!" said Annie as the shadows overtook them and though she'd said it lightly, it *was* creepy. It was as if the atmosphere around them was changing – somehow getting thicker, more oppressive. When they appeared into the light at the far end of the rabbit hole where it joined the main road, Annie thought the sense of being squeezed would stop. It didn't. It grew as Jack drove through the country lanes and Annie could see he was feeling it, too.

"This feels weird, Jack..." she began, but he finished her sentence,

"Like something bad's about to happen?"

"Yeah, but I can't put my finger on what."

"I thought it was just me," said Jack. His jaw was tense. Usually, sharing something strange can make you less anxious about it, but for some reason, knowing that it was happening to both of them at once was more disquieting. This wasn't an internal, subjective feeling, this was a reaction to something real and outside them. Jack slowed the car and parked opposite a small, grey church with a squat tower.

"Come on, maybe we'll feel better outside," said Jack, opening his door and taking his black wool and cashmere overcoat from the back seat. He was glad of it, as his breath billowed in the cold, damp air. Annie came around the car and took his hand,

"I'm not feeling any better, Kiddo," she said, looking up into his strained face.

"Me neither."

They walked across the road and down a farm track skirting the wall of the churchyard. On the other side of the track, they were able to see over the hedge where the river Wey wended through the soggy grassland. They walked about a hundred yards and stopped.

"This is it," Jack said.

"What?"

"Where I almost got trampled to death by cows."

"What, this is *the* field?"

"Yup. And right down there is where I went through the barbed wire."

Annie looked at where he was pointing – just beyond was the bridge where he'd lost at Pooh sticks. The fields in winter were not at their best – scraggy grass, slumping under its own weight, clods of mud and pools of black water that still hadn't drained since the last heavy rains. Coupled with the light, which seemed to be fading by the minute even though it was still only mid-morning, the whole scene was oppressive. Annie shivered. She was used to New York winters, but damn, this English cold seeped into your bones! Jack noticed her reaction and said,

"Let's keep walking. We can get in through the bottom gate and you can meet my loved ones."

Annie shot him a quizzical look, but followed his lead.

As they walked, the cemetery wall, which had been about seven feet high at the start of the path, got lower and lower until Annie could see over it. Ancient gravestones stuck out of the ground like bad teeth, all appearing at odd angles where subsidence and tree roots had had their way. Apple trees, which would look lovely in spring and summer stood, skeletal among the graves, and, inevitably, a few great yews towered darkly, silently watching over the dead. Annie felt as if part of her life force was being drained by this dreadful place that had been the home of death for hundreds of years.

"How old is this church?" she asked.

"Dates from sometime in the twelve hundreds. It's seen everything from the Black Death to two World Wars."

"Cheery!"

"Well, you did ask."

Annie did a swift calculation and figured there were eight hundred years of death right there beside her. Great!

It wasn't long before they reached the low iron gate, which later the hearse would presumably use to access the graveyard. Jack opened it and the metal of the hinge grated horribly.

"This place just gets better and better!" said Annie, trying, but not quite managing to force a smile.

They headed off to their right, making sure not to step on the graves and then Jack noticed something up ahead.

"Oh shit! I forgot that they'd be burying him with mum."

Sure enough, the space in front of one of the headstones had been excavated and a large pile of earth stood next to the hole. Jack wasn't prepared for this – what if they could see his mother's coffin? It had been twenty-six years – what if it had broken up? What if they could see her? No. Don't be daft! The gravediggers wouldn't do that! Even so, he approached with caution and only looked over the edge of the hole with reluctance. Nothing. Just a hole in the cold, dank earth. And that was where his beautiful, loving mother was. It didn't seem right.

Then, Jack remembered his manners and cleared his throat,

"Annie, this is my mum, Sylvia. Mum, this is my wonderful wife, Annie."

This caught Annie slightly unawares and she stammered out a

"Hi... er, pleased to finally meet you... kinda."

"And the two people to her left are my grandparents – Katharine and Rufus. Nanna, Granddad, this is Annie."

"Hi," said Annie, giving their plain headstone a little wave.

"Aside from you and Harry, all the people I've ever truly loved are here," said Jack. His eyes were thick with tears and Annie felt her throat constrict. Jack pulled out a handkerchief and blew his nose,

"Anyway," he said gruffly, trying to keep his emotions in check, "There's a lot of news to catch up on: I got married, obviously, I've become an American – sorry – we live in New York and we have a son... and he's amazing..." and there Jack broke down, unable to hold back the tears. He turned and held Annie, crying on her shoulder as she squeezed him tight. They stayed like that until his sobs subsided and he straightened up, wiping the tears from his face and then blowing his nose again.

"Sorry about that," he said.

Annie shook her head,

"Stop being so British! If you can't cry at your mother's graveside, where can you cry?"

"Yeah. It's just... it's only now, when I think of all the good times we've had and how lucky we've been with Harry that I realize how much they've missed – and how much I've missed them. You wanted to know how come I'm not a total fruit loop because of what my sisters did to me – the answer is, these people. They were good people and, thank God, they've been the biggest influence on my life. They grounded me. Kept me sane. I just wish I'd had more time with them... especially mum," Jack had tears in his eyes, but he had mastered them. Annie gave his hand a loving squeeze.

"It's a bloody disgrace!"

The harsh, male voice jangled the couple out of their little world and they turned. Just behind them, a clean-shaven old man in a green waxed jacket and a tweed cap was standing with his feet apart and a walking stick planted truculently on the ground between them.

"Sorry?" said Jack.

"It's a bloody disgrace them burying that bastard within a mile of that woman," he said in an accent with a distinct country burr.

"You knew her?" Jack asked.

"My dad stabled her parents' horses and I looked after 'em. I knew Sylvia Hicks when she was young and had the world at her feet. Great equestrian! Great at everything. Then she threw it all away for him and his evil brood," he said bitterly, indicating over his shoulder as if Jack's dad were standing back there,

"How did you know her?" the old man finished belligerently.

Jack stepped forward and held out his hand,

"I'm Jack Kidd – I'm afraid I'm one of the evil brood."

Annie was amazed that the old man took this in his stride. There was no hint of embarrassment that he'd just trash-talked most of Jack's family, he simply shook Jack's hand and looked him in the eye.

"Little Jasper. I remember you – took you and your mum riding more than once..."

A memory, long forgotten, but sparked by the old man's words flashed up in Jack's mind – a hot, blinding afternoon in late spring, trotting through the woods on a pony with his mum ahead and one of stable hands behind.

"A'course, it was only ever you and your mum. Your dad had no interest and your sisters spooked the horses. Funny, that," he mused, looking into the past, "They'd had some talent – 'specially the older one – but then summat' changed. Curdled 'em. My guess is it had summat' to do with that man. Whatever it was, suddenly them horses wanted nuthin' to do with 'em. And the feelin' was mutual. So, it was just you, me and your mum. Good to see you've turned all that fat to muscle," the old man continued, patting Jack's shoulder with a hand experienced in appraising horse flesh,

"I'm truly sorry for your loss – of your mother, I mean – but I stand by what I said about your father."

"Don't worry," said Annie, stepping forward, "There's no offence taken. Jack hasn't spoken to his dad for over ten years. I'm his wife, Annie," and she shook the dry paw of the old man, whom she already liked.

"Pleasure. I'm Mark Fry. Some say I'm too blunt. Some say I'm summat' that rhymes with blunt..."

Annie and Jack exchanged the briefest of glances.

"...But that's how I am and now I'm old, I'm not changin'. And when it comes to David Kidd, I'm happy to speak ill of the dead," and his jaw jutted defiantly as he looked up at Jack.

Annie glanced at her man and could see he was still shaken by the feelings for his mother and grandparents that had overwhelmed him. She had to take charge of the situation.

"You know, Jack's kinda raw right now, so why don't you and I take a walk and you can tell me exactly what you think," she said, offering her arm to the old man. He softened a scintilla and replied,

"How can I refuse?" and he took her arm in his to walk back to the lane.

"Jack never talks about his family – tell me about his mom," Annie said as they weaved through the graves.

"Well, she was special. You know she could've gone to the Olympics?" Fry said, looking across at Annie.

"Really?"

"Oh yes. Modern Pentathlon. She had it all, that girl! Fast runner, crack shot, could make a horse do whatever she wanted, handled a blade like Zorro and swam like no one you've ever seen. Oh yes..." and he looked again into his memories, where something made his brown eyes twinkle,

"But back in those days they didn't let ladies do that. Not 'ladylike'. Load of sexist bollocks, if you ask me. If you've ever seen a woman on a horse jumping cross country, sweating, covered in spume, muscling a tired horse over fallen trees and such, then you know they can do anything a man can."

Annie nodded in agreement. He had that right!

"So, what happened?" Annie asked, accepting his offer for her to go through the gate first.

"David bloody Kidd, that's what happened!" and Fry turned and spat as if the name had left a bitter taste,

"He seemed all right when he first came along. Quiet, but nice enough. Thinker. Played sports, but he was no countryman. He wanted a traditional wife and when the children came, she was happy to be one. Stopped competing, but kept her hand in for pleasure. Then, like I say, summat' changed. We all saw less of her and when we did, she seemed... taut. Like wire, ready to snap. Summat' was happenin' at home that she didn't want to talk about. But being a blunt old bugger, I asked her once, straight out, 'Is that bastard hitting you?'. 'No,' she says, equally blunt, but I could see there was summat' wrong there – summat' very, very wrong!"

Annie was listening intently and cast a glance over to Jack, who was staring into his mother's grave. Perhaps she could get more insight into him from a different perspective.

"And then Sylvia drowned. And that was crazy! She was such a strong swimmer. When I heard, I just couldn't believe it. It couldn't be possible! Drowned? Sylvia? Nonsense! But it happened. And after that, the stories started."

"Stories?"

"About them girls and their carryin' on. Shagging their way through every boys' school in the area."

"Yeah, Jack did mention they were... forward with their charms," Annie fished for words that avoided 'sluts' or 'hoes'.

"That weren't the worst of it. Their cleaner and their gardener – they had tales to tell even before Kidd fired 'em. He was evil. What they claimed he did with those girls... pure evil. And now he's taken the coward's way out."

"You mean..." Annie was struggling to take in so much at once.

"He committed suicide, yes. Ghastly, apparently, but no less than he deserved. Couldn't live with the knowledge of what he'd done. Should've been kept alive and forced to re-live his guilt, if you ask me. You know what they used to do with suicides in the old days?"

"No."

"They'd bury 'em at a crossroads with a stake driven through their hearts!" and Fry clearly delighted in the thought of David Kidd receiving that treatment.

"No way!" Annie couldn't believe it.

"It's true, all right. Even up to the 1820s. No religious ceremony – just stake 'em and bury 'em. They weren't allowed to bury 'em in daylight until damn near nineteen hundred. That's what Kidd deserves. But what are they going to do? Bury him on top of one of the most wonderful women who's ever graced the earth. Fucking bastard!" and Fry spat again.

Annie watched him closely. His face, deeply lined from a lifetime of outdoor work was set in hatred. He had no tears for Sylvia, only a loathing of the man she had married. Fry glanced over to the grave.

"I held a candle for her – can't pretend otherwise – but it weren't to be. We wouldn't be here now if..." and he trailed off, imagining the other reality beyond the sliding doors.

Annie gave him a sympathetic look, which made Fry react,

"No, don't get me wrong – I'm not some dewy-eyed unrequited sap. She had me, all right. By God, could she go! But it was only physical."

Annie's laugh was involuntary. The man was outrageous! She held his shoulder as she laughed and, thankfully, he laughed with her.

"You are... unique!" said Annie as she recovered herself.

"That's one way of putting it," Fry smiled, but it faded as thoughts of David Kidd rose up in his mind again.

"And burying him next to her parents..." he shook his head, "It beggars belief! It's a slap in the face of decency! He took her away from 'em and when she died, he wouldn't hardly let them see young Jasper. He was their favourite, y'see? So obviously, Kidd wouldn't want them near him. Packed him straight off to a boarding school in Wiltshire."

"Nice thing to do to a boy who's lost his mom," Annie felt her own anger kindle.

"I used to chat to his granddad about it. Jasper was what they call a 'full boarder', so he'd be at school all term and only come home for Christmas, Easter and the summer. So, Katharine and Rufus – that's his grandparents

– would sneak down some weekends and take Jasper out without telling his dad. Rufus told me he even bribed the headmaster to make sure Kidd never found out. Even in the holidays Kidd wouldn't let him stay with 'em. Fortunately, Elstead's only a few miles away and Kidd couldn't control where Jasper went on his bike, so he spent a lot of days with 'em."

"Good for Jack!" Annie said, looking over at him, standing like a black shadow under the towering evergreens near his family's graves.

"A'course, there was a reason why Kidd didn't want Katharine and Rufus to see him – he knew they'd notice in the end," Fry's voice was dark with conspiracy. Part of Annie didn't want to know, but she forced herself to ask,

"Notice what?"

"The bruises," and that was all Fry had to say.

Annie understood and the old man could see it in her face.

"But it all ended one Christmas. Katharine had got Kidd to agree to join them for Christmas lunch, but come the day, he cancelled. Didn't give much of a reason. Well, he never did say much, so that's not very surprising, but Katharine had a feeling summat' was off. So, they drove over there and dropped in unannounced. Jasper got to the door before his dad. And there he was, a twelve-year-old boy with a gash across his forehead and a massive black eye. Kidd was a few yards behind him in the hall. Rufus told me they all just stood there, looking at each other. They all knew. There was nothin' to say that would make a difference. Katharine took Jasper's hand and led him to the car. Rufus said Kidd's eyes were black as coals. He didn't say a word. Didn't try to stop 'em. Just watched with his dead, black eyes as they took his son away."

Annie was barely breathing as she pictured the scene.

"Kidd had hit him with one of them big glass ash trays. Miracle he didn't break his eye socket. And then it all came out: the beatings, the punching and kicking, the starvation diet – once, he even dragged Jasper up the stairs by his hair, just so he could push him back down 'em."

"Son of a..." Annie's fists were clenched hard and her knuckles were white.

"Didn't even have the excuse of being a drinker. He was just a bastard. Fortunately for Jasper, his grandparents were a good deal richer than his dad, so he wasn't able to cut up rough when they sent men round to fetch all Jasper's stuff. He lived with them just over that hill," Fry indicated the steep slope beyond the bridge,

"Stayed at the boarding school, but had good holidays. Dunno if he ever went back to see his dad. I know his sisters almost never came to visit him. Queer fish, them two..." Fry looked past Annie as he thought about them.

"They'll be here soon," said Annie, checking her watch.

"In that case, I'd best be off," Fry said briskly,

"I only came to give this to Sylvia," and he gently drew a single rose from inside his coat pocket,

"Will you lay it on her headstone?"

"Sure," Annie replied, accepting the proffered flower.

"If I stay here, I might get myself into trouble. Pleasure to meet you. A true pleasure," and Fry shook her hand warmly before walking purposefully off in the direction of the bridge.

Annie returned to the graveside and showed Jack the rose.

"From Mr. Fry," she said, laying it along the top of the simple headstone. Then she took Jack's hand. It was much warmer than hers, so she wrapped both of hers around it.

"You all right?" she asked.

"Yeah, just lost in my thoughts. What did the old man have to say? Looked like an animated chat."

"It was!" and she outlined the conversation, though she paused before telling him that his father had taken his own life. Jack's reaction to the information was neutral, as if it was something that had no bearing on him at all. Maybe he was numb from the overload of memories and being back where so many bad things had happened to him. She continued to relate what Fry had told her, until she finally looked up into Jack's face and said,

"I'm sorry your dad hit you."

"What can you do?"

Annie thought for a moment and as she did, her anger flared,

"Let's skip the funeral. Fuck your father. And your sisters. They don't deserve to have you here. Let's do a three-day tour of Cornwall."

Her sudden outburst took him aback. Her eyes were glittering fire,

"Um…" Jack began, but Annie interrupted,

"Don't overthink this, Jack. What good is this going to do you? Huh? You don't need to see those fucking harpies and why should you pay any respects to that child-beating psycho?"

Jack sighed deeply, his breath curling around his head

"God knows, I'd love to cut and run, but I think I need to see this through. Closure. Maybe I can bury all my bad memories with him?"

Annie looked at him keenly,

"Only if you're sure."

"Yeah, I'm sure," Jack said and leant over to kiss her.

They stood for a few moments, silently contemplating. Annie looked down the river valley – it probably looked lovely in summer, but right now… then she had a brainwave,

"If you want, we can come back in the night and piss on his grave," Annie said.

Jack laughed.

"I'm serious! We go to a pub, down a few pints - as you Brits say - and then take a big leak all over that sick son of a bitch."

"We might get arrested."

"In that case, why stop there? I say we dig the fucker up so I can beat him to death…"

"Still not legal."

"Why not? Do the dead have human rights? Two hundred years ago, he'd've been buried at night at a crossroads with a stake through his heart! Surely we can string him up from a tree with a sign saying, 'Abusive asshole' hung around his neck?"

Jack found Annie's fervour amusing and endearing in equal measure, but he had to draw the line at grave robbing.

"Let's do one thing at a time. Funeral first, potential abuse of the dead, second. Okay?"

"I guess..." Annie said, calming slightly, "But I still think it's a good plan."

Before Jack could question this last statement, the church bell tolled and the sound swept away the levity they had just shared. They turned and looked up the hill to the church, surrounded with grey, haphazard gravestones. The bell tolled again and the dark clouds above the church tower seemed to visibly drop downwards at the sound. Jack's face set with resolve,

"Showtime!"

Chapter Sixteen

A Fond Farewell?

When they reached the top of the lane, they found a very different scene to the one they had left. The sleepy little village had gone, replaced by a paparazzi nightmare. The narrow street was blocked by photographers, reporters, cars, motorbikes and security personnel – there was even a drone camera hovering about thirty feet above the mayhem. Three black Range Rovers were lined up alongside the wall at the front of the churchyard and Jack noted that each was modified by a different company – Revere, Kahn and Overfinch.

"Rosalind's here," he said, pointing out the cars, "Definitely her style."

"She's over by the gate," Annie pointed to a scrum of paps, who were being held back by a team of eight very burly men in black suits. Just behind them, standing in the gateway and framed by overarching ironwork from which a carriage lamp was hung, stood a stunningly beautiful blonde woman in a perfectly tailored black trouser suit. She was posing for the photographers, giving them a vision of poised dignity and mourning.

"Makes you want to throw up, huh?" Annie said.

"Yup!"

And then Veronica arrived.

From around the corner of the road came the unmistakeable roar of a Ferrari engine and then, with a beeping of horns to clear a path, two Ferraris prowled into view. The first was a grey Purosangue with four big men in it and the second was a Ferrari-red Roma Spider, driven by a woman and with a man in the passenger seat. They pulled up opposite the church and the four big men were quickly out of the first car and holding back the paps and hacks that were flocking towards the Roma Spider. Unlike Rosalind's security detail, who all looked like hard-bitten ex mercenaries, Veronica's security team seemed to have been picked as much for their looks as their size. Annie couldn't help murmuring,

"Wow! They're buff!"

Jack shot her a look.

"But they are!" Annie protested.

Jack's smile quickly faded as Veronica emerged from the Roma and was immediately flanked by her impossibly handsome passenger-cum-security guard. Veronica stood in four-inch black heels in a short, black clingy dress that simultaneously displayed her ample cleavage, generous curves and long legs. She was, of course, wearing black stockings and, as a nod to the chill of the day, her guard laid a black mink stole across her shoulders – but only after the paps had got some good photos of her famous cleavage.

Then she was on the move, stalking across to the church with her team parting the press before her. She joined Rosalind in the gate of the church-yard for more photos amidst the racket of the shouting press corps. And they were a paparazzi wet dream: two stunning women, one with blonde hair down to the middle of her back and the other with raven hair cut short in an impossibly alluring urchin style. Each had a different kind of beauty, and the pictures of them together would sell magazines!

"Hello, sister," Veronica said as she put on her mournful face, "A sad day."

It was hard to tell if Rosalind's stony-faced look was for her sister or the photographers, but she didn't sound friendly as she replied,

"And a day we wouldn't be having were it not for you, sister."

"Not here," Veronica murmured, putting her arm around her sister's shoulder in apparent condolence.

Rosalind turned and took her sister in her arms for a sympathetic hug, giving the paps a picture that would make the little people think how good it was to see such warmth and humanity from the rich and famous, and how family is *so* important.

"Your unending selfishness has ruined everything, yet again," Rosalind whispered into her sister's ear as she held her tightly enough to convey her fury.

"Yes, it's always MY fault, never yours. *I* have a life, too, you know. Perhaps if you'd taken a moment out from playing at princesses, father would still be alive?" Veronica hissed, squeezing her sister back.

They parted and looked hard into each-other's eyes. This wasn't over. Not by a long chalk. But for now, they would put on a united front for the cameras. They turned briefly back to the hyenas, who duly barked and howled at them to 'look over here', 'put your heads together', 'put your arms round each other' and a bunch of other nonsense. Then, holding hands, they walked regally towards the low porch of the church, where the short, rotund female vicar was standing. With every step, the day got blacker, and a vicious wind squalled around them, so that by the time they had reached the porch, the vicar was having to fight to hold down her surplice in the gale.

"Welcome!" she said, looking up at the two women, who towered at least seven inches above her. Rosalind and Veronica - unruffled by the wind - turned their implacable gaze upon the ridiculous woman with her scruffy hair and fat, red cheeks.

"Good morning," they said as one.

Penelope Hatchell, vicar of this and two other parishes, was so unnerved by their presence, that she found herself reaching to her faith with a silent prayer. Then, after an awkward silence, she stammered,

"Er... well... I'm, er... sorry the weather isn't playing its part."

Rosalind and Veronica regarded her with faces of granite, their unworldly eyes boring into her. They seemed to be waiting for something. The vicar felt a terrible crawling sensation in her stomach that had nothing to do with the double-chocolate muffin she'd wolfed down ten minutes earlier.

"Welcome!" she said again, and the wind caught her surplice and blew it over her face. She fought the urge to swear and scrabbled to get the white surplice back down over her black cassock. The sight of the two women looming over her made her wish she'd left the surplice over her head. She started to sweat in spite of the freezing wind, which was howling around the porch. Rosalind realized that the woman needed goading,

"May we...?" she began.

"Oh yes, please do!" Penelope gushed,

"Come in and find yourself a seat near the front – either side will do."

And finally, Veronica and Rosalind sashayed insolently into the church.

Jack and Annie watched them go inside and, no sooner were they in, than the heavens opened. Huge drops of cold rain drove in sheets upon the crowd outside the churchyard.

"Shit! Come on!" Jack shouted to Annie and, realizing there was no way through the melee by the gate, he vaulted the low wall separating the churchyard from the road. Annie was over in a flash and they sprinted to the church, where the vicar had retreated into the dark but dry shelter of the porch.

"Sorry!" said Jack as they tumbled into the porch, already soaked by the ferocious wind and rain.

"It's all right," the vicar said, regaining her composure, "It's an occupational hazard of February funerals."

She took in the handsome couple before her and offered her hand,

"Penelope Hatchell."

"Pleased to meet you," Jack replied, trying to wipe off the worst of the rain before shaking the vicar's hand,

"I'm Jack Kidd, the son of the deceased."

"And I'm with him," Annie smiled as she shook the vicar's hand.

"Do you know if anyone else is coming?" the vicar asked, bending towards them in a confidential manner,

"It's just that this is a rather unusual ceremony in that I've had no communication from family whatsoever. This has all been organised by a firm of solicitors from London. Most unusual!"

"I'm afraid we're as much in the dark as you are," said Jack.

The vicar shrugged.

"Oh well, just have to play it by ear, I suppose," and she glanced at her watch,

"I'll give it another five minutes and then we'll start," then she looked out at the squall engulfing the church and the mass of the press corps,

"Those poor souls! I'd let them in, but I fear it would be an unseemly bunfight. Can't have that at a funeral!"

They looked back at the maelstrom of the press pack as half of them ran for shelter while the rest jostled for the best view for when people came out.

"I think it's for the best," said Jack.

"Yes," agreed the vicar,

"Now, do go in and take a seat near the front," and then she suddenly remembered,

"Oh, there is one thing,"

Jack and Annie paused and looked at the vicar, who was clearly embarrassed,

"I'm afraid I have made a change to the requested service. One of the readings didn't seem very... appropriate. Genesis Chapter Nineteen, Verses twenty-four to thirty-six,"

The blank expressions gave her all the reply she needed,

"Um... anyway, I've switched that for something more becoming – I do hope you don't mind," said the vicar, looking hopefully at them.

"I'm sure it will be fine," Jack smiled and was pleased to see the relief on the vicar's face.

"Thank Go... well, thank him in there, I suppose," the vicar effused,

"So, I'll see you in a bit."

Inside, the church was lit only by candles, which would have been fine on a normal day, but because of the sudden darkness of the storm outside, the result was a Stygian gloom. Once Annie's eyes had adjusted, she could see that it was an unpretentious, rural church. An arcade of simple arches, supported by squat pillars ran up the left side of the nave, separating the main body of the church from a smaller chapel, while above them the vaulted ceiling was a looming mass of dark oak and massive beams. As they turned to walk up the aisle, the clouds of their breath eddied as they walked through them. Annie wondered how it could possibly be even colder in the church than outside, but somehow it was! Straight ahead of them, the coffin lay on a pair of wooden stands in front of the altar. Directly to the right of it, a small choir of boys were sitting quietly in the choirstalls. Annie thought they looked angelic, while Jack wondered whether any of them were surreptitiously playing games on their phones. As she walked forward, Annie couldn't work out which was worse - the stifling silence, or the fact that it was only being broken by the sound of their shoes on the flagstones.

Then, the strangest thing happened. As her eyes fell upon the two figures in black sitting in the front pew, Annie felt her hackles rise. Literally. All the hairs on the back of her neck stood out and she felt an instinctual reaction to danger. She had seen pictures of these women for most of her life and heard Jack's account of their brutality, but to be near them in that space was like nothing she'd ever experienced. They exuded a sense of threat, which made her muscles tense. Fight or flight? She was ready for either. The women were sitting to the right of the aisle and when the moment came, Annie made sure she steered Jack to the pews on the left and placed herself between him and his sisters. They sat looking straight ahead. While Jack was lost in a swirl of the dark memories he had so carefully sealed and stacked away, Annie was in the moment and alert to anything that might happen. Her right leg wanted to twitch, but she wouldn't let it. She looked at the stained-glass window above the altar, but couldn't concentrate enough to work out what it depicted. She looked abstractedly at the choir. There were some women in the back row, but no men. A choir of boys and women? Maybe it was a British thing? Then she picked up the folded piece of A4 paper, which was the order of service, and didn't so much look at it as stare through it. And all the while, her concentration was drawn towards Jack's sisters. Finally, she couldn't stand it anymore and flicked her eyes across to look at them. The split second was like a click of a camera shutter and it was all she needed before snapping her eyes forward again.

The mental picture was unsettling. Rosalind and Veronica were no longer sitting looking forward. Both had turned a few degrees and were looking directly at Jack and Annie. And the more she reviewed the mental image with her keen photographer's eye for detail, the more menacing it became. On the surface, they were two strikingly attractive women, who were looking across at their brother, whom they hadn't seen in years. Beyond that, the devil was in the detail. First of all, they were sitting perfectly straight. Not relaxed, not slouching, not affected by grief, but ramrod straight as if they were ready to act in an instant. To do what? Annie couldn't guess. Their sharp jawlines, so perfectly highlighted by the cut of their collars and their choice of earrings, indicated their lean strength and hinted at a certain cruelty. The lips of both women were slightly parted, revealing rows of perfect, white teeth in what amounted to a barely disguised snarl. Their faces were set with disdain, but it was their eyes that were most unnerving. Aquamarine and sea green – Annie had never seen such vivid colours before even in the thousands of close-ups she'd taken of people's faces. Beyond the colours, it was the way the lines radiating from the outer edge of their irises to the rims of their pupils seemed to flash with energy that was so aberrant. They weren't fixed patterns like those of other people, but were a constant lightning storm of shifting lines. Their eyes were charged with a crackling volatility that made it impossible to read what they might be thinking – or what they might be about to do. The overall effect of these different features was truly menacing and gave the sisters the hungry, unnaturally alert look of a pair of Dobermans waiting for the command to attack. Annie swallowed hard and reached for Jack's hand, which she squeezed tightly. What the hell had she gotten herself into?

The sudden blare of Bach's Toccata and Fugue in D minor from the church organ made Annie literally jump an inch off her seat. As she collected herself, she didn't see the smile that passed between Rosalind and Veronica – whoever this person was with their brother, she would be no match for them.

"You ok?" Jack whispered into her ear.

"Yeah, fine. The organ caught me unawares."

Jack smiled as he listened to the music. Even in death, his father was being dark. The organ played for the best part of ten minutes, during which the vicar came to take her place near the altar. Finally, as the last, fat note filled the church, the vicar stepped forward,

"We meet in the name of Jesus Christ, who died and was raised to the glory of God the Father. Grace and mercy be with you."

The stillness within the church contrasted with the howling gale outside it. The vicar paused for a moment to run a nervous finger around the inside of her collar, then continued,

"We have come here today to remember before God our brother David Joseph Kidd; to give thanks for his life…"

Jack couldn't help but grind his teeth at this,

"To commend him to God our merciful redeemer and judge; to commit his body to be buried, and to comfort one another in our grief."

At this, Jack very deliberately leaned forward and looked at his sisters for the first time and found them looking right back at him. He looked them both in the eye. First Veronica, then Rosalind. His gaze was steady, theirs was the gaze of Furies, barely containing their urge to wreak havoc. Inside, Jack was laughing. It was nice to see they hadn't changed a bit!

"Almighty God, you judge us with infinite mercy and justice and love everything you have made," the vicar said, but before she could draw breath, there was a flash of white light from outside the church and an explosion of such force that Jack could have sworn he saw the stained-glass window behind the altar bow inwards and snap back. God, it seemed, wasn't in complete agreement with that last sentiment.

"It's all right," said the vicar quickly to calm the jittery choirboys,

"Just a bit of lightning. Nothing to worry about," although the look on her face as she turned back to the 'congregation' was one of concern and she couldn't help but hurry through the next part of her address,

"In your mercy turn the darkness of death into the dawn of new life, and the sorrow of parting into the joy of heaven; through our Saviour, Jesus Christ. Amen."

"Amen," repeated the choir, Jack and Annie. Rosalind and Veronica remained tight-lipped.

"Please stand for our hymn, Eternal Father, Strong To Save," said the vicar who, wiping the sweat from her face, walked across to conduct the choir as the organ took up the song.

The congregation of four stood up and with the choir they sang,

"Eternal Father, strong to save,
Whose arm hath bound the restless wave,
Who bid'st the mighty ocean deep
Its own appointed limits keep;
O hear us when we cry to Thee,
For those in peril on the sea."

Annie wondered how the proceedings would have gone without the choir, because Rosalind and Veronica barely bothered to mime and, as the first verse drew to its close, their faces were as thunderous as the storm outside. This anger built up as the hymn progressed through Father, Son and Holy Ghost quelling the raging waters, ending their tumult and shielding brethren in danger's hour. By the end, the sisters looked fit to burst into the screaming rage so recently quelled by the Lord. Normally, Annie would have found such impotent fury amusing, but there was nothing funny about Rosalind and Veronica. They had the look of two people who would exact revenge for their discomfort. But why, Annie wondered, were they so discomforted? It was a song about the sea. So what? Why should it get under their skin? From what she knew of them (from magazines and the tabloids) neither really had much to do with the sea or sailing. It was bizarre.

As for Jack, he had cast a glance across at them as the hymn had begun and was relieved to see they had decided not to sing. The fact was, their singing was dreadful, tuneless and simply wrong – as if their voices were calibrated for a different set of scales to those used in most music. There was something about their singing that had always made him feel physically sick, so at least they were spared that! As the service progressed, Jack tried to think of any happy memories of his father. Incredibly, there were none. He couldn't remember a single moment when his father wasn't either absorbed in work, arguing with his mother or being vile to him. He wondered for the hundredth time why his mum had married him. He remembered that his mum was sensible and could be funny, so surely the man she'd married couldn't have always been like that? Something must have changed, though what it was barely mattered now. Now he was being buried and only four people cared enough to witness it – and of them, one had only bad memories and another had already suggested a plan to piss on his grave, dig him up and hang him. So much for a celebration of his life!

The reading was Ecclesiastes Chapter 3, 'To every thing there is a season, and a time to every purpose under the heaven'. Having been forced to attend Chapel every Sunday at boarding school for eleven years, Jack was familiar with it. He'd always found it rather hypnotic, with its rising and falling cadences – like listening to the classified football results... A time to love 3, and a time to hate 0; a time of war 1, and a time of peace 2. Even today he was finding it making him drowsy, despite the hammering rain and the rumbling thunder. Then, the vicar came to the last verse and Jack became wide awake.

"Wherefore I perceive that there is nothing better, than that a man should rejoice in his own works; for that is his portion: for who shall bring him to see what shall be after him?"

And it lodged in Jack's mind. His father would never see what would be after him. If there were a God, David Kidd (child-beating, sadistic SOB) would certainly not be going to spend a happy eternity with them. So, he would never see that in spite of the beatings, the verbal assaults and the mental cruelty, his son had turned out a happy, healthy, nice person. His father had failed. He'd failed to break him, he'd failed to sour him and he'd failed to turn him into some emotionally stunted mini-me. Most of all, he'd failed to make Jack pass on the cruelty to his son, Harry. Jack knew that Harry would grow up with all the love and support that he would ever need to chart his own course through life. Jack wished his father could see that, could see that cruelty ultimately ends in failure. But David Kidd was lying a few feet away, blind, deaf and dumb in death. Even his attempt to control his own funeral had failed. What was the reading supposed to have been? Genesis Chapter nineteen, verses twenty-four to thirty-six? Jack made a mental note to look it up later.

By now, the vicar was most of the way through a short sermon about the importance of family and how, as Christians, we are all part of one family in Christ. Annie looked across at her sisters-in-law and hoped that the Christian family wasn't anything like as dysfunctional as Jack's. Then a horrible thought dawned on her – these people weren't just Jack's family, they were hers, too. And, worse, her son's family. That thought set off a bloom of white heat in her gut. Having spoken to Mark Fry and having seen Rosalind and Veronica up close, Annie could understand exactly why Jack had insisted that Harry be kept as far away from this family as possible. The heat within her flared into a fire of determination to protect her son and her husband. From what? From anything! From whatever his sisters might conjure. She looked at them again and this time, they returned her gaze. Annie gave them an upward nod to say,

"Sup, bitches?" and then turned her eyes deliberately back to the vicar, who was ending her sermon with something ridiculous about how the trust of family is the greatest trust of all.

"Yeah, and if we all wish hard enough, we'll get a unicorn!" Annie thought.

There was no eulogy and the service finally wound up with a blessing and an invitation to follow the coffin down to the graveside. The undertakers made their way solemnly up the aisle, then made a good job of the technical difficulties of safely getting the coffin off the stands and onto their shoulders.

"Nothing worse than dropping the coffin," thought Jack, who decided he ought to tip the undertakers, the vicar and the choir, who were singing the coffin out to 'Guide Me Oh Thou Great Redeemer'. The vicar led the pallbearers and, as they were walking past, a thought occurred. Jack whispered into Annie's ear,

"Do you want to go ahead of my sisters or behind them?"

"Behind!" she hissed. There was no way she was going to let those two blindside her!

And then the procession was past them and they were directly facing Rosalind and Veronica. Fortunately, being arrogant (and 'up themselves' as Annie thought), the sisters immediately glided into place behind the coffin. They were the older sisters. They were famous. They were important. They were also unable to see Annie make faces at them as they walked out of the back door of the church and down to the graveside.

The downpour had stopped and the wind was dropping, which made the vicar very happy, because her vestments were a nightmare to dry out. Soon they were down at the graveside and committing the body to the earth.

"We have entrusted our brother David Joseph Kidd to God's mercy, and we now commit his body to the ground: earth to earth, ashes to ashes, dust to dust..."

Jack lost himself in thought. In some ways, he'd already done this on the day he'd left England for America. He had buried his father and everything he'd done to Jack as a boy in a deep, deep grave and tried to forget him. By and large, he'd been pretty successful. Now, standing over his actual grave and watching the coffin being lowered in, he found a distinct lack of feelings. He wasn't angry or sad, he wasn't really anything. He was just standing there looking at a box that would now be covered by earth forever. And that was all there was. Some end to a life!

"...who died, was buried, and rose again for us. To him be glory for ever. Amen."

"Amen," Jack said, then threw a handful of earth onto the top of the coffin. He was impressed that the sexton ensured the earth was kept dry in spite of the rain. He would need a tip, too. This funeral was getting expensive.

Annie followed his lead and threw a handful of earth, then noted that this was clearly beneath Rosalind and Veronica who couldn't possibly sully their perfectly manicured hands, even for their dear, departed father.

"We'll leave you to have some private moments," said the vicar,

"But I'll be waiting by the door of the church if you have any questions, or anything..." she trailed off as she caught Veronica's eye, blushed and then bustled off, followed by the undertakers.

Silence and a chill descended on the graveside. The four people stood looking at each other. A casual observer (or a paparazzo up a tree in the next field with a long lens) might have seen a group of people joined together in a moment of contemplation at the loss of a loved one. The casual observer and the hundreds of thousands of people who saw the picture in the glossy magazines the following week would have been hopelessly wrong.

"Who is this?" Rosalind said icily, not taking her eyes off Jack and indicating Annie with the slightest movement of her hand.

"This is…" Jack began, but his wife took the ball off him and ran with it,

"Annie. Annie Ingels – Jack's wife, your sister-in-law. Thrilled to finally meet ya. I'm so sorry for your loss," and she was around the grave, shaking Veronica's hand very firmly and staring into her eyes before her victim had time to pull her sharp heels out of the soft earth and take evasive action.

After three firm shakes, she didn't so much let go of Veronica's hand as throw it aside so she could move on to Rosalind. The older sister refused the outstretched hand, but Annie wasn't done – she was going to run that ball right into the endzone.

"Of course, what am I doing? Shaking hands? We're family!" and with a climber's speed and accuracy, she was onto Rosalind and giving her a crushing hug before she could move.

"I really hope we can become good, good friends," she said with her head pressed against Rosalind's shoulder. She felt her trying to break free but was pleased that she didn't seem to have the strength to. Touchdown!

Annie let go and stood back to look at them both. They were simultaneously nonplussed and furious. Perfect! Jack came round and joined her, and now that he was right up close to his sisters, he realised that Annie was right – attack was definitely the best form of defence.

"Good to see you both looking so well, terrible circumstances, of course, but I suppose nobody lives for ever. Impressive that the old man organised the service ahead of time. What did you think of it?"

"Too long," said Veronica severely as she extricated her treacherous left heel from the soft grass.

"And you've been married how long?" Rosalind enquired in a tone that made it clear she didn't give two shits either way.

"Ten wonderful years," Annie said, bringing Jack's hand to her lips and kissing it.

Jack smiled as he looked at Annie with unbounded love and admiration. She was standing proud and getting the better of these two much taller women who were used to always getting their way.

"Really? You should have invited us to the wedding," Veronica said pointedly.

"Well, you haven't invited me to any of the six weddings you've had between you, so I guess that makes us even," beamed Jack. God, he'd forgotten how unpleasant it was to be so close to them! They wanted to intimidate him, to treat him like the little brother they'd tortured, but they couldn't and their anger was palpable. Being within the pall of that anger was frankly horrible, but he'd stick it out, so they'd be under no illusions that they had any power over him anymore.

"You must work to keep the family's failed artist in protein shakes, so what is it you do?" asked Rosalind, levelling her uncanny, electric eyes at Annie.

"You do know that Jack is a leading website designer?" Annie replied. Each of the sisters minutely raised a precision-plucked eyebrow in response,

"But me? I'm a photographer," Annie finished.

"Like *them*?" Rosalind indicated the badly camouflaged paparazzo up the tree across the field.

"Not quite – I shoot action sports."

"Ah," said Veronica, with contempt dripping from her scarlet lips, "It's like they say – those that can, do. Those that can't, take pictures."

Annie laughed lightly and replied,

"So true! But here's the thing – to take pictures of people at the top of the Matterhorn or Everest, or K2, you gotta climb up there with them. So, what's the biggest thing you've scaled recently – an airport escalator, or that handsome bimbo you pulled up with?"

"Giancarlo is not a bimbo!" Veronica snapped and she would have lunged for Annie had her heels not sunk back into the ground.

"Really, sister," Rosalind chided, holding an arm across Veronica,

"You shouldn't let someone so insignificant goad you. Remember, she is beneath you."

"But not in the same way that I'm guessing you like Giancarlo to be beneath you," Annie countered.

Jack couldn't help snorting with laughter. Watching Annie in action was priceless! And now his sisters were flashing with indignation.

"Aren't you going to say something, Jasper?" asked Rosalind.

"I think Annie's saying quite enough for the both of us."

"It's pathetic to see a big man under the thumb of such a little woman," Veronica needled.

"Oh!" said Jack in apparent surprise, "Well, if you really want me to say something..."

Veronica's venomous eyes dared him to,

"You, Veronica, can go and shove your head right up Rosalind's arse-hole," where Annie had wielded a rapier, Jack favoured the sledge-hammer approach and, before his sisters could react to the first blow, he added,

"From what I've read online, Ros loves to take it up the arse, so it should be nice and roomy for you."

Even Annie's jaw dropped.

Rosalind and Veronica made noises somewhere between a snarl and a strangled scream.

"How dare you!" Rosalind hissed.

"Little fucker!" Veronica had taken the gloves off,

"You always were a nasty little shit."

"One click of this," said Rosalind, holding up a lighter-sized device,

"And my security team could put you in that grave along with father."

"In the glare of the tree-cam, the drone and the long lens from up on that hill? Be serious!" said Jack, though he could see that she *was* deadly serious. If she thought there was a chance of getting away with it... but there wasn't.

"Why did you even come today, Jasper?" Veronica asked, "Father hated you. We all hated you."

"Mum didn't," Jack replied softly, "Or Nanna and Granddad."

"Yes, and we all know where that got them," said Rosalind, jerking her thumb across her throat with a 'cccchhhh' noise.

Annie felt Jack stiffen – that one had hit home and the sisters knew it. They decided to quit while they had some sort of advantage,

"Delightful as this has been, we have important things to do before the reading of the will," Rosalind said, starting to move.

"Not that he'll have left you anything. Your presence will be pointless, as per usual," Veronica added, trying to make a dignified exit, but failing because her heels kept sinking, with the result that she looked drunk as she walked across the grass.

"Unless you have the self-respect to stay away, we'll see you at three," Rosalind tossed the remark over her shoulder, and then they were on the path and marching quickly back up through the graveyard to the church.

"Love you, too!" Jack called back.

Then, when they were out of earshot he and Annie started laughing.

"Oh my God, that was incredible!" Annie enthused,

"After the build-up you gave them, I was expecting them to be unpleasant, but they are spectacularly nasty!"

"I know – and you were brilliant!"

Annie gave a small curtsy,

"I thought – go for it!"

"Such a strong move! And they were all like, 'Eurgh! Who is this pauper touching us!', it was perfect," Jack laughed,

"And when you hugged Ros... fucking classic!"

"And you – where did that stuff about Veronica sticking her head up Rosalind come from?"

"Years of pent-up anger, I guess."

"The looks on their faces! I hope that photographer caught it," Annie said excitedly,

"Let's ask him! I'll buy it as your Christmas present!"

"I'd rather have the new Burton step in boots and bindings, but okay," and they turned to go. They could see the photographer just starting to extricate himself from the branches of the tree, so they moved quickly.

"I do have one serious question, though," said Annie as they got to the gate.

"What?"

"How do people online know that Rosalind likes anal?"

"Apparently there's a leaked video of her and her racing driver husband doing it on Pornhub. Thank Christ I haven't seen it, but according to what I've read, she really begs him for it."

Annie thought for a moment and then nodded, "Respect!"

Chapter Seventeen

Down The Boozer

The pub was quiet. Thursday lunchtime is never rush hour in a rural pub, so Jack was immediately able to gain the attention of the barman.

"We're with the Kidd party – I believe there's a room booked?"

"Yeah, it's in the Tavern Room – follow the corridor round and it's at the end."

"Thanks..." then he stopped and asked, "Are there drinks laid on?"

"Champagne on ice, white and red and a range of soft drinks and hot beverages. Plus food."

"In that case, two pints of ESB, please."

"ESB?" Annie asked as the barman pulled the pints.

"Fuller's Extra Special Bitter. Makes Dom Perignon taste like gnats' piss – you'll love it!" smiled Jack, whose eyes lit up as the pints arrived. He reached for his wallet, but the barman held up his hand,

"Open tab on the bar 'til closing time."

"Wow!" Jack was impressed, "Thanks," and they took their drinks and headed for the Tavern Room.

"Trust dad to only start being generous after he's dead," Jack said as they got to the door.

The room was fairly large and of the traditional country pub style with lots of wooden beams across the ceiling and on the walls between white painted plaster. Horse brasses, old copper cooking utensils and the usual rural stuff that tourists love adorned the walls. Across one side, long trestle tables groaned with food and drink, while half a dozen round tables with chairs were dotted throughout the room.

"Cheers!" said Jack, looking Annie in the eye as he took a long pull at his pint,

"Oh yeah! I've missed you, old friend!"

Annie tried hers with a bit more circumspection, but immediately succumbed to its rich, malty charms.

"Nice," she said.

"Nice? Nice!" Jack said with mock ferocity, "It's the Ninth Wonder of the World! The pinnacle of human achievement and all you can say is, it's 'nice'? What a heathen!"

"Okay, it's wonderful – happy now?"

"Yes, but be careful, it's quite strong and it creeps up on you."

"Sounds like your courtship technique."

"Hey, don't knock it – it worked on you, didn't it?"

Annie looked around,

"So, this is your dad's wake? Good crowd!" she was still hyped from the altercation at the graveside and ready to giggle at anything,

"Let's see what they've laid on – I'm starving!"

There was a good selection of sandwiches, crisps and, under a large silver lid, a plate of hot pigs in blankets. This would do nicely! They were just loading up their plates when the door opened and the vicar came in. She'd changed out of her vestments and now sported a chunky Norwegian jumper in patterns of blue, red and white.

"Come on in!" Jack cried, "Champagne?"

"Oh, well, seeing as it's lunchtime and I've already written my sermon for Sunday, why not?"

Jack did the honours while Annie chatted easily to the vicar, who was looking a good deal happier than she had been during the funeral.

"So, how does that rate on the weird funeral scale, Penelope?" Jack asked when they were ensconced with their food and drinks at a table.

"It certainly had its moments! That lightning! We nearly lost the choir there! But at least no one fell in the grave, I've had that before," she replied cheerily.

"In the grave?" Annie exclaimed.

"Yes, I think they'd started the wake early and this chap just tottered in. Nightmare!" and then Penelope's smile faded slightly as she looked over her shoulder and asked,

"No offence, but your sisters aren't coming to this are they?"

Jack laughed,

"Never in a million years!"

"Oh good..." she sighed, then realised she'd said it out loud and back-tracked, "I mean, that is to say..."

"Don't worry, we can't stand 'em either," Annie said, giving Penelope a nudge.

"I hope you don't mind my saying, but they are a bit..." she fished for the right words.

"Yes, they are a bit..." said Jack and they all laughed.

"I've been a vicar for twenty years and have met a hell of a lot of different people from dear little old ladies to serial rapists – I used to have a parish in central London," she added in response to the looks of surprise on their faces,

"But I've never met anyone who gave me the collywobbles quite like them."

"I know what you mean," said Annie and she recounted how she'd felt during the service.

"There's definitely something off about them," said Penelope finally, then mused,

"But this whole thing's been very strange. Not just the funeral being organised by lawyers, or my having to change the reading, but the back-ground," and then she stopped, clearly worried she might have said too much.

"How do you mean?" asked Jack, and then, seeing her hesitancy, he added,

"Don't worry, we'll be going back to America on Sunday, so we're not going to tell anyone."

Penelope thought for a moment and then decided – they were family and ought to know.

"Well, the whole thing's been rather... dark. You see, I've only been in the parish for two weeks. Parachuted in after the death of the previous vicar, Reverend Thompson,"

Annie and Jack offered condolences and Penelope continued,

"He had been approached by your father a few days earlier, just before his own death. According to my predecessor's diaries, your father wanted to give a confession, but obviously being an Anglican, the vicar couldn't do that. But your father was insistent. He had to give it to the priest of this parish because of the links to his wife's family."

"I suppose it makes sense. We never went to the church in Elstead. Christmas and Easter we'd come here," said Jack.

"His need went beyond that. I've been piecing things together from Reverend Thompson's notes and diaries, and it seems that your father's desire to confess was wrapped up with the deaths of your mother and grandparents."

Penelope took a sip of her drink. Silence sat heavy on the room and all the levity they had shared was squeezed out.

"It seems he felt responsible for their deaths."

"But they were accidents," said Jack.

"Yes, but nevertheless he thought they were his fault in some way," Penelope replied.

"Hang on, wait – what? Your grandparents died in an accident, too?" Annie was shocked.

"Yes," this was definitely something Jack had not wanted to talk about, but he forced himself,

"Coming back from Farnham, they were turning right into Kennel Lane when an articulated truck behind them decided that was the moment to try to overtake. T-boned their little Honda Jazz. Crushed it beyond recognition. They were killed instantly. The truck driver said they didn't indicate."

Annie looked at Jack in horror.

"I was going to tell you, but I thought you'd probably heard enough depressing crap from me for one lifetime."

"I'm so sorry..." she said. Jack smiled weakly back at her, then turned to Penelope,

"But I still don't see what my father had to do with it. Or with the death of my mother. I was there. In fact I was with him when it happened, so I know he had nothing to do with it."

"Unfortunately, Reverend Thompson didn't leave details of why your father felt that way..." she paused, wondering whether to tell any more,

"But there are details about... about your sisters."

"What about my sisters?"

"Well, I'm new to the Parish, but it seems there were a lot of rumours spread around. Obviously, there are a lot of gossips out here in the country – it's the only entertainment some people get. However, the rumours concerning your father and your sisters were very serious. Your sisters were accused of sleeping around with boys in the local schools. The rumour was your father knew and encouraged them. And then," again Penelope paused,

"And then, there was the other rumour. Incest."

Penelope looked at Jack to see how he'd taken this information.

"Yes," he said, "I'm aware of that."

"That's why I had to change the reading, you see?"

Jack gave a 'dunno' shrug.

"Genesis Chapter nineteen, Verses twenty-four to thirty-six. The story of Lot escaping from Sodom and Gomorrah with his family," Penelope explained.

"Oh! Yes, Lot's wife looking back at the destruction of the cities and being turned into a pillar of salt," said Jack.

"Yes, that is part of it, but it's what happened after that which is most pertinent to today's proceedings. You see, Lot escaped into the mountains with his two daughters, and then: 'The firstborn said unto the younger, Our father is old, and there is not a man in the earth to come in unto us after the manner of all the earth: Come, let us make our father drink wine, and we will lie with him, that we may preserve seed of our father.' And that's just what they did. First the older, then the younger – 'Thus were both daughters of Lot with child by their father'."

Jack exhaled heavily,

"Blimey! They never dwelt on that bit during Sunday chapel at my school!"

"So, you see, with all the rumours swirling about your father and your sisters, I couldn't possibly allow that passage to be read. And especially since I know from Reverend Thompson's papers that your father's relationship with his daughters was central to his desire to confess. Although Reverend Thompson couldn't take his confession as such, I know for a fact that he did hear him out, and that whatever he heard shook him. Your father killed himself the following day. The day after that, one of your sisters paid a visit to Reverend Thompson – the dark haired one according to the housekeeper."

"Veronica," said Jack with an unsurprised tone that said 'it figures'.

"Yes, well, that seemed to take a terrible toll on him. What he put into his diary that night was virtually illegible. His hand was usually so firm and elegant, but that night it was hardly recognizable. It looked like he'd had a stroke. The housekeeper said that he was a nervous wreck the next morning - could hardly speak. She said he was like a man having an internal battle with himself, but losing. The only thing she could get out of him was that he had to get to Portsmouth to speak with the Bishop about a point of maritime law. Why, nobody will ever know. He drove his car off the road at full tilt and straight into the petrol pumps at Liphook services. As you can imagine, the whole place went up. And that was that," Penelope drained the rest of her glass at a single gulp, poured herself another and quaffed half of that in one.

In the stillness that followed this news, Annie decided the vicar had it right and downed the rest of her pint. Jack, meanwhile, stared into his and slowly his mind clicked things into place.

"So, my father does his best to keep his incestuous activities secret," he said deliberately, "Even to the point of firing household staff. But then suddenly wants to confess all, AND point it out in public through this Bible passage, with the two victims sitting right there to hear it? It doesn't make sense."

"Victims?" Annie cried, "You're calling your sisters victims?"

"Of course," said Jack, "He was the adult. They were the children. Therefore, they are the victims."

"Unless he was trying to tell the world that *he* was the victim," Annie countered.

"But abusers do that all the time," said Penelope, "I've seen them deny wrongdoing and accuse their victims of tempting them into acts of evil when, in reality, they've done it because they're fucking scumbags... oh, er... pardon my French!" Penelope added, blushing furiously and taking solace in another gulp of champagne.

"Whoever is the victim in all this, the fact is that he suddenly changed years of habit trying to keep this secret and then ended it all. Why?" Jack wondered aloud.

"Does it matter?" Annie asked.

"I don't know," Jack admitted, then he finished his pint and looked at his watch,

"We'd best be off – don't want to be late for the moment where I'm told officially that he's left me nothing. Thank you for everything, Penelope, I thought everyone did a great job today," and now they all got up and started shaking hands.

"My pleasure," she replied, "All in the line of duty!"

"And if I want to leave a consideration for you, the choir, the organist, the undertakers and the sexton, how should I..?"

"Transfer the total amount to the church, with a direction for how it's to be split and I'll see to it."

"Great!"

Then he and Annie set off for the door, but just as he opened it, he turned and said,

"By the way, we've got an open bar until closing time for anyone involved, so it would be a shame to see it go to waste."

"Goodness, no! I'll let the relevant people know," said Penelope and she waved as the door closed. When they were gone, her hand went straight to her phone,

"Come on... pick up... Phil! Yes! Phil, it's Penny. You know that eleven-o-clock we had? Yes, well the wake's on at the Badger, I'm the only one left and I've got five words for you – open bar 'til closing time!"

Chapter Eighteen

The Bermuda Covenant

A nnie stared in silence at the heavy iron gates looming fifteen feet above them, at the broad gravel drive ending in a wide turning circle in front of the big, red brick Georgian house. It stood, implacable in the gloom, encased in a black skeleton of leafless Virginia creeper.

"And this is where you spent the *happiest* days of your childhood?"

"Yup!"

"Sheesh!" Annie rolled her eyes.

"Don't judge a book by its winter cover. Most of the year the house is decked out in greenery and in autumn – that's fall to you..."

Annie gave Jack a sour look, which he rode,

"It's a blaze of colour. And anyway, it's what goes on behind closed doors that matters and I had a lot of fun with my grandparents. So, this is my happy place. Now, let's go to my least favourite place on the planet – my dad's house," Jack said, turning the car around.

"We could still skip it," Annie said, "The lawyers will contact you if there's anything important."

"Yeah, but I want you to see it, and anyway, my father might have left some sort of clue as to why he suddenly changed tack and wanted to tell the world about his relationship with my sisters. I want to know why – don't you?"

Annie wasn't so sure. There was something going on here that made her want to leave it alone.

"Maybe, but it seems to me that too many people have met with accidents for them all to be accidents. And I don't like it."

They fell back into silence as they drove over an ancient bridge and then passed a pub next to a triangular grassy village green. Annie thought that on a sunny day it would have been achingly pretty. They crossed another bridge and began to go uphill away from the river.

"I agree that when you take them all together, it seems like something's off, but they didn't happen all together. There were ten years between my mum's death and my grandparents' accident, and another fifteen or so years from then to the vicar," Jack reasoned.

"Okay," Annie conceded, "It could be I'm jet lagged, or I'm overwhelmed by suddenly being submerged by all the crap you've been through, or meeting your sisters when I know what they did to you, but something's giving me the creeps. If all those accidents really are just coincidences, then why do I feel like I'm walking into the death zone?"

Jack glanced across at her – she meant it. She'd entered the death zone three times, climbing above eight thousand metres, where the human body starts to die cell by cell from lack of oxygen. Stay too long and you never leave.

"Really?"

"Truly," she replied with grim-faced certainty, "Climbing is dangerous. Every climber knows it. You know that one day you might be cut loose from a rope to save a party, or that you might have to cut a friend loose to save yourself and others. I've had to climb past more than one dead body frozen to the side of a mountain. It's something we all deal with in our own ways."

Annie then turned slightly, so she was facing towards Jack,

"But when you're in the death zone, that's something different. You've gone beyond where humans should be. You feel you're on borrowed time. I always feel that the mountain I'm climbing has finally noticed me and is turning all its attention to my every move. I feel its all-encompassing presence and unimaginable power. I know that any moment it could shrug me off. So, with every painful step, I pray to the mountain. It's strange up there, Jack. Things happen up there that are beyond our capacity to understand. On Everest, one team member started veering off away from the group and we had to get him back. He could see we were pissed off, but he said he had to go, because Mallory and Irvine were showing him the way to the summit."

"Isn't that just lack of oxygen?" Jack asked.

"Yes... and no. Up there, it's... a world beyond. Time, space and the laws of nature become fluid. It's uncanny, Jack. And so is this."

As if to emphasise the point, Jack turned off the main road and up a narrow, single lane track that was completely overhung by vast laurels and evergreen trees. Gloom turned into near darkness under the thick canopy.

"What the hell is this?" Annie didn't like it. And she really didn't like the way the ground to the right of the road was beginning to slope sharply away as they went up the hill.

"This is the road I grew up on," Jack replied, concentrating as it rose and fell, twisted and turned. The evergreens were thinning out and now the woodland was becoming mixed. The darkness lifted somewhat. There on the right was the entrance to a driveway. She couldn't see the house, as the drive doubled back almost parallel to the road, but the gap in the trees gave Annie the chance to see across a steep-sided valley to the heavily wooded hills beyond.

"Who lives up here?" She wondered out loud.

"Rich people who value their privacy."

They passed another driveway. Somewhere below them through the thick woodland there was a glimpse of a huge house. Yes, these would be perfect for very discreet, very strange people to indulge their desires beyond prying eyes. Who would want to come snooping up here? In places, the road was barely wider than the little Abarth. Her Beast would've been half off the track already.

Then the road got steeper and they came to a hairpin. Not like the wide, sensibly designed bends you get on Italian mountain roads, no, this one was sharp and narrow. There would have been no way for her camper van to get round it.

"What do people do when they move in? No truck can get past this," she said with mild indignation on behalf of unsuspecting road users. What idiot designed this road anyway?

"The people moving in at this end of the road come up the way we came. Everyone on the other side of this bend has to get their removal vans to come from the other end of the road. It's okay, the locals all know how it works. Sometimes you find a delivery truck in problems at this corner, but they're never from round here," said Jack as he threw the Abarth into the corner. It skidded happily around it, then raced up the hill like an over-excited puppy. Annie didn't share the car's exuberance as they were once again going through a dingy tunnel of evergreens. Every now and again, high gates loomed at the side of the road, marking the entrance to another large house.

"The houses aren't exactly close together," Annie observed, "Does anyone here know their neighbours?"

"We didn't, but I can't vouch for everyone," said Jack as the trees crowded the road, low and menacing, "But some of these houses are set in twenty or thirty acres, so your nearest neighbour might be hundreds of yards away. Anyway, does your mum know all her neighbours in Southampton?"

"No," Annie admitted, "I think the richer people are the less neighbourly they become. Except the super-rich. They always seem to chum along pretty well."

Jack reigned in the car and indicated right. Between ten-foot-high hedges of rhododendron, yet another black, iron gate barred entry to the property beyond. While Jack pulled up next to the intercom and called the house, Annie looked through the gates at the drive which went straight for about thirty yards and then swept to the left. More rhododendrons flanked the drive but she could see some very tall pines behind them with apparently lifeless trunks, topped by great, green crowns.

"Come on up," said a crackly voice through the intercom and then the gates opened and they were driving back into Jack's childhood. Apparently, nothing had changed. The driveway had always had the mature rhododendrons on either side and now, as then, they made Jack feel uneasy. They were the kind of bushes prowlers could hide in and he remembered that the worst bit of any cycle ride was coming home at dusk or in the dark and cycling up the unlit driveway. With nothing but a small bike light, the darkness had seemed to envelope him and he'd felt that one day it would gobble him up and he'd never be seen again. Driving through the mid-afternoon gloom, with sunset barely two hours away, Jack decided to take decisive action and switched the lights onto full beam. What he wouldn't have given to have been able to light up the driveway like that when he was eleven!

Finally, the house came into view. It looked like it had long forgotten the sound of laughter. Its black upper windows stared hollowly at them. Christ! It was even bleaker than his memories of it, Jack thought. There were some lights on in the lower rooms, but most of the action seemed to be in the vast parking area in front of the house, where Rosalind's Range Rovers, Veronica's Ferraris and an unknown silver Audi A8 were lined up. It was like driving into a 'Who's got the biggest dick' competition. And speaking of dicks, the two security teams had already stationed themselves around the house, looking tough. Jack parked near the Audi and they got out and walked to the front door to be greeted by one of Rosalind's toughs and one of Veronica's pretty boys.

"They're in the study," said the tough, who had a South African accent.

"Thanks," Jack smiled amiably. The tough grimaced back at him as if he were working out the best way to pull Jack's spine out of his body.

Annie winked at Veronica's guard, who looked less pretty and less friendly up close. He grunted and opened the front door.

And there it was. There, opposite the front door, against the side of the stairs was the panetiere. Annie couldn't help but stare at it. The door was tiny! She looked at her broad shouldered six-foot husband and couldn't help but exclaim,

"How the hell did you fit in that?"

Jack smiled as he looked down on it,

"I was much younger then."

Annie took in the lifeless hall and imagined what it must've been like for the little boy to have been locked in there with this as his only view. What a fucking nightmare! Before she had the chance to start badmouthing his bitch sisters, a brisk voice, with a hard Yorkshire accent interrupted,

"Mister Kidd? We're ready for you in here."

They looked over to the study to see a blonde woman in her late forties, impeccably dressed in a dark grey trouser suit, beckoning to them from the door.

"Great," said Jack and they joined her,

"Janet Warren, your late father's solicitor," and she held out a dry, strong hand for them to shake, before closing the door behind them.

The room itself was a symphony in dark wood panelling, with floor-to-ceiling bookshelves filled with tomes on engineering. In one corner there was an antique wooden globe and across one wall, a picture window looked out onto the garden. Four chairs had been arranged in front of his father's broad oak desk with its surface inset with green leather. Two of the chairs were occupied by Rosalind and Veronica, who looked up at the latecomers with barely concealed animosity. Ms Warren took her seat behind the desk, produced some papers from her briefcase and then gave the family a look of professional welcome that was friendly, but in keeping with the sombre circumstances of the day.

"Thank you all for coming today to hear the reading of the last will and testament of David Joseph Kidd. Please accept my sincere condolences for your loss. Now..."

But Rosalind coldly interrupted,

"I thought Norris and McNulty were our father's solicitors."

"They were," Ms Warren replied with perfect poise and professionalism despite the rudeness of the interruption,

"But your father approached us about eight weeks ago and transferred the handling of all his affairs to our company. May I?" she extended Rosalind the courtesy of allowing her to continue. Rosalind nodded.

"Thank you," and she took up a document and began to read,

"I David Joseph Kidd, being of sound mind do hereby declare this to be my last will and testament. I hereby revoke all former Wills and other testamentary dispositions..."

At this, Veronica shot a look of concern at Rosalind, who acknowledged it minutely, but flashed her eyes back to the lawyer.

"I appoint the firm of Warren, Mortimer and Scott of 4 Fleet Place, London ECM 7RD to be the sole executors and trustees of this my will,"

Another look somewhere between anxiety and rancour passed between the sisters. What was this? This wasn't what they'd been expecting. This was something that was now beyond their control.

Although Ms Warren seemed engrossed in reading the document, she had noted the sisters' reaction. It was exactly as Mr. Kidd had predicted. She continued reading in a business-like tone. Annie thought she sounded like a female version of Sean Bean.

"Subject to their surviving me, I give devise and bequeath the whole of my estate (including property over which I may have a general power of appointment exercisable by will) (and including all stocks, shares, bonds) (subject to the payment of my just debts funeral and testamentary expenses) unto my daughters Princess Rosalind Diana Constance Stahlberg and Veronica Phoebe Artemis Matser, to be split equally between them."

Jack could see relief suffuse his sisters faces and now they looked smug and self-satisfied. He wondered why he'd bothered coming. Of course his father would leave him nothing! At least nothing pleasant. He could imagine his father directing the lawyer to make sure the reading of the will was done in this room, from behind that desk, which Jack remembered all too well. One of his father's favourite punishments was to strip Jack down to his underpants and make him lie face down over the desk, so that his feet were still on the floor and his outstretched hands hung over the other side of the desk. He would then tightly tie Jack's hands and feet together with rough twine so that there was no way the boy could writhe out of what was coming. And what was that? A beating! He had an array of implements in a cupboard set into the wood panelling behind the desk. He would open the cupboard, which Jack could see clearly from his trussed position. His father delighted in choosing the tool of his torture, quietly listing the virtues of each before finally taking one out. It could be the cane, with its hard ridges; the flat paddle with the hole in the middle; the whip; the rattan carpet beater; the martinet with its ten leather lashes, each tipped with a sharp, silver triangle; the thick length of rope with its heavy, knotted end; or the simple sports sock with the bar of Wright's Coal Tar Soap inside. His father would then step around the desk, pull down Jack's underpants and set to work on his buttocks, the backs of his legs and across his back, depending on the weapon of choice. Jack felt like spitting and his teeth ground hard at the memory.

There was more, as Ms Warren continued,

"Subject to his surviving me, I discharge to my son, Jasper Algernon Charles Kidd the full estate of Katharine Elspeth Hicks and Rufus James Algernon Hicks,"

What? Suddenly the room became electric. Rosalind and Veronica stiffened. Jack was shocked and Annie sat forward in her chair.

"Including all stocks, shares, bonds and properties held by the deceased at time of death. Properties include The Glades, Shortfield Common Road, Frensham, and Cliff House, 1, The Drive, Warwick, Bermuda, which have been held and maintained in trust according to the will of Katharine Elspeth Hicks and Rufus James Algernon Hicks, to be passed to Jasper Algernon Charles Kidd on the event of my death."

"What?" Veronica screeched.

"No, that cannot be correct!" said Rosalind, starting out of her chair.

"I'm sorry," Ms Warren clearly wasn't, "But it is correct. Your father left his entire estate to you and your sister, but followed the stipulations of your grandfather's will to leave *his* entire estate, including the house in Bermuda, to your brother."

"It can't be!" Veronica raged, "That house should be ours! What right has he to it? He only went there twice. We have memories there. It's our heritage!"

"Be that as it may..." Ms Warren began, but was cut off,

"I want to speak to your boss - get him on the phone right now," Rosalind ordered.

"I'm afraid that isn't possible," Ms Warren replied calmly. Mr Kidd had fully prepared her for this outburst and she withstood it like a rock scattering the spray of thundering waves.

"Oh, it is possible and you will do it," Rosalind was leaning forward with her white knuckles on the desk and her eyes flashing dangerously, "I will speak to the man in charge at once!"

"There is no man in charge," Ms Warren said flatly, but with a triumphant gleam in her eye,

"We are an all-female practice and I am the senior partner. As far as this matter is concerned, I am the alpha and the omega. Mr. Kidd was my personal client, this is his will and I am the executrix of it. I have not finished reading that will, which now requires you and your sister to leave the room, so that I can continue the last part with your brother and his spouse alone."

"No!" Veronica roared,

"How dare you tell us to leave, but allow *her* to stay," and she directed a poisonous glare at Annie.

"This is an outrage!" Rosalind shouted.

Ms Warren's reply was to pick up the document, flip the page and read aloud,

"If, after being requested to do so by my representative, my daughters do not quit the room within one minute and without violence of word or action, I hereby direct my representative to invoke the following clause: to disinherit them both and pass the entirety of my estate to the Royal National Lifeboat Institution."

That quelled the storm.

Ms Warren looked up from the paper at the fiery hellcats in haute couture before her,

"And your time starts now."

"You fucking..."

"Hush now, sister!" Rosalind snapped, "We don't want to lose everything because of our tempers."

Jack watched in some amusement as Veronica physically struggled to control her fury.

"This is not over," Rosalind continued, staring down at the solicitor,

"My lawyers will tear this to pieces and your precious company with it. By the time we've finished with you, you'll be begging on the street."

"Thirty seconds," Ms Warren replied, implacably.

Rosalind turned on her heel and led Veronica out of the room, while the latter walked backwards, never breaking her vicious gaze on the lawyer until the door closed behind her.

"Now," said Ms Warren, smiling at Jack and Annie,

"I suppose you're wondering how much your grandfather's estate is worth?"

Jack wasn't, but Annie was – purely out of intellectual curiosity of course, it wasn't like she was a gold-digger... although there was that exquisitely sweet, but oh-so-expensive new snowboard by Jones that she'd been coveting all winter. Maybe Jack could get that for her birthday?

"Your grandparents' house in Frensham was not sold but has been leased since their deaths. The current occupants have six months left on their lease. After that, if you so wish, the property can revert back to you," said Ms Warren.

Annie was screaming internally: yes, but what's it worth? Get to the point for Chrissakes!

"So, after management fees and tax, the cash sum from leasing the property over the last fifteen years stands at ten million, three hundred and five thousand pounds. The house itself was recently valued at six point five million pounds," Ms Warren said calmly.

Well, that'll keep us in snowboards for a few seasons, Annie thought.

"The house in Bermuda has also been leased and, after management fees and tax, the cash sum stands at one million, eight hundred thousand pounds. The estimated value of the property is two point seven million pounds."

New snowboards, skis, surfboards and a Dodge Charger Hellcat Redeye flitted through Annie's mind. She couldn't help it! Yes, this was turning into one hell of a day...

"Meanwhile, your grandparents' stocks and shares have been managed by a trust since their deaths and all dividends have been reinvested. Their current worth – and I'm afraid it's not what it should be, but given the current turmoil it's hardly surprising and they are good stocks, so they should bounce back..."

Get-to-the-point! Annie screamed internally.

"Their current worth as of nine a.m. this morning is," and at this point, excruciatingly for Annie, Ms Warren had to sift through a couple of documents to find the right sheet, "Ah, here we are – four million, nine hundred and fifty-three thousand, seven hundred and seventy-six pounds and eighty-two pence."

"Wow!" Jack was shellshocked. This he did not expect!

Annie somehow suppressed her urge to do a loud and exuberant touch-down celebration and merely nodded seriously at the news. What a result! Jack's sisters could both suck it!

"Now we have three final matters to clear and then we are done. The first is this," Ms Warren took an envelope from the neat stack of documents at her elbow and handed it to Jack. It clearly had some keys in it. He opened it and let the keys drop into his hand.

"The keys to Cliff House," Ms Warren smiled, then handed him another envelope, "And here is the second. This was part of your grandfather's estate and should have been given to you on his death. Unfortunately, his solicitor mistakenly thought that, like the properties, it was to be held in trust until your father's death. They failed to mention any of this to your father, as, legally, he held no claim to any of it. As a result, only your grandfather's solicitors knew of its existence. I discovered this error when they contacted me after your father's passing. I'm sorry for any inconvenience this might have caused."

Jack opened the envelope and a simple leather cord necklace with a small jade porpoise slipped out into his hand. There was a letter inside. Jack read,

"Darling Jack, this has been handed down through the men of my family since 1640. Remember how I always wore it?"

Jack stopped reading and said, "I do. It was always there around his neck. He said he wore it for protection from the devils."

Annie gave him a 'What?!?' look.

Jack shrugged,

"I don't know! I thought he was just trying to scare me. But I never saw him without it. Anyway..." and he read on,

"Now it is yours. You <u>MUST</u> wear it. It has protected me my whole life from the devils and now it will protect you. Please do this for me and wear it always. All my love, Rufus."

Jack looked at Annie with tears in his eyes and she reached out to gently stroke the back of his hand. She could see that he was barely able to contain the surge of emotion as he re-lived the grief of his grandparents' sudden deaths.

"And finally, this covenant from your father. Please open it and read it aloud," said Ms Warren, handing Jack a third envelope. At the mention of his father, his eyes hardened and the tears receded. It was typical of the vicious sod to have something to say even after he was dead. Jack opened the envelope angrily, having just stopped short of snatching it from the solicitor's hand.

"Jasper, I have left you one pint of my blood in cold storage at the George the Second medical centre, 53 Point Finger Road, Bermuda. It is the least I could do to try to protect you and your family. My blood will finish it, but you must be careful."

He stopped reading and looked up in bewilderment.

"What the fuck? Do you know what that means?" he asked Ms Warren. She shook her head. He looked at Annie, who looked as nonplussed as he felt.

"Why didn't my dad show me any concern like this when he was alive? Treats me like shit my whole life and now he's carked it, he's suddenly all 'be careful, protect your family'. He never once tried to reach out to meet you or Harry. Fuck! I hate these mind games! Do I have to read the rest of this?" he asked.

"I'm afraid so, yes," said Ms Warren, "He was very clear that I should witness you reading it. He said it was to ensure your safety," Ms Warren replied, trying not to sound dramatic.

"Okay..." Jack looked down at the paper with unconcealed malice and continued,

"I know you undoubtedly hate me, but there is something you must do for the sake of you and your family. You must meet the people on this list and talk to them about their loss. Once you have done this, you might understand why I did what I did. I do not ask for forgiveness, only understanding. You must talk to them all. Only then can you end it. Good luck and I am truly sorry... and then there's a list of names – Mary Brewer, Giulia Mazzoni, Skylar Judd and Josephine Paget – with their addresses. And that's it." Jack threw the piece of paper on the table.

"Right," said Ms Warren, putting her briefcase onto the table and opening it, "That concludes our business here today... oh, except for one thing I need to see you put the necklace on."

"You need to see me put it on?"

"Yes, your grandfather's instructions are absolutely clear on that."

"Okay..." Jack said and put the necklace on. The jade porpoise felt strangely warm against his skin.

"Thank you," said Ms Warren, putting various documents into her case, "You know, this is without a doubt the weirdest job I've ever undertaken," she continued, loosening up a bit.

"You mean all will readings aren't like this?" Annie asked.

"No, I've never been threatened by family members before, or had my client kill themselves in such a spectacular fashion."

Jack couldn't help but ask,

"What was spectacular about it?"

Ms Warren looked at Jack with a level gaze and coolly described what had happened in detail. Before she got to the part with the shotguns, she reappraised her audience: Jack was staring straight ahead, while Annie looked back at her with little emotion. Ms Warren decided they could take it and described the last moments of David Kidd's life, finally ending,

"Cause of death was bleeding from the gunshot wounds that severed his legs. His suicide note simply said "I deserve this", but what he did to deserve it, one can only imagine."

Jack could certainly think of a thing or two.

The silence that followed was deep. No one wanted to catch another's eye and the three people stared blankly at different parts of the room for a few moments. Every time Annie thought things had got as unpleasant as they could, the broken elevator they seemed to be riding fell a few more floors. Jack was imagining the scene. He knew the workshop well, knew exactly where the chair would have been placed. Ms Warren was thinking about the bottle of 2003 Margaux waiting for her in her apartment in the Barbican. If ever she deserved a drink, it was tonight! She allowed the silence to settle for about ten seconds and then briskly finished filling her briefcase and snapped it shut.

"I'm sorry," she said again.

"Don't be," Jack replied and his voice was hard,

"It was in keeping with who he was – a sadistic sod, who enjoyed inflicting pain,"

Jack stood and walked around behind the desk, then felt along the side of the bookcase, found the button and pressed it. The secret cupboard in the wall swung open to reveal the array of torture implements of which Jack had intimate knowledge. Still there, ready for action.

"These are what he used on me when I was a kid. He got exactly what he deserved," Jack said bluntly.

Annie and Ms Warren stared in disbelief at the collection.

"And on that note, I take my leave," said Ms Warren, shaking their hands,

"My card. I will be in contact with you to complete the legal documents necessary for the transfers," she handed Jack her card,

"I look forward to seeing you again in less stressful circumstances," she smiled and walked out of the room.

The shouting started as soon as she opened the door. Rosalind and Veronica accosted her with threats, but the sounds became muffled when the door clicked closed behind her. Annie looked at Jack and at the cupboard full of implements.

"He used those on you?"

"Yes," said Jack flatly, "I hated this one the most," he pulled out the martinet and ran the lashes over his hand, then picked out one of the silver triangle ends between his fingers. He held it up so that it glinted in the light,

"The cuts these made would hurt for days afterwards. He was very scientific in his punishments."

Annie went to him and gave him a hug,

"Sadistic asshole!" she said fiercely.

"And now he wants me to track these people down and talk to them?" Jack held up the piece of paper.

"Fuck him! Let's go home!" Annie urged, looking up into Jack's face, but she could see that he was hooked by his father's final mind game.

"I don't know why, but I need to understand what this is all about. All I do know is that we can't tell my sisters anything," he said, pocketing the letters and the list of names and addresses.

"Ya think!" Annie exclaimed, "I wouldn't trust those two as far as I could throw 'em."

The words were hardly out of her mouth when the study door burst open and Rosalind and Veronica crashed into the room with a breaking wave of curses and threats.

"Don't think you're ever going to take residence in that house!" Rosalind snapped,

"My lawyers will tie you up so badly, your grandchildren won't even get in there."

"No need for lawyers, sister," said Veronica slyly as she glided towards Jack,

"I think we can persuade Jack ourselves."

And before he or Annie could react, Veronica was standing right in front of him, fixing him with her uncanny, electric eyes.

"You don't want the house in Bermuda, do you, Jack? No, you understand that it is ours by right and you want to give it to us."

Annie almost laughed out loud. *This* was Veronica's play? Some half-baked hypnotist routine? She was about to say something cutting, but her smile faded as she looked at her husband. His face was going slack and his eyes were becoming glassy.

"Maybe I don't want the house in Bermuda..." he droned, like someone talking in their sleep.

"Of course you don't," Rosalind purred, joining her sister and fixing the power of her eyes upon him,

"After all, it's such a burden. And why would you want all that responsibility?"

"Who wants a burden?" Jack droned again.

What the fuck? Annie was momentarily frozen by the sheer surprise of what she was witnessing.

"Give it to us and you will be happy," Veronica soothed, stretching out a soft, perfectly manicured hand to stroke his cheek.

"Hey! Get your hands off him!" Annie suddenly found her voice and stepped forward, but Rosalind blocked her.

"This is none of your concern. We are talking to our brother, not *you*," and she loaded the final word with so much derision and intense hatred that Annie felt it like a slap in the face.

"I'll be happy..." Jack drawled, then changed in a split second, "...to tell you to get stuffed."

Veronica recoiled.

"This shit never worked on me when I was growing up and it won't work on me now. So, unless you've got something sensible to say, get out of my face, because we're leaving this nightmare house right now."

"Yeah," said Annie, leaning up towards Rosalind's face,

"And if you ever talk to me like that again, I'll punch your teeth so far down your fucking throat, your dentist will have to sift through your shit to find 'em," and she barged Rosalind out of the way.

Annie caught up with Jack as he entered the hall. He was bristling and said,

"I would give you the tour, but this place makes me sick. Suffice it to say, they locked me in that bloody thing," pointing at the panetiere,

"My dad pushed me down those stairs, he hit me over the head with a plate in the dining room, assaulted me with a frying pan in the kitchen and beat me unconscious in the drawing room while those two sat on the sofa watching Top of the fucking Pops!"

At Jack's raised voice, the South African guard opened the front door and stood with his right hand hovering inside his jacket just under his left armpit. His eyes flicked from Jack to Rosalind, who was standing in the doorway of the study.

"Oh yeah, and here's a little newsflash for you and all your psycho buddies," Jack said, marching towards the front door,

"Carrying firearms is illegal in Britain and for handguns it's a minimum of a year in jail. Now, shift it before I call the police."

Hesitation flickered across the guard's face, but a nod from Rosalind made him relax his hand and stand back from the door.

"Clever boy," said Jack as he and Annie walked out. In a few seconds they were in the car and Jack was reversing out of the space to turn in the driveway. He stopped for a moment to look at the house one more time in the rear-view mirror. He ground his teeth at all the terrifying memories it contained. Well, those memories could stay right there in that dismal shithole. He revved the engine into the red, launched down the driveway with the tyres screaming and then they were gone.

Rosalind and Veronica stepped out just in time to see the Abarth's tail-lights round the corner of the drive.

"We have a problem," said Rosalind.

"And I have a solution," Veronica's eyes flashed in the gloom of the dusk.

"Not yet. We must find out what they discussed. Then you can have your fun."

Veronica was frustrated by having to delay her gratification, but realized her sister was right,

"How do we do it?"

"I know a man. Very efficient. Very discreet. Very persuasive. He can have a chat with Ms Warren. I'll make sure he's waiting for her when she gets home tonight," and Rosalind clicked her fingers. Her guard passed her a burner phone and she dialled a number.

Chapter Nineteen

An Evening With Janet Warren

W ine, cheese, bath, bed. These were the thoughts that were going through Janet Warren's head as she pulled into the underground car park. It was already past eight and she was cursing her own diligence. Why had she gone back to the office? She could quite legitimately have gone straight home, as she hadn't got into central London before six. But no, she just had to drop by the office, and naturally there was work to do. There was always work to do! She loved it, but occasionally she did wonder whether she let it take up too much of her time. The whole point of living in an apartment in the Barbican was easy access to the mass of cultural events from concerts to poetry recitals that took place on the site. How many had she been to in the last year? One – and that had only been because a friend had given her tickets to a show they couldn't make it to. She decided this year would have to be different, as she drove around under the yellow light that gave everything in the underground lot an unpleasant pallor. It made the concrete walls, ceiling and floor seem simultaneously drab and menacing – like some Soviet bunker from the 1950's. The only thing that gave the game away that this wasn't a Cold War facility was the array of Porsches, BMWs, Bentleys and other high-end cars crammed together down there.

She wondered whether to see some music or dance as she made the last turn before her space.

"Shit!" she said angrily as she realised there was a battered old Ford Transit parked in her space. To add insult to injury, it was badly parked! Now her neighbours would think she had a crappy van and parked like a cretin. She pulled up and was thinking about what to do when one of the doors of the van opened and a man got out. He was wearing a baseball cap and paint-spattered overalls that were very much in keeping with the van. She pushed a button and her window went down,

"Hello! Sorry, but you've parked in my space. Could you move, please?"

The man, who was of medium height and looked to be in his early fifties, changed direction and approached her open window.

"Sorry, luv, I didn't quite catch that," he said in a hoarse East London accent as he sauntered over. He looked like an ordinary middle-aged bloke, so Janet thought he was bound to see reason,

"I said, you're in my parking space. Everything on this level is reserved for people who live here. The public parking is on the upper floors only."

"Oh, I'm sorry about that. I must've missed the signs. It's hard to read down her with these lights," he said as he got to the car and his face was open and friendly.

"Don't worry, it's easily..."

The left cross caught her flush on the side of the jaw and knocked her out instantly. The man quickly undid her seatbelt, pulled her out and dragged her round to the boot of the car. He lifted her in with relative ease – she probably only weighed about fifty kilos and that was nothing to him. With well-practised moves, he cuffed her hands behind her back and gaffer taped her mouth shut. Satisfied that she couldn't do anything annoying if she woke up, he shut the boot. He checked that she hadn't lost a shoe or dropped something out of her pocket. No. Good to go. He got into the car, adjusted the seat, drove calmly back to the exit ramp and then took the long spiral of blank concrete with its yellow tinge under the dingy lights up, up and up. Within two minutes, he was out of the car park and into the night. Within thirty, he was out of the city and in countryside, beyond the prying eyes of traffic cameras. His car awaited him in an isolated copse off a narrow lane. He pulled up next to it, got out and went to see how his cargo was doing. The flailing foot as he opened the lid of the boot told him that she was very much awake. No, he couldn't have that! As her foot darted out a second time, he slammed the lid down on it. There was a muffled scream and the car rocked slightly as the woman writhed in pain. He opened the boot and looked down at her,

"Try that again and I'll break it," he said without anger, but as a firm statement of fact.

Janet Warren whimpered and was still.

"Good."

A strong hand in a latex glove grabbed her hair and dragged her, whining, into an easier position for him to get his hands under her arms and then she was out of one car and bundled into the boot of an old Mercedes. The man with the friendly face looked down at the terrified woman and put his finger to his lips,

"Ssssh."

And then he closed the lid. Again, a quick check that nothing had fallen from the woman between one car and the other. All good. And now it was the last leg. In fifteen minutes, she was in the basement of his house. The van had been stolen months ago. It couldn't be traced to him and, when he'd parked it, he'd worn a COVID mask and shades while he disabled the security camera covering that section of the car park. So, there was no way the police could later see exactly what had happened or who was involved in the kidnapping. Yes, they would be able to piece together the journey of the car by security cameras across London, but it would all go cold, because ten minutes after he'd abandoned the car, it was on a low-loader under a tarpaulin. An hour after that, it had been crushed to nothing in a breaker's yard. Janet Warren, senior partner of Warren, Mortimer and Scott had vanished from the face of the earth.

Chapter Twenty

Known Unknowns

"Timber!"

Jack fell back onto the bed like a mighty pine crashing to the ground in a primeval forest. Oh, but the bed felt gooood! It had been a long, strange and draining day, and now his body wanted sleep. The only snag, as he lay there staring up at the off-white ceiling, was that his mind was still very much awake. In fact, it was racing, trying to assimilate all the information and experiences that had engulfed him during the day. Since he and Annie had left his father's house, it was safe to say they'd gone through a lot of emotions. On the one hand the anger and distaste of being near his sisters, the horror of remembering what had happened to him in that house, the shock of the details of his father's death... but also the joy of finding they were now officially rich. It was effectively a lottery win in the midst of a miserable day and the resultant cognitive dissonance was affecting both of them. During dinner they'd hardly known whether to laugh or cry. They'd chattered a bit too loudly, like over-excited children, and had to shush each other at various points when they noticed other diners turning to stare at them. But the whole day had been so crazy, they just couldn't help themselves. In the space of a couple of hours they'd discovered his father was basically a paedophile; buried him; been given a mysterious list of names to track down; and been told there was a pint of his dad's blood awaiting them at a medical facility in Bermuda. Then, to top it all, his granddad makes them millionaires.

"This is fucking nuts!" said Annie as she came out of the bathroom and flopped onto the bed next to him,

"What are we going to do, Kiddo?"

"Buggered if I know," Jack sighed, "I guess we could track down the first name on that list – Mary Brewer. She's only over in Puttenham and that's barely ten miles away."

"But what are we gonna say when we get there? 'Oh hi, your name was given to us by a dead guy who thought you'd be able to enlighten us about his twisted life and gruesome death,'. Yeah, good luck with that!"

"When you say it like that, it does sound nuts," said Jack.

"It is nuts. This whole thing is nuts," Annie exclaimed, "So right now, maybe the least nutty thing to do is follow that list. At least that gives us something to aim at. Otherwise we're gonna be flailing around in the dark."

"Yeah, I guess..." Jack didn't know what to think.

"Lookit – after what happened today, are you gonna be able to put that to one side and drive me around the place showing me the sights?" Annie asked.

"No."

"Hell no, Jack! Hell no! We've gotta lean into this... this... well, whatever this is," Annie said firmly,

"We've gotta get out there and find out what's going on. And you need to book yourself a flight to Italy."

"But I can't go gadding off on a whim, my clients..."

"You're a millionaire now! You've gotta start thinking like one. Screw your clients. You don't need their money."

"But I quite like my clients," said Jack in a deliberately small and slightly whiney voice.

Annie rolled towards him and propped herself up on an elbow to look him in the eye,

"I know you do, but how long did you say their feedback was gonna take?"

"Two weeks."

"That's plenty of time to visit these four women. Then you can finish this and get back to designing your pretty little website."

"It is doable," Jack mused, "Although what I'm supposed to be 'ending', I don't know."

He sat up and reached for his father's letter on the bedside table,

"You must talk to them all. Only then can you end it... what does that even mean? And where does his blood come into it?" he asked, looking to Annie for answers.

She shrugged,

"It's like the man said – there are known unknowns and unknown unknowns. And we've got a bunch of both here."

"What man said that?"

"You know, that guy back in the Gulf War – Rumsfeld!"

"Who?"

Annie gently took his face in her hands and said,

"You're focusing on the irrelevant. The point is, we're in something we don't understand, right?"

"Right."

"And we've got a choice – let ourselves float along and get washed up somewhere we don't wanna be. Or plan and take actions to get to where we wanna be at the end of this. It's like climbing a mountain, Jack. You plan and train to get to the top of the mountain and back down again safely. In between, you've gotta improvise. You never really know what's waiting for you up there. But in the end, my ultimate goal is to get back down safely. That's what we need to do here. Now come on, grab the iPad and let's get planning."

Two hours later, the lights were out and Annie was snoring gently with her naked body half wrapped around Jack's. He was lying flat on his back and just starting to feel his eyelids get heavy. Annie's soft, warm body felt delicious against his. He was lucky. Very, very lucky. Together they had planned their itinerary and now every flight, car, and hotel had been booked. Tomorrow, Friday, they would track down Mary Brewer. If they couldn't, they had Saturday as a spare day to find her. On Saturday, they'd also need to do some shopping, as Jack only had clothes for a couple of days and he needed his own suitcase. When Annie left for home on Sunday, he would be off to Italy. While he was tracking down Giulia Mazzoni near Lake Como, she would get Harry back from her mom and try to get some time off work until their bizarre adventure was over. Then Jack would come back to New York, spend a couple of days with her and Harry to get over his jetlag, and take a flight to see Skylar Judd in Charlotte, North Carolina. After that, he would come back to New York, rest and recharge for a day before jetting off to Bermuda to find Josephine Paget. Then… well, he didn't exactly know what, but hopefully they would be able to finish it and move on. That was a nice thought - locking all of this up into secure boxes in his mind and moving on. He slipped into sleep with a hint of a smile on his face.

***

Once she had let her attack dog off the leash, Rosalind had booked herself into the biggest suite in the most exclusive hotel in the Surrey hills. She had eaten alone at a Michelin starred restaurant and gone to bed at ten – about the same time that her acquaintance was getting to work on Ms Warren. Like Jack, Rosalind couldn't sleep, but for very different reasons. She was incandescent. Her anger coursed through her veins and, as she lay in the dark, her eyes flashed with dangerous malice. How could her moronic little brother have stolen what was rightfully hers? He'd walked back into her life and ruined everything. How dare he? Who was he? No one! Nothing! She would put him firmly in his place. And how could her father not have told her about grandfather's will? It didn't make sense. Up until six weeks ago, he'd always told her everything. Or had he? Now, alongside her anger, a fear rose up within her – what else had he kept from her? She had to know *everything* that lawyer knew, not just the names on the list. She exhaled angrily, threw the bedcovers off and marched to the door. She opened it,

"You, come in here," she said brusquely to the big South African tough standing to the left of her bedroom door. He followed her inside without a word or hesitation, leaving her other guard to stand alone outside.

Rosalind flicked on the lights and held out her hand,

"Phone."

The guard handed her the burner phone she'd used earlier. She dialled the number and waited. With each unanswered ring, her face took on the look of a storm gathering out at sea. Piet van Wyk, a former mercenary who'd spent ten years providing 'security services' for corporations exploiting the resources of the Democratic Republic of the Congo, tried not to look like he was checking Rosalind out. Of course, he was. He'd only joined her security team two weeks ago and this was the first time he'd been alone with her. He scanned the bay window of the big ornately decorated room, then swept his gaze past her to the area with a sofa and easy chairs. In doing so, he allowed his eyes to linger on her just a little bit longer than they needed to. She was wearing a shimmering, gold satin nightdress that stopped just below the knee. All perfectly proper. Except that it clung to her body and accentuated every curve. His pulse beat harder. Nothing covered her perfectly toned arms and for a moment he imagined taking his sharp commando knife and cutting the two thin straps that held the nightdress in place. She made an inarticulate noise of frustration after four unanswered rings and turned away from him. Now he could look at her without her knowing, and he felt his throat constrict. The line of her shoulders and cut of the nightdress created a silhouette of female perfection that was like nothing he'd ever seen. And the way the material accentuated her perfectly rounded ass was spectacular...

"Finally!"

Rosalind's exclamation made Piet jump slightly and he was relieved that she'd been looking the other way.

"It's me. Listen. I need to know *everything* she knows about my father as well as the other information. Yes, whatever it takes. Add ten thousand. Call me the moment you finish."

Rosalind turned and held out the phone to Piet, who took it and put it back in his jacket pocket. Now it was her turn to look at him. Yes, he was good. Very good. He certainly filled out the suit nicely. Six two, about two thirty pounds, sandy coloured hair, a brutish face with a broken nose and big hands with thick fingers. He was feeling awkward, trying not to look at her – how adorable!

"Look at me," she ordered.

He did so and was instantly caught by her eyes. They were like nothing he'd ever seen. Deep oceans promising unknown pleasures...

A licentious smile twitched the corners of her lips. There was no way she was going to sleep until her man had called her back, and she wasn't the type to bed down with a good book. No, there was really only one thing to do. She moved in close without breaking eye contact and slipped a soft hand across his muscular chest and down his right flank to his thickly muscled buttock. She squeezed it, feeling it for power. Oh yes, that would do nicely.

Piet's breath had quickened. He was lost in her eyes and, now that she was up close, enveloped in her scent. She was like gentle sea breezes on the beach at Durban. Intoxicating.

Her left hand went to his crotch to size him up. He was hard as rock and straining to get out. Yes, that would be quite sufficient.

"I want it hard," she said, staring with unquenchable need into his eyes. It awakened some animal instinct beyond his conscious mind and now it was like he was a passenger, watching his body move and hearing his mouth speak. He drew his knife from its concealed sheath in his jacket saying,

"I'll do you like a Kinshasa whore," then cut the straps of the nightdress.

"You'd better," Rosalind warned as it slipped to the floor.

***

By two a.m. it was clear that Ms Warren had nothing more to say. In the white tiled basement room with a floor that gently slanted to a central drain, the middle-aged man with the friendly face walked to the stainless-steel table on which his tools were lined up. Among them was his phone. He picked it up and dialled a number. In a second a voice demanded,

"Tell me."

And he did. In clear but quiet tones he outlined what Ms Warren knew, occasionally consulting a somewhat blood-spattered notebook for exact details. She had given him one name – Mary Brewer. There were three others, all women, but she couldn't remember their names. There was some nonsense about a pint of blood in Bermuda. Yes, Bermuda. No, she didn't know anything more than the fact that there was a pint of blood waiting for him there. No, she couldn't remember the exact details of where. No, none of her documents could shed light on it either. Jack had received the keys to a house in Bermuda and his grandfather had given him a necklace with a... yes, a jade porpoise on it. At this point he had to wait for the vicious swearing at the other end of the line to stop before he could continue. Beyond that, there was nothing Ms Waren could add to what was revealed at the reading of the will. As to her relationship with Mr Kidd, there wasn't much at all. He had come to her only a few weeks earlier and directed her to set everything up for his will and the funeral. No, he hadn't mentioned anything about Rosalind or Veronica beyond warning her that there might be some unpleasantness at the reading of the will. No, he didn't leave any other documents, diaries, voice recordings, films or electronic storage devices in her possession.

"Good," Rosalind sounded satisfied, "And you can dispose of her?"

"Yes."

"Then our business tonight is concluded. Good night," and Rosalind hung up without waiting for a reply.

The man turned his friendly face to Ms Warren, who was stripped down to her bra and pants, bound and gagged, and hung upside down from a meat hook by a chain above the centre of the room. Her body was covered in welts and burn marks, and large bruises were beginning to bloom all over her back and torso. All her fingers were horribly broken. Blood was spattered across the floor. The man took a butcher's knife from the table and approached her. Even through the grotesque bruising on her face, he could see the terror in the woman's eyes.

"Don't worry, luv," he said and with a single quick slash, he cut her throat. He stood back as the blood gargled from her, then a thought struck him.

"Tea," he said to himself and turned to walk to the door. He'd have a nice cup of tea while she bled out, then force out as much blood as possible before butchering her into a set of five-kilo bags. He could get those over to Phil in Canvey by seven and she'd be feeding the fish in the Bay of Biscay by tomorrow. Thus, would begin the eternal mystery of the disappearance of Ms Janet Warren. There'd probably be a podcast about it in ten years.

"And that deserves a chocolate hobnob," he said as he walked up the stairs.

Chapter Twenty-One

Thanks For The Memories

The morning was cold and dank with a fog which looked unlikely to lift before lunchtime.

"Great day for it," said Annie as she slipped into their little car.

Jack grunted in reply as he squeezed himself in.

"You do know how ridiculous you look in this car, don't you?"

"Don't care," Jack replied, "It's fun to drive. You can have a go if you want."

"Not right now. Having to watch you contort your way out of this tin can would be too tragic. C'mon, Jeeves, get going and don't spare the horses."

The Abarth growled into life and Jack pulled out of the car park. As he eased the car across the bypass and up the hill past the station, he said,

"And it's James, by the way."

"Hmm?"

"Jeeves is a butler's name. The driver or coachman is always called James. As in the phrase 'home, James'."

Annie smiled,

"You Brits and your funny formalities. And I suppose this," she flung a critical hand towards the windscreen and the grey murk beyond it, "Is what you call a 'pea souper'?"

"No, this is just fog. Pea soupers were the urban fogs mixed with smoke from coal-fired power stations. You couldn't see your hand in front of your face, let alone drive in them."

"Oh," Annie sat corrected and they fell into silence.

Soon they were out of the town and driving along the Wey valley, parallel with the river as it wound its way through water meadows.

"Wow! It's certainly atmospheric," said Annie as she looked across the grasses and meadow plants that looked thoroughly tired of winter. She could just see the black river through the mist, but could only make out vague, dark shapes beyond it. A couple of horses were standing patiently near a feeding trough. Annie hoped their feet weren't wet. Shouldn't leave horses in wet fields.

"And if you can see it, we've got a historic landmark coming up on the right," said Jack, "The ruins of Waverley Abbey."

"Oooh!" Annie 'ooohed' with what she hoped was the requisite respect, then,

"Why's it ruined?"

"Good King Henry the Eighth."

"The psycho with a love of chopping his wives' heads off?"

"The very same – have a gold star," said Jack and Annie beamed back at him.

"So, he needed cash and he decided that the best thing to do was steal it from the church. He appropriated a lot of their land and the income from it, kicked the monks and nuns out of their monasteries and abbeys, and let the locals break up the buildings for the materials."

"Psycho!" said Annie with a sing-song delivery.

"There it is," said Jack as they approached a left hand turn in the road that would take them over the river.

Annie looked at the ruins looming in the mist. Yeah, that made her feel cheery!

"I could pull over if you..."

"No, very happy to get out of here, thanks," she interrupted.

As they passed over the river, it had widened into a mill pond. On the surface, the water was still and black, but where it narrowed into the mill race, it foamed white. Just beyond on the far bank, a massive shape lurked in the fog, a troll guarding the bridge. This view, of what she presumed was a huge tree, reminded Annie of Rosalind and Veronica's burly security teams, and that set her thinking. In the chaotic avalanche of events the previous day, there was something that had struck her, but that she hadn't mentioned – partly because she wasn't sure how to start the conversation. As they drove up a heavily wooded hill where the fog hung still and silent among the trees, Annie decided to just come out with it,

"What was that thing with your sisters yesterday?"

"Which one?" there were a lot of 'things' to choose from as far as Jack was concerned.

"Where they tried to hypnotise you into handing over your inheritance."

"Oh, that! Yeah, what about it?"

"Is that something they do? Does it ever work?"

"On me? No. They've been trying that one on me since I was little. Really pisses them off that it doesn't work. I remember they visited my grandparents one summer when I was sixteen and they hadn't seen me for over a year. I'd grown about four inches and I'd started doing weightlifting and wrestling at school, so I was bigger and stronger than them for the first time. And I could tell that they were almost scared of me..."

"They probably thought you were going to get them back for all the shit they did to you," Annie interjected and there was a touch of fire in her voice. She wouldn't forgive them for that!

"Yeah, probably. Anyway, so we were in the garden by the pool and my grandparents were in the house, and they came over to me and started doing that mojo thing. So, there they are in skimpy bikinis, you know Rosalind was twenty-seven and Veronica was twenty-five and they were really coming onto me,"

"Eeew!"

"Exactly! They were standing there like a sixteen-year-old's wet dream, but they're my sisters, right? And they're encouraging me to take off my trunks and get in the pool with them and saying how hot it is on the patio and how great it'll be in the pool, and all the things they'll do for me when

we're in there, and how they'd make me a man if only I'd get in the pool...
and I laughed at them."

Annie guffawed,

"And how did they take that?"

"Oh, they were off the scale of angry! Veronica practically exploded and
made the hilarious mistake of trying to push me in. She didn't know I'd
been doing Greco-Roman wrestling, so when the push came, I slipped it
and used her momentum to throw her into the pool."

Annie laughed again,

"God, I wish I'd seen that!"

"It was spectacular. And, for good measure, I picked Rosalind up and
chucked her in, too. Then I went back in the house and left them screaming
blue murder."

Jack slowed the car for a junction joining the road from the left, then
motored easily through the fog and woodland, while Annie enjoyed imagining the scene with his sisters.

"Okay, so it doesn't work on you, what about on other people?"

"It works on men. I've never seen them try it on women. But on men...
those two can get them to do whatever they want."

Annie was shocked at his blasé attitude to it,

"And you don't think that it's kinda fucking weird?"

"I guess, but they've always been like that. They could always just wrap
men round their fingers."

"What about your grandfather?"

"No, not him. He seemed immune to their dubious charms."

"So, what you're saying is that aside from you, the only man you've ever
seen resist your sisters is your grandfather. The grandfather who, it turns
out, always wore a necklace with a jade porpoise on it, to protect him from
'devils'. A necklace he specifically gave to you to protect you. Are you doing
the math, Jack, or am I gonna have to walk you through this?" Annie eyed
him sharply as she spoke.

"Suggesting my sisters are devils isn't exactly news to me," said Jack.

"But what if..." Annie stopped. Was she really seriously entertaining this
thought?

"What if what?"

"What if, somehow, they're more than simply twisted and vicious? What if..." she still couldn't say it.

"They *are* 'devils'?" Jack declared dramatically.

"I know how it sounds..."

"Stone dead crazy?"

"Yeah... but what if?"

The thought forced a laugh out of Jack, but then he stopped short when he glanced across at Annie, who had a very serious face on,

"Hold on, are you seriously suggesting that there's something supernatural going on here?"

"Why not?"

"Because it's batshit crazy?" Jack suggested.

"Okay, yeah it is batshit crazy. I'm not denying that. But it might also be true," Annie replied insistently,

"They might have powers and given what they did to you, they're clearly nasty. Why can't that add up to something... unnatural?"

"But I'm their brother. If they're supernatural, why aren't I?"

"I don't know," Annie admitted.

"And if they're genuinely evil, why aren't I?"

Annie shrugged,

"I don't make the rules," she said, "But bad things seem to happen to people around them. You've gotta admit that – they've got three dead husbands between them for Chrissakes!"

Jack shook his head. He couldn't believe it, "I think they get men to do what they want because they're incredibly beautiful and exude a 'fuck me' vibe that men can't resist. As for the deaths, I think they've just been unlucky."

"Unlucky? There's a trail of bodies behind them. And I don't know whether you've noticed, but they always seem to come out with whatever cash is going."

They were approaching the left turn that would take them to Puttenham, but Jack drove past it. After a couple of hundred yards, he took a right and they went along a driveway next to a section of the river Wey that had been widened into a pond before narrowing back into the river. They crossed a bridge over it, then the driveway swept around into a gravelled car park set among the open fields of the floodplain. Jack parked in a space with a view of the front of a red brick four-storey building that announced itself as 'The Mill' in large gold letters across the gap between the second and third floor windows. Water ran out from beneath the building through two stone archways and into the pond they had passed.

"I want to show you something," Jack said, opening the door and con-torting himself to get out. Annie followed suit,

"So is this…" she left it hanging.

"Yes, come on," and he sauntered over to the far side of the building.

There was a well-kept lawn that ran down the side of the river and a number of big wooden pub garden tables attested to the fact that this would be an idyllic place to sit and have lunch on a nice day. On this foggy day, the tables were covered in water droplets, but the mist added atmosphere, shrouding the river and the surrounding trees. Jack walked down to the water's edge and looked at the back of the building. Just as he remembered it. There was a patio across the back, which could only be accessed through the pub and allowed guests to sit and watch the river come straight at them before disappearing through metal grates and under the building.

"We were picnicking about thirty yards down there," Jack waved his arm at a point on the bank upstream,

"Being young, there came a point where I needed the loo, so my dad took me into the pub. When I finished, he asked if I wanted to see the view from that patio. I said 'yes' and we stood looking back up the river at the water. I waved to my mum and she waved back. Then we looked down at the water as it disappeared under the mill. I asked my dad why they had the metal grates and he said it was to stop branches from coming in and getting stuck in the mechanism of the mill wheel. Then suddenly we heard my mother shout 'Veronica!'. I looked up and saw my mum kick off her shoes and dive into the river. Veronica was nowhere to be seen and Rosalind was sitting on the picnic rug about five yards away. My dad shouted something and ran back through the pub to get round here to see if he could help. And

I stood right there and watched and waited for my mum to come back to the surface, but she never did. I think the whole place was in uproar, but it was like I was in a frozen moment, holding my breath waiting for my mum to come back up. Minutes passed with people trying to throw lifebelts in and doing what they could without endangering themselves too. And then I looked down. There was something white down in the water, caught against the metal poles. Whatever it was, was being rolled around and held down there by the force of the water and then it turned, and I could just make out my mum's face. Then you know what happened?" Jack looked at Annie, who was unable to speak,

"Veronica slaps me on the shoulder and says, 'What're you doing, brat?'. Totally unaware anything had happened. As you can imagine, I had something of a melt down and I don't really remember much of the rest of the day. Turned out, Veronica had been in the ladies' sneaking a cigarette and missed the whole thing."

Jack turned to Annie, who looked very pale and cold standing on the wet grass in the fog.

"I'm sorry," he said, "I never wanted to tell you that, because I didn't want to upset you."

"Me? Christ, Jack, what about you?" Annie pulled him to her and held him tight,

"I'm so, so sorry. That's... it's..." she couldn't find the words and settled for kissing his cheek and snuggling her face into his neck. After a few moments, they separated and he said,

"The reason I told you that is to show you this stuff that's happened around Veronica and Rosalind might have nothing to do with them. When my mum drowned, I could see everything. Rosalind was nowhere near my mother and Veronica was in the loo. Why she shouted 'Veronica' and jumped in, I don't know. But it wasn't because they made her. It happened and the water did the rest – even though she was a brilliant swimmer. It was an accident."

Annie looked at him. She wasn't about to argue. How could she? He was an eyewitness and all she had was a cockamamie theory about devils.

Here, outside in the cold and the damp, her theory seemed as insubstantial as the mist rolling across the river.

"Want to go in and get a coffee before head off?" Jack asked.

"Or maybe a large scotch?"

Jack smiled and took her hand. It was freezing.

"Come on," and he led the way.

***

At about the same time and only five miles away, a woman entered the roughest civilian pub in Aldershot. Unlike most pubs across rural Surrey and Hampshire, it wasn't quaint, pretty, ancient, or a mix of all three. It had no exposed beams, hung with horse brasses or old-time drinking vessels. There were no old photographs charting the pub's history, no uplifting or amusing signs like 'Now Wash Your Shoes' outside the gents toilet, and there were no 'craft' beers on tap or bottled at the bar. The floor was an easy-clean, hard-wearing, non-slip linoleum knock-off that made it easy to clear up blood, vomit, piss, shit and broken glass. The walls were a plain dark magnolia and were unadorned with pictures or mirrors, because they had always ended up used by regulars when fights inevitably broke out. Before the smoking ban in 2007, the place would have reeked of stale smoke and booze. Now it smelt of urinal cookies. Even for Aldershot, a military town, where whether you were a local or a squaddie, walking into the wrong pub could result in you getting part of your cheek bitten off, this pub was a shithole. At barely half past ten, there were men drinking at the bar. And none of them were workers who'd just come off shift.

The woman allowed the door to close behind her. She was wearing black stiletto heels; skin-tight black jeans that perfectly showed off her long legs, well-proportioned hips and jaw-dropping rear; a black cut off T-shirt that simultaneously displayed her lithe midriff and the promise of her ample breasts; and a black, battered biker jacket with the colours of the Bakersfield chapter of the Hells Angels to indicate that she wouldn't take any shit. She stood at the door and scanned the room through black sunglasses. She wasn't impressed with what she saw. The five men drinking at the bar were all fat, tattooed, middle-aged, wearing football shirts and sporting few teeth. No, they wouldn't do at all. And now they were staring at her like hungry dogs salivating at the sight of a juicy steak. Sorry, boys, but steak's off the menu for you today! She looked over to the pool table at the far end of the stark room. No, the so-called men there were no better. She turned her gaze to a dark corner beyond the bar, next to the exit for the lavatories. There was a table with three young, twitchy-looking lads. They had clearly taken something pharmaceutical before coming to the pub for the thin, cheap lager. Yes, they'd do.

She walked across the pub with supreme confidence, followed by the eyes of every man in the place, and finally stood before the gawking lads with her hands on her hips. With the sunlight behind her, she was framed as a dark goddess, come to earth to fulfil desires and wreak havoc.

"Why don't you get me a large Jack Daniels on the rocks?" she said, pointing a long finger with a crimson nail at the lad who looked the weakest,

"And then we can all get to know each other."

The lad, jaw slack, hair askew, shirt half tucked in, made an inarticulate noise and quickly scrambled to the bar while the woman took a seat, leaned in to the other two lads and told them what they were going to do.

***

It was around eleven-thirty when Annie and Jack arrived at Mary Brewer's house. Annie had decided she should give driving a go and the journey through the country lanes had been a much-needed dose of fun, as the Abarth had reacted to her every gear change and pressure on the gas pedal with the excited obedience of a border collie. Jack had made a show of putting his hands over his face and looking through his fingers as she'd taken some corners with more exuberance than necessary, but it was all in jest.

"I want one!" Annie smiled as she locked the car, "It can be the Beast's crazy little brother."

Jack laughed,

"Suits me!" he said, then consulted the list of names and addresses, "Yes, this is it."

Behind high hedges, broken only by a low, wooden gate, stood a funny little end of terrace house, which seemed to be all roof. Only the ground floor had windows, with the gutter resting an inch above them and then about two storeys of roof angling up towards the sky. At one end, the roof seamlessly joined that of the next house in the terrace, which had gable windows in its second storey, but an equally vast expanse of tiles above them. The front garden was woefully neglected and was home to little more than brambles, which had overrun both sides of the path to the house. It was quite out of keeping with the other houses on the narrow main street of Puttenham (cunningly named 'The Street'), which were neat and tidy even in their winter desolation. As he opened the gate and led the way up the garden path, Jack didn't like the way the strange house seemed to look at him through the beady little eyes of its meagre windows. Between that and the garden, the whole place stank of 'crazy'.

"Here we go," he sighed and rang the bell.

Inside, the muffled sound of the chimes of Big Ben filtered to them through the door. There was a pause. Jack looked at Annie and Annie looked at Jack. If he was going to press the bell again, that was his call – she didn't want any part in that decision. His finger hovered. Then came the sound of shuffling from within, a series of bolts being drawn and the door opened to reveal a red-faced woman who looked like she'd been dragged through a hedge backwards. Her long, grey hair was a wavy tangle of knots; her thin face was careworn; her thick jumper in all the colours of the rainbow was faded, stained and full of holes; her fingerless black woolly gloves were filthy; her brown corduroy trousers looked like she'd spilled porridge down them at some point in the past and her bare feet were swollen and livid, with purple scabs.

"Can I help you?" she asked in a surprisingly cultured and friendly voice.

"Mary Brewer?" Jack tried to inject as much friendliness into his words as possible.

"Yes," the woman replied, but now her voice was wary and her eyes alert.

"I was wondering whether we could possibly talk to you? My name's Jack Kidd…" but before he could offer his hand, a look of panic took the woman's features.

"Your sisters aren't with you, are they?" she demanded, looking past him to the road beyond.

"No, it's just me – and my wife, Annie."

"Hi," Annie smiled, trying to look as unthreatening as she could.

"Thank God! I've been dreading the day they might come knocking, but I'm ready for them!" and she reached to the side of the door and produced a shotgun.

Jack and Annie recoiled with their hands raised.

"There's no need…" Jack began,

"Oh, put your hands down!" Mary Brewer snapped as she put the shotgun back in its place, but then lingered with her left hand on it as she said,

"Unless you're them in disguise… No, but you wouldn't tell me if you were, would you? That would defeat the whole object of the disguise. Come on, Mary! Stop being dozy. Even those two can't shape shift. Not here, anyway. So," she said, finally turning her thoughts back to Jack and Annie,

"You say you want to talk – what about?"

"Er…" that question caught Jack on the hop, "Well, my father, who's now deceased…"

"Good riddance! Used to be a top bloke, your dad. Top bloke. Then he became a complete cunt."

Annie almost choked at the sound of the word coming from such a well-spoken old lady.

"Anyway, do go on," Mary Brewer said in a kindly tone.

"He left me an instruction in his will to talk to you, so… here we are," Jack ended limply.

"Right, well, you'd better come in. Can't have all the heat leaving the house – especially on account of that arsehole David Kidd. Call me 'Maz'.

Come on! Come on!" and she ushered them past her and into the cramped hall.

"Door to your left," he said as she closed the front door and treble locked it behind them.

Annie gave Jack a look that said,

'The crazy lady with the gun just locked the door', but Jack thought she was indicating for him to go first, so he did. Annie mentally slapped her forehead in despair at Jack's lack of awareness and followed him in. They entered a small sitting room packed with too much furniture, which had clearly been bought for a bigger, grander house. One side of the room was taken up by a vast mahogany sideboard, which groaned with bottles of booze and expensive looking glassware, while the rest of the room seemed to consist mostly of chairs. So, where to sit? There were so many choices! The overlarge, filthy sofa, or one of the three overlarge filthy armchairs? Or maybe one of the five dining chairs that were strewn randomly about?

"Pop yourselves on the sofa," Maz ordered with cheery bonhomie.

They did so and Maz flumped into an armchair opposite them, causing a cloud of dust to rise out of it and then gently settle in a fallout of filth.

"I remember when you were born," she said, pointing a finger at Jack, "Oh, your parents were so happy! Finally, a boy to carry on the Kidd name. Your dad was particularly pleased, because he'd finally be able to get a four for mixed doubles. Your mum was never a one for tennis – too busy on horses. But him and your sisters, yes, they were pretty good players. Yes, yes, all of you were happy. And so were we – me, Geoffrey and Katy. See?" and she pointed to a framed photo of her as a younger woman with a man, and a girl of about eight,

"See how happy we were?" then her gaze turned inward,

"Of course, it all went to rat shit in the end. If only we'd known, we could have held onto each other that bit harder... cherish every day!" she said, abruptly coming out of herself and looking at her guests perched on the edge of the sofa.

"You bet," Annie smiled and took Jack's hand to squeeze it with what she hoped he'd realise was growing disquiet.

"So, David's reaching out from beyond the grave to make you talk to me? Bloody typical. He was always a bit odd, but your mum adored him. And why not? He was good looking, solvent, wonderful with the three of you, and she said he was a wiz in the bedroom," and she noted with glee the way her young visitors shifted uncomfortably.

"You see, Sylvia and I were at school together. I think we'd be labelled BFFs, these days. We had no secrets. And back when we lived in Elstead, we were in and out of each other's houses all the time. We were three houses down from yours – on the more fashionable side of the street, I might add. God, yes! Happy times. But then it all stopped. And you know why?"

Jack shook his head,

"Why?"

"Because of that bloody holiday!"

Chapter Twenty-Two

A Jolly Holiday

Remember 1993? It's the year the Montreal Canadiens win their 24th Stanley Cup; the year Bill Clinton becomes President; the year dinosaurs roam the earth again in Jurassic Park; and the year QVC launches the first shopping channel on British television. A monumental year!

And it certainly is for the group of tourists stepping out of the terminal at Bermuda airport into the bright April sunshine. In the lead is David Kidd, looking fit and healthy in light chinos and a pink linen shirt with the sleeves rolled up, laughing at something his beautiful wife has just said. Sylvia Kidd is looking ravishing in a light summer dress - so full of love and life... but wait! There's something odd. Two girls – one with blonde hair, the other with raven hair – are each holding onto a hand of a pudgy little boy and happily swinging him between them with a 'Wheeee!' sound. Can that really be Rosalind and Veronica? They seem so happy and carefree – and glad to be with their brother! And bringing up the rear, the girl from the photo on Mary Brewer's mantlepiece. She's about six years older than in that picture and is becoming a young woman, but it is definitely Katy Brewer. And she's happy, too, especially now she's getting a go at swinging little Jasper. How exciting for them. David is piling their luggage into the boot of a taxi and they're going to head across the island to Rufus' house. It's the perfect start to a wonderful holiday!

They drive over the Causeway across the shimmering turquoise waters of Castle Harbour, then up Blue Hole Hill and left at the roundabout onto Wilkinson Avenue. It's nice that they drive on the left and all the road signs are the same as you'd find in England. Perfect if you want all the familiarity of the mother country with none of its weather. Katy is super-excited about it all and, while Rosalind and Veronica are playing it cool, because this is the fifth time they've been, secretly they're excited too. And why not? It is spectacular. Everything is so green and full of life as if every nook and cranny has a plant or flower growing in it. The journey is a constant swirl of lush vegetation, pastel-coloured houses in pink, yellow, blue, peach and green all with white roofs, and the ever-changing sea, apparently offering a different shade of blue at every turn. They skirt Harrington Sound and head towards South Road, which takes them down to Warwick Parish and their final destination. The journey doesn't take long, because it's barely ten miles, and soon they are turning off the road and onto a drive which winds up a short hill. At the top is an elegant, two storey house in pastel pink. They've arrived at Cliff House.

The children spill out of the taxi and rush towards the front door and, while David gets the bags out of the taxi and pays the driver, Sylvia lets the kids into the house. It is instantly transformed from an empty building silently awaiting their arrival to a home away from home, filled with a riot of shouting, running and laughing as the children find their rooms, jump on their beds and dump their hand luggage and toys all over the floors. Sylvia smiles and walks from the hallway into the living room with its two large bay windows looking out over the edge of the cliff and across the endless sea. She crosses the polished wooden floor of a room furnished with understated elegance and unlocks the door onto the patio. She steps out and luxuriates in the sunshine and heat, kicking her shoes off as she walks towards the swimming pool. Her urge is to take her dress off and dive straight in, but with the arrival of children and responsibilities and having to be 'sensible', she has to put that old habit aside and satisfy herself with sitting on the edge of the pool and dangling her feet in. The water is a delicious temperature.

She rests back on her hands and looks around. The garden is surrounded by a two-foot-high picket fence, which is really only there to stop toddlers or drunk partygoers from stumbling over the edge of the cliff. Beyond the patio and pool, the lawns are dotted with land crab holes and she makes a mental note to remind the children to be careful when running about.

To the right, the garden slopes gently up to some whistling pines where a couple of hammocks have been slung. Nearer the house there are Bermuda palmetto trees and fan palms, while the beds around the house are planted with succulents and 'spiky plants', as the kids call them. To the left, the garden starts to slope down and, from the gate in the fence, a narrow path angles steeply down the side of the hill to the crescent of pink sand that is the private beach they share with a dozen other properties. She can't see the beach, but she can see across the gap to the high promontory on the far side. It's covered in scraggy grass and is a perfect place to indulge in one of Bermuda's favourite pastimes – kite flying. It's that promontory and the cliff of Cliff House that make the beach so private, as only the bravest of free climbers would dare try to get around them. Even at low tide, the rocks and cliffs keep hoi polloi at bay. Sylvia tilts her face up to the sun and smiles as the warm breeze blows through her golden hair.

"Kids, get your swimming costumes on! The pool is lovely!" she shouts.

From inside there are gleeful cries and the sounds of running feet. Then the children burst out into the garden and rush for the pool.

"Ah, ah, ah! Where are your cossies?"

"In the big bag," says Rosalind.

"What? But I said 'put your cossies in your hand luggage so you can swim when we get here'. Weren't you listening?"

The three girls all shake their heads and Jasper copies them even though he doesn't know what's going on.

"Oh dear, well you'll just have to wait," says Sylvia,

"Wait for what?" says David, coming to join them after taking all the luggage to their respective rooms.

"Until we've unpacked before we can go swimming."

"Why?" says David, taking off his shoes and laying his keys and wallet on a nearby table as he walks towards the pool,

"You see, I always think that the key to a perfect holiday is total relaxation."

Sylvia sees a cheeky glint in his eye,

"Now, David..."

But he keeps walking,

"And the best way to relax is..."

As he gets to the last word, he steps over the edge and straight into the water, fully clothed. Then, when he bobs up, he continues,

"...by getting into the pool. Come on, kids!"

And with cheers, the three girls leap into the pool and start splashing around with David.

"Well, if you can't beat 'em..." Sylvia says as she pulls her dress over her head, leaves it on the side and slips off the edge and into the water. It is lovely. Divine! She dives to the bottom, swims along it, then reappears near the steps, where Jasper is tentatively edging into the water.

"All right, my little water baby, mummy's here," and she grabs him and holds him close as she brings him into the pool. He can't swim yet, but he knows the moves and, with a pair of water wings and flippers on, he's pretty good.

And so, the family plays without a care in the world, without worrying about drying out the clothes or what they're having for dinner, or what they're going to do tomorrow. They're in the moment, revelling in the water and the bright sunshine.

"Hey, Jasper, you want to fly high?" David asks, holding out his hands to his son.

"Yes, fly!" he squeals, splashing his mum with his feet as he tries to power over to David.

"All right, you little wriggler!" Sylvia laughs as she hands the boy over, and immediately David launches Jasper high into the air and catches him as he comes down with a huge splash into the water. Jasper is in heaven! Again and again, he is thrown high and lands with a splash. Jasper is laughing and giggling and screaming for joy as he flies high and comes down. Yes, his joy is infectious and his dad has come down with it in spades! The light in David's eyes is wonderful to see. His son is his world.

After nearly an hour playing in the pool, good sense prevails and the party breaks up. Everybody squelches out onto the patio and struggles to pull off their soaked clothing. Everybody except Sylvia, who hops out of the pool, picks up her dress, turns away and whips off her soaking bra, then quickly puts the dress on over her head. It's then the matter of a moment for her to slip out of the soaking underwear before it can get the dress wet, and there she is – dressed and ready to tackle the rest of the day. David doesn't take his eyes off her throughout this quick change. He clearly fancies the pants off his lovely wife and, when she turns to see him lying topless on a sun lounger, it's clear she feels the same about him.

"Right, stay there kids while I get the towels. No coming into the house with wet clothes," and Sylvia runs into the house, while the children lounge in the hot sun. What a perfect start to a perfect holiday!

And it is perfect. Two weeks of playing in the teal sea or lounging on the pink sand of their own private paradise. David and Jasper build sandcastles of epic proportions; Sylvia snorkels with the girls; they hire a moped (or as they call it, 'the putt-putt') and David ferries the girls one-by-one to Horsehoe Bay, Cambridge Beaches and Gibbs Hill Lighthouse, while Sylvia opts for cabs to take Jasper out on their escapades; the girls spend time playing with Jasper in the pool, teaching him to swim and showing off their diving skills, which he is totally unable to emulate; they go to the Crystal Caves, the aquarium, enjoy a tour in a glass-bottomed boat to look at the fish, and have a day out shopping in Hamilton, where the girls quietly laugh at the passing businessmen in their smart work jackets, ties and Bermuda shorts. And there is always Cliff House to come back to – elegant, cool, welcoming. After their long day in Hamilton, David and Sylvia, relax by the pool looking out at the sea as the sun sets. It's a quarter-to-eight and, remarkably, the kids have gone to bed, exhausted. It's the perfect moment for a Dark 'n Stormy, which the pair are both sipping while holding hands. They aren't talking. They don't need to. They're letting the dark rum unwind them gently while the stunning view soothes their souls. And there they sit, together in a shared wonder until the stars come out over the ocean. Finally, David says,

"Come on, let's go in before we get cold," and they stand, but before they go in, he draws Sylvia to him gently and kisses her. She responds and presses her body into his as they kiss, then they walk hand in hand to the house. Tonight, they will make love and it will be beautiful. Neither of them realises that it will be their last time.

The morning of their penultimate day arrives with cloud and a stiff breeze. It's not really a day for the beach, although Jasper does do some sandcastling with daddy in the morning, while the girls walk down the road to a nearby beach that has a game arcade. By lunchtime, the weather is turning decidedly unpleasant and high winds lash Cliff House with heavy rain. The girls arrive back looking bedraggled and are shooed into the utility room by Sylvia who gets them dried off.

"It's all right, mummy, the rain's quite warm," says Veronica.

"Yes, but I don't want water all over the house," Sylvia replies, towelling her hair,

"Did you have fun at the arcade?"

"Yes," Veronica says happily and then, quietly so that only her mother can hear,

"Ros and Katy even talked to some *boys!*"

Sylvia gives a melodramatic gasp,

"No!"

"Yes!"

"Who were they?" Sylvia whispers conspiratorially.

"Just some boys on holiday from America. Mummy, where's Des Moines?"

Sylvia's brow furrows,

"I don't know, darling. Somewhere in the middle."

"That's where they said they were from," Veronica whispers and then buries her head in the towel when Rosalind looks at her suspiciously.

Much of the afternoon is spent reading, drawing, playing Cluedo and listening to the storm rage outside. At about five-o-clock, the rain subsides and David goes out to take a look around to see if there's any damage on the property. He's wearing a light anorak over his T-shirt and shorts, and the moment he's out of the house, his hair is blown every which way from Sunday. He opens the door a crack and calls inside,

"It's still blowing a hoolie out here, but it's lovely and warm," before firmly closing the door behind him. He walks all around the house and is glad to see there's no damage. But there is something. What is it? It's like something on the wind. In the air itself. A sound. But what? There's such a cacophony from the palms clattering that it's hard to tell. He comes out to the pool and listens. Well, the whistling pines are certainly living up to their name! The wind really is whistling through them. He tries to cock an ear, but can't pinpoint anything particular. Is there something nestled in the soundscape between the crashing cymbals of the fan palms and the whistling pines? Or is it higher? He is drawn to the edge of the property and stands in front of the low fence about five yards from the cliff. He should have a look over. That's his gut instinct. Go to the edge and take a look. Go on... what's stopping you?

David stands at the fence for more than a minute. Wondering. Why not take a look?

Because there's a howling gale and you might get blown over the edge.

Nonsense! A big man like you? You'll be fine. Go and take a look.

But it must be dangerous – that's why there's a fence here.

That's just to stop kids! You'll be all right. Come and have a look.

And then he lifts a foot and steps over the fence. As soon as he does, he wonders why he had any qualms at all. It's perfectly safe! Nothing's going to happen. He walks to the edge and looks down. Seventy feet below, the waves are crashing over the rocks in great explosions of spray. Wow! It's amazing! He should get the children and take them down there to get a closer look. It's a once in a lifetime opportunity. Yes, the children need to get down there. That thought becomes lodged very firmly into his mind and he turns to go back to the house.

"It's amazing out there!" he declares as he opens the door and now everyone is looking at him,

"I went to the edge of the cliff and looked down at the waves on the rocks – it's incredible! The children have to see it," he enthuses.

"I'm not sure they should go near the cliff edge..." Sylvia begins,

"No, of course not," David jumps in, "We can go down to the beach and look at the waves from there – I bet it's even more spectacular. What do you think, kids, do you want to see the amazing waves?"

The children cheer and look to their mother for permission. Sylvia considers it and then says,

"Okay, but don't go near the cliff edge and stay safely on the beach. Don't get too close to the water."

"We won't, mummy," says Rosalind happily.

"I'll stay here with Jasper and get dinner going."

No one argues this plan. A stormy beach is no place for a three-year-old.

Two minutes later and David is leading Rosalind, Katy and Veronica down the steep, winding path to the beach. The girls are excited and a little bit of fear is added to it when they get down to the sand. They really feel like they're in the storm. The sea is a boiling, foaming chaos. Where it was a beautiful teal colour yesterday, today the sea is a brooding gunmetal grey. The waves boom as they break, then hiss as they claw up the beach towards the little group, who are standing at a safe distance. Then a thought comes to David,

"Let's get over to the rocks!" he shouts against the wind.

He points to the rocks on their right, under the cliff they just climbed down. These mark the end of the beach and stand about six feet above it. Their tops are fairly flat and, because the cliff bulges out into the sea beyond them, they are a safe distance from the breaking waves, but will give those brave enough a grandstand view of the big breakers on the rocks and cliff beyond. The girls look at each other. It's a bit frightening to get that close, but after all, they have been clambering all over those rocks for the last two weeks. The girls all nod and follow David to a point where the rocks meet the cliff face and there are a couple of easy footholds. They all clamber up onto the rocks and now they really are in the heart of the storm! The wind is fully in their faces and the spray of every wave is being blown twenty feet into the air and over them. They can taste the salt and feel the power of the sea, so close and yet they're safe from it. It's like being next to the lion enclosure in the zoo. They know that just there is a power that could tear them to pieces, but it can't reach them.

"It's amazing!" Katy shouts to Rosalind, but her words are scattered in the wind and noise. She taps the other girls on the shoulders and gives them both a thumbs up.

Rosalind and Veronica both look as exhilarated as she does and excitedly give her a thumbs up back. It's incredible! The sheer energy of it makes them giddy with nervous laughter. There they are, getting soaked and it's brilliant! And now David is venturing further out towards the waves. He can see exactly where the highest reach of the waves has been and he steps carefully across the rocks to it. He turns back to the girls and shouts,

"Come over here!" and he gesticulates to them to join him. They stand, hesitant.

"Come on! It's perfectly safe!" he shouts and somehow his voice is cutting through the storm to them.

It's Katy who makes the first move and a moment later, all three girls are cautiously crossing the rocks to join David. Now they are part of the storm, standing with the fury all around them and able to see the waves smashing against the rocks in front of the bulge in the cliff almost side-on. A big wave crashes on their part of the rocks and its foamy fingers almost reach their feet.

"See? We're all right here!" David yells with a very wide grin and they feel an intense thrill, yet safe with him at their side. But as he turns back to the sea, it's almost as if he comes to his senses. He shakes his head and his eyes seem to see the scene properly for the first time. He turns back to the children. He's going to get them away, get them somewhere safe... then a wave rears up like a great hand reaching out from the sea and sweeps them into its power.

David feels his feet taken from under him and he's suddenly engulfed. Simultaneously smothered and blinded by the sea, churned over and over, he can't tell which way is up and then he feels himself surging headlong forwards. He hits something hard and is scraped along it by the swell. The skin is torn off his knees and thighs, now his feet and his toes. Then he's turned over and dragged along his back and his shirt is flayed off him. Suddenly, he's in deeper water. Panic-strength gives him the power to claw his way to the surface and he gratefully drags in a deep breath. Good Christ! He's now thirty yards from shore and has already drifted down as far as the bulge of the cliff. But where are the children? A dreadful terror explodes within him at the thought that his babies are drowned. He desperately starts to front crawl towards the rocks they were swept from, but in the rise and fall of the swell, it's hard to keep going in one direction. And now another wave is coming and again his legs are being dragged over rocks. He throws out his hands to protect himself and in a moment they're bloody. Now he's pulled away from the shore again. He's no longer a man, with a life and a job and responsibilities and respect and self-determination. He is flotsam to be thrown wherever the sea chooses. But where are the girls?

There! There's a head! Is it? Yes, it's Katy and by some miracle she's being thrown back towards the rocks they were standing on! David front crawls towards her, then breast strokes so he can look – yes! She's tumbled up onto the rocks by the wave, but she's thrown further than he was and he can see her scrabbling at the rocks. Come on! Grab a hold! Please for the love of God! Yes! She's done it! The wave is hissing back into the sea and she's crawling towards the cliffs. But what about Rosalind and Veronica? If Katy has survived it, surely they can, too? But now he's in trouble again and the swell is taking him back to the cliff and he's tumbling over the rocks that are grazing, cutting and stripping his skin. As he's pulled back out, his fingers find something sticking up and he grabs it. He can feel the water all around him, trying to pull him back into the tumult, but he's fighting with every ounce of his strength and suddenly he knows he's won! The water reluctantly gives him up and he's crawling, scrabbling across the rocks to where Katy is lying safely above the furthest reach of the sea.

The girl is a mass of blood and cuts, but doesn't seem to be badly injured, so David wobbles to his feet and looks out to the sea. Nothing but a boiling nightmare of surging water and flying spray. David shouts his daughters' names into the storm. What if only he can hear it? He must try!

"Rosalind! Veronica!" he screams, almost bending double with the force of his cry. He scans the sea with eyes of desperation and panic. Whatever possessed him to bring his babies out into this churning desolation? Why did he go so close? Was he out of his mind? He paces up and down along the line of the highest wave, shouting, screaming, oblivious to his bleeding, flayed skin. He looks back at Katy, who is gingerly getting to her feet. My God! She's a bloody rag! David runs up to her,

"Katy! Can you walk?"

The girl is terrified and staring in horror at the sea.

"Katy!" he shouts, grabbing her face and forcing her to look at him,

"Can you walk?"

She nods.

"Then get up to the house," he shouts through the storm, "And tell my wife there's been an accident. Tell her to call an ambulance and the coastguard. Yes?"

She nods again and then she's moving. Good girl! In fact, she's already running, throwing horrified glances over her shoulder as she goes. Now she's jumping down from the rocks and dashing across the beach – she's running away from terror, not running to fetch help.

David turns back to the furious sea and shouts for his daughters again. Over and over, with a prayer between each. But each time his hope seeps away like a falling tide. And now the real fear starts to grip him. Not the fear that attacks from outside. Not the fear for one's own life. Not the sudden, reactive fear of being confronted with the terrible. This is the fear that rises from the bowels and slowly grasps each and every organ, working its way up the body until the entire being is filled. David is feeling the worst fear of all – the fear that he has brought disaster on the people he most cherishes and loves. He tosses his head violently, as if he's hoping to shake the fear out of his brain, but it's no use. Every fibre of him is screaming with condemnation. He has done this. This is all his fault. His children are dead, his family, his life, are shattered and all for what? He can't even remember! Yes, he wanted to see the storm, but never so close!

"Rosalind! Veronica!" it is a wail now, not a shout. Hope has gone and he is wracked with great sobs.

Then, though the blur of tears and sea spray something appears, bobbing in the water. It's black and round. And there! Just a few yards away, a dot of dirty gold. It's them! And they're alive! Their arms are flailing, trying to swim to shore. Without a thought, David runs into the waves, diving over a crashing breaker and swimming hard towards them. If he can just grab them both and hold onto them, maybe they can all get to the rocks together? He can't feel the sting of the salt water on his lacerations, he is all effort as he powers out. He keeps losing sight of them in the swell, but suddenly, miraculously, he is with Rosalind. Without a word, he takes her arm and puts it around his neck. She holds on tightly and he strikes out to where he thinks Veronica is. Thankfully, she has seen him and is swimming well. They find each other and she grabs onto David. He reorientates them so that they're facing the shore and shouts,

"Kick!"

And the three of them kick for their lives. Yes, they're on the right line! David glances behind them. Good God! A huge wave is building and will be on them in a matter of moments. He and the girls kick and then the wave picks them up and launches them at the rocks. Now they're tumbling across the hard, sharp surface, cutting, slashing, stabbing. The monster wave is so big, it throws them out of the sea, across the rocks and right up to the cliff. When the water recedes, they are high and dry. They are a bloody mess of crumpled clothes, but they are alive.

"Come on!" David shouts, pulling his daughters up and leading them to the safety of the beach, where they stumble and fall onto the pink sand, slowly turning it red.

The next hour is an excruciatingly painful blur of dragging themselves back to the house, the ambulance and then the hospital. Wounds are washed and disinfected, tears are shed, checks are made. It is a miracle! An honest to God, five-star miracle. Although they are covered in cuts and some of them are deep, they have no major injuries.

"You are lucky," says the doctor to David as he makes his final checks before the nurse can dress the wounds,

"The sea threw you back."

David wonders whether this is how fish feel when they're caught by a sport angler. He decides there and then he'll never fish again.

Outside in a quiet corridor, under harsh strip lights, Katy sits alone on a bench. She is a mass of bandages and is covered with two blankets, but she is still shivering. Apart from telling Sylvia about the accident, she hasn't said a word. She is staring at nothing. Terrified. An ambulance crew break through the double doors at the end of the corridor and unhurriedly wheel in a gurney and park it opposite her. A nurse comes out to meet them,

"What have we got?"

"Girl about ten. Washed up near Tucker's Town. There was nothing we could do."

"DOA," says the nurse, "Okay, we'll take it from here. Got any more coming in?"

"You bet! With all these tourists here for Easter, we're up to our ears in idiots out there!" laughs one of the ambulance men, who immediately looks ashamed when the nurse glares at him and indicates Katy.

"Sorry," he says quietly.

"Good luck," says the nurse, turning on her heel and bustling down the corridor.

The ambulance men leave to get themselves another gurney. As they go, one of them accidentally catches the edge of the cloth covering the dead girl's face. They walk out, unconscious that the cloth has been fully drawn back. The double doors slam. Katy sits, shaking and looking straight ahead. The girl's face is slightly turned towards hers. One dull eye is staring at nothing, the other closed. Her half open mouth is filled with sand.

Chapter Twenty-Three

The Musings Of Mary Brewer

"Didn't say a word for a fortnight," Maz Brewer said forcefully as she sat forward in her big chair, fixing Jack and Annie with a pugnacious look.

The cramped, dirty room filled with oversized furniture was, if anything, darker than when she'd started her story forty minutes earlier.

"Our doctor said it might be PTSD and recommended a psychiatrist. He got her talking, but in some ways I wish he hadn't. I'd rather have a silent, living daughter than..." and she trailed off, looking at the photograph on the mantlepiece,

"You see, we all thought – and I mean us and your parents – that the children were different because of a normal accident. Terrible, of course, but normal. Something that could've happened to anyone. Because your sisters were different, too. They were speaking, but they weren't themselves. They were... odd. Started calling each other 'sister' rather than using their names and calling your parents 'father' and 'mother'. And after that holiday, Katy refused to see Rosalind again, which seemed crazy, because they'd been inseparable like me and your mum, but the fact was Katy was terrified of her!"

"Terrified?" Annie said before she could stop herself.

"Yes, once she started talking again, she said she wanted to have nothing to do with Rosalind or Veronica. She even made us take her out of the lovely school they were all at, because she didn't want the risk of seeing them. Right pain in the arse for us, I can tell you. Do you know how hard it is to get a place in a new school part way through the summer term?"

Annie and Jack shook their heads.

"Almost bloody impossible!" Maz exploded, "But Katy was adamant," then she stared off into space. She seemed to be remembering happier times.

"Eventually, she told us why," and Maz leant forward and lowered her voice as if someone might be eavesdropping outside the front window. Jack caught a waft of scotch as she came in close,

"She said that your sisters were literally different. She said that when the wave swept them all off the rock, your sisters were dragged to the bottom of the sea by two... now, what did she call them?"

Annie wanted to shout 'who cares what she called them! What the hell were they?', but she managed to suppress the urge.

"Not mermaids, the other ones... no, it's gone. Anyway, two creatures of the sea grabbed them and dragged them down and started to suck out their souls... or something like that. Katy couldn't be sure because she didn't see the whole thing. Once they got to the soul sucking bit, Katy was caught up by another wave and the rest of it was a blur of foam, rocks and being tumbled about. But the point is that she was convinced that while your sisters bodies came out of the sea later, it was no longer your sisters living inside them."

"So, these things possessed my sisters?" Jack was dumbfounded.

"Yes, and they have been living their lives ever since. God, I wish I could remember what they're called. My memory's buggered. Combination of Famous Grouse and lazy veins in my legs – no, don't look at them, they're ghastly!" Maz cried, because Annie and Jack had naturally looked at her swollen red feet and ankles with their dark scabs.

"Sorry," said Annie, looking up into Maz's florid features.

"The creatures are mythological," Maz continued,

"Greek. You know, they were the ones that Odysseus tied himself to the mast for... Oh, it's right on the tip of my tongue..."

"Sirens?" Jack suggested.

"Yes!" cried Maz with such force that Jack and Annie jumped in fright, causing a plume of dust to burst from the sofa cushions.

"Sirens! That's it! Katy said they were sirens. Well, of course the psychiatrist thought she was totally doolally. Thought it was all part of the mental scarring from the accident. It was nonsense to say that the girls were possessed, and to insist upon it showed that her mind wasn't right. But, bless her, she *did* insist upon it. Swore that she'd seen it with her own eyes. Couldn't understand why nobody believed her."

Maz paused. In the silence, they all considered what she'd just said. It was fantastical. It was crazy. It could be a story made up in the brain of a girl to make sense of a horrible accident. Or it could be... No. No, that would be insane! Sea creatures possessing people's bodies and taking over their lives? That *is* doolally!

"We tried to understand," Maz sighed, "But she could tell we didn't really believe her. And in some ways, I think that's what ultimately drove her to drugs. They were the only way to numb it all. She ran away. Barely seventeen. Whole life ahead of her. Of course, the police were no bloody help! Couldn't find their own dicks with a map... so we spent a fortune on private investigators. By the time they found her she'd already been selling her body for heroin. God, it's all so bloody stupid!"

Tears were building and she put her fist to her mouth and bit it to stop them coming.

"So, we had to kidnap our own daughter, get her home and get her clean. But you know how it is. The addict has to want to change. And Katy didn't. By the time she was twenty, she'd been in and out of rehab three times. The cost was frightening," and Maz looked again at the photograph of her happy family,

"We had to sell the house and downsize, and then dear Geoffrey took the easy way out – heart attack. At the bloody theatre, of all places. Christ! I haven't been able to show my face at the Yvonne Arnaud since. And then everything bloody unravelled. Katy got sectioned, and I thought 'Thank God! At least she's safe,' then they sodding released her! How can you release someone who's convinced there are mythical creatures walking the streets in the bodies of the living?"

Maz looked at her visitors for the answer, but Jack and Annie had nothing.

"She was back on the heroin before you could say Jack Robinson. Six months later, I got the dreaded phone call. Could I come and identify a body. And that was that! All our lives down the shitter."

With that, Maz reached across to the sideboard, grabbed a bottle of Famous Grouse and a small glass, filled it and downed it.

"Do you...?" she asked, waving the bottle at them.

"No, thank you," Jack said, although he suddenly felt like a large scotch was the sensible choice.

"This is my self-destructive weapon of choice. Problem is, I'm cursed with a robust constitution, so I'll probably last another ten years."

She filled the glass again, but this time sipped at it.

"For me, the worst of it is, that the more I've heard about your sisters, the more I believe that Katy was right. Your sisters seem to be able to make men do anything. And all those rumours about them and your dad... that would make sense of it. David had been lovely and then he was an arsehole. Treated your mum so badly. By God, if I'd been a man, I'd have given David the thrashing of his life for what he did to Sylvia!" then Maz realised she was ranting and calmed herself,

"Sorry."

"No, it's fine," Jack soothed.

"We ain't fans," Annie added.

"And why would you be? If the rumours are true, he used to beat the hell out of you."

Jack nodded.

"And that's just the thing. I know people change, but David became a different person. I'm not suggesting he was possessed by anything, but if two sirens were inhabiting your sisters' bodies, wouldn't they want to control your dad first? And if you or your mother threatened that control, wouldn't they make him punish you?"

Jack didn't like this. He was sitting in this crazy, dirty house with a woman who was both deeply traumatised and semi-sozzled, and he was seriously wondering whether she might be right. Did that make him as crazy as her?

"All I know is this," Maz said with a note of finality, "Something evil entered all our lives that day in Bermuda and it destroyed *my* family, and it destroyed *Sylvia's* family. Now I think it would be better if you left, because I'm going to drink the rest of this bottle of scotch."

Two minutes later, Annie and Jack were standing out in the cold, having waved goodbye to Maz Brewer from the end of her path. They walked back towards the car in stunned silence and got in. Annie started the car,

"Where to?"

"Let's get some lunch in Farnham. The measley moo should be good."

"The measley moo?"

"The Spotted Cow pub. A lot of locals call it the measley moo."

Annie still looked confused.

"Spots – measles. Spotted cow – measley moo."

"Got it. You Brits and your so-called humor!" she sighed.

"Just go back the way we came and I'll direct you when we get close," said Jack.

Annie pulled out, did a quick three-point-turn and started to retrace their steps. After about five seconds, a silver BMW M3 pulled out of a parking space just down the street and set off in the same direction.

"So!" said Annie, somehow managing to get 'So, what do you think of that wild story of insanity from the drunk, crazy lady with the weird legs?' into one syllable and two letters.

"So-o-o-o?" Jack extended the word and changed the note with an upward lilt halfway through to effectively reply 'Holy crap, there was so much madness to unpack, I don't know where to start, but I think that maybe there might be the possibility of something in there, maybe'.

"On the one hand, she's clearly traumatised, so most of what she said could be nonsense," Annie proposed.

"But on the other hand, given how weird my sisters are and the circumstances surrounding my dad's death, it would explain a lot," Jack replied.

"It would explain a lot," Annie nodded, taking a right and heading up out of Puttenham along a narrow road with high hedges.

"But then again, we'd have to buy into the whole 'malevolent sea creatures that can possess the souls of the living actually exist' argument," said Jack, "Are we ready to do that?"

"That's the million-dollar question," said Annie, making a nifty gear change to allow her to take the corner at the top of the hill at speed and then power out even faster into the straight beyond.

"Part of me wants to believe it," said Jack, "Because then it wouldn't be my sisters who are these vile, manipulative bullies, but some nightmarish 'things'. And that would also mean my dad wasn't a paedophile arsehole, but that he was bewitched into doing it. It would make them all victims of evil instead of being evil themselves. That's so tempting..."

"But you don't buy it," said Annie.

"No," said Jack flatly, "It's too abnormal. This sort of thing doesn't happen. If it did, it would be all over the news. I mean, for this to be true, we have to throw out biology, physics *and* religion. What's the biology of sea monsters that suck out the souls of the living? That's number one. Two: how does the physics of them possessing a human body even work? Three: we don't have any scientific evidence of the existence of souls, so scientifically, this soul-sucking stuff doesn't add up. Four: if these really are sirens, then they've been around a good deal longer than Christianity and are part of a pantheistic world. And if *sirens* are real, what if all the other Greek Gods are real too? And where does that leave Christianity, Islam and Judaism? Intellectually, it puts our entire world view into a blender."

"How'd you know so much about the Greek pantheon?" asked Annie.

"I read Mythos by Stephen Fry on my Kindle last summer."

"Oh... did it cover how a Greek mythical being can end up five thousand miles away off the coast of Bermuda?"

"Funnily enough, no, it did not," said Jack dryly, "And that's another hole in the theory. What the hell are they doing all the way out there?"

They had come down the hill from Puttenham Common and Annie slowed as they came down between the two ponds at Cutmill and approached a crossroads. She stopped, checked all around and then released the Abarth, which leapt across the junction and sprinted onto the road beyond and through the thick woodland.

"So... what do you think?" Jack turned it back to Annie.

"I think there's a lot we don't understand in this big old world. And some places have an ancient power that defies science, logic and popular religions. Mountains, the sea, deep forests – anywhere on the fringes of human influence. They've all got a power beyond us. The stories mountaineers and sailors tell... if only *some* of 'em are true, there's a lot of weird shit going on out there. Even hard-bitten scientists can feel things when they're out in the deeps of the ocean that make no rational sense."

"You really think my sisters are sirens?"

"I'm saying the jury's out," said Annie, taking a right and heading back to Farnham,

"And until it returns to deliver a verdict, we need to plan and act like all possible scenarios could be true."

"How do we plan for my sisters being sea creatures from Greek mythology?" Jack exclaimed.

"You got me there, Kiddo..." then Annie looked hard into the rear view,

"What the hell's wrong with this guy?"

A silver BMW M3 was coming up fast behind them, flashing its lights and sounding its horn.

"Someone's in a hurry!" Annie said with a touch of annoyance as she eased off the throttle and made some room for the car to pass. It didn't. Instead, it pulled up right behind them and sat on their rear bumper, filling the rear-view mirror.

"Ah, crap," Annie sighed as she looked up to see the faces of the three hyped-up lads in the car behind.

"What?"

"Our friends in the car back there look coked up to the eyeballs."

The car was still hooting at them and the lights were still flashing.

"There's nothing I can do, dickwads!" Annie said, raising her voice.

"You know they can't hear you, right?"

"Yeah, but it makes me feel better," half of Annie's attention was now focused on the car behind, which finally made to pull out,

"Yeah, c'mon go now before we get to the blind corner," she encouraged, but the driver decided not to bother and pulled back to his position almost touching their rear bumper.

"Idiot!" Annie spat.

Now their speed was increasing. Annie was unconsciously adding pressure to the accelerator as a natural reaction to the closeness of the BMW. Although they were being assholes, Annie could see why they couldn't simply overtake. The problem was that the road was a series of sweeping turns, which would tempt an impatient driver to start an overtaking manoeuvre, only to run out of road before a blind curve. So, that was a possible reason why they weren't overtaking. Why they were sitting on her tail and screwing about was anybody's guess – although Annie was sticking to her drug-addled assholes theory. She decided the best thing to do was keep a good pace and then let them go by when it was safe.

"Oh, we could always have lunch at the Donkey..." Jack remembered, but too late as the entrance to the pub driveway came and went, and now they were going up a hill through heavy forest.

"It's okay, the road straightens out at the top of the hill, so they'll have plenty of time and room to pass," he said.

"Good, because I don't like the way the driver is eyeballing me. He's staring at me in the mirror."

"Really?"

"Oh yeah! He's doing it now. What a nutjob!" Annie said, then nodded her head slowly while smiling and keeping eye contact with him,

"Yes, you're a fucking nutjob who should get his licence revoked," she hoped he could lipread, but from his expression of staring frenzy, she doubted it.

When they crested the hill and saw an empty quarter mile of straight road, Annie breathed an inward sigh of relief. Once the bozos had overtaken, she'd be able to relax and enjoy the view of the tall beech trees in the woods on either side of the road. Finally, the driver pulled out and started coming alongside them. For someone in such a hurry, he certainly was taking his time to do it. Annie lowered her window to beckon them past,

"Go for Chrissakes!" Annie shouted, "The road's clear. Go!" and she gesticulated angrily out the window for them to get on with it.

But they didn't.

As the BMW crawled up the side of the Abarth, Jack could see two youngish blokes in the front and a third in the back. Their eyes looked wild and they were all shouting and whooping with the thrill of the chase. As they came alongside, two of the lads started making 'wanker' and other gestures at them.

"Yeah, real mature!" Annie shouted, suppressing the urge to give them the finger.

The driver kept glancing across at her as they drove neck and neck down the road, then Annie saw exactly what she'd been afraid of. A big truck appeared on the road ahead, travelling towards them.

"He's gonna have to overtake now, or he'll end up a hood ornament on that truck," she said.

"I wish he'd shift it!" Jack replied. They were rapidly approaching the truck.

"Go, you moron!" Annie yelled as the other driver resolutely refused to overtake. Now the truck was sounding its deep, mournful horn. Annie eased off the gas, but the BMW did the same.

"What the..." suddenly this had got deadly serious. What was the other driver trying to do? The truck began to loom and Annie tried to spot where she could veer off. The trees lining the left side of the road were only set back a couple of yards, but they'd been planted in clumps with gaps between them. Beyond them was a space of about fifteen feet to a low picket and wire fence, then into fairly open woodland made up of youngish trees. Yes, she could dive off to the left and end up in the woods without too much danger. She picked a spot ahead.

"Brace yourself!" she said firmly, as the BMW held its ground

And the truck kept coming on – why the hell didn't *he* stop? Fuck! She was gonna have to do it? Motherfu...

And suddenly the BMW shot past them through the narrowing gap with the oncoming truck. Annie took her foot off the gas as they coasted, watching the idiots in the BMW disappear into the distance as the sound of the truck horn filled their ears.

"Fuck!" she screamed, shaking herself back and forth with the steering wheel, "What the fucking fuckers? Fuck!"

"Well done," Jack said quietly.

"I hope you wrap it around a tree!" Annie shouted after them, but they were out of sight.

"Bloody joyriders. If that's their car, I'm the Dalai Lama," said Jack.

"Like today isn't fucked up enough already! Aaaargh!" Annie yelled in an attempt to get all the fright and nerves out of her, "When we get to the pub, I'm drinking and you're driving home," she added as she slowed to about twenty miles an hour and pottered along.

"Sure thing," said Jack and then the two of them excitedly jabbered at each other, as people so often do after a near miss.

A mile further on and they were still debating whether hanging was too good for idiots like that, when they came to a dogleg in the road before the river crossing next to Waverley Abbey.

"Oh yeah, I know where we are," Annie said with satisfaction as she took the corners. What they didn't see, was the silver BMW hidden by the trees about thirty yards up from the junction on the corner of the dogleg. Annie drove easily across the river. By now, the fog had mostly dispersed and she could see that the 'troll guarding the bridge' from their trip out was a magnificent weeping willow. They rounded the corner, still couldn't properly see Waverley Abbey across the fields, and followed the road along the side of the floodplain. The road was cut into the hill about ten feet above the fields that were patched with ponds where the river had spilled over. For the next half mile, there was no room for manoeuvre on the left side, because a stone wall buttressed the hill rising above it.

"Oh great!" snarled Annie, looking in the rear-view.

"What?" but Jack got his answer from the sound of a car horn being repeatedly hooted behind them.

"Ah shit!" he said, "They must've waited for us."

"Motherfuckers!" Annie said with feeling as she looked back at the car flashing its lights and its passengers bouncing up and down, egging the driver on,

"Fuck you! You wanna be dicks, then just sit there behind me," she growled as she stared into the rear-view at the all-encompassing BMW.

This time, they weren't content to stay on the tail of the Abarth. Suddenly, there was a crunch and the little car jolted forward.

"Son of a bitch!" Annie yelled looking back at the hyped-up jerks behind them. As soon as they made contact, they dropped back, then came up fast again.

"What the fuck?"

The Abarth was thrown off centre as the much bigger BMW bumped them again and Annie had to fight to keep it straight.

"Fuck this shit!" Annie said through gritted teeth. Then she floored it.

The Abarth leapt forward and raced along the flowing, serpentine curves of the road as Annie quickly ran through the gears. Her move left the BMW for dead and Annie gave a hard smile as she looked at it disappearing in the rear-view.

"Suck that, bitches!"

Her bravado was short-lived. The BMW rapidly reeled them in and was soon right on their tail. They braced for another bump, but this time the driver behind them started to pull alongside. Annie's foot tried to bury the accelerator further into the floor, but she didn't have any more. And now they were side by side again, but this time as Jack looked over at them, there was none of the shouting or gesticulating. This time the passengers' eyes were like dinner plates and they were fixed on him and Annie. The driver's eyes flashed occasionally towards them, but he was reading the road ahead – hardly surprising, given that the BMW was fully in the oncoming lane. If a truck appeared now, the result would be catastrophic. He and Annie had no 'out' to the left. They'd be crushed into the wall and smashed to pieces.

Annie was blessed with excellent peripheral vision and quick reflexes, so when she saw the front of the BMW twitch towards them, she slammed on the brakes. What happened next was over in about two seconds, but seemed to last an age. The driver of the BMW had turned in to crush the Abarth against the wall, but by slamming the brakes on, Annie had ensured that there was nothing for the BMW to make contact with. Instead, the BMW slewed across the lane where the Abarth should have been and angled into the wall. The impact smashed the left side of the car, which rebounded out of control back across the road. As the Abarth skidded to a screeching halt, Annie could see the BMW driver frantically trying to turn the steering wheel to no effect. The wall had broken the front axle. The car was across the road in an instant and smashed into a massive oak tree with a shattering crunch. The front of the BMW concertinaed into the unyielding tree and the back of the car reared up six feet into the air, before coming back down with a crash of metal and glass. Despite the airbag, the driver was crushed by the steering wheel. The front passenger, who hadn't been wearing a seatbelt, went straight through the window and his head exploded into the tree, leaving nothing but a messy stump driven into his shoulders. There was no sign of the third passenger. Annie sat motionless and staring, gripping the steering wheel with all her strength. No one spoke and the only sound was a sort of ticking from the remains of the BMW. The tree would have a scar, but in two years its bark would grow out and no one would know it was a killer.

Chapter Twenty-Four

Dwayne Stebbings Takes A Trip

What they never show in action movies about the police is how much bureaucracy follows a serious accident. By the time Jack and Annie were allowed to return to their hotel, it was past eight in the evening and they were exhausted. Once the police, fire brigade and ambulance arrived at the scene, the questions came thick and fast, and they had to repeat the same information over and over again to different people. When it became clear they were foreigners, things got even more complicated. They were driven back to their hotel for their passports and then it was off to the police station in Guildford for seemingly endless checks about who they were, why they were in the country and, apparently most important of all, when they were due to leave.

"Welcoming bunch, you Brits," Annie said dryly to Jack as she came out of the interview room for the nth time to join him on an uncomfortable bench in a waiting area.

"They don't really like foreigners here anymore," Jack replied, "Especially when they think they caused an accident."

Around five-o-clock, the atmosphere changed. It turned out that the BMW had been stolen and that the two dead lads were known to the police for minor drug offences. Suddenly, Annie and Jack's claims of being chased were taken seriously and it was finally confirmed that the damage to the back of their car was consistent with being rammed. Miraculously, the third lad in the back seat had nothing more than a few cuts and bruises and two broken ribs from where his seatbelt had saved his life. After spending the afternoon in the hospital, he appeared at the police station around six. He was wearing handcuffs and was led straight to the interview room. Annie and Jack didn't know it, but he was the weak one who had bought the goddess the drinks in the pub in Aldershot. Once they had someone in custody and an obvious explanation of events, the police officers began treating the Americans as simple, idiotic tourists, rather than some existential threat to the British way of life. They even offered them a cup of tea, and at seven p.m. their duty of care to the victims of what Annie had spent the afternoon vociferously describing as 'attempted murder' kicked in and a medic checked them over. It was too late to give them blankets to keep them warm if they were in shock, so the medic advised them to take some paracetamols or ibuprofen if they were in pain and that was it.

"No lunch!" said Annie bitterly as she tucked into her beer battered fish and chips.

They were sitting in the elegant, but sparsely populated hotel dining room and had just made it in before the kitchen closed.

"They don't pay nurses enough to live on, so they're hardly going to waste public money feeding potential criminals," Jack replied, chewing on his burger and fries.

"Mmmm," Annie ruminated, then after a silence,

"Dangerous roads in this neck of the woods."

Jack could tell this was more than a comment on the day,

"How so?"

"Kinda convenient that the day after you inherit an expensive property in Bermuda and your grandfather's fortune, three kids do their utmost to run us off the road."

"Yeah, that does stretch coincidence."

"Almost as convenient as your grandparents being taken out by a random truck?"

This was met with silence, as Jack chewed his mouthful longer than he needed to.

Annie wanted to say more but held back until the water had been tested.

"The thought has crossed my mind," Jack said at last.

"Almost as convenient as a competitive swimmer jumping into a river for no good reason and drowning?" Annie watched Jack's face carefully. Was she overstepping?

In the morning, he'd said 'no' to such a thought, but since the conversation with Maz Brewer and the events of the afternoon...

"It could be," he said, "Right now, I don't know. If Katy Brewer saw what she claimed she saw, then I'd say you're right. Rosalind and Veronica aren't my sisters and they've orchestrated the murders of most of my close family. And they tried to kill us today. But we can't be sure. I need to talk to the Mazzoni woman, Skylar Judd and Josephine Paget. Maybe everything will become clear. In the meantime, we need to be on a war footing."

"Assume that your sisters want us dead and act accordingly?" Annie said, looking hard at Jack.

"Yes..." then he sighed and scrubbed his face with his hands, "What a nightmare! It was bad enough coming back here with all these God-awful memories, but to add this supernatural stuff to it makes it almost impossible. I mean, what do we do if they are sirens?" he asked, dropping his voice on the word 'sirens'.

Annie shrugged.

"Can we kill them? Are they immortal? Do we need to perform some ritual?"

Annie snapped her fingers and her eyes flashed,

"I bet that's what the blood's for!" she said in a low but excited voice, "Somehow, your dad broke free from their influence long enough to work out what was going on and what to do to beat them. For some reason you need his blood to do it."

"Then why didn't he just phone me or write me a letter?"

"Would you have believed him?"

"Probably not. I'd've thought it was another one of his mind fucks."

"Exactly! So, he decided to lead you on a journey to figure it out for yourself. And eventually, you'd have the tools to finish the job."

"But how could he be sure I'd do it?"

"He couldn't," said Annie, "That was a gamble he had to take."

"I'm really struggling with the idea that my father's trying to do the right thing," Jack said.

Annie looked at him kindly. She could see the tiredness, confusion and swirling mix of emotions were putting a strain on him, but she knew how tough he was.

"Try not to think about it. When all this is over, go to a shrink and sort it out. Right now, we need to be focussed and frosty, because that's what those bitches will be," she said, with determination glittering in her eyes.

"Okay... okay," said Jack, looking inward and nodding his head as if to tell his mind that that was the way it was going to be.

"We need to do some research. Tonight. Now. Find out exactly what we're up against," Jack said, "Come on, let's finish up."

"Woah, woah, woah there Kiddo, hold your horses!" Annie said, putting her hand out to stop Jack getting up,

"You might be happy to leave half of your dinner, but some of us are still starving. I'm gonna eat my English fish and chips, then I'm gonna have the triple tier chocolate delice – whatever that is – with a double espresso and then, and only then, am I researching mythical creatures."

"Fair enough," Jack smiled and took another bite of his burger.

***

"The Isle of Devils," Jack said dramatically.

It was an hour later and Annie had been as good as her word and stuffed herself silly. She'd even ordered the cheeseboard to go on top of everything else.

"What is?" she replied through a mouthful of well-aged brie and celery, which she was eating while perched on the side of the bed.

"Bermuda. According to this..." Jack said, lying on the bed propped up with pillows and consulting his iPad,

"Bermuda was known as the 'Isle of Devils' back in the seventeenth century, because of its treacherous reefs and the strange noises that could be heard all around the island."

"What kind of strange noises?" Annie wanted details!

"It says here, 'they were probably made by seabirds such as the Bermuda Petrel and wild hogs left by Spanish and Portuguese sailors in the 16th century'. But here's the thing – before it was discovered in 1505 by Juan de Bermudez, it was uninhabited."

"Really?" intriguing, thought Annie, while she looked up 'sirens' on her phone.

"There are more than three hundred known shipwrecks around the island..."

Annie laughed.

"What's funny?"

"Guess what sirens do for shits and giggles," she said, then before he could guess, "They lure sailors onto rocks with their bewitching songs, so that they can devour them," and she gave Jack a knowing look.

"Sounds like they've been doing a roaring trade around Bermuda, then," he said, "No wonder the Spanish and Portuguese didn't try to colonize it. They only used it to stop off for provisions."

Annie thought about this for a moment,

"So, what you're saying is Spain and Portugal - the greatest colonizing superpowers of the sixteenth century, who were busy taking over every-where they could find from Mexico to India, decided to give Bermuda a miss for no good reason?"

"No, they had a reason – they were scared shitless by the devils that lived there," Jack replied.

"Oh, that's nice. At least it's a rational reason and not some disturbing, supernatural one," Annie said sarcastically.

She looked across the room at the window. The curtains weren't drawn and seeing the darkness outside felt like someone putting a cold, wet towel over her shoulders. She shivered, stood and went to close the curtains.

"It took over a hundred years before the English decided to colonise," Jack said, summarizing what was on the webpage,

"And then they only did it because the flagship of a flotilla ran aground on the reef during a storm. The people made it to shore and decided that it was a nicer place to be than Jamestown, which was where they were heading for. They'd left England thinking Jamestown would be great, but on the way, the sailors told them what a shithole it was."

"Hey!" said Annie with mock hurt, "That's my country you're talking about!" as she went back to the bed and took a slice of Stilton with a grape.

"It's not my words, that's what the sailors said," Jack smiled, "So, they set up the colony and Bermuda was claimed by the English…"

"You Brits were good at claiming things that didn't belong to you," Annie interjected.

"Sorry, babe, you can't blame the Brits for that. Britain didn't exist until the Act of Union in 1707."

"What, it says that there?"

"No, I know it, because I did history A-Level. British and European history 1450 to 1715."

"Wow! And here was I thinking that all you had in your head was computer coding and pretty pictures," Annie said, taking a grape and giving it a provocative lick before popping it into her mouth.

Jack shook his head pityingly and continued,

"Then the colonists did what the English liked to do in the seventeenth century,"

"Which was?"

"Bring slaves to do the work and burn women as witches."

"Ah," Annie nodded, "Caring, sharing bunch those Brits… sorry, English. Was it as bad as Salem?"

"Nowhere has been as bad as Salem," Jack replied, "But this says that Jeane Gardiner was tried because she put a spell on a mulatto woman that struck her blind and dumb for two hours."

"Oh," Annie became serious, "And what happened?"

"They tested her by throwing her into the sea, but she kept bobbing back up like a cork, so they executed her."

"Yeah, that sounds like a fair test. In salt water, where people are naturally more buoyant."

"She also had a blue 'witch mark' in her mouth, which didn't bleed when they pricked it," Jack added.

"Of course, that makes perfect, rational sense."

"In the sixteen fifties, they didn't really do 'rational'. And in Bermuda, between sixteen fifty-one and fifty-five, ten women and two men were accused of witchcraft, with four of the women and one of the men executed. According to this, the man was John Middleton, whose wife had already been accused of witchcraft, but been acquitted."

"Good for her."

"Turned out *he* was the witch all along. He had witch marks all over him and during the trial, he apparently became convinced they were right and that he had unwittingly become a witch and the accomplice of Satan."

"How do you do that unwittingly?"

"It doesn't say," Jack admitted, scanning through the web page,

"But it does say that he confessed to all sorts of heinous crimes and claimed that there were too many witches in Bermuda. So, he gave them a few names and two women were tried and executed as a result. It seems that at that point, Bermuda was more or less in a state of anarchy."

"Sounds like a perfect situation for sirens to get away with murder," said Annie, and then she had a thought,

"Speaking of…" and she spoke as she typed into her phone, "How do you kill a siren?"

And she hit 'go' with a flourish.

"Crap!" she exclaimed.

"What? Are they unkillable?"

"Pretty much. They seem to be immortal… It's hard sorting out the Role Playing Game bullshit from actual myth – I'm guessing there isn't such a thing as a 'Trident of Dark Tides' outside fantasy gaming?"

Jack shook his head.

"In which case… ooh, wait! What have we here? Paydirt!" she said with satisfaction. Jack waited and watched the excitement in her eyes.

"According to this site, what you need is a bronze dagger and… guess what?" she said, looking up at him with triumph.

"What?" said Jack, "Come on, babe, you're killing me."

"A bronze dagger dipped in the blood of someone the siren has infected!"

Jack felt his stomach sink. If that was the case, then maybe his father really had thought all this stuff was true! So far, Jack had only thought of it on an intellectual level. Now, as things were apparently falling into place at speed, he was having to cope with the reality of it. Sirens really and truly existed and his sisters had really and truly been taken over by two of them. Not only that, but his father had been convinced enough to leave Jack a pint of his blood so that he could kill them.

He looked at Annie, who still had the glitter of victory in her eyes.

"Pretty conclusive, huh?"

"Depends on the web page," Jack said warily and secretly hoped it was some wacked out crazy website so that he wouldn't have to admit the reality staring him in the face.

"It's not just one page, Kiddo. I've got half a dozen pages here. They seem to disagree on some of the siren's powers… so, for instance, would you say your sisters have the power to read people's minds?"

"Men, maybe; women, no; mine, no; each other's, strong probability."

"If they are caught in a mirror, can you see their true, horrible face?"

"No. That's bollocks," said Jack firmly, "Those two have spent more time in front of mirrors making themselves look perfect than professional supermodels."

"Are they able to shape shift?"

"Not to my knowledge. Although, what was that thing Maz said?" and Jack wracked his brain, "That's it, she muttered something about them not being able to shape shift, or at least not here. I wonder what that meant?"

"Maybe they need to be near water or something?" Annie suggested, then continued, "But here's the deal: all these pages disagree on the powers, appearance and myth behind sirens, but they all agree on the bronze dagger and the victim's blood."

"Okay… that does seem indicative of something."

"*And* they agree that when the sirens are stabbed with the bronze dagger dipped in the victim's blood, they immediately release their hold on all their victims."

"Shit! Do you think this might be real?" Jack asked, turning towards Annie and hoping that she'd say 'no'. She looked right back at him and, without hesitation, said,

"Yes. Yes, I do."

'Sod it!' thought Jack, knowing that now he'd have to face the reality of a world that contained actual mythical creatures.

"Bugger!" he said.

"I know," said Annie, shifting across the bed to get close to him, "We're in a situation that shouldn't exist, but... it does. And the bitch is, we can't even tell anyone without sounding..."

"Doolally?"

"Yup! Whatever that means, that's how we'll seem. So, it's just you and me, Kiddo," and Annie looked deep into his eyes.

In that moment, they made their deepest bond. They could see that they had both accepted the insane truth, that they were alone, that they could tell no one, that they were up against an evil they couldn't fathom, but that each would always be there for the other and they would do everything in their power to protect each other and end the madness. They rested their foreheads together, then kissed.

"Tomorrow morning, we should try to talk to the joyrider who survived," said Jack.

"Will they let us do that? Earlier today they wanted to kick us out of the country – remember?"

"Yeah, but we've got to give it a try, don't you think?"

"Here's another fine mess you've gotten me into," Annie sighed.

**

Guildford Police Station was the sort of building that the East German Stasi would have loved. It was a ten-storey block of grey, brutalist menace set in the heart of the otherwise picturesque cathedral city. At precisely eight a.m. on Saturday morning, a woman in a very sharp, black trouser suit and sensible shoes entered through the main doors and strode up to the reception desk. The Sergeant looked away from his paperwork at the redhead standing looking up at him. Her eyes were the most incredible pale blue he'd ever seen.

"Morning," she said in a sharp, upper-class voice that was clearly used to command, "I'm here to see Dwayne Stebbings, the boy who survived the joyriding accident yesterday."

"And you are?" asked Sergeant Nicholls in what started out strongly, but which ended up dreamily. He was getting lost in those eyes…

"I'm his brief, Margaret Smythe – court appointed, of course. I need to see him and then afterwards, you and I need to have a little chat," and she ended with a smile that lit up her beautiful face. Sergeant Nicholls felt a bloom of warmth in his chest, as if no other man had ever been smiled at in such a way before.

"Of course," he said, "Go to interview room one. Straight down the hall, second on the left. I'll have him brought up from the cells."

"Thank you. Excellent fellow," said the barrister and then marched down the hall.

Rosalind, decked out in a very fetching red wig and her most sensible suit, sat in interview room one for almost ten minutes before the second door (which presumably led to the cells) finally opened and a somewhat bleary-looking Dwayne Stebbings appeared, accompanied by a big guard. Rosalind got up and went straight over to the guard, ignoring Dwayne. Holding the guard in her gaze she said,

"You didn't see me. If anyone asks, you don't remember bringing Dwayne Stebbings up here. Understand?"

"Yes," said the big man in a small voice.

"Now stand in the corner looking at the wall until I say otherwise."

"Yes…"

Having dealt with the guard, Rosalind turned to Dwayne Stebbings, who looked twitchy, exhausted and in pain. She sat down opposite him and fixed him with her aquamarine eyes,

"What have you told them so far?"

Dwayne quailed under her scrutiny,

"Nothing," he gasped – God, she was the most beautiful thing he had ever seen.

"Nothing about why you stole the car or who told you to do it?"

"Nothing at all," he said in an accent that mixed the worst of estuarine sub-cockney with country yokel, "I can't hardly remember. All I know is, it was very important to steal the car, go to the house in Puttenham, follow the people in the little car and run 'em off the road."

"Right, well, you can start by forgetting all of that," said Rosalind, putting power and intent into every word,

"What are you to forget?"

"I dunno," Dwayne said, like a man half awake.

"Good boy! Now, here's what I need you to do..."

She talked for two minutes and he listened very carefully. As he did so, he thought that if only he could kiss her, his life would be complete! When she finished with,

"Do you understand?" he replied,

"Yes, but could you please kiss me, mistress?"

Rosalind glanced at her watch.

"All right," and she stood up and slipped around the edge of the table in such a provocative way that Dwayne got an instant hard-on.

Rosalind took fistfuls of the shirt on his chest and pulled him up out of the chair. She slipped one hand to the back of his neck and the other down to his crotch. He was so hard!

"Mmmm," Rosalind gave a low growl, savouring his youth and his ever-so-hard manhood. It had been a while since she'd had one as young as this. Yes, she really must do this more often... and then she pulled his face towards hers and kissed him deeply.

For Dwayne, it was as if his life had finally found its meaning. It was a feeling of total and rising pleasure. Rosalind felt it.

"Now, let's not waste that!" she said and instantly dropped to her haunches, unzipped his fly and enveloped him in her mouth just as he came hard in a series of long spasms, white light bursting in his brain. Oh yes, she'd forgotten that power, that seemingly endless vitality that young men had. She'd spent so long mastering older, successful men that she'd neglected youth. She made a mental note to rectify that from now on. She zipped him up, stood up and said,

"Good boy. Wait here," then, running a cultured forefinger across her lower lip, she turned to the guard in the corner,

"You, turn around."

The guard did so with a glazed expression on his face.

"Take him back to his cell, but before you put him in, give him a pen."

"Yes," he said blankly and took Dwayne Stebbings away.

A few moments later, Rosalind was back at the reception desk with the Sergeant.

"I need you to take me to the room with all the CCTV equipment."

"Of course, Miss. Follow me," and he led her to the lift.

They went down two floors with the Sergeant staring at her throughout. For her part, Rosalind was going to hold off on this one. He was in late middle age and had little of the spark she craved, so she simply held his gaze without giving him any further encouragement. On arrival in the second sub-basement, he led her to the operations room. Inside, two men in their mid to late thirties were manning the multiple banks of the building's security cameras. As the newcomers entered, one of them turned and said,

"All right, Charlie, what can we... do... you... for..." the man's cheery welcome ground to a halt as Rosalind instantly took control of him.

"Look at me!" she ordered, and the two technicians and the Sergeant all fixed their eyes on her,

"I need you two to wipe any trace of me from all your cameras. Got it?"

They nodded. Whatever the goddess wanted, that is what they would do for her.

"I'm going to leave now, so make sure that you wipe everything for the next five minutes, too."

Again, they all nodded, even the Sergeant, who knew nothing of how the CCTV system worked. Rosalind smiled a cruel, arrogant smile. Men were very, very weak! And yet, she did crave them so! She turned on her heel and beckoned the Sergeant to follow her. As they walked back to the lift, the doors opened and a female officer came out. Rosalind's lip curled in a snarl and she fell into step behind the Sergeant as the woman approached.

"Morning, Charlie!"

"Morning, Val, you all right?" the Sergeant said merrily.

"You know me – muddling through," she said as she passed and, as the vacuous exchange took place, Rosalind managed to slip around the far side of the Sergeant so that he was always between her and this 'Val' woman. A moment after she had passed by, Rosalind was in front of the Sergeant and seconds later had made the lift unobserved. They went back to the reception desk without incident and within a minute, Rosalind was out of the building and beyond the electronic eyes of the external security cameras.

Ten minutes after Rosalind had left the building, Dwayne Stebbings got up from his bunk and looked around his cell. It was small and from floor to ceiling, the walls were tiled in large, brick shaped off-white tiles. At one end of the bed, a four-foot high, tiled wall, which sloped down to the floor after a couple of feet, delineated the space for the toilet. Dwayne took the steel Parker ball point pen out of his pocket and stepped across to the opposite wall of the cell. He made a fist and put it side on to the wall so that he was looking down the curl of his fingers with his thumb pointing towards him. With his other hand, he slipped the pen into the tunnel made by his fingers until it was braced against the wall. He squeezed his fist tightly around the pen, the point of which was at eye-level, and took a deep breath. She said he had to ignore the pain and get the job done. When the job was done, he would be rewarded. Pain was the price he would pay, but the pleasure would be ten times greater. He drew his head back. Then, with every ounce of strength he had, he smashed his face into his fist. The tip of the pen instantly burst his eyeball and fluid exploded across the tiles. Dwayne suppressed a scream of agony, holding the pen in place and using his head like a hammer to drive it further into his eye socket. The impact against bone was so excruciating he almost passed out.

Dwayne had failed. He was bleeding badly and, with his good eye, could see blood all across the wall and over the green, easy-wipe flooring. His breathing was ragged and he was lurching about the cell, gripped with pain. But the goddess had told him that failure was unacceptable and would lead to unimaginable agony. Could anything be worse than this? He knew that

She could inflict worse. He didn't dare try it with his other eye. What if he blinded himself? How would he look on her beauty then? No, he had a better idea. In a frenzy of suffering, he pulled the pen out of his eye and staggered to the low wall between the bed and the toilet. He shoved the pen as far up his nose as he could, took aim and slammed it with all his force into the sloping top of the wall. There was a burst of white as the steel pen punched through to his brain and he knew no more. Before he fell, Dwayne Stebbings had inflicted two horrific injuries on himself, but had failed. Neither injury was fatal. He was still alive and would survive if he fell to his right, where he would hit the side of the bed and fall to the floor. But he didn't. He fell head-first to the left and onto the toilet. His face hit the far edge of the rim and his full body weight twisted his face up and around as he fell. The dull crunch of vertebrae sealed it. Seconds after his neck broke, his bladder and sphincter released. Instead of living forever in the shining light of the goddess, experiencing pleasure beyond all imagining, Dwayne Stebbings' mangled body was found twenty minutes later in a pool of urine, blood and faeces.

When Jack and Annie arrived at the police station around ten a.m. the entire place was in uproar. Uniformed officers were rushing about like ants whose nest had been poked by an inquisitive boy with a stick. Some of these were holding back a gang of reporters, who were on the front steps shouting questions and taking photographs. As they got closer, Annie and Jack exchanged a questioning glance. There was no way to get up the steps and into the building, so they hung at the back of the crowd of reporters.

"What's happened?" Annie asked the nearest one, a young man in jeans, T-shirt and heavy anorak, who looked about a week out of college.

"Been a suicide in one of the cells. Some joyrider."

Well, that certainly grabbed their attention.

"Any details?" Annie pressed.

"Rumour is that he got hold of a pen, put one end up against the wall of his cell and head butted it. Went straight through his eye and into his brain."

"Jesus!" Annie exclaimed.

"But it didn't kill him. They're saying he did it a second time through the other eye. And that's what killed him," the young man said in a tone bordering on glee,

"Can you believe it – and this is my first week at the Farnham Herald!"

"Congratulations," Annie said, patting him on the shoulder, and he moved away to get a better view of the mayhem.

Jack and Annie left him to it.

"I don't know how they got to him, but they did," said Jack.

Annie looked around them. Suddenly, she was very aware of their surroundings.

"Feeling like a sitting duck?" she asked.

"Yeah, and I'm not enjoying it."

"I say we get into our dented, fast little car and get the hell out of here. Disappear into London."

"Suits me fine," said Jack as they hurried back to where they had parked. He clambered behind the wheel and they were soon in the Saturday morning traffic. Annie looked in the wing mirror,

"I think we've got company – black Range Rover about five cars back."

"I see it," said Jack and he kept one eye on it as they headed through the town and out towards the A3 for London. The Range Rover was certainly following their route, but maybe they were going to the A3 for perfectly normal reasons? At the last set of lights before the turn-off, he was pleased to see the Range Rover head straight on, while they'd turned left.

"I think we're in the clear," he said, taking the long, sweeping turn to join the road to London. He didn't notice the anonymous green Ford Focus estate that ghosted along a couple of hundred yards behind them from Guildford to London.

Chapter Twenty-Five

Tea At The Dorchester

Jack and Annie were not the only people who had decided that a trip to London was just the ticket. By the time they were leaving Guildford, Rosalind – minus the red wig – was just stepping out of her custom Revere Range Rover and walking into a hotel on Park Lane. She ignored the various salutations of 'Good morning, madam' from the phalanx of flunkies in the reception area and went straight to her suite. This was spacious, elegant and exceedingly comfortable. Rosalind did love comfort. Almost as much as adoration and drawing off the life spirit of men. Those three things were her driving urges – though, of course, the latter was the most important of all. Yes, to draw the strength and vitality from a man was quite delicious and temporarily staved off the constant, gnawing hunger for it. That young man from the police station had certainly whetted her appetite, so when she approached her suite and saw a valet come out of a door further along the corridor, she called out,

"You!"

The man turned towards her and was immediately spellbound. Rosalind approached, appraising him with a haughty expression as she did. He couldn't have been more than twenty, about five foot ten, neat, dark hair, slim build. Yes, he would do nicely.

"Come with me," she ordered and he obeyed, following her to the door of her suite, which was flanked by two of her security team.

"See that we are not disturbed..." and she began to enter, then paused, "Unless it's my sister, in which case let her in. I'm sure she'd enjoy some of this," then she led the valet into the suite and closed the door.

Rosalind was right that Veronica was going to pay her a visit, but it was mid-afternoon when she arrived, by which time the valet, dishevelled and utterly spent, had already left, to be yelled at by his boss for going AWOL. The unfortunate man had no idea what had happened, couldn't account for his whereabouts and was summarily fired. Veronica phoned ahead and the sisters agreed that the most sensible thing to do was meet at The Dorchester over afternoon tea. Veronica swished into the elegant 'Promenade' at the Dorchester like a fresh spring breeze. Her outfit was classic 'new look': a red jacket with the collar turned up and pinched at the waist; a black, pleated skirt; cream three-inch heels; fine, emerald-green leather gloves, all topped off with a broad-brimmed emerald-green hat. She noted the way every man watched her as she approached her sister's table. She could almost taste their desire and she savoured the power.

"Sister," she said simply as she sat down next to Rosalind on the plump, three-seater sofa that curved around one side of the table.

"Sister," Rosalind replied and they kissed. Not a double-sided air kiss, so beloved of the rich, but a kiss on the lips. An elderly gentleman across the room choked on his tea as he sat, transfixed by the sight.

"You taste of youth," said Veronica.

"Yes, a vigorous valet from my hotel... and one of your joyriding boys."

"Ah yes, the weak one. You should have tried the other two. They were delightfully piquant."

"I'm sure," said Rosalind, raising an eyebrow, "I'd forgotten how fun they can be when they're only just ripe."

"I try to have a couple every week. Although variety is the spice of life, so I always have something well-aged every now and again," Veronica replied, turning her commanding gaze on the elderly gentleman across the room. He stared back and suddenly Veronica's deep, sea-green eyes were his world. His hand went slack and the cucumber sandwich he'd been about to bite slipped from it and landed back on his plate. Veronica sized him up – mid-seventies, suit from Saville Row, clean-shaven, slightly overweight and undoubtedly married to the fat frump in the hideous flower-patterned dress sitting opposite him. Yes, she'd try him later.

"Sister," Rosalind said insistently and Veronica broke her gaze and turned back,

"Business first, pleasure later."

"Of course."

Waiters came and brought them the best tea, cakes and sandwiches that London can offer, all against the backdrop of the opulent space - the white and grey marble floor, softened by a thick, elegantly patterned carpet in which gold and eau de nil dominated, walls in gold and white, black marble columns with gilded tops, pretty and unchallenging artwork, gilded mirrors and strategically positioned pot plants between tables to give everyone the impression of privacy in what was effectively a communal area. Rosalind and Veronica tucked into everything put in front of them and happily ordered more as they went. In fact, their enthusiasm for the food was such that the casual observer might have found it off-putting. Was there an element of desperation in the way they devoured the food? How could two slim, beautiful, stylish women eat like a couple of herring gulls that have happened on a discarded bag of fish and chips?

"Your plan failed," Rosalind said bluntly after the waiter brought the second round of sandwiches.

"True," Veronica replied, through a mouthful of gravadlax, "But the plan was sound – it worked on our grandparents, after all. Of course, I was able to take my time and choose the right man for that. This was a rush job and I had to make do with what I could find on the day."

"We should assume that they know about us," said Rosalind, "Especially after their trip to Mary Brewer."

"Will they believe that mad old cow?" and Veronica's eyes flared with hatred.

"She would have filled their heads with Katy's stories," Rosalind replied, "And perhaps between that and father leaving Jasper his blood, they might now have put it all together."

"How could father betray us like that, after all the pleasure we gave him?" Veronica snarled. It's not easy to look murderous while sipping Earl Grey tea from a fine bone china cup decorated with pink roses, but Veronica managed it perfectly.

"Sister, you know exactly why – we left him too long, he came to his senses and realised what we had done. If you had followed my instructions..." Rosalind left that hanging.

"As Brego's muse, I couldn't very well *not* go to Papua New Guinea with him. You were only a couple of hours' flight away, *you* could have gone to see him," Veronica said in a terse whisper.

"I was on my honeymoon!" Rosalind muttered angrily.

"Your third honeymoon. It's not like it's anything special. You could have gone to father's and back without your Prince noticing. Anyway, what's done is done. What next? Shall I try and liquidate them again?"

Rosalind sat back and stuffed an entire mini chocolate éclair into her mouth, which she hardly seemed to chew before swallowing. She washed it down with Earl Grey, then replied,

"No. On reflection, trying to kill them was a tad precipitous. We need to know who else is on the list that father gave him. Any of them might be a danger to us, and we can't have that, can we?"

"No," Veronica replied firmly.

"I say that we follow Jasper, find out who he's speaking to and *then* eliminate them."

"Yes, and we can start with Mary Brewer," Veronica hissed.

"No," Rosalind said flatly.

"Why not?"

"Because if we do it now, they might suspect something. No, we want them to carry on and lead us to the others. Once we know who they all are, then we can take care of them. As for Mary Brewer, we can deal with her at our leisure. Her bitch of a daughter almost ruined everything and soon it will be time for her to pay."

"What about Jasper's poisonous little whore?" Veronica's lip curled at the thought of Annie's insolence at the reading of the will.

"I think we should dispose of her as soon as we can. If he's alone, he'll be easier to deal with," Rosalind said with a crooked, unpleasant smile.

"Such a pity he has the necklace, otherwise this would be over already," said Veronica.

"Yes, damned witches!" Rosalind snapped, and the two of them fell into silence, lost in their memories.

When the human race was young, it had always been so easy. They had been able to pick off the unwary without any real consequences. People had been too afraid or disorganised to hunt them down. Throughout antiquity, they had been able feed well on sailors, but as humans had inexorably filled both land and sea, the risk of discovery and retribution had become greater. And so, they had flown across the sea to find new lands. They had found Bermuda and made the empty island theirs. From there, they had been able to raid the east coast of the Americas from Newfoundland to the Caribbean preying on the local tribes. And then one day, the winds brought European sailors to them. That was a happy time. A hundred years of explorers and pirates to drain and devour. Then came the first settlers and that had been good, too, because they were men... but then came wives. And some of those wives were 'wise women'. They were the ones with Power, who had knowledge of the Secret Art. They were the ones who could tell when their men were being controlled and had some inkling of how to stop it. So, the only thing to do was influence the men to hunt the wise women down and execute them as witches. This was a success. How Rosalind and Veronica had delighted in watching the men hanging and burning the very women who were trying to save them from true evil. It had been priceless to see! But one of them had been cunning. She had not shared her power with anyone so there was no way for Rosalind and Veronica to know that she was working against them until it had been too late. She was the one that created a powerful spell to protect men from the sirens' powers. The witch had even learned to contain the spell in objects that could be worn for protection. Mistress Hicks had given them to every man in her family and now Jack wore one that she herself had made in the 1640's. But in the end, all her spells couldn't protect her. She had been collecting roots down at Hog Bay at midnight under the full moon, when Rosalind and Veronica caught her. They appeared to her in their true forms – half woman, half sea bird – and using their vicious talons, they had torn her to pieces. They could still remember the taste of her flesh.

And then, for nearly three hundred years, life had been very good. They'd had all the men they wanted, fearful slaves to prey on and civilization at arm's length. But then came progress and world wars and, worst of all, aeroplanes. Suddenly, their quiet island backwater was a short flight from America and the tourists flooded in with their cameras. The sisters had had to be careful. They could not risk discovery. They were forced to pick and choose their moments to come out and feed – almost always when storms hit. The authorities expected disappearances and deaths at such times. Even so, pickings were slim for almost forty years, but then one day they found David Kidd and his two daughters. Such a handsome man! They watched him from the sea with hungry eyes. So virile! They *had* to have him. A plan formed in Rosalind's mind to do something they'd never tried before. For reasons she hadn't been able to explain, she felt that they would be able to take over the bodies of the two girls. When they were close to the shore or swimming in the sea, she had been able to feel a power between her and them. Veronica felt it, too. So, why not try to take their bodies? The girls were attractive and once their souls were removed, it would be easy to get all the men they wanted without having to hide. Then the fateful storm had come and... they had been sitting pretty ever since. Of course, they had always lived with the danger of being found out. They had already had to silence five journalists who had got closer to the truth than they'd liked. Also, they would eventually have to inhabit new bodies. If they stayed looking as young as they did for another twenty years, people would start asking questions, but that was a bridge they would cross when the time came. Right now, though, they were living well and had no intention of going back to the intense hunger they'd experienced before taking over the lives of David Kidd's children.

Their silence was long and the rest of the room continued its comings and goings around them as if they were in stasis. At last a waitress arrived,

"May I clear these away, or would you like something else?"

"Champagne!" Veronica declared, breaking out from her reverie.

"Of course, madam, although the service does stop at six and it's now a quarter to..."

"We shall take it away with us if we haven't finished it by six... Sadie," Veronica said coldly, reading the waitress' nametag and making a mental note to get her sacked.

"Of course," Sadie replied. The words 'you stuck up bitch' were left unsaid as she started clearing the scattered remnants of the enormous tea.

When she had gone, Veronica asked,

"Do we know where they are now?"

"Most likely somewhere around here. I had them followed. They went to Heathrow and dropped off their car, checked into one of the airport hotels for the night and then took the tube into town. I told my man to follow, but he lost them. To make up for his failure, he has gone back to the hotel and is going to bug their room and put trackers in their luggage."

"Better than nothing. I will keep a couple of my men available to track them if needs be," said Veronica.

"Where are you staying?"

"A few doors down the road in the penthouse suite of that modern monstrosity. The views of the park from the floor to ceiling windows are outstanding. And there's nothing quite like being taken from behind with your breasts pushing into the cold glass with every thrust... Yes?"

The waitress had returned with the champagne and was standing with an appalled look of shock on her face,

"Er... your champagne, madam," she stammered, trying to pull herself together and fumbling the glasses.

"Don't strain yourself. We're leaving, so we'll take it as is," and Veronica stood, plucked the bottle from the waitress' hand and swept over to where the old man was sitting. He looked at her with dumb awe as she approached him and whispered in his ear,

"Tell your wife you're going to the lavatory and meet me outside," and then she swept off towards the exit.

Meanwhile, Rosalind stood up, roundly ignored the waitress and walked up to the maître d',

"Two hundred ought to cover it, with a little something left over for you, Andrew," she said, smiling as she passed him the folded fifty-pound notes.

"Thank you, your highness," the maître d' stammered, as Rosalind followed her sister out.

Fifteen minutes later, the sisters were standing in nothing but their heels and their expensive underwear in the stylish sitting room of Veronica's suite. They were inspecting Sir Reginald Brady, who stood naked and unashamed before them with a wicked gleam in his eye. If truth be told, the ravages of time had started work on his body. He was saggy in all the wrong places, with a fold of skin between his belly and his groin. His shoulders and arms which had once been his pride when he had rowed for Oxford, were now slack and wrinkled with random tufts of sprouting hair. His skin was covered in liver spots and worryingly large moles, his legs were knobbly with varicose veins, the nails of his feet were thick and yellowed, and his man boobs sagged morosely. But as Rosalind and Veronica circled him, assessing every inch of his body, their eyes were aflame.

"Oh yes," purred Rosalind as she sniffed in his direction.

"You see? They develop such depth of flavour," Veronica said, "I think it's the years of being fertile but not being able to sow. I'm sure he loves his walrus of a wife, but when was the last time she allowed him to give her a good seeing to?"

"November the twelfth, two thousand and eight," said Sir Reginald, who didn't seem at all put out that they were discussing him in such an offhand way or calling his wife a walrus.

"Oh, you poor man," Veronica said with a genuinely sad look on her face, approaching him and holding the underside of his chin up with a long, scarlet nail as she looked into his eyes,

"And masturbation doesn't quite scratch that itch, does it?"

"No," he said glumly.

"And now here we are," said Rosalind, who had prowled up behind him and was pressing herself into his buttocks while slipping a hand around his chest,

"Fifteen years of pent-up virility. Whatever shall we do with it?" she whispered into his ear, delicately biting the lobe as she finished.

"I think part of you knows exactly what it wants to do," said Veronica, not breaking the electric contact with his eyes, but reaching a hand down to the one part of him that was very hard indeed.

She was right – it did know what to do - and, as the evening progressed, they squeezed every ounce of suppressed desire, hunger and vigour out of him. Yes, they fully enjoyed the aged delights of Sir Reginald Brady. And before his heart finally gave out, Rosalind even experienced the feeling of her breasts pressing hard against the window as Sir Reginald took her from behind. Veronica had been right – there was nothing quite like it.

***

While the rich woman who paid his wages was having her jollies against the window of the penthouse suite of a hotel overlooking Park Lane, Vincent Chambers was sitting in his green Ford Focus estate in the car park of a hotel near Heathrow airport. He was wearing headphones and had been there since two in the afternoon. After he'd bugged Jack and Annie's room, he'd bought himself a bucketload of snacks and drinks, and settled down with his Kindle to read another Maigret detective novel. By the time Annie and Jack returned to their room after a day shopping in London, Vincent Chambers had finished 'Madame Maigret's Friend' and was three quarters of the way through 'The Misty Harbour'. Since he had not left his listening post for a moment, he had also half-filled a two-litre bottle with something that looked like apple juice, but definitely wasn't. As a fan of Maigret, he had also been smoking his pipe in the car, which now reeked of stale sweat and Kendal Gold cherry and vanilla tobacco. He liked to think of himself as similar to his hero detective – solid, dogged, unflappable – although the reality was that he was shorter, fatter and wasn't a brilliant detective, but just a bloke who did surveillance work for anyone who'd pay. Most of his clients were journalists on tabloid newspapers.

As soon as his headphones crackled into life with the opening of the door to the room, Vincent put his Kindle aside, started his recording device and set his entire being to listening and imagining the people and the room.

There was a rustling of multiple plastic bags and the bump of... what was it? There it was again – an empty suitcase! Yes, one of those hard plastic ones with wheels and a pull up handle. So, that was one thing they'd been out to buy. More rustling of bags – this time it sounded like they were being dumped on the bed. From the sound of them, they seemed to be full of clothes.

"Jeesh! I'm done in!" came the voice of the woman – what was her name again? Ah, yes – Annie.

"What is it about walking around through crowds of people that's so damned tiring? We've barely covered ten miles, but I feel like I've run a marathon," she complained and then there were two distinct thuds, followed by a groan of relief. Must've been taking her shoes off...

"And I know city people always say this about tourists," the man – Jack – began, "But why do so many of them stop at the top of escalators? Do they really not understand that the mechanism keeps going after they get off? Do they really not understand that the people behind them are going to start piling up the second they stop to admire the view? They drive me mental!"

There was a loud 'whumpf' and a long, satisfied 'Aaaaah' from Jack as he undoubtedly let himself fall backwards onto the bed.

"Hey, we mustn't get too comfy!" Annie said, "We've got to pack tonight. We wanna be able to wake up and head straight out the door. You've got to check in for your flight to Milan at eight – and remember, it's Malpensa..."

"Not Linate. Yes. Blimey, I make that mistake one time and you never let me forget."

"Only because it was such a spectacular mistake. Milan's got two airports and you managed to fly us into one of them, but book the car hire in the other. That cost me half a day's snowboarding, Kiddo. And when it comes to snowboarding, I never forget – or forgive," said Annie darkly.

Vincent made a note. So, the bloke was flying to Milan Malpensa! His client's team would be able to find out which exact flight he was booked on.

"Are you gonna move?" asked Annie.

"Eventually," said Jack, but from the sound of it, it wouldn't be any time soon.

Vincent Chambers strained his ears. He imagined the room. Although it was a famous name hotel, the room itself was little more than a box with a king-size bed in it. The door opened directly into the main space and almost immediately on the right was the door to the small, sterile bathroom in white, light grey and dark grey with its not-quite generous shower, sink and toilet. The decor of the main room was a symphony in bland – oyster coloured carpet, off-white walls, mid-silver curtains and a faun headboard for the bed. There was a grey office chair 'for the executive' to work at the long, white worktop which ran along the wall opposite the bed. On that wall, a fifty-inch flatscreen TV took pride of place so that you could watch it in bed while propped against the faun, faux suede headboard. There was a minimal amount of room between the bed and the window, so any packing would need to be done in the space between the door and the bed.

"Okay!" said Jack suddenly, and the bed creaked as he got up. And now there was a lot of rustling as the many plastic bags were unpacked and the contents laid on the bed. Then the hollow, plasticky sound of the empty suitcase being positioned on the floor and opened.

"You're going to need this..." said Annie, "No, don't just throw it in, fold it. Maximise space!"

"Okay," Jack grumbled and more rustling followed.

"Take the tags off."

"Why?"

"Because you've got more time here than you'll have in Italy. Here, use these," Annie said.

This was followed by the sound of tags being snipped.

"Could you pass me the bin, please," Jack said.

Vincent Chambers' face registered approval. Whoever these two were, they clearly respected each other. Once, many years before, he might even have had a vague sensation at the back of his mind that maybe what he was doing was in some way wrong. He didn't have that sensation anymore. What he had was a house with the mortgage paid off, five more years until his pension kicked in and a static caravan in Rhyl with no outstanding payments.

Through the ether, the packing continued in the unseen room. Finally, after about ten minutes of the sort of filler dialogue normally only found in afternoon plays on Radio 4, Vincent's ears pricked up as Annie said,

"Okay, that's that. Got your ticket?"

"Yup."

"Passport? E-boarding card and car hire stuff?"

There was a rustling of paper.

"Yes, yes and yes," Jack replied and then it sounded like he put it all away.

"Map?"

More rustling.

"Yes... and that's another weird thing that's been bugging me..." said Jack, and Vincent allowed himself a smile as Jack continued,

"No address for this Mazzoni woman, just a grid reference."

"Yeah, that is weird... but so's everything else, so I guess you've gotta roll with it."

As Vincent noted down the name 'Mazzoni', the Oasis song 'Roll With It' started going around in his head and would be there for the rest of the night.

"I wish I didn't have to break in these walking shoes on the hike up there. Remind me in the morning to get some blister plasters from the pharmacy, just in case," said Jack.

"Ok."

"What time's *your* flight again?"

"Eleven. Should get me into New York by two their time," Annie replied, "Then I'm on the road and should be in Southampton by four. Maybe four-thirty."

"Will you stay for dinner?"

"Not sure. I think yes. Mom will have a lot to tell me and Harry will be excited, and Doctor Bob will be there. So, we'll eat, I'll get Harry sleepy, bundle him into the Beast and homeward bound."

"Long day."

"Nah! I'll try to catch some sleep on the flight."

Vincent Chambers was writing quickly. Yes, this was what the careful planning and hours of waiting were for – gold dust like this. It would more than make up for his earlier mistake. Who knows, his client might even pay extra.

"Okay, I'm gonna hit the shower," said Annie, and the next half hour offered nothing more than two people taking turns in the bathroom and getting ready for bed, interspersed with functional language. Eventually, they had finished their ablutions and the rustling sounds of covers made it clear that they were now in bed. Suddenly, Vincent Chambers was listening very hard.

"You know," said Jack, "I've got no idea how long this Italy thing is going to take or when we're going to see each other again, so..."

"So, maybe we should give each other something to remember?"

And then there was the sound of kissing.

Vincent Chambers slowly drew his tongue across his top lip. Oh yes, this would be good. His furtive eyes flicked down to his recording device to make sure it was on. Yes, all good there. He wouldn't want to miss this. He had seen the owners of the two voices and had already undressed the woman in his mind, so it was easy to imagine the action of what he was hearing in glorious technicolour. His ears strained for every movement, every caress, every change of position. By God, they were keen! As he listened with sweat beading on his forehead and his erection pushing against his trousers, he knew that this one was a keeper. This one would give him wank fantasies for years. And the sounds she made as she climaxed again and again were spectacular! Oh yes, he knew some people who would pay good money for a copy of this. Sod the celebrity sex video with its dodgy camera work, shaky pictures and dismal lighting – this was what the real connoisseur wanted. High quality audio where the listener's imagination could provide the pictures in perfect HD. This one would be up there with the audio of Jude and Sienna, Johnny and Amber, and – of course – Harry and Meghan. As Vincent Chambers listened for the next hour and a half, he knew this was worth more than the rest of the job put together. When the couple finally finished and went to sleep, he slumped back into his seat, took off the sweaty headphones and stopped the recording. He stared at nothing, thinking of how he could edit that into the hottest half-hour that had ever been caught on tape. And how much money he could make from it.

"You beauty!" he said, then picked up his phone to call his client and tell her their plans.

Chapter Twenty-Six

Passeggiata

Gianfranco Cacciatori settled into his business class seat on the nine-o-clock British Airways flight from Heathrow to Malpensa and winked at one of the female cabin crew. She smiled back. Not because it was her job to keep the passengers happy, but because the guy in seat 4A was gorgeous – albeit in a sort of rough way. The fact was, Gianfranco was a magnificent specimen in his perfectly tailored Armani suit: six two, broad shoulders, narrow waist, dark hair which tumbled to his shoulders, chiselled Italian features and big, brown eyes with pretty lashes. They were the instant hits that had got him into so many beds. A longer consideration, however, had always led sensible women to leave him as a one-night stand or avoid him altogether. There was an air of menace about him. Yes, his nose had clearly been broken a couple of times and he had a scar through one of his eyebrows, but those could easily be old rugby injuries. No, there was something in the tight set of the jaw that might be indicative of a hair-trigger temper and there was an other worldliness in his gaze. It was the false reassurance of the slaughterman as he looks at an animal to calm it before the kill. Yes, the eyelashes were pretty, but they were camouflaging the eyes of a stone-cold killer.

His job for the next couple of days was simple. Get to Malpensa before Jack Kidd, wait for him, follow him and find out who he was seeing and where. Then he had to interrogate that person to get every last iota of information from them – that was the important part - then kill them. How he did that was up to him and, as the flight took off, he daydreamed about what he might do. He would be aided in his endeavours by the fact that while Jack and Annie had been at breakfast that morning, Vincent Chambers had sneaked back into their room and planted a tracker in Jack's new suitcase. And when Jack had finished his business in Italy, Gianfranco could return to his usual duties as the personal bodyguard of the goddess. Being away from her was almost painful. She was his world. Only one thing was important – the happiness of Veronica Matser. Yes, she was married to that idiot artist, but it was Gianfranco that she came to when she wanted muscular sex. And he always gave satisfaction. Now he was away for a few days, he was free to indulge himself with other women, but he knew deep down that none of them would even come close to Veronica. He would do anything for her and had already happily dissolved the bodies of two snooping journalists in acid. For now, though, his target was Jack Kidd.

So, when Jack finally strolled through passport control at Malpensa a few hours later, Gianfranco was fed, watered, had hired a fast car and was ready to go wherever his prey led him. The first place was a car rental booth. Gianfranco hung back, apparently reading La Gazetta dello Sport. His team – Inter Milan – would be playing Udinese later in the day. They needed to get it together if they were going to catch Napoli for the title, but he wasn't really reading. His sharp eyes were on the booth. Jack was having to stumble his way through the interminable paperwork with only Google Translate as his guide. Watching the booth was easy, where it would be trickier was when Jack got the car. Gianfranco would have to spot which car Jack was going to be in, then move quickly to get his own car out of the garage and in a position to follow. As it turned out, this was easier than it could have been, because by a stroke of luck, Jack had chosen the same car hire company, so Gianfranco could slip over to his car, watch Jack leave and, after a suitable gap, follow him. Also, Jack decided to practice putting the snow chains onto the wheels. This took about twenty-five minutes of faffing and swearing, which gave Gianfranco plenty of time to be ready.

Jack's faffing told Gianfranco something important - they were going to the mountains! That would be the only reason to check the snow chains. Even in February, the roads down on the plain rarely required chains, but up in the mountains they could be vital. Gianfranco hoped they weren't going to a ski resort. He hated skiing, and skiers, and crowds, and tourists, and crowds of tourists. The thought of crowds of skiing tourists made him grip the steering wheel tightly. As a native of Milan, he had grown up within a hundred kilometres of some of the best ski slopes in Europe, but for him, they'd may as well have been on the moon. His family were poor, so no skiing for him. He didn't even like the countryside or hiking. These were activities for soft people who had the time and money to waste on such things. Almost all his life had been spent skirmishing to make a living on the dirty backstreets of Milan. Ever since he was a kid – first stealing from shops, then working as a lookout for the local drug dealers, then, as he'd developed into a big, strong man, becoming one of their enforcers. Finally, two years ago, he'd bribed his way into a security job at the Milan Fashion Week and that's where Veronica had spotted him. She had opened up new worlds for him, but at heart he was happiest in the grime and hustle of the big city. However, it looked like there would be none of that for him today, because they were off to the bloody mountains.

Once he'd stowed the snow chains back in their box, Jack took a bottle of water and poured it over his hands. He shook them and wiped them down his jeans. He could see from the grid coordinates on the map that the place he was going to was up in the mountains. He had no idea what the conditions were like up there, but he didn't want his first time putting on the snow chains to be halfway up a mountain in a snowstorm. Anyway, he knew how they worked now, so that was a plus. He'd hired an Alpha Romeo Stelvio in the hope that since it was named after a mountain pass about fifty miles from where he was going, it would cope with whatever the conditions might be up there. He got in, started the engine and drove out of the car park to find the main road. He checked the rear-view and didn't see anyone behind him. That was good. Ever since he'd left London, he'd felt like someone was watching him. Given what had happened, he was sure that he'd be followed, so the feeling was natural.

After getting away from the nightmarish tangle of roads around the airport, he headed west along the Autostrada dei Laghi – the Lake Highway that shuttled tourists to most of the great Italian lakes from Como to Maggiore. It was a lovely afternoon, with bright, winter sun shining through scattered clouds above. The view from the road wasn't anything to write home about yet, but once he turned north and headed to Lake Como, all that would change as the heavily wooded mountains emerged out of the plain. As he drove, he kept checking his mirrors. Nothing seemed out of the ordinary, but...

"Goddammit!" he erupted, slapping the steering wheel. He hated all this nonsense! After the shitshow of his youth, all he'd wanted out of life was to design, draw and have a happy, quiet time. And he'd done brilliantly at carving that out. But now... now he was deep in the shit. He'd had to think very carefully about where to stay, and not for nice reasons like 'where's got the best views?' or 'where can I get the yummiest dinner?'. No, he'd had to work out where would be the best place to stay if he was being followed by someone who wanted to kill him. What the fuck! What sort of screwed up nightmare had he fallen into? The question he'd had to ask was 'should I get as close as possible to the place I'm going'? But that would invariably be a small town or even a village, where the arrival of a single American tourist would be impossible to hide. He'd be a sitting duck. Instead, he'd decided to make a larger town his centre of operations. There were plenty of lovely towns around Lake Como where he could stay, but would he be safe? Because, and here was the kicker, his sisters were apparently water devils, so if he stayed near a big lake, their powers might somehow be intensified, thus putting his life in peril. He wasn't in Switzerland, but he certainly felt like he was in a cuckoo clock.

"Fuck me!" Jack swore, slapping the wheel again.

In the bright light of the Italian sun, it all sounded totally and utterly in-fucking-sane! And yet... and yet... something deep within him was squirming with fear that it was all true. His mind was saying 'Don't be ridiculous', but his gut was saying 'Sorry mate, this is how it is, however crazy it may seem'. And he was being torn between them. He wished Annie was with him. She was sure it was all true and that confidence gave her clarity of thought and action. Unconsciously, his left hand went up and touched the porpoise hung around his neck. Then he realised what he was doing and placed the hand back on the steering wheel. And there was that, too. Had his grandfather, one of the best and most rational men he'd ever known, really believed that this necklace protected him from devils?

"What a mindfuck!"

So, where to stay? In the end he'd plumped for a larger town nowhere near the lake, but fairly near his destination. Sondrio was in the Valtellina and big enough to some chance of anonymity. It was in a valley at the top of Lake Como, which left him a choice. Take the western route up the side of the lake, through all the beautiful towns with their dreamy views, or take the eastern route where brilliant Italian engineers had tunnelled through half a dozen mountains to create a road that cut the journey time up the lake by about two hours? So, which road to take? The winding, picturesque road next to the lake where Jack's water devil sister had probably drowned the brother of the woman he was trying to find... or the motorway through tunnels that kept half a mountain between him and the water? It hadn't been a tough choice. When the first turn off for Lake Como (and the town of Como itself) came up, Jack ignored it and motored on. He skirted around the north of Milan until he got to the road that would take him past the town of Lecco and up the eastern shore of the lake. Now he was driving straight towards the distant mountains, dark against the skyline. It was three-thirty and the light was becoming watery. As he drove on, he couldn't shake the feeling that he was literally driving into darkness.

By the time Jack got to the top of the lake, the light was fading. The twenty or so miles of fast tunnels, with their overhead and wall lights flashing past, made driving feel like a video game, so he was glad when he popped out into a land of lakes and mountains. The head of Lake Como was to his left, its waters still and dark, as the sun had already disappeared beneath the mountains in the west. He swept right and into the Valtellina. The road led him up the middle of the valley, which had been gouged out of the earth by mammoth glaciers. The surrounding mountains rose sharply to two thousand metres and their hulking presence in the dying light dampened Jack's already low spirits. He had been checking his mirrors all the way, but couldn't see any cars that stood out. He shrugged. Maybe it was all in his mind? Maybe there was nobody following him? The mountains, ancient and brooding with their snowy winter caps glowered at him mockingly. They had been here for aeons. They knew truths about the world that Jack could only guess at, and yet here he was trying to dismiss supernatural ideas because they didn't fit his view of 'reality'.

"What a young fool," they seemed to mutter, "Soon he'll go back to dust and yet what will he have learned in his brief little life? Nothing. But, of course, he'll still prattle on about his opinions and beliefs like they matter. He's a deluded ant, scurrying he knows not where or why. And after he's gone, and all the generations of men have disappeared and been forgotten, we will still be here. Watching."

Perhaps that was one reason Annie liked climbing so much – so that she could reply to the mountains: 'Yes, you will be here long after me, but you will always have to live with the knowledge that I, a mere ant, climbed to your summit and stood on your snowy peak and looked out to see what you see. I stood higher than you ever will. Remember that!'

It was dusk when he reached Sondrio and, although he couldn't get much of the flavour of the town in the gathering gloom, he was impressed by the palatial nineteenth century hotel he'd booked into. Since he was now officially rich and also officially in danger of being killed, he thought he'd might as well spend it while he could. Once he'd checked in, had his car parked in the underground lot and been shown to his spacious but quirky room up in the eaves of the hotel, he decided to go for a short stroll to stretch his legs. It would give him a chance to check his bearings and break in his new walking boots. He stepped out of the impressive hotel entrance and into a bitterly cold evening breeze. It was below freezing and the biting wind was doing its best to cut through him. However, he was nicely bundled up and had brought some good gloves with him, so the experience was more on the side of refreshing than miserable. He walked to the centre of the piazza in the front of the hotel and looked all around. The Piazza Garibaldi was elegant and beautiful, but it made him feel small. Like the hotel, the other buildings were all on a grand scale and behind them loomed the shadowy mountains that crowded over the valley. It was as if everything was there to put him in his place.

"No!" he said firmly.

He wasn't having this! He'd beat the blues and he knew exactly how. He would enjoy a passeggiata and check out the swankiest of the local shops.

He headed towards the twinkling lights across the square and was soon engrossed in a world of expensive shoes, watches, clothes and knick-knacks. Although he only spoke a smattering of Italian, he had been to Italy a few times and knew one important thing about shopping there – in Italy, shop assistants are keen to assist you and most of them don't mind if, having got a half-dozen items out for you to look at or try on, you walk out without buying anything. So, when he walked into Intimissimi and explained he was looking for a present for his wife, the assistant (who was in her fifties and thought how lucky his wife must be) was happy to spread a vast array of items on the long counter for him to look at. In the end, he walked out with some sensible winter nightwear for Annie, some racy and not-so-sensible nightwear and some underwear that he knew she would look incredibly sexy in.

The temperature was still dropping, but it was a drier cold than in England. Jack looked to his right as he came out of the shop and wondered momentarily whether the well-dressed man about fifty yards down the street bent a little too quickly to tie his shoelace. A shoelace which seemed to be taking a long time to tie... Jack turned the other way as coolly as he could and walked with all the nonchalance he could muster in the direction of the hotel. Inside, his heart was pounding. He knew that man. It was one of Veronica's bodyguards. It wasn't the muscles bulging under the tight suit that had given him away, but his hair. No businessman would ever have his hair that long or so carefully coiffed into that 'just had sex' look. No, that was the heavy who had got out of the car with her at the funeral. Jack was trying not to panic, but only just managing it, keeping his movements deliberately easy and slow. Then he saw the perfect place to help him.

He opened the door of the tourist centre with a cheery,

"Buona sera!" to which the young woman behind the counter replied in kind. Jack then set about looking through the various leaflets in a rack that was tucked down the side of the room. It gave him a perfect view of the people coming past the shop without their being able to see him unless they stopped and looked for him. Sure enough, a few seconds later, the heavy came walking past in his expensive suit and stupid hair. He was trying to look like he wasn't looking for Jack, who registered that it was definitely the guard, and then looked down at the brochures. In the street, Gianfranco spotted his target obliviously reading through a tourist guide and walked on about twenty yards, then ducked down an alley. He would pick him up again when he came out. The main thing was that his target clearly hadn't noticed him. Inside the tourist centre, Jack wondered how long he would have to keep 'reading' the leaflets before he could safely look up. He left it thirty seconds and then did so. The man was nowhere to be seen. Good.

Jack heaved a sigh and was just about to move on, when a leaflet caught his eye:

'Val di Mello – rock climbing paradise'.

He stopped and took one of the leaflets. What a stroke of luck! According to his map, the coordinates he'd been given were somewhere high up in the Val di Mello. This could give him some useful information. Pleased with himself, he was about to leave, when a thought struck him and he went back to the rack. He took out leaflets for a dozen different places and attractions around the Valtellina, Lake Como and the Valle Spluga. He put them into one of his shopping bags, thanked the assistant and left. As he walked back to the hotel, he was finding it difficult not to keep looking over his shoulder. The thought of that paid thug tailing him made his stomach flutter in an unpleasant way. What should he do? Pick up and leave at once? But where could he go? And could he give the guy the slip? He'd already managed to tail Jack without his knowledge all the way from Milan... no, wait! All the way from England. How in hell did he manage that? Annie was the only other person who'd known he was coming to Italy, so how had this guy done it?

Jack was desperate to get back to the hotel, but kept up his pretence of being an interested tourist, sauntering through the town. Another shop caught his eye. Yes, that might be useful. He spent ten minutes inside, then reappeared and continued his stroll across the wide piazza in front of the hotel. It was only when he was through the front door of the hotel that he picked up his pace and hurried to the lift. The short ride up to his floor seemed to take an age and when it finally released him, he almost sprinted to his room and gratefully shut the door behind him. He dropped the shopping, grabbed the chair from in front of the desk 'for the executive' and wedged it under the door handle. Good! That made him feel a bit safer. But hang on – all of Veronica's guards looked like they were armed. What if this fucker had a gun? Jack looked at the chair wedged against the door and realised he was totally out of his depth. Shit! And he still couldn't explain how they'd known where he would be. It was like magic. What if his 'sisters' *were* telepathic? He'd be royally screwed. This was all too much! And then a truly terrifying thought struck him – if they knew exactly where he was, did they also know exactly where Annie was?

It was one of the few times in his life when he could say he felt his stomach drop. Really and truly drop, weighted by a terrible sense of dread that something catastrophic was happening. He took out his phone and began to dial, then stopped. Where would she even be right now? He started to frantically calculate in his head – she took off at eleven am UK time, it was a seven-and-a-half hour flight, so she wouldn't land 'til at least six thirty UK time and he was now an hour ahead of them, so it was still only five-ish there...

"Fuck!"

She'd still be in the air for another hour and a half! Okay, he'd have to leave her a message and hope she got it. He continued dialling the number, but before he hit the call button, he stopped. He needed to sound calm and together. The last thing she needed was him squawking nonsense down the phone at her. He then did something that would have left the casual observer thinking that he'd finally lost his marbles. He placed the phone on the bed, then stood up straight with his feet shoulder width apart and his fists on his hips, striking the classic Superman pose. He stayed like that for a full three minutes and, at the end, he was calm and thinking clearly. It was (according to the TED talk he'd seen) a proven way to clear cortisol, the stress hormone, from your system while raising adrenalin and other hormones to reduce stress and increase focus. Whatever the science, it had calmed him down and now he picked up the phone and hit 'call'. He spoke to the answer machine calmly but quickly, explaining the situation he was in and warning her to be on the look-out. He ended with, "The main thing is that you and Harry have to stay safe. I'm really sorry I got you into this, babe. Call me when you get the chance. I love you."

Then he rang off.

He sat on the edge of the bed and thought hard. If Veronica's man had known where Jack was every step of the way, and if they wanted him dead, then why hadn't he done it already? There'd been plenty of opportunities for an 'accident' on the way. Why wait until he got up into more sparsely populated areas where his death might garner more attention? Unless... they weren't really interested in him at all. Of course - they wanted to know who he was trying to see. But how could they know about the list of names the lawyer gave him? Again, his mind pivoted towards the 'they're mythical creatures with psychic powers' explanation. This was bad. Really bad. And he didn't know what to do. He just didn't know. And then he slapped his forehead,

"Wanker! How could you be so stupid?"

Unwittingly, he and Annie had made the classic mistake. They'd split up to cover more ground. And now, they couldn't support each other or protect each other's back. Now their enemies could pick them off at their leisure.

Jack swore for about a full minute, by the end of which his system was so brimming with cortisol that no amount of 'superman posing' could flush it out. He paced around the room thinking. So, they wanted him to lead them to the person on the list. They knew what he looked like and what car he was driving. So surely all he had to do was drive out in the morning in disguise in a different car? He went to his suitcase and rummaged through it – yes! The Boston Bruins cap that he'd brought but hadn't worn on the trip so far, and a COVID mask. Add to that some shades and the fact that all the clothes he had for the hike were new, and he'd look a different man! It might work... he picked up the bedroom phone and dialled reception,

"Buona sera. Parla Inglese?"

And twenty minutes later, he'd organised a new hire car that would be delivered to the hotel's underground car park within the hour. Since the hotel had all his credit card details, the whole thing was simple. He would leave the Alpha there (and pay a fortune to have the company pick it up, but so be it), pack everything into the new car first thing in the morning and head off without Veronica's goon being any the wiser.

"Stick that up your arse, Veronica!" he said loudly, just in case she was psychic or had super-hearing or whatever.

Then, feeling very pleased with himself and somewhat more relaxed, he went downstairs and had an excellent meal in the hotel restaurant.

When he got back to his room, his disquiet was rising once more, and he approached his room with the caution that someone might be waiting inside. He unlocked the door with infinite care, then flung it open suddenly to catch anyone inside unawares. The empty room laughed at him, but he still went through and checked the bathroom and under the bed, before wedging the door with the chair again. He laid out all his clothes for tomorrow, stripped, put on a bathrobe, and packed the clothes he'd been wearing that day along with everything else. He then piled the bags across the door. At least if anyone did force their way in, they'd be hampered by clutter and that might give Jack the advantage he'd need to... to what? Disarm them? Beat them up? *Kill* them? He didn't like it. Even though he still wrestled regularly at the New York Athletic Club, he didn't fancy going toe to toe with someone to the death. He shook his head to put it out of his mind. He went into the bathroom to have a shower and was glad to find that if he left the door open, it gave him a clear view to the main door of the bedroom. Then he clicked his fingers as he remembered something and went back to the clothes on the bed. Under the hat, there was a large pocketknife with a smooth walnut handle and shiny brass ends. He opened its four-inch blade. The locking mechanism gave a reassuringly solid 'click'. He went back into the bathroom and placed it on the sink within easy reach of the shower. He'd bought it from the last shop he'd visited. Insurance against the unthinkable.

Jack didn't linger in the shower. This was a shame, because it was a good one with strong jets and plenty of hot water. Once he was done, he went to bed, placing the open knife under one of the pillows he wasn't using. He pulled on his boxers and slipped between the soft sheets, then picked up the leaflet for the Val di Mello. It was a cheery piece, with vibrant photographs of the valley in summer with climbers 'bouldering', which seemed to simply involve scaling the massive boulders that scattered the valley floor. Apparently, they had a festival of it in May. It was all very happy, until he reached the final paragraph:

'But visitors must respect the valley, or the Gigiat, the great mythical beast of the mountains – part ibex, part chamois, part lynx - will have its revenge!'

"Oh great!" Jack sighed, "More mythical creatures to deal with."

He picked up his phone and Googled 'Gigiat'. Yes, there it was – a huge goat-like creature rearing up in front of two terrified men. Jack read page after page of different websites on the subject and pieced together its story.

High up in the mountains, beyond the realms of human influence, lived a spirit of the earth and the protector of the Val Masino, the Val di Mello and the heavily wooded mountains around Bagni di Masino. The Gigiat. No one could be truly sure what it looked like. Yes, it was excessively hairy – on that everyone could agree – and yes, it had great horns like the ibex and its goat-like stench was overpowering, but beyond that, eyewitness accounts differed. Some said it had the face and arms of a man. Others, that it had the legs and paws of the lynx, but the face of a chamois with the horns of the ibex. Others still, that it was a gigantic combination of ibex and chamois, with four hooves and huge horns. But no one could agree. Even its name – Gigiat – meant 'strange thing' in the Valtellinese dialect. But the local people all knew it was there. It lived among the high peaks, roaming their dense forests and crossing entire valleys in just a few bounds. Silent and swift, a master of camouflage and cunning, only a very few had ever seen it… and fewer still had lived to tell the tale. For although, like the ibex and chamois, its natural food was mountain plants, it was known to devour those foolish souls who had ventured into its domain alone. But it was not indiscriminate in its killing or seen as evil by the local people. It was the protector of the mountains and it only preyed upon those who came to the mountains with evil desires in their hearts. It was a hero to the mountain folk. In the autumn, those who had mountain huts that they only used in summer, would leave bowls of chestnuts and hang hay outside their dwellings to feed the Gigiat throughout the coming winter. The people respected the mountains and revered the Gigiat as a divine protector from the ancient age of pagan gods. And, in spite of mechanisation, population increase and tourism, the Gigiat still protected the mountains. Guides spotted it from time to time and everyone walking in the valleys and forests could feel its presence with them, just beyond their sight. Always watching. Always ready to judge men's hearts and bring swift vengeance on the wicked.

Jack put his phone down and switched off the light. Three days ago, he'd have put the whole thing down to superstition and gone to sleep. Tonight, he couldn't. Now that there was even the possibility that water devils existed, what if this Gigiat existed too? What if he was about to walk to his doom at the horns and hooves of this mountain spirit? And on top of that he had the very real problem of giving Veronica's hired bruiser the slip. He had also heard nothing from Annie and she hadn't returned any of his calls. This was what worried him most as he lay in the dark, desperately trying to fall asleep. Although she'd had a lot to do, what with getting home and driving all that way to pick up Harry, surely she would've had time to answer the phone or listen to her messages? What if something had already happened to her? What if his 'sisters' had done her harm? Then, on the other hand, what if her phone had simply died after the long flight and she hadn't had the opportunity to recharge it? What if the problem was with his phone and it wasn't taking incoming international calls? What if? What if? What if? The questions swirled around his head until finally, sometime around 2, he fell asleep. But that was no comfort. He spent the deep watches of the dark in a swirling nightmare of drowned bodies and his sisters rising up from Lake Como to drag him into its depths, wrestling with Veronica's thug and being shot in the side, then stumbling down mountain paths with a giant unseen thing chasing him. There was no rest in sleep, there was only death, devils and the ever-lurking presence of the Gigiat.

Chapter Twenty-Seven

Wild Thing

J ack was glad it was a glittering, sunny morning. Not only because the light cheered him after a dreadful night's sleep, but also because it allowed him to wear shades without looking out of place. As he pulled out of the underground car park in the anonymous silver Opel Corsa, with his Bruins cap down low, his shades on, a white COVID mask across his face and the collar of his new black climbing jacket pulled up, he felt sure he'd be able to give Veronica's thug the slip. And he was right. Gianfranco Cacciatori had chosen a guest house with a view of the hotel car park exit. As he sipped his double espresso by his bedroom window, he thought nothing of the little silver car as it left. He idly wondered where the American might be going later as he lit a Lucky Strike and opened the window to let the smoke out. It wasn't until an hour had passed that he thought to check the tracker device.

"Che cazzo?" he swore, shaking the electronic tracker. This couldn't be right! It placed the American in a village somewhere up in the mountains. He thought for a moment, then hurried over to Jack's hotel.

As he walked through the doors, the woman on the reception desk became instantly alert. This guy was good looking, and the way he moved...

He approached in his perfectly tailored grey suit, his shiny black leather shoes beating out the rhythm of his strength and determination on the marble floor.

"Good morning, can I help you sir?" she smiled – wow, he was even more dreamy up close.

"Hi, I'm due to be meeting a friend of mine here in the lobby, but I'm early. Could you please let him know I'm here?" Gianfranco gave the plain woman behind the counter a smile that warmed her.

"Of course, what name?"

"Mister Jack Kidd,"

The receptionist consulted her screen. Her face clouded,

"I'm sorry, Mister…"

"Cassetti," Gianfranco lied with a winning smile.

"I'm sorry, Mister Cassetti, but Mister Kidd checked out about an hour ago."

Gianfranco made a performance of being exasperated,

"Oh, Jack! Why do you do this to me! You know, that man has a mind like a Swiss cheese – all full of holes!"

The receptionist giggled politely.

"Did he say where he was going?"

"No, I'm sorry."

"Not to worry, I'll call him. Thanks for your help – you've been an angel," Gianfranco said, taking out his phone and pretending to dial a number. He walked towards the front door and said loudly,

"Jack! Where are you? Guess where I am!" and he turned back towards the receptionist with a 'what an idiot he is!' gesture. She laughed and watched him leave,

"I'm at the bloody hotel, aren't I, you dozy donkey!"

As soon as Gianfranco was out of the hotel, he jogged to his car. Before he got in, he did a fast check of his equipment – phone, tracker, gun, two spare magazines for it, wallet, keys… no coat! It was up in the room. He hesitated a moment, caught between going up to get it and taking his chances with the cold. He was already so far behind that maybe a couple more minutes would make no difference – but then, if he failed to find out who Jack was seeing, he'd get into trouble with Veronica. And that was the last thing he wanted. Then he remembered he had a puffer gilet in the trunk. He could wear that under his suit jacket. Yes, that would keep him warm, especially if he had to track the man on foot.

"Okay," he said, got in the car and sped off with a screech of tyres. As he drove, he tried to figure out how Jack had got past him, but he hadn't a clue. All he could do was put his foot down and hope to catch him up. His Audi A5 ate up the miles on the highway, but started to lumber when he got to the switchback curves of the mountain road up to San Martino. This was why the man had got the Stelvio. It must have been perfect taking on the twists and turns of the steep road. Gianfranco cursed again as the Audi barely made it around a curve in one turn. He was angry and if he got the chance later, he would take that anger out on whoever Jack was trying to find.

An hour earlier, Jack had also been cursing when taking on the curves of the road. The Corsa one litre was one of those cars that made a lot of noise while hardly breaking thirty miles an hour. It had dawdled along the highway and now it was on the steep, twisting roads it had slowed to a crawl and was complaining every inch of the way. Jack wondered if it would get up there at all if he had passengers. But no, he was being harsh on it. There was a real possibility that this little car was saving his life. He should be grateful and he tried to raise a smile. He had ditched the COVID mask as soon as he'd got out of town and the shades not long after, as the sun had disappeared behind heavy clouds. A light drizzle was falling, which the windscreen wipers couldn't quite cope with as they smeared the windscreen, rather than cleaning it. At one turn, Jack made the mistake of looking over the edge. God, that was a long drop down. After what seemed an inordinate number of hairpin bends, the road straightened out a bit and headed up the steep sided valley. At that level, most of the forest was deciduous and the stark, leafless trees seemed to claw at the air. He drove through a concrete tunnel, one side of which was galleried and the light strobing across his eyes was unsettling.

After the road crossed the river to the western side of the valley, the view to the mountains ahead opened up and Jack could see the snowline clearly. If it was drizzling down here, it would be snowing up there. He'd certainly be glad of all the hiking gear he'd bought, and he was very impressed with the walking boots, which were giving him no problems at all. "Little victories," he said to himself as the Corsa grumbled its way through the town of Cataeggio and on to Val Masino, where the deciduous trees were now thinning and pines and larches were starting to take over. The mountains were looming all around him, dark and heavy against the grey sky and at the head of the valley, the sharp peaks jagged up as if they were trying to pierce the clouds. In summer, with a picnic, some wine and his family by his side, this would be a glorious view, beckoning him to come and enjoy the delights of nature. Today it was bleak and the mountains grimaced at him. These weren't tame ski mountains. This wasn't a winter playground. This was where life ground out the cold, harsh months starving and scraping its way through until spring. He had left the soft world of the Piazza Garibaldi far behind and was entering a world of tough survivors. Jack hoped he had it in him to be one of those.

Up in San Martino, the town put on a good show of cheer amidst the gloom with its buildings in various colours from terracotta, to yellow, to red and white. Jack considered stopping at the jolly looking Bar Albergo San Martino for a quick espresso, but thought better of it, just in case he was still being followed. He drove through the town and then swung right onto the road that would take him up into the Val di Mello. According to the map, there was a tourist car park about a mile up the valley. A mile less to walk would suit him fine. But what if his was the only car parked up there? That would make things easy for his pursuer. In fact, it might make things nigh-on impossible for Jack. The guy could just wait down by the car and jump him when Jack came back from the mountain.

"Bollocks!" he said, doing a three-point turn and heading back to the town and the parking area by the river, which had about fifteen cars in it. On the way, he passed a twenty-foot-high mural of the Gigiat. Great! That reminded him of another reason he might not be alone on the mountain. At the car park, he squeezed the Corsa into a space between two rather badly parked cars. This was good. Parking on the end would make him easier to spot. Now it looked like his car had been parked there all week. He checked he had everything he'd need, then left the car and started the hike.

Although it was still drizzling, Jack was very comfortable in his waterproof camouflage trousers and black jacket. He was also glad of the snowboarding gloves he'd bought. Although they were a bit bulkier than he needed, they were waterproof, warm and he needed a new pair anyway, so wins all round. He crossed the river and soon found the hiking path that wended its way up through the last of the silver birches. It was narrow and within a few hundred yards, it had climbed up from the valley floor and was little more than three feet across, with the steep slope down to the river on his left and the steep slope up the side of the valley on his right. Aside from the swish of his waterproofs and the distant sound of the river, it was very quiet. Even the birds seemed to have forsaken the forest. He suddenly felt very alone. However, one consolation was that there were only two ways that someone could come at him – from directly in front or directly behind. He had a clear view ahead and, in the stillness, it would be impossible for anyone to sneak up on him from behind. All the same, Jack's senses dialled up their alert level to 'ridiculously high'.

After a while, the path wound its way down to the river level and ran alongside it. Then Jack came to a bridge. He could cross it to the road and follow that up to the car park, or stay on the slower path by the river. Jack chose the latter. At this stage, keeping away from other people was the best idea. Without glacial melt, the river at this time of year was little more than a stream and, as it burbled and babbled along beside him, it was good company. He had walked up into the area where he guessed the 'bouldering' began. Large rocks – some of them almost the size of houses – seemed to have been scattered across the valley floor. Their appearance was bafflingly random and some of them stood slap-dab in the middle of the river. Jack guessed they had all tumbled down from the high peaks around him at various times through the years and he vaguely wondered whether rockfalls were more likely in winter or summer. Then he stopped himself. He had enough to worry about without adding falling rocks to the list.

'Still', he thought as he passed a real whopper, 'you wouldn't want to be under one when it came down'.

The mile up to the tourist car park took about half an hour because of the gradient and the twists of the path. As it opened out into a twenty-yard wide stretch of grass next to the river, he could see the tourist car park ahead on the other side.

"Yup!" he said to himself quietly as he hiked past it. Not a car in sight. Had he parked here, he'd've been a fish in a barrel.

The going was much easier for this stretch, as the valley floor was fairly wide and had flattened out. Jack was able to pick up his pace and he was glad to, because the trees were sparse here and there was little cover for about three hundred yards. He passed a gaily coloured restaurant on the other side of the river and again thought how wonderful it must be to sit at an outside table in the height of summer with a beer in hand enjoying the spectacular views of the mountains. Beer. That would be nice. He smacked his lips and realised he was getting thirsty. He took the tube from the CamelBak he was carrying and had a quick drink without so much as breaking step. The faster he could get into the trees up ahead, the better.

When he reached the trees, he hid behind one to look down the valley. He crouched and scanned the valley floor. Nothing. Not a soul. Good. He got up and marched on, keeping as fast a pace as he could without tiring himself out. He still had about two miles to hike and he had no idea how difficult the terrain might get. As he walked, the cover changed constantly between woodland and more open scrubby pasture. He passed a pretty little place where the river opened out into a pond, then came upon some houses, which were all closed up. Summer homes. He was glad that the path he was following took him through the trees to the right of the open ground near the river. The rest was pasture and he would have been very exposed. He could see the main tourist path across the other side of the river. Yes, that was best avoided! He was experiencing a strange mixture of feelings. On the one hand, he felt desperate isolation. He was a lone speck in these great mountains - small, frail. With a flick of a boulder, the mountains could end him. And yet, on the other hand, he had the horrible feeling that he was not only being watched, but stalked. He knew there was a man out there who might be pursuing him, but this was a feeling of something more. It was a presence that seemed to be pushing down on him. It filled the valley. He could see exactly why the locals felt there was a spirit here. All he could hope was that it saw he was coming in peace.

Like it or not, our decisions channel the course of our lives. Jack's decision to hike up from San Martino was about to have a very direct effect on his. When Gianfranco Cacciatori had left Sondrio, he had been an hour behind. By the time he pulled into the car park where Jack's Corsa was, he had made up fifteen minutes. He wasn't able to pinpoint which car was Jack's, but he could be sure that the suitcase with the tracker was in one of them. Since the Stelvio wasn't there, it was clear that Jack had switched cars, which meant that he knew he was being followed. Gianfranco swore. He'd screwed this up, but could he salvage the situation? Okay, so the bag was somewhere here, which meant that Jack had to come back to it, but that wouldn't help in finding the person Jack was meeting. Gianfranco couldn't interrogate Jack, because he still had to lead them to two other people. What a balls up! He parked and jogged over a bridge to the café in the town.

"Good morning," he cried cheerily as he entered the dark, but welcoming café.

"Hi," said the man behind the bar.

"I'm looking for a friend of mine. We're supposed to be meeting here, but I can't find him. Have you seen any strangers this morning?"

It was a funny request, but then the café owner was used to crazy city folk coming up and asking stupid questions. He thought about it for a moment.

"I did see one guy go off hiking about forty-five minutes ago," and he pointed vaguely in the direction of the mountains.

"That could be him. What was he like? Big, small?"

"Big, I'd say – although I only saw him from here, so..."

"That's okay. Is this the only way to get up the valley?"

"No, and that's why I remember him. See, there's a car park a couple of kilometres up the hill. Most winter hikers drive up and start from there. But this guy didn't. Seemed funny."

"Thanks!" Gianfranco smiled and quickly left.

'Stupid city types,' the café owner thought and went back to cleaning glasses.

Gianfranco flayed the car up the empty mountain road and was pulling into the car park five minutes later. He didn't know it, but he was only about fifteen minutes behind his quarry. He parked and slipped on his gilet. It was a little tight over his Beretta, but that couldn't be helped. He buttoned up his jacket and, as the drizzle started to seep into it, he wished he'd gone back for his coat. Soon he'd be damp. He looked down at his shoes. They'd probably get ruined in the inevitable mud.

"Fucking mountains!" he cursed and headed towards the wide, well-kept path that led up the valley. There was a noticeboard with a picture of the Gigiat rearing up in front of two men. What the hell was that all about? He put it out of his mind and walked quickly on. He was on the main path up the mountain, with the river to his right. The path was clear and easy – even in fashionable city shoes – and with every step he was gaining on Jack, who had taken the narrow, winding path on the other side of the river. Had Gianfranco known any of this, he might have been happier, but as it was his face was set in an angry scowl and he had violence in his heart.

Soon he was passing a restaurant. There was no one around and it gave him the creeps. It didn't help that his shoes were click-clacking on the stone path. Then came a pond, summer homes locked up tight, and now he was in pastureland. He was constantly scanning the way ahead, looking for the slightest movement, but he seemed to be alone. Or was he? For some time, he'd had the distinct feeling that he was being watched. More than that, he felt that in some way he was no longer the hunter. His hand instinctively went to his left armpit where his Beretta was snugly holstered. It felt reassuring, but he couldn't help looking up and around him at the mountains. There was something about this place that set him on edge. The appearance of first one, then two, then three restaurants, all locked up for the winter, did nothing to improve his morale. Clearly, all the sensible people had left the valley to itself for the cold, dark months, so what the hell was this idiot American tourist doing leading him up here? And who, in their right mind, would be living up here at this time of year? Gianfranco didn't like that thought and tried to put it out of his head. He hated crazy people. They were unpredictable and, if he was going to torture information out of one, it would be hard to tell what was the truth and what was mere crazy talk. And then, to top it all, just as he was slogging towards another closed up rifugio, the drizzle turned to snow. Fica!

When Jack had reached that point about five minutes before, the drizzle magically turning to snow had made him smile. He loved it when you could see natural physics in action. Here it was cold enough to snow – there it wasn't. For some reason, that sort of thing tickled him. His path took him wide of the rifugio, although there was a small bridge across the river to allow summer hikers to cross and enjoy a break. Soon the snow began to settle. First it was barely a dusting, but within a couple of minutes it was about four inches deep. Now, here was another problem. He was leaving footprints that anyone could follow. He was in fairly open ground again, but about three hundred yards ahead, a wall of pine trees marked the end of man's influence on the landscape and the beginning of the true wilds. He decided that once he got into the trees, he would leave the path and bear to the right. His final destination was only about a mile away and, according to the map on his phone, it was somewhere up on the right-hand side of the valley. He picked up his pace and, when he got to the trees, he crouched behind one to examine the open ground back towards the restaurant. No one. Then he turned and walked away from the path and up into the stillness of the dark pine forest.

Gianfranco was fuming about the snow as he plodded on, but then something dawned on him – the snow on the path ahead was untouched. In fact, looking around him, none of the snow showed any signs of footprints. There was no way anybody was ahead of him. Had he really come all the way up here on a bloody wild goose chase? Christ! He stopped and looked back at the little bridge over the river. Was there a path over there? He walked back down to the bridge. Well, no one had been across it, that was for sure. He walked over it, but had to catch himself when the shiny sole of one of his shoes slipped on the snow. Bastardo! Gianfranco seriously considered ignoring his orders and shooting this fucker the minute he caught up with him. He stumbled over rocks until he found the path and there, finally, he saw something that made him smile – fresh tracks! A big man had recently been walking up here through the snow and the tracks led into the trees. He drew his Beretta and took a good look ahead. There was no one between him and the trees and he couldn't see anyone lying in wait, so he followed the tracks. His joy was short-lived, because it was clear that the person ahead of him had left the main path the moment he'd entered the forest. That was a pain! What should he do? Stick to the path or leave it? And if he left it, which way to go – left or right? Left would leave him wedged between the path and the river. Right would be best. And so Gianfranco, in his scuffed shoes, his soggy Armani suit, and clutching his compact Beretta 92G Elite, left the path and worked his way through the trees.

Leaving a path to walk through a wild forest is no simple task. Especially a forest interspersed with boulders. Jack quickly found that there was no such thing as a straight line. There was always a fallen branch or a tree or a rock in the way and he was constantly having to crouch down to avoid obstacles. In the forest it was uncannily still. Beneath Jack's feet, the thick carpet of pine needles muffled his movements, while the snow in the trees above acted like a blanket, shutting out light and sound. The result was that it was as gloomy as dusk under the trees. This, added to the jumble of trees, meant that his visibility in any direction was limited. After ten minutes of clambering and zig-zagging, Jack wondered how long it was going to take him to do this last mile. He felt like he'd only gone about two hundred yards, but he also felt like he'd already been in there for ages. Time and distance were different in the forest, and in the dim light his eyes started to play tricks on him. What was that? Jack ducked down and crouched, not breathing. He'd caught something moving out of the corner of his eye and turned his head very slowly to the left to look for it, while he listened with fierce concentration. He could hear the snowflakes as they hit the trees above him. These weren't big, fat flakes but tiny, hard and granular – more like fine sand, pattering down in a steady drizzle. He looked hard all around. There was nothing to see. Only the gloom and the jumble of branches, fallen trees covered in snow and moss, and the three-foot-high mound of what was clearly an enormous ant's nest. Yes, he'd better look out for those. The last thing he needed was to blunder into one. Would the big wood ants be hibernating? He didn't want to take the risk of disturbing them.

He slowly let his breath out as silently as he could, then slipped his hand into his trouser pocket and quietly pulled out his knife. He was now one hundred percent sure that he was not alone in the forest. He opened the blade, while keeping his thumb on the locking mechanism so that it wouldn't make that satisfying 'click'. He checked it was locked open, then looked all around. Fuck! Everything looked the same – just a jumble of trees and lichen-covered rocks. Were it not for his phone, which was guiding him up towards his destination, he wouldn't have had the first idea which way he was going. Now he could easily understand how local people might have developed a legend of a beast haunting the mountains. There, isolated in the gloom, hemmed in by the trees, his eyes and brain were trying to pick out patterns from the forest chaos, seeing things that weren't there and missing things that were. It was easy to imagine there was something out there just beyond his sight, and if even an ordinary sized ibex were to suddenly loom up out of the forest, surely it would seem huge and terrifying?

Jack's mouth and throat were now very dry. He gently took the tube of his CamelBak and quietly took some grateful sips. The water was now icy cold. So was his nose, which was starting to drip. He couldn't risk blowing it, so he wiped it on the thumb of his glove, which was covered with a section of fleece to allow a snowboarder to clear their goggles with a sweep of the hand. Right. Got to keep moving. Slowly, he got up and continued on. Christ! The sound of his waterproofs must be giving his position away. They seemed so loud in the silence. But what could he do? He had an almost irresistible urge to run away. Just run, screaming and flailing his arms back down the valley. Back to the car and then drive as far and as fast as he could until the mountains were a speck in his rear-view mirror. But he couldn't. He had to keep putting one foot in front of the other. It wasn't easy. He was still heading up the valley, but he was also climbing up the side of it now, as he followed the phone's directions. The pine needles were treacherous underfoot on the slope and he was thankful for his boots with their flexible soles and chunky grips. And then, out of nowhere, there came a gust of wind through the trees.

It was so sudden in the midst of the stillness, that it felt as if some huge thing had passed low overhead. Jack slipped forward and stayed on his belly with his face almost on the bed of pine needles as snow dislodged from the trees above and fell to the ground in lumps all around him. He lay totally still, not breathing. Then his eyes widened and the hairs on his neck stood up as terror gripped him. There was something big right behind him breathing heavily. Jack couldn't move even if he'd wanted to. He was frozen in fear. There was something there and the length of its breaths told him that it was much bigger than any man. It was coming closer... this was it. He was going to die. His back was exposed and all it would take would be a blow to the right place and that would be the end. It was pointless. It was stupid. He'd thrown away his life, and endangered those of his wife and son, and for what? He could see the knife in his hand just in front of him. It was laughable that he'd ever thought a mere knife could be any defence against... what? He didn't want to think it, but the word wouldn't go away. Gigiat. The breathing came closer, as if he was being examined. Jack wanted to pee, but somehow held it in. Then there was a snort and another gust of wind, and the presence was gone. But Jack couldn't move. He lay still for how long? A minute? Ten? An hour? Then his shoulders started to heave as he silently sobbed.

Gianfranco was quietly cursing. This bloody forest! Everything was against him. His shoes slipped on the shiny pine needles and he kept having to stop and pull ones out that had jagged down into the sides of his shoes. Branches snagged at his trousers and jacket and had torn at least two holes in them. One twig had damned near had his eye out, when he'd walked into it end-on, so now he had a cut above his left eye. He'd barked his shin on a fallen branch and slipped and grazed his right knee scrambling over a rock. He hated it all, but what he hated most was the way it made him feel – small, useless, incompetent. He was Gianfranco Cacciatori, for Christ's sake! He was a feared killer. He was a rich man with a Ferrari. He was a mighty lover with a big, bullying cock. He had a gun... and yet this forest mocked him for all that. And he couldn't shake the feeling of being hunted. Ever since he'd stepped into that dismal place he'd been hearing things, now ahead, now behind – rustlings in the trees and, whenever he'd turned to face them, there was nothing. And he was freezing. His bare hands were painful and his right ached from gripping his pistol, while his feet were like blocks of ice. Now he'd decided that whatever happened, if he caught up with the idiot American, he was going to empty his Beretta's magazine into his face and damn the consequences!

Then out of nowhere came the wind. A sudden gust overhead that shook the trees, dumping snow everywhere. What the hell? Then a low moan to the left as it blew down towards the river. And then... Gianfranco turned in a circle, following the sound as it rose from a moan to a howl heading down the valley and then... no, it couldn't... Holy Christ! It was coming back! How could it? Wind didn't do that! He was staring back the way he had come, searching for whatever this thing was, howling towards him. Now the trees were moving, as if some great hand was sweeping through their tops. And it was coming straight for him. The sound and the unseen presence passed above him and, as he craned his neck to follow, he almost fell over backwards. It blew up towards the mountains and then turned again. That was the final straw. Wind couldn't do that. This was something beyond the natural. Something beyond imagination. Gianfranco fled. Slipping, stumbling, falling, it didn't matter so long as he was heading down that bloody mountain. He could hear the wind rushing down again and he knew it was coming for him. He fought his way through the trees, but it was no good. He couldn't outrun Fate itself! The wind howled over him again and then...

Stillness. Jack, lying with his face on the forest floor had heard the wind howling up and down the mountain, but hadn't dared move. But now the fury had suddenly stopped. He listened, then jolted in fright as a high-pitched scream pierced the forest. Then came the unmistakable pops of a pistol. More screams, more small arms fire. Shouting and the distant sound of branches breaking. Jack didn't want to stick around to meet whoever owned that gun and he was on his feet and scrabbling up the slope in a flash. Now his focus was total as his brain worked overtime to plot his way through the chaos of the thick forest. He was moving fast, vaulting fallen branches, side-stepping roots and rocks, swiping pine branches aside in his headlong rush to his goal. Something inside was urging him on, not to run away back down, but to keep going up. More gunshots – distant now. Whoever it was must've got out of the woods and onto the pastures. But what did Jack care? He was heading up and away from whatever was happening below. All that mattered was the moment and his dash through the trees.

Chapter Twenty-Eight

Beyond The Realm Of Man

The house didn't look like it had been built, but more like it had grown out of the mountainside. The chunks of granite that were its walls and the grey slates of the roof were all rough-hewn and different shapes and sizes. It was an intricate jigsaw puzzle in which each piece was perfect for its place. The squat chimney did not open straight out to the sky, but had its own little roof of tiles, below which smoke was pluming out from an opening in the side of the chimney. Everything was spotted with lichen and moss, which acted like a camouflage and added to the impression that this was part of the mountain itself. The windows were inset, with deep external ledges and dark wooden shutters, which were open. The front door was of heavy wood, studded with iron. As it materialised out of the forest ahead of him, Jack slowed his pace and tried to get his breath back. He had pretty much run almost a mile uphill through the forest and was gulping in the freezing air as sweat dripped down his face. He took out his handkerchief and dried his face and neck as best he could. After all the effort he'd made to get here, the least he could do was try not to look a sweaty wreck. After folding his knife and putting it back into his pocket, he approached the front door and was about to knock when it opened.

The woman who stood framed by the doorway was slim, with long, dark brown hair flecked with silver and was dressed in faded jeans and a thick polo neck jumper. She stared at Jack eagerly,

"Did you see it?" she said in English, with only a trace of an Italian accent.

"I'm sorry – see what?" asked Jack.

"The Gigiat!" she said with a hint of pride.

"No... I..." what could Jack say? Something told him that total honesty was the best policy,

"I didn't. I was too frightened to look and buried my face in the ground."

The woman looked at him hard and nodded slowly,

"Wise man. The Gigiat respects those who are able to admit that they are in the presence of a power far greater than theirs. But for those who cannot admit that... looking upon the Gigiat might be the last thing they do."

"So, I didn't imagine all that..."

"No."

"Are you Giulia Mazzoni?"

"Who is asking?"

"My name is Jack Kidd," and he half expected her to slam the door on him, but instead she laughed.

"The brother of the creature! It is a miracle that you are alive - come in and we can talk. I expect you have a lot to ask me," and she beckoned him into the house.

He walked up to the door and stepped into the main room of the house - a large kitchen cum living room. The main focus was a magnificent iron stove, set into a large granite chimney breast, which presumably heated the house. To the right of it, by the window, there was a small dining table in front of a corner banquette. To the left there was a large stone sink with an ancient hand water pump next to a granite worktop with cupboards underneath. One corner was curtained off – a makeshift bedroom? And in the other corner there was a door. The rough stone walls were hung with animal hides and tapestries and the inside was lit only by oil lanterns and candles. There was a comfy looking couch, placed at an angle between the front door and the chimney, and from the looks of it, Giulia Mazzoni was using it as a bed so that she could sleep near the stove. She closed the door behind them and now they were cocooned in a cosy world of warm light and shifting shadows.

"Take off your waterproofs and hang them on this," she said, taking a folded airer from a hook on the wall by the door and setting it up near the stove.

"Thanks," said Jack, gratefully handing her his jacket, trousers and gloves.

"Coffee?"

"Yes please."

And she busied herself emptying a large Bialetti coffee maker of its old grounds and pumping water by hand to clean it in the sink.

"I am sorry that I do not have comforts like electricity or running water, but this is what one has to do to survive when one is pursued by the devil," and she turned to see his reaction – hardly a flicker,

"Aha! So, you know," she said, smiling.

"I think I'm getting there," Jack replied. There was still some part of him, some rational scientific being that was denying that any of this could be true.

"For some people it takes longer to accept. Me? I was thrown into the deep end. Milk? Sugar?"

"Yes, please. Dash of milk. Two sugars."

"Rum?"

"Yes, please!" that was music to Jack's ears.

Soon the coffee was brewed and they were sitting at the table, one on each side of the corner banquette.

"So, you were followed," said Giulia.

"Yes, I'm sorry. I thought I'd given him the slip. God knows how he found me."

"Do not worry. That is why I am here, because the Gigiat sees into men's hearts and destroys the wicked. It does not protect me, it protects the mountains. My protection is merely a corollary of that. But I offer it what I can. I think my belief makes it happy. You know, it isn't always terrifying..."

Jack's expression must have indicated that he felt otherwise and Giulia laughed,

"Seriously. I have seen it playing in the trees with squirrels."

"Really?" Jack had to stop himself from laughing.

"Truly. And there are mountain guides that have told me they've seen it dancing with the marmots in the spring to celebrate the end of winter."

Jack couldn't believe it, but Giulia looked certain.

"How long have you been here?" he asked.

"Since the day your sister killed my brother – fourteen years."

"Fourteen years!" Jack exclaimed - it was incredible, "Fourteen years here?"

Giulia nodded in reply.

"But how... why?" Jack was, in the British vernacular, gobsmacked.

"How, is complicated – why, is simple. Fear. No... terror," she corrected herself, then took a long sip of her coffee and rum.

"I'm sorry, but I never liked your sister," she began, but Jack cut in,

"Don't worry – I've known her almost all my life and I've never liked her. And a few days ago, I think she tried to kill me."

"Good, so I can talk as I like," she said with relief, although Jack didn't see what was 'good' about his attempted murder,

"From day one, I could see she had bewitched my brother, Luca. We were very close. I ran the company with him, until Veronica arrived. It didn't take her long to convince him to ease me out. I didn't know what was happening, he no longer wanted to talk to me, no longer trusted me. Within two months, he had paid me off with twenty million dollars and served me a restraining order to keep me at least five hundred metres away from him. It was madness. But I have always believed in the occult, so I consulted with a trusted medium. She told me something I couldn't believe – that a devil in human form had latched onto my brother to drain all his virility and creativity from him."

She looked directly into Jack's eyes. Yes, he was starting to believe now...

"At first, I couldn't accept it. Yes, I had thought that Veronica had some occult powers, but I had always thought that she was merely a woman. Never did it occur to me that she wasn't human."

Jack thought 'Why would it? That would be crazy. But that's where we seem to be', but he kept silent and gratefully sipped his drink. The rum was calming him down after his brush with the Gigiat.

"But without knowing what kind of devil she was, there was little we could do. I had her and my brother watched. And I also watched. My family have a lakeside villa just along from Bellagio, so I took an apartment in Cadenabbia, right across the lake from it. It isn't far – less than two kilometres across the water. And with a telescope or powerful binoculars, I could keep track of all their comings and goings. My God – the orgies would have sickened Messalina. There would be fifty, sixty men including my brother, and Veronica would be the only woman. She would wear them all out. And she didn't care if they were seen, because even the gutter press could not use the pictures. I watched my brother degenerate before my eyes until he looked like nothing but an empty shell. And then..."

Giulia paused and took a pouch of tobacco from her pocket.

"May I?"

"Of course," said Jack and he watched as she rolled a cigarette and lit it. She drew the smoke in gratefully, but rather than exhaling, she spoke. Now smoke curled up from her lips to bear her carefully chosen words into the room.

"Then one day I finally saw her. Not the woman you know as your sister, but the real creature. She was sunbathing – naked, of course - on the lawn by the water. My brother decided to take his Riva out onto the lake. It was a beautiful, still day and he must have wanted to race. I watched him from my window with envy. I used to drive the very same boat and I could feel the thrill of the wind and the water, and the music of the engine. So, he raced down towards Como. After about twenty minutes, he came back and stopped in the middle of the lake – relaxing in the sun. Then I turned my binoculars back to her... and saw the devil!" she said fiercely, with smoke rising from both sides of her mouth as she poked towards Jack with the tip of her cigarette.

"Veronica was lying unconscious and it was standing on her chest. It had a woman's head and face, but the wings and torso of a cormorant – black as evil itself. It had thin, scaly legs and webbed feet with vicious talons.

But what made it truly hideous was its face - haggard and bony, like it was starving, with those electric, staring eyes filled with hateful frenzy that distorted all its features... God, just thinking of it still freezes my blood. I knew at once that it had come out of your sister, that it was somehow living inside her. Then this half bird, half woman opened its black wings and flew low and fast across the water to my brother's boat. There was nothing I could do but watch. It went for him with its talons, grabbed his head and shoulder, and dragged him out of the boat. Maybe I imagined it, but I thought I heard him scream, and then I watched that... thing drown him. It held him under the surface and I could see him struggle, striking at it with his fists until he struggled no more. Then it pulled up his face and it looked like it was going to kiss him. It didn't. It tore his face off and ate it right there. Then it looked over its shoulder with its face covered with my brother's blood and leered at me. I swear, it looked me right in the eye. It disappeared under the water with his body, which was never found. I believe it took it to the bottom of the lake and ate him. I ran. Straight to my car. Got in. Drove up here. Not along the side of the lake. I couldn't take the risk. I went up round Lugano into Switzerland and then back over the Splugen pass to Chiavenna and so to here. I know it is impossible to believe, but you must!" Giulia's eyes were full of urgency and she reached out to grip Jack's arm with painful force,

"I saw her face – her true face. The devil's face. You must understand – she is not a woman. She is not your sister. She is a creature living in your sister. A devil of the sea..."

"A siren," said Jack, hollowly.

Giulia stared into Jack's eyes and then let his hand go.

"Now, finally, you believe!" she said.

Jack nodded like a convicted man hearing an inevitable sentence of death.

"Yes. I believe. I don't want to, but I do," he said quietly.

"You have researched?"

Jack nodded again.

"I had learnt of the sirens when I was a child, so when she emerged from your sister's body, I knew instantly what she was. It is a lot to comprehend all at once, here..." Giulia said, taking the rum bottle and tipping a large measure into Jack's mug. There was no coffee left, but he drank it down gratefully.

"I could not believe it at first – and I believed in the occult. I believed in the Gigiat, yet still I could not believe what I had seen with my own eyes. I thought I was going mad. But then men started to come here looking for me, asking questions in the town. Of course, no one spoke. My family are mountain people. This house has been in my family for generations. No one in the town would have sold me out. Had Veronica come herself, that might have been different. Her power over men is absolute. She would have been able to turn them against me. But she won't come up here, because of our friend," and she jerked a thumb towards the window,

"Her power is the power of the sea, but here the mountains rule. She knows the Gigiat would destroy her."

She sat back and lazily rolled another cigarette, lit it and took a strand of tobacco from the tip of her tongue, which she carelessly flicked away.

"And now you come, bringing evil with you, waking up the Gigiat. Why are you here?"

Jack told her about his father's death and the covenant in his will.

"But all he gave me was your name and some map coordinates. No more. No instructions on what to ask and no reasons why," he finished.

"Perhaps he thought that talking to me would be enough," Giulia mused, "But clearly, he doesn't want you to hide like me. He wants you to kill them."

"Yes."

"And you must!" Giulia said with sudden, startling force,

"You do not want to go through what I have in the last fourteen years. You must be strong and cunning, and make sure your family is safe. They will go after them. They are your weak point. But you must be like the rocks in these mountains – immovable in your determination. Anything less than total ruthlessness on your part and you will fail. Attack them like you'd attack a snake threatening your child. If you succeed, then I, too, will be freed from my luxurious prison," and she indicated the room with her cigarette.

"How have you coped?" Jack asked.

"Well enough. The beauty of the mountains is endless. The air is clean. The water is freezing, but it can be heated. I even have limited electricity from a solar panel further up the mountain. I get regular supplies from friends in the town and, down the years, some of the mountain guides have been my special friends," and she gave a sardonic smile,

"So, it is a very pretty prison, but I would love to live fully again."

"I feel I'm out of my depth," said Jack – out of his depth and totally bewildered by this new world he'd been thrown into.

"Of course you are, but it doesn't matter how much water is below you so long as you keep swimming."

"But sirens, mountain spirits – it's all so at odds with reality."

"Listen, before radio was invented, the thought of being able to speak to people on the other side of the world was nonsense. And yet the ability to do it was always there. It's not like humans suddenly invented the physics of radio. This is the same. The existence of these beings shouldn't shatter your world view, but add to it. The existence of the Gigiat doesn't change any of the laws of physics. The Gigiat, the sirens and whatever else is out there, they are governed by laws just like everything else. The difference is they exist in the areas between the laws we know and are governed by ones we haven't yet discovered. Do you know how your iPhone works?"

"Not really," Jack admitted.

"Are you afraid of it?"

"No."

"Then you should be no more afraid of these other things."

"Yeah, but my iPhone isn't trying to kill me," Jack replied.

At this, Giulia laughed long and hard. It was infectious and soon Jack was laughing, too. Finally, as their laughter subsided, Giulia said, wiping a tear from her eye,

"Yes, true! You have me there. What I mean is just because you don't understand the principle of how your iPhone works, it doesn't make you fearful of the world. The same with these entities. Okay, so you don't know how they work, but that shouldn't ruin the world for you. You understand?"

"Yeah, I get it."

"Good, because you need to think clearly and act resolutely."

"Yes."

"And from now until those devils have been dispatched, you cannot trust any man. They are too weak to resist them. Except you. What makes you so different?"

"Maybe it's because I grew up with them, or because of this," and Jack reached into his shirt and produced the porpoise necklace. Giulia took out some reading glasses to look at it more closely. Now that she was so close to him, he could smell her – she smelt of pine sap and moss.

"Yes, yes, I can feel its power. Perhaps this is why the Gigiat came to sniff you over. It was intrigued by it. Now, what is the time?" Giulia said suddenly.

"Almost two."

"Then you must go – unless you want to stay the night? We can talk, I can make pizzocheri, we can share a bottle or two of Sforzato..."

But before Jack could reply, she turned on a dime,

"No!" Giulia said firmly, "They might come back in greater numbers and if they were to intercept you in the town..."

"We don't want that," Jack agreed.

"Okay," said Giulia, getting up,

"You need to move, because you do not want to try to navigate your way down the valley in the dark."

Jack nodded as he got up.

"All dry," she smiled, handing him his waterproofs. He put them on and followed her to the door. Before she opened it, she turned to face him,

"Let me look at you," and she cast her eyes over his face and body, gripping both his shoulders,

"Yes, you can do it. That is why they fear you," then she let go of his shoulders and slapped him on the top of his left arm,

"Good luck, Jack Kidd. May we meet again after you have freed us."

Giulia kissed him on both cheeks and gave him a powerful hug, which he returned.

"I'd love to come back here for a picnic in the summer," he said.

"It's a date!" she laughed, then opened the door. The cold instantly sharpened his senses after the rum.

"My prayers go with you," she said as he stepped out, waved a thank you and began to pick his way back through the forest.

"And look out for the Gigiat," she called, "It likes you!"

***

The same could not be said for Gianfranco Cacciatori. His escape down the valley had been a nightmare. Something huge had come at him out of the forest and thrown him backwards twenty metres. He'd shot it. Again and again, but it had kept coming. So, he had fled through the forest with the gatekeeper of hell at his heels. He had bludgeoned his way through the trees and, with the beast breathing down his neck, he had burst out of the forest and run across the pasture. Now he could hear the pounding of hooves behind him and he didn't dare look back. It was that thing. The thing from the picture down in the car park. Half ibex and half demon. And it was coming for him. But he was fast. Terror gave him wings and, when he got down to the river, he didn't even bother with the bridge, but ran through the shallow water so that there was no chance he could see the thing chasing him. Somehow he knew that if he looked at it, it would tear him apart. Down he ran, along the well-kept path, past the restaurants and on through pasture and trees down, down, down the valley. His lungs were bursting, his feet in their ruined city shoes were crying out in pain, and he was a mass of cuts and bruises from his headlong rush through the forest. And all the while, he could feel the great presence right behind him, hear it snorting and smell nothing but it's sickening, animal stench. Finally, blessedly, there was the car park and the Audi.

As he ran, he took out the keys and unlocked it. The lights flashed and he put on an extra turn of speed. He wrenched the door open, dived in and slammed the door with one hand while pressing the starter button with the other. The car stirred into life and he immediately banged it into reverse. Although he didn't want to, he couldn't help looking out through the windscreen. There was no creature to be seen! It was as if he'd been chased down the mountain by his own imagination. Gianfranco screamed out a torrent of curses as he stared out through all the car windows, craning his neck to see where his pursuer might be hiding. Nothing. Son of a bitch! He was overcome with rage that he'd been terrified by nothing more than a mountain. He lowered his window and screamed curses at the wilderness, firing his gun at Nature until the magazine was empty. Then he heard a bellow like that of a huge, furious stag cascade down the valley towards him. That was it. He threw the car into Drive and stepped on the gas. The tyres churned up the stones of the rough surface of the car park, then the car lurched forward. He was safe! Or no. Even over the engine, he could hear the incensed roar of the mountains' primal anger as he drove away and then, bang! Something huge came down on the back of the car, shattering the rear window. Gianfranco looked behind him, but there was still nothing there. He gripped the steering wheel and flew down to San Martino, skidded his way through the town and floored the Audi down and away from the Val di Mello.

His journey back to Lake Como, down through the tunnels along its side to Lecco and then back up the other side to Bellagio was a jumble of images blurred by speed as he broke every law of the road to get back to his mistress and safety. Veronica, who had flown in even before Jack had left London, saw Gianfranco's arrival from an upper room of her villa. His car howled up the driveway and skidded to a halt outside the enormous picture-perfect palace. He tumbled out of the car and went round to the back. The window was shattered and the rear section of the boot crushed. Gianfranco stared with eyes wide with terror. There, clear as day, was the imprint of a giant hoof in the twisted metal. That was the last straw. He fell to his knees and was sick. Veronica shook her head. She snapped her fingers and the guard at the door stepped in,

"Get Gianfranco cleaned up and then bring him to my bedroom," she said in her brittle, glassy voice.

"Yes, Principessa," the man said, bowing curtly.

An hour later, a much-recovered Gianfranco Cacciatori was standing before his mistress. He had showered, been patched up and was looking good in a light grey Armani suit. Veronica looked like she was ready to go out, wearing a pair of 'fuck me' heels and a full-length black mackintosh, tightly belted at the midriff. Her bedroom was the size of two squash courts, with a high ceiling covered in lewd frescoes. A line of tall windows along one wall gave incredible views of the lake, and a pair of French windows opened out onto a large balcony with luxurious chairs on it to soak up the sun. At the far end of the room was a custom-built four-poster bed, which could easily sleep six, and near it, a door led into an opulent bathroom. The floor was beautiful parquet, which usually had a number of Persian rugs laid across it to lend warmth and softness, but which had been taken to Milan for specialist cleaning. Now, Gianfranco was standing in the middle of the room, to where Veronica had beckoned him, and she slowly prowled around him with her heels clicking sharply on the floor with each step. He was used to this sort of assessment and stood tall and proud. He knew that Veronica valued strength above all and, in spite of his nightmare, he had pulled himself together and was projecting all the strength he could.

Veronica had been told the tale of his escape from the mountain by one of the other guards and it made sense. Jasper must have come looking for Giulia – presumably so she could tell him about the day Veronica had eaten her brother. So, father wanted the little brat to know everything! And it proved what she had suspected all along - that Giulia had hidden in the mountains. Veronica's eyes flashed dangerously as she walked slowly around Gianfranco. She wanted Giulia dead so badly that she could taste it, but even she wouldn't dare to go up there. The mountains were ancient and powerful – what did they have to fear from spirits of the sea, when they collected the very water that fed the oceans? No, she would leave the bitch Giulia hiding in her mountain until she had become an insane old hag. Yes, that was it. The longer Veronica lived, happy and rich and draining men of their power, the more Giulia would wither. The thought twisted Veronica's mouth into a fiendish smile. But now she had Gianfranco to deal with. What to do? He had failed and she hated failure. And yet, she thought as her eyes devoured the spectacular man standing in front of her, she had always enjoyed Gianfranco. He was so vital, so willing, and he tasted exquisite.

"So," said Veronica as she finally stopped prowling and stood in front of him, "You failed in your task."

"Yes," he wanted to add that he had met an unexpected and supernatural foe, but he knew that she didn't want excuses.

"Apart from the fact she's up a mountain, you have no idea where the bitch is?"

"No."

"Strip," she said, fixing him with her electric, sea green eyes.

He did so without hesitation, leaving his clothes in a neat pile on the floor nearby. This was far from the first time she had given him that order.

"Good," Veronica said, giving him a predatory look. He really did have a magnificent body: beautifully muscled shoulders, a strong, but not overdeveloped chest, a perfect six-pack tapering to a narrow waist, which drew the eyes to his impressive manhood. Like all her other guards, his pubic hair was closely cropped and his heavy balls were clean shaven. Veronica stepped in close to him and started running her hands all over his body, feeling every muscle, every angle, every line. Oh yes, he was a truly incredible specimen! She ran her hand down towards his crotch, but stopped just above it, fluttering her fingers lightly across his skin. She could feel the skin tighten minutely and smiled, then stepped back.

She very deliberately untied the belt of her mackintosh, then let it slip off her shoulders and kicked it away across the floor. Gianfranco was unsurprised to see that, aside from her high heels, she was naked. The sight had an immediate effect on him, and the part of him that had been merely interested now became eager and straining. Inside, Gianfranco was filled with raging desire to take her, but he knew better than to make the first move. That was for her. She slid in close again and kissed him lightly, playfully taking his bottom lip between her teeth, then letting go.

"Let's see what we can do with this," she said, taking him in hand. Then, without relinquishing her grip, she slowly worked her way down his torso, kissing, licking, sometimes biting until she was down on her haunches in front of him. The scent of him sparked a flash of desire in her. Yes, this would be delicious! She took his balls in one hand, kissing them, then sucking one of them gently. Gianfranco's head fell back as he groaned. God, he felt ready to burst. Then Veronica let it slip from her mouth,

"It's incredible when you think about it," she said, "The way men trust women with their balls."

Gianfranco looked down at her and their eyes locked as she said,

"They trust them not just with their virility, but with their entire future, with every possible child they could ever have," then she opened her mouth wide and took them both in.

This time Gianfranco's head snapped back and his entire body strained in ecstasy. Veronica released them, weighed them in her hand and looked at the straining shaft that had given her so much pleasure.

"Yes, this is going to taste good," she said quietly to herself, running her hands around to grasp his perfect ass. In a flash of movement, she lunged forward. Her mouth seemed to elongate as her lips drew back to reveal barracuda teeth, which flashed out and engulfed his cock and his balls. The move was so quick and the cut of the razor teeth so clean, that for an instant, Gianfranco didn't even realize what had happened. Then the explosion of agony, the scream that didn't seem to be his own and the horror of seeing the elongated fish mouth as it gulped down his manhood. Then the face went back to normal and he stared, unbelieving at Veronica as his blood sprayed across her face and naked body. Before he could pull away, she dug her long nails into his buttocks and attached her mouth to the gaping hole where his genitalia had been, guzzling down his lifeblood. Now Gianfranco tried to break free, to somehow escape the searing pain that had suddenly become his entire universe, but Veronica's nails were buried deep into his flesh and as he moved, she moved with him. His bare feet slipped in the blood and he fell backwards, a tree being felled. Veronica held fast, sucking at his mutilated groin and grunting with delight. His terror and his fast-fading life tasted so good! Gianfranco was trying to buck her off, but his immense strength was dissipating and she clung on, a giant leech, impossible to shake off. Now his limbs began jerking as his body went into shock and still Veronica pressed her face into his hot, spurting flesh.

But good things never last. Within a few minutes, Veronica was having to actively suck the blood, as Gianfranco's heart finally gave out. His last experience was pain, the misted view of the ceiling fresco of four nymphs dragging a satyr into a pool, and the animal slurping and grunting from the creature sucking his life out of him. Veronica finally eased her nails out of his flesh and wiped the blood from her face into her mouth. She stood and surveyed her work. The bloody, mutilated corpse with its ghastly, tortured expression hardly resembled the tough, beautiful demi-god in a sharp suit. But then, of course, he wasn't a demi-god. He was just a man, and men die. Veronica scooped some of his blood from her belly and licked it off her fingers. Yes, he had tasted great, but there would be other tasty men and she would enjoy the interview process for this one's replacement.

"Guard!" she called and a moment later, an impossibly attractive, yet clearly tough man entered. He didn't flinch at the sight – he knew better than that.

"Feed that to the dogs," Veronica ordered, then turned on her heel to go to the bathroom and wash the rest of the man off her.

Chapter Twenty-Nine

Doctor Bob's Bedside Manner

Annie's flight back to New York had been perfectly straightforward and it had given her plenty of time to think. By the time she touched down, she was even more firmly of the opinion that Rosalind and Veronica were sirens hell bent on killing her and her husband. As she'd gone through the banalities of security and baggage reclaim, she'd been like a caged tigress. Her mood wasn't helped by the fact that her phone had died on the way over. Being an iPhone, the slightest bit of lint caught in the power port stopped the phone from charging. She'd gone to bed thinking it was filling up on electricity, but when Jack had left her and she'd tried to send him a good luck message, she'd discovered the problem. Now, as she unlocked her apartment door, she had a clear plan – dump her suitcase, clean the stupid phone, grab a charger and go fetch Harry. She left the case just inside the front door and dashed up the stairs. She decided that since she was home, a quick change of clothes would help. She didn't want to see Harry smelling of planes and stale sweat. After changing everything, even down to her shoes, which were pinching after the flight, she took a couple of minutes to pressure blast the phone's power port clean, then she was off on the road again with a charger in her hand.

The drive over to Southampton was easy and although her iPhone had coughed into life after a few minutes of charging, she didn't check it while she was driving. The last thing she needed, after narrowly escaping a car accident in the last forty-eight hours, was to cause a pile up by checking her phone. After the dreary English weather, it cheered her to be driving in bright sunshine with blue skies above. It was also nice to be in the Beast. Unlike the Abarth, there was no way something as puny as a BMW would be able to run her off the road. She felt genuinely safe for the first time in a couple of days and the grunt and growl of the Beast reassured her even more. She wondered how Jack was getting on and was tempted to pull into a gas station to give him a call. What time would it be there? Around ten p.m.? No, she'd leave it until she arrived. Most of all, she wondered how Harry had been with her mom and Doctor Bob. Probably having more fun than when he was with her and Jack. Grandparents had it lucky – carte blanche to spoil their grandchildren, then hand them back having encouraged bad habits, which they could then blame the parents for. Yes, Annie was very much looking forward to becoming a bad grandma when she was old.

It was around five when she pulled up in front of her mom's house. Should she listen to the messages her phone was telling her she had, or head straight in? The likelihood was that she'd only get part way through the message - Harry must have heard the van and soon he would be running out to see her... Funny! No one coming out. Maybe they *hadn't* heard her. She picked up the phone and listened to Jack's message. Her face, which had been relaxed, quickly became tense and her sharp jawline tightened all the more. Jack sounded calm, but the urgency of his words made it clear he was in trouble. And here she was, half a bloody world away! Dammit! Maybe they should've stayed together? She finished listening to the first message and wondered whether she had time to listen to the other two. She looked up at the house. There were lights on inside, so someone must be in, but it was strange that Harry hadn't come running out. Something inside her was ringing an insistent alarm bell. Was there really something wrong, or was it simply the result of a crazy few days playing on her mind? Either way, she decided Jack could wait and put her phone in her pocket.

"Hello? Anyone home?" Annie called out as she entered the front hall. The house was unnaturally still and her feet sounded loud on the hard-wood floor. She looked around. Everything seemed perfectly normal. The hall was, as always, freakishly neat and tidy. The hall table, nestled against the side of the staircase, was undisturbed with its bowl of car keys and fresh cut flowers in a smoky glass vase. She glanced through to the elegant dining room with its American Chippendale chairs and table, and the 18th century mahogany sideboard which displayed her mother's pride and joy – a solid silver Georgian tea set from England. Nothing out of place there. Annie listened to the silence again. It was as if no one was there at all – and yet the door hadn't been double locked.

"Mom, you here?" Annie called again, trying to keep her voice sounding bright and breezy, even though she was getting an unpleasant fluttering sensation in her stomach.

"Hello?" said a man's voice from another room.

"Bob? It's me – Annie."

"In the kitchen. Come on through!" Bob called out cheerily. Annie walked across the hall and found him fussing about in the big kitchen.

Doctor Bob was a shortish, slightly tubby gentleman, with neat little feet, small hands and a face that clearly favoured laughter over frowns. His shiny black shoes, formal trousers and bow tie indicated that he'd been at work that morning, but the brown and beige diamond-patterned sweater vest he was rocking showed he'd been home long enough to relax at least a little bit. He was standing next to the kettle, which had just started to boil. Two mugs were sitting on the worktop next to it and as Annie entered, he turned and smiled at her, saying,

"Tea? Coffee? Hot chocolate?"

"Tea please," Annie replied and she went over to him and they hugged. He was about her height and she always found it funny to feel his little pot belly against her stomach when they hugged. She idly wondered whether Jack would feel like that when he was older and fatter.

"How are you doing? And how's Jack bearing up? I was very sorry to hear about his dad," Doctor Bob said with sympathy drawn across his face.

"It's been an emotional roller coaster," Annie replied – and boy, had it ever!

"So, he didn't come back with you?" asked Bob, busying himself with getting tea bags and milk while the kettle made its usual racket. Why didn't mom get a new one? And why didn't Bob give up on the 'Just For Men' and allow his hair to go grey? It looked far too dark to be real.

"No, he had some family business to clear up. He should be back in a couple of days."

Annie looked around. Was everything right here?

"Where are Harry and mom? I expected to be mobbed the second I pulled up."

"Nancy took him into town. She wanted to get a cake for your return. They should be back soon," Bob smiled.

See? A perfectly reasonable explanation. Just relax and sit at the table. But why was Bob only smiling with his mouth?

"You okay?" she asked.

"Me? Fine. Just a bit tired today. I like the money I get for practising on a Sunday, but sometimes I think I might let it go. Too much hassle."

And that was a perfectly reasonable answer. Nothing wrong here at all, just an ordinary Sunday. But why wasn't he meeting her eye?

Bob squeezed out the teabags and placed them neatly in the bin.

"Here we are," Bob said as he brought the mugs, the milk and the sugar bowl over to the big, rustic table.

"Thanks," Annie added a dash of milk and three spoons of sugar to her tea. Usually, Bob crinkled his nose at this habit and made a remark about diabetes, but not today. Today he seemed to be watching her movements. Not overtly, but sort of out of the corner of his eye. He sat down opposite her, smiled and took a sip of his tea. Did his face cloud minutely when Annie set her mug aside to leave it to cool for a moment?

"So, Jack's still in England?" asked Bob, trying to pitch his level of concern correctly.

"No, he went to Italy."

"Italy? Do tell!" said Bob, sitting forward.

"Oh, it's all very complicated and not very interesting. Something to do with his father's will."

"Ah, I see. I've only ever been once – to Rome. Did the whole nine yards – the Colosseum, Trajan's column, St Peter's Square, the Trevi Fountain. Beautiful! Is Jack there?" Bob smiled.

"No, he's up north somewhere," Annie replied. Why did this feel like a very polite, very friendly interrogation?

"When are you expecting him back?"

"Not sure," Annie replied honestly.

"Oh well, I'm sure he'll turn up," said Bob, who then became flustered, saying, "Not like a bad penny, of course. I'm not saying that. Jack's great," and Bob coloured a bit.

The conversation sagged and silence filled the void. Annie reached for her tea and blew on it. Bob smiled and took another sip of his. The kitchen clock seemed to be ticking more loudly in the thick silence. There was something not quite right about it, as if... as if... What? Annie brought the mug to her lips but stopped. Now she knew. The silence was wrong. It didn't feel like the silence of an empty house. It felt like the silence of an afternoon siesta. She had stayed with friends in Italy, Spain and Mexico where the family would retire for their siestas during the day and their houses would have this kind of silence. Not empty, but full and resting. Annie got a horrible creeping feeling in the pit of her stomach as she realised there was more.

"How come you had two mugs?" she asked.

Bob looked confused,

"How do you mean?"

"When I came in, you already had two mugs by the kettle."

"Oh, well, we knew you were coming over this afternoon, so I thought I'd be ready for you in case you arrived while Nancy was out."

"But you didn't get plates out for the cake. She's coming back with cake, right?" Annie said.

"Er... you caught me on the hop – I hadn't got them out yet," said Bob, looking tight around the mouth and flashing a glance at the mug of tea Annie was holding in front of her mouth.

Annie put the mug down very deliberately.

"What's going on, Bob?"

Bob looked at her in mild confusion.

"I don't understand."

Annie looked at him hard, then without a word got up quickly and was over by the door before he could say,

"What are you doing?"

"Gotta go to the bathroom," she said and stepped quickly into the hall. A glance at the bowl of car keys confirmed her suspicions – both sets were there. She could hear Bob mobilising behind her and she dashed up the stairs two at a time. She had a terrible sense of dread. The first room at the top of the stairs was her mom's and she opened the door as Bob was getting to the hall. Nancy was lying on the bed, on top of the covers, fully clothed and with her shoes on. Annie was straight over to her and feeling for a pulse. Thank God! There it was and she could see her mom's chest gently moving. What the... then Bob puffed into the room. Annie slithered back from him towards the dressing table by the window.

"What the fuck?" said Annie, feeling slightly detached from the words by the mixture of fear and anger gripping her.

"I can explain," said Bob, holding his hands up in supplication.

"Where's Harry?" Annie's voice was shrill and loud.

"He's here and he's going to be all right."

"What have you done to him?"

"Nothing."

"Nothing? Like you've done 'nothing' to my mom?"

"Nothing to worry about. He's in his bed having the best afternoon nap of his life," Bob was getting closer, backing Annie into a corner.

"What...?"

"Sssh!" Bob soothed, "They're only interested in you. Your mom and Harry will be fine."

"They? Who are they?" Annie demanded.

"Oh, I think you know exactly who *they* are," Bob kept coming, "All they need is information. Is that so difficult to give?"

Annie pulled out her phone and Bob shouted with sudden menace,

"Give me that!" and he lunged at her, grasping the hand that didn't have the phone in a painfully strong grip.

"Get off me!"

"Give me the fucking phone!" Bob yelled, trying to grab it out of her left hand. Fuck, he was strong for a tubby little middle-aged man. Annie managed to turn them as they struggled so that he was in the corner. He had a grip on each of her wrists, but didn't quite have the strength to overpower her. She was trying to pull away, but didn't have enough strength to get away. Their movements slowed as a stalemate ensued. His face was red with effort and sweat was dripping off his jowls into the top of his collar.

"Why the fuck are you doing this?" Annie hissed through gritted teeth.

"I have to," Bob grunted as he strained to gain the advantage, "She promised me so much."

She? Fuck, it must be one of those bitches.

"Just tell me who Jack's seeing. Tell me who's on the list and this will all be over," he said, putting more effort into bending Annie's arm back.

"Fuck off!" Annie screamed in his face as she brought her knee up hard into his groin.

Bob twisted with more speed and flexibility than might be expected from a man of his age and shape, so that Annie's knee connected with the fleshy part of the top of his left thigh.

"Bitch!" he shouted, kicking out at her shins but missing. Back to deadlock. They were both starting to tire, both breathing hard, but this was where Annie's age and fitness started to tell. She could just feel that his strength was ebbing. Yes, he wouldn't be able to keep this up much longer.

"Shit!" Bob swore as he realised it, too. He suddenly put in a Herculean effort and caught Annie off guard. She was being bent backwards and if he got her to the ground, she'd be in real trouble. His straining face was right in front of hers. Crunch!

The sound of her forehead smashing into his nose was like someone crunching a mouthful of tortilla chips.

Bob cried out and staggered, relinquishing his grip on the hand with phone. Annie instantly used it like a blunt dagger, stabbing it again and again into his face and neck. Bob went down under the welter of blows, trying to fend them off, but now Annie was kicking him in the ribs and screaming abuse at him. There was a split second's pause when the hitting stopped and Bob tried to get up. The solid seven-ounce bottle of Chanel Number 5 Annie had whipped off the dressing table was a blur to him as she smashed it into his face. The first blow shattered his front teeth and he howled, spitting blood and bits of tooth. The second blow caught him flush on the forehead and that was lights out. He slumped backwards.

Annie drew away from him, shaking. What the shit? What had just happened? She put the bottle of Chanel back on the dressing table with a trembling hand and looked down at Bob. Lovely, cuddly Bob, who was so good with Harry and the perfect partner for her mom, and who had just drugged her mom and her son and then attacked her. As she stood trying to process it all, her whole body felt wobbly. Then she remembered Harry.

"Fuck!" she turned to run to him, but stopped. No. There was no way she was letting Bob out of her sight unless he was hogtied. She looked around the room quickly for something to tie him with. Nothing. No, wait – there! Her mom's need for lavish home furnishings came to the rescue. Not content with long, heavy curtains, she just had to have opulent, gold-coloured twisted rope curtain tie backs. They'd do. In a flash Annie took them off the curtains and went back to Bob. He wasn't moving, but she didn't want to get caught out if he was playing possum. She took up the Chanel bottle again and held it ready, then gave him a firm kick in the ribs. Nothing. She put down the Chanel and heaved Bob onto his front. Then, with a mountaineer's intimate knowledge of ropes, hogtied the son of a bitch.

Seconds later, she was in the spare room and holding her unconscious boy in her arms. Now the tears came. Tears of anger, fear and relief. After a few minutes, she calmed herself enough to think. She had to call the cops and an ambulance. Her iPhone was smashed to shit, so she used the landline. Within fifteen minutes, police officers were reviving Bob so they could arrest him, while paramedics were putting her mom and Harry into the back of an ambulance.

"I don't know what he's given them, but there might be some in the cup of tea on the kitchen table," Annie said to the paramedic who had 'Jean Dubois' on the ID card clipped to his shirt pocket.

"Thanks, okay Andy, go find that and put some into this," and he threw his colleague a plastic container.

"Can I ride with you to the hospital?"

"Fine by me, but you need to clear it with the cops."

"Okay, just give me a minute," said Annie and she walked in something of a daze over to the police cruiser into which they'd just put Bob.

"May I go to the hospital with my mother and son?" she asked the senior officer, a tall, rangy man with sullen eyes.

"Yeah, but we'll need a full statement from you tonight. I could send an officer to the hospital to take it from you if you want."

"Please," Annie nodded eagerly.

"And you really have no idea why he'd drug your mother and son, and then attack you?"

"Not really," Annie semi-lied. The truth was so ridiculous, she might quickly find herself in a straitjacket.

"I only flew in from England at two."

"Well, I'll be!" he said, looking into the cruiser at Bob, who was in a sorry state even after being cleaned up by the paramedics,

"It's always the quiet ones you gotta watch out for..." then he turned back to Annie, "We'll send someone over in a couple of hours, okay?"

"Thanks!" then, just as she was about to turn away, she had a thought, "Could you send a female officer, please? I'd feel a lot more comfortable."

"Sure thing."

And with that, Annie climbed into the ambulance and took Harry's hand.

Chapter Thirty

Annie Makes Plans

Annie hated hospitals, but for once she didn't mind being in one. The doctors and nurses worked quickly and efficiently to ensure the safety of her mother and son, while taking blood samples to find out what the hell they'd been given. Then it was simply a question of waiting until they came to. They were given a room to themselves and Annie sat on a chair between the beds holding Harry's hand in her left and her mom's hand in her right. She stroked the backs of their hands softly with her thumbs and talked to them, telling them how much she loved them, that everything was going to be all right and that they'd soon wake up. Under the subdued lighting, their skin looked yellowed. They both looked older and fragile. Annie thought of all the times she'd risked her life on mountains or in the sea and wondered whether her mom had ever felt as she did in that moment – sick with fear. Annie was also feeling something she almost never felt any more – guilt. It was an old adversary from her teenage years, when her parents' marriage had collapsed. Guilt brimmed inside her. This was her fault, wasn't it? The result of her choices? No. Goddammit! It was those creatures. How in hell had they got to Doctor Bob? How dare they attack her family? Now she turned all of that brimming guilt into anger and, had Rosalind and Veronica walked through the door at that moment, they would have turned and run. Annie's beautiful face, framed by her tumbling, copper-coloured hair was set in terrible wrath. She was no longer a woman, but an avenging angel tasked by God himself to send those two creatures back to hell.

Her brain went into overdrive, plotting and running different scenarios. But how do you outwit beings that might be thousands of years old? Surely they'd seen everything and would be ready for any counter-move? No, that wasn't the way to think! Okay, so they had the wisdom of the ages, but this wasn't their time and this wasn't their world. They still acted like this was a world where only men had power, but they were out of date. Yes, men still held most of the cards, but women had the freedom to choose what to do with their lives, and Annie was ninety-nine percent sure that the sirens hadn't got that through their heads. They underestimated women and Annie would see to it that that would be their downfall. A plan was crystallising in her mind and it was one that she felt sure would blindside those bitches. If it worked, it would give her the infinite pleasure of being able to stand over them with her foot on their throats and look them in the eye before she dispatched them.

The handle of the door started to move and Annie let her mom and Harry go, ready to spring to their defence.

"Annie Ingels?" asked officer Debbie Benson as she put her head round the door?

The woman sitting between the beds visibly uncoiled and her face changed from one of fury to relief.

"Yes?" said Annie.

"I've come to take your statement. We can do it right out here if you like."

"Sure thing," Annie replied and left her mom and Harry with one protective glance before she gently closed the door behind her. In the corridor, the lights were bright and harsh. Annie had to blink before her eyes got used to it. Officer Benson was a serious and strong-looking woman of around thirty, who was reassuring in her uniform with its various items of lethal and non-lethal defence. They sat on the bench opposite the door and Annie gave her statement. She held back nothing except the part about ancient sea spirits that were out to kill her and her family.

"Has Doctor Bob said anything?" asked Annie, once she'd gone through the events of the afternoon.

"Who? Oh, Doctor Harrington... no. Hasn't said a word. Just stares in front of him. The only weird thing was, when he made his phone call he burst into tears at the end of it. And no lawyer has appeared."

"Weird," said Annie, looking into space.

"Yeah, the whole thing's weird. He spent a typical Sunday morning at work; his secretary said he was in a great mood..."

"Doctor Bob's always in a great mood," Annie interjected.

"That's what his receptionist said. Always smiling. So, nothing out of the ordinary happened. The only thing was, he had a new patient come in and request an immediate consultation,"

Annie became very alert.

"According to the receptionist, the woman was tall, very elegant – clearly rich – and paid in cash. But the receptionist didn't warm to her. Said she had weird eyes."

And that was the clincher! So, either Rosalind or Veronica (or possibly both of them) were in Southampton. Annie's right hand unconsciously balled into a fist and her knuckle turned white.

"After that, he had two other consultations, nothing out of the ordinary, and then they closed up shop and went home."

"Excuse me," said a young, male doctor approaching them holding a clipboard, "The toxicology results are back."

Annie and officer Benson stood and gave him their attention.

"I'm doctor Gupta, by the way – good to meet you..." Annie and officer Benson nodded, but clearly wanted him to get on with it,

"So, your mom and your son were given safe, but large doses of sedatives. However, that wasn't what was in your mug of tea. That contained sodium thiopental."

Annie gave him a quizzical look.

"Basically, sodium pentathol."

"The truth drug?" Annie exclaimed.

"In spy films, it is used as a 'truth serum'," he said, putting the clipboard under his arm to put air quotes around the phrase,

"But it's really an anaesthetic, although it could make you kind of talkative. Thing is, it's also used in lethal injections," and he let that sink in before adding,

"And that brings us to the syringe he had prepped and ready in his medical bag. That contained pancuronium bromide."

From the look that crossed officer Benson's face, this was a bad thing.

"That's another drug used in lethal injections," Doctor Gupta said, trying not to sound too dramatic,

"And the amount would have killed you. Sorry to have to break that to you, but that's what it is," he finished, trying to give Annie a kindly look.

"So, this is looking like attempted murder?" asked officer Benson.

"I can't comment on what the intention of Doctor Harrington was, but if you did want to kill someone, this would be a very effective way of doing it."

"Has that report been sent to…"

"Yes, it's all done and your chief is across the details. But I thought that since you're here, you should be made aware of the situation."

"Thanks."

"No problem. If either of you needs me, I'll be down by the nursing station for the next half hour, then I'll be on my rounds but the nurses can page me," he said, then he gave Annie an encouraging smile,

"Your mom and son will be totally fine and won't remember anything. And you have had a very lucky escape."

Annie nodded her thank you and then he turned and walked away.

"I think I'm done here, too," said officer Benson, turning to Annie.

"Okay, but if you need anything else from me, you know where I am."

"Thanks, and if you need any psychological support, call any of the numbers on this card. They're twenty-four-hour lines," then she looked long and hard at Annie. She knew there was something being held back. Maybe it would come out when she'd had more time to process the events of the afternoon,

"And remember, it's kinda like he said – focus on the positives. You're all okay. And that's always a win."

"Thanks," said Annie, "You've been a real help," and she gave officer Benson an unexpected hug.

"Okay," said the flustered policewoman as she broke free, "I'll look in on you in the morning but in the meantime, get some rest. You look beat."

"Will do," said Annie and she went back into the room.

Rest was the last thing on Annie's mind. Fortunately, her mom's phone had been in her pocket when they'd brought her in and now Annie put it to good use. Safety was her first priority. She knew that she couldn't fully trust any men except Jack, so she needed some protection she could rely on. It took a few calls, but she finally secured the services of an all-female bodyguard agency. And, although it was crazy expensive, they would be able to send two 'operatives' to the hospital within three hours. That would give Annie the chance to sleep, knowing that she was safe. However, her conversation with the head of the security company went far beyond that. Annie had a plan to secure her family's safety and the security company were at the heart of it. Once that was taken care of, she checked her watch – nine o-clock. That would make it three a.m. in Italy. She couldn't bring herself to wake Jack up in the middle of the night, so their conversation would have to wait until the morning. Instead, she busied herself with maps of Vermont, looking at airline websites and trying to work out how the sirens had figured out where she'd been going and how to get to her through Doctor Bob. And then there was Bob – what would happen to him? If he had been bewitched (as it looked likely) was it fair to press charges? And how could she or her mom ever trust him again? These were the thoughts she was wrestling with when the two tough-looking women from the security company arrived. After a brief and practical conversation, they stationed themselves outside the door and Annie was able to make a nest for herself on the big chair between her mother and son and go to sleep.

It was seven when Harry woke up. He looked around, confused, and then saw his mom snuggled on a chair next to him.

"Mommy!" he cried in delight and although it startled Annie out of a dream, it was the most wonderful thing she'd ever heard in her life.

"Harry!" she said with bleary eyes before enfolding him in her arms,

"How are ya doing, little man?" she asked, getting into bed with him.

"Hungry!"

Annie laughed,

"You should be. You've been asleep a very long time."

"Gamma's sleeping, too," Harry said, pointing.

"Yes, she is," Annie said, her voice hitching. There was something about the innocent observation that brought home how close she had come to losing everything.

"But she'll be up soon. Now, what do you want for breakfast?"

"Bekkfast!" Harry cried triumphantly, missing out the 'r' as usual.

"You want breakfast for breakfast?"

"Bekkfast!"

"Well, I guess that makes sense. C'mon, let's see what we can get you."

Annie slipped out of the bed, picked him up and carried him to the door.

"And we'd better change you while we're at it," she said, then opened the door and explained the situation to Beth and Amy, who were standing guard.

When Annie and Harry returned half an hour later, they found Nancy sitting up in bed. Sunlight streamed through the open curtains and she looked refreshed.

"So, my husband drugged me?" she said, almost cheerily once Annie had got Harry interested in a picture book.

"Yeah," Annie nodded.

"Son of a... not even your dad did anything that shitty to me."

"Maybe it's not all his fault..."

"What, it's my fault?" Nancy protested.

"No, no. It's just..." Annie hesitated and that was all her mom needed to turn her X-ray specs on her.

"Okay," said Nancy, "There's something huge you're not telling me. And it's not Jack, but something to do with Jack. Right?"

Annie sighed,

"Yes. As always!"

"So why can't you tell me? Clearly it's serious enough to induce my husband to drug me and my grandson. I think I ought to know."

Annie hesitated again,

"Look, if I tell you, you've got to promise not to weird out."

"I can't promise that. If what you say weirds me out, then I can't stop that," Nancy said.

"Okay, at least promise me you won't have me committed," Annie countered.

"All right... at least not immediately. But if you've gone crazy as a loon, then I reserve the right to have you committed later for the safety of your son."

"Agreed," Annie smiled. She was truly blessed with a practical mother.

"Hold onto your hat, this will get strange," and Annie launched into everything that had happened in the last few days, that had felt like weeks.

Nancy's emotions swayed from shock, sympathy and anger about what Jack's sisters had done to him as a child, to horror at the revelations of his father's behaviour. She was already wrung out by the time Annie began to broach the idea that Jack's sisters were some sort of mythical sea-devils who had bewitched Doctor Bob into drugging her and trying to kill her daughter.

"Holy sh...moley!" Nancy exclaimed, narrowly avoiding swearing in front of Harry, even though he was paying them no attention.

"You gonna have me committed?" Annie asked tentatively.

"It all sounds like crazy talk – you do know that, don't you?"

"Yes."

"Good. Then that means you haven't gone crazy," and Nancy gave her daughter a very big hug.

"Does that mean you believe me?"

"Yes," Nancy admitted reluctantly,

"If they send you to the booby-hatch, they'll have to take me, too."

"Really?"

"You betcha. What choice've I got? I can believe you, my brilliant, practical, wonderful daughter who's telling me that my husband has been possessed by the same creatures that tormented Odysseus... or, I can believe that for no good reason, the man I love, a truly good man who's been nothing but delightful to me, suddenly turned rabid and decided to drug us and try to kill you. The fact is, I can't believe that of him. So, by a process of elimination… sirens are trying to kill us. I hope straitjackets come in size four."

Annie couldn't help but smile.

"What now?" Nancy asked, searching Annie's face to gauge her confidence.

"I've got a plan. Whether it'll work, who knows? First, I gotta talk to Jack. If he's okay. Because if they can know where I'm going and get here first, you can bet they've done it to Jack, too," said Annie.

Nancy thought she looked too old for her age and hoped that once this was all over, the experience wouldn't weigh on her.

"Better get on with it," said Nancy, "Don't mind me – unless you're gonna talk dirty to each other, in which case, please leave the room."

***

By the time Jack got down to the car park in San Martino, the light was fading and it was murky. Even though it was barely above freezing, he was hot and sweaty, and he was glad to strip off his waterproofs and throw them onto the back seat of the Corsa. He looked back up the Val di Mello, whose forests were dark and hung with pockets of mist. Far above, he could just see the snowy peak of Monte Disgrazia looking benignly down on the valley. For the mountain, this had been just another day to add to its hundred-million-year life. For Jack, it had been life changing. He got into the car, reversed out and headed down the mountain as fast as the Corsa could go. After the first ten minutes constantly checking his mirrors, he decided that he wasn't being followed. When he got back down to the Valtellina, he decided to copy Giulia's idea of avoiding Lake Como. He would continue up into the safety of the mountains, over the passes and into Switzerland. Then he would go to Zurich and take the first flight back to New York, although he wasn't sure what his next move after that should be. As he skirted the Lago di Mezzola on his way north, Jack felt a frisson of anxiety. It fed directly into lake Como and Jack wondered how dangerous it was for him to be so close to the water – especially if Veronica was nearby. She must surely be stronger near water and as he drove, he couldn't help but keep throwing glances at the black, glassy surface. Jolly lights were already coming on outside lakeside restaurants and bars as dusk hunched itself over the mountains. All very nice, but what the hell might be lurking in the black depths of that lake?

Jack didn't relax until it was miles behind him. He was driving through Chiavenna and had just taken the turning to Switzerland and St Moritz, when his phone rang. He looked across at it and his stomach instantly dropped. Nancy! Why would Nancy be calling him? He pulled over nervously, his mind throwing out innumerable scenarios, all with very bad endings involving Annie being injured or killed. He exhaled firmly, then took the call,

"Nancy?"

"No, it's me!" Annie's voice sounded small.

"Thank God! Are you safe? Why are you using your mum's phone?"

"I kinda smashed mine up beating Doctor Bob unconscious..."

"What?"

Jack's incredulous tone deserved a full explanation and Annie gave it to him, with her narrative occasionally punctuated with Jack's exclamations.

"But you're all okay now?" he asked with deep concern when she'd finished.

"Yeah, we're good. I'm paying through the nose for kick-ass female bodyguards, so I'm feeling pretty safe," Annie replied, "How about you?"

"Funny you should ask..." Jack smiled and told her his news, which Annie punctuated with a liberal selection of exclamatory swearing.

"And right now, I'm in the mountains driving to Switzerland," he finished.

"Are we in some weird nightmare?" Annie asked, "Are we gonna wake up to find everything's normal and there's no such thing as sirens or bizarre mountain goat-gods?" and her timbre was almost pleading with Jack to make it so.

"Sorry, but I think we're stuck with this. But our plan's up the spout. If Rosalind and Veronica are tracking both of us, then we can't go and see the other two women on our list without endangering their lives."

"And we've got to make sure mom and Harry are safe," said Annie, "But I've got a plan for that..."

Annie outlined her plan and Jack listened hard, making suggestions here and there.

"That is a very elegant plan," Jack said when she'd laid it all out, "Sounds expensive."

"Yeah, it's gonna cost a frickin' fortune, so you can kiss goodbye to a chunk of your inheritance."

"Yay!" said Jack dryly.

"But what are we going to do about these women on the list?"

"I'll phone them. I know dad wanted me to visit them, but let's face it, the rule book's out the window,"

"Yeah, along with sense and reason!" Annie added.

"I'll see what I can get out of them, but I'm gonna have to get to Bermuda. Everything leads to it."

"Yeah," said Annie, "But I still can't figure out how they knew where we were going. They can't be mind readers, otherwise they'd've already killed everyone on the list. So how?"

"And how did that guy track me up the mountain after I'd switched cars? There was no way I was followed up there, because there's a point on the road up to the mountain where you can see at least a mile behind you. There was no one else on that road."

"Maybe it's not something supernatural. Maybe they've put a tracking device into something we've got."

"Can't be the phone. Mine never left my sight," said Jack, thinking hard.

"Yeah, nor mine. But here's the thing – I've got nothing with me right now that was on me when we left England."

"Not even your underwear?" Jack asked with a leer.

"No, not even my underwear," Annie said and she rolled her eyes at her mom and covered the receiver, "Sorry, he's got a one-track mind."

"Get it while you can, honey!" Nancy smiled.

"But my point is," said Annie, turning her attention back to Jack, "Even if, say, they got into our room in England and put a tracker in any of my stuff, I'm clean. Once I'm out of their sight, I'm gone."

"That's great for you," said Jack ruefully, "But what about me?"

"It doesn't matter…"

"Nice! Love you, too, babe."

"It doesn't matter, because we want them to know where you are. You're the bait."

"Yeah, good point. So, I carry on and play the toothless tiger, and when they least expect it…"

"Boom! We take the fuckers out – sorry mom!" Annie said hurriedly.

Jack smiled. He could imagine the look Nancy had just given her daughter. Although Nancy was no prude, she wasn't big on swearing.

"Okay, so we're clear on the new plan?" asked Annie.

"As crystal. You do what you need to and I'll let my fingers do the walking. Listen," and Jack's tone became more tender,

"Before we do this, I want you to know how much I wish I hadn't dragged you into it… and how much I love you."

There was a moment's silence, then Annie's voice came back with a slight hitch,

"Yeah, I love you too," then she gathered herself and said severely,

"So you'd better take care of yourself, because otherwise there'll be hell to pay!"

"Don't worry, I'll be super careful."

"Love you," Annie said softly.

"Love you, too," said Jack, ending the call.

Jack sat in the car at the side of the road in Chiavenna, watching the traffic go by for a minute or two. What a mess! How quickly had his carefully constructed life been torn down! And now he was facing more danger. It was a serious situation. He didn't know it, but in Bellagio, Gianfranco Cacciatore's freshly dismembered corpse was a testament to just how serious it was. Jack could feel anger and resentment growing inside him. All those feelings from a brutalised childhood that he'd so carefully crated up and stacked away were well and truly out, but instead of being swept away by the maelstrom of emotions, the threat to his family was giving him the strength to focus the storm. He was concentrating every moment of hurt and fear towards a single goal – the total destruction of the evil that threatened his family. He would tear them apart with his bare hands and if any of their guards got in his way, he would kill them, too. Gladly. He was no longer Jack, the happy-go-lucky web designer with a love of abstract expressionism. That Jack had stepped into the shadows for the moment and given the floor to the raging beast. This Jack would kill them all, bathe in their blood and display their skins on his wall. But first, he had a job to do. He picked up his phone again and started to dial.

Chapter Thirty-One

Donny Judd Takes A Drive

Skylar Judd should be a beautiful woman. She's about thirty and her body is delightfully proportioned. As she steps out of her impressive four-bedroom home into the bright North Carolina sunshine, she should easily be rocking that combo of Daisy Dukes and tight T-shirt. With her straight, blonde hair riffling in the breeze as she walks down to the mailbox, she should be stunning. But she isn't. She's shuffling along like an eighty-year-old, and her face, which might be kind and pretty, is blotchy and her blue eyes are puffy from crying. Mechanically, she checks for mail and pulls out three letters. She stares through them with a look that signals that none of it matters - not even if they were from the lottery company telling her of three jackpots she's won. She closes the mailbox and shuffles back to the house. She looks exhausted. Then comes an unmistakable sound from inside the house – the rising wail of a teething child. That must be it. The poor thing is wrung out from multiple sleepless nights. She doesn't change gear when the wailing starts, but simply shuffles up to the house with its combination of mid-brown brickwork and beige clapboard, and closes the front door behind her.

Inside, the front door leads into an open plan entrance hall-cum dining room-cum sitting room. These are the 'formal' rooms, with big, plush furniture set on the dark, reddish wooden floors. Skylar walks through them like they aren't there, as she does every day except when she's cleaning them. She goes through to where the action is – the huge kitchen/diner/living area in the back. She crosses the kitchen, dropping the letters on the honey and white marble of the island and shuffles towards the playpen next to the broad sliding patio doors. There's the baby girl sitting on her diaper-fattened rump wailing like a good 'un. Her left cheek is bright red, shiny and so swollen it looks fit to crack. The poor little thing is beside herself in pain and doesn't even register her mother's arrival. Skylar gets into the playpen and picks her daughter up.

"Oh, honey, don't cry. Momma's gonna fix you up right now," she says kindly, with an unexpectedly soothing tone, given how distraught she looks herself. She takes her daughter over to the kitchen island and the magic tube of teething gel, which contains a mild local anaesthetic. Of course, little Emmie will have nothing of it and turns her head away, squirms and kicks the moment Skylar gets her little finger with the magic gel on it near her mouth. Again, Skylar doesn't get cross, but is patient, cooing to and soothing her darling girl until, at last, she is able to get the finger in and apply the gel to the gum where the jagged first tooth is forcing its way through. Then she rocks her baby, singing gently to her. It's a slowed down, folksy version of AC:DC's 'Whole Lotta Rosie'. Not quite 'Hush Little Baby', but it's doing the trick and Emmie calms down sufficiently for Skylar to change her diaper. Yes, as suspected, that stinky friend of teething – diarrhoea – has paid a visit. Skylar cleans up the mess with the practised hands of a woman with her third child in seven years. She lifts Emmie up from the changing mat by her feet and slips a fresh diaper under her. Then, just as she's in the process, of putting it on, Emmie lets rip a fresh stream of sputtering, squittering light brown liquid. Despite her obvious exhaustion, Skylar's hands move fast to ensure the diaper catches it all. And then the process starts again.

Within ten minutes, Emmie is asleep on the sofa and Skylar is sitting next to her, talking on the phone. She's crying intermittently,

"I know my Donny's seein' another woman... no, I ain't caught him at it, but I just knows. A wife knows..."

There's a pause as the person at the other end of the line has their say. Skylar takes the chance to wipe her nose with a tissue, then her eyes flash with anger,

"You bet! I got a darned good idea who it is – Billy Payton's goddam wife... Yeah, Rosalind. The stuck-up English bitch! I don't know why she married him. She don't understand racin' and every time she comes to the track, she's lookin' down her nose at everyone – even at Billy. I think she does it to make him mad. You know what they say - she likes it rough. And the madder Billy gets, the rougher he gives it to her. We've all heard them going at it in his trailer – yeah, right there by the track – her screamin' and the whole thing rockin'. She don't even have the class to wait 'til they get home. But that ain't enough for her. Now she's gotta go after my Donny. And he ain't her type. He's kind and gentle... but the last three weeks, he's been so cold. Walks past me like I ain't even here. Don't hardly talk to the kids... this week, Becky says to me, she says 'Momma, have I done somethin' bad? Daddy don't love me no more'..." then the tears come and she's listening to the person at the other end of the line.

Skylar then has her say,

"Yeah, but what if Billy finds out? First, he's gonna kick Donny's ass and second, he's gonna can him. And then we're screwed. We'll lose the house and there ain't no guarantee Donny's gonna get another job in racin'. You know how it is. I'm worried sick and I ain't hardly sleepin'. Emmie's got her first tooth comin' and it's a S.O.B."

Then comes the sound of the front door opening and Skylar hurriedly ends the call,

"Listen, Donny's just comin' through the door. I'll call you later. Bye," and she ends the call and quickly puts the phone onto the table. She gets up and catches a glimpse of herself in a mirror. She looks dreadful and tries to wipe all the tears from her eyes before Donny comes in but as he does, it's clear he's been crying, too.

"Donny?" there is fear and uncertainty in Skylar's voice as she comes around the sofa to meet him halfway across the kitchen.

Donny is in a daze and only half sees her,

"Billy's dead."

"What? Oh my God!" and she holds Donny in a hug, which he doesn't reciprocate,

"What happened?"

"Hit the wall in practice and flipped. Went up in flames. He was already dead when we got there," Donny says, staring straight ahead and seeing it all in front of him.

"Oh, Donny!" she says and tries to comfort him again with a hug, but again he doesn't respond.

"It's all my fault," and he sounds hollow.

"No, baby, don't talk like that. It's racin'. It's dangerous. Billy knew that."

"No," Donny says firmly, and sees Skylar for the first time as he looks her in the face,

"I did it."

"Did what?"

"Just like she said."

"Who? Just like who said?" and Skylar is holding his shoulders and shaking him.

"I made it look like an accident. A worn brake line. Pinprick in the fuel line, then let her rip. And boom... she did."

"What are you saying?"

"I killed him. Killed him as surely as if I'd put a forty-five to his head and pulled the trigger. Oh God, what've I done?" and now tears are rolling down his cheeks.

Skylar is distraught and freezes. What is this? What's happening?

"But I ain't finished. I gotta go. Tell the girls I love 'em," and he turns and walks over to the door that leads to the garage.

Something about the way he says it snaps Skylar out of her indecision and she's immediately after him,

"Donny! You stay here! We can work this out,"

But he's already got through the door and locked it before she can follow. She tries the handle. No use. She bangs on the door and calls to him. Then she hears the Challenger roar and she runs to the front door. As she runs down the hot flagstones of the garden path, the garage door is almost fully open and Donny is easing the black Challenger out past his pickup on the drive.

"Donny!" she screams and the look he gives her as he drives past is one of tragic finality.

"No! Come back!" she shouts as she runs after him up the street.

He watches her diminishing figure in the rear-view with teared eyes. She doesn't understand. This is something he has to do. He has no choice. He must demonstrate his faith and this is the only way. He drives across town to a specialist store and picks up a hundred yards of half-inch diameter steel winching cable, then he drives into the countryside – to a quiet place he knows on the way to Mooresville. The road has led him into woodland and it ends in a big turning circle from which a number of paths lead into the trees. At the weekend people park here, but today it's just him. Donny's tears are gone now and he looks as if he means business. He turns the Challenger around, then backs towards the trees and stops so that he's facing directly down the strip of asphalt he's just driven up. He heaves the cable out of the trunk and carries it to a big tree that's about ten yards in a straight line from the back of the Challenger. He runs the cable round the thick trunk of the tree, pushes the end through the eyelet and then has the laborious task of pulling all the cable through. By the end he's sweating, but he's finally able to pull the cable tight around the tree.

Satisfied, he takes the end of the cable and walks back to the car. He reaches into the trunk, pulls out an escape safety hammer, closes the trunk and protects his eyes as he smashes out the rear window. It is a matter of moments before he is threading the cable through the car to the front seat. He leans in through the open door and removes the driver's headrest, then takes the cable and wrangles it into a noose, which he leaves hanging over the seat.

Donny steps away and walks back to the tree. He gives the cable a tug. Yup, that'll do it. Then he walks along the length of the cable to the car. All good. Just one thing to do now... but first... he stops and looks around, taking in the trees, the sunshine, the sound of birds, the scent of summer in the air. Isn't the world beautiful? Yes, that's how he's going to remember it. Then he walks around the Challenger, puts the noose around his neck and gets into the driving seat. He buckles himself snugly into the racing harness he's had fitted and adjusts the noose so that it's snug around his neck. Donny closes the door and starts the engine. Oh, that sound! What a thing of beauty. He revs the engine, just to enjoy that muscular grunt and roar, then looks down the road. It's straight for three hundred yards. More than enough road to take him to his destination. And where is that? Into *her* arms. She explained it all to him. With Billy gone, Donny will be her sire forever, but he has to pass over to the other side first. She is an immortal and he can only have her fully if his soul is free. And he wants her so-very-much. More than Skylar. More than his children. More than life itself. He slams the car into Drive and pushes his foot to the floor. The Challenger surges forward, an unstoppable flash of metal with the cable running out behind it. There it goes, running out like quicksilver, but it's only a matter of seconds before... suddenly, it's taut. In that moment, the cable stops Donny from going forward with the car and tries to lift him backwards out of his seat. But the racing harness holds him firm. The struggle is intense but short. Cable and harness will not relinquish their prize and the only thing between them is Donny's neck. It gives in an instant and his head with part of his neck are ripped off his body. The head with its stump of neck is pulled out of the rear window of the Challenger, flicking Jackson Pollock blood trails as it bounces across the asphalt. Inside the car, blood sprays out of top of the torso, painting the windscreen red, and now the Challenger starts to slow and veer drunkenly off the road into the trees. Twigs and branches crack until it comes to rest. The engine cuts and the sound of the woodland fills the void. Already, a crow is eyeing up Donny's head. His only destination is oblivion as his sightless eyes stare at the sky. His mouth is open and his face still holds the look of strangulated surprise that was his last experience. A piece of gravel is stuck on his open left eye. The crow hops over and picks it off before starting on the soft bits with its strong, sharp beak. Within a week, even the Challenger will be nothing but scrap metal.

Chapter Thirty-Two

Josephine Paget Stays At Home

"**S**uicide 'invalidated his life insurance'. That's what the man from the insurance company told me, anyways," said Skylar into her phone as she sat in a battered folding chair next to her trailer. She was wrapped up in a big puffer jacket and smoking a Pall Mall, flicking the ash onto the patch of wet, scrubby grass that passed for a garden.

"I'm sorry," said Jack from the roadside in Italy.

"I lost the house. The investigation of Billy's accident found what Donny had done, so I got nothin' from the racing team. And now here I am, five years down the line - three daughters to bring up and no money left to bring 'em up with," said Skylar, taking another long drag. The five years had been hard and now her hope and her beauty were all but gone.

"You still there? You hearin' what your bitch of a sister did to me and mine?" she said angrily. If people wanted to ask for her life story, they should goddam listen!

"Yes, sorry," said Jack quickly, "God, what a nightmare."

He was very sad for her and felt strangely responsible for what had happened. To get her hands on Billy Payton's money, Rosalind had left a trail of collateral damage.

"It's a nightmare twenty-four-seven. Thanks for callin' to remind me," Skylar said sourly as she lit her next cigarette off the embers of her last and then stomped the dying one into the ground.

"Listen, I won't take any more of your time," Jack said, "But may I keep in touch with you?"

"I guess it's a free country," she sighed, billowing smoke.

"Thanks. And for what it's worth, I'm truly sorry for what's happened."

"Yeah, whatever."

Before Jack could reply, Skylar had rung off, leaving him sitting in his little car at the side of the road, with the windows all steamed up. He shook his head sadly. He hadn't heard about it before. He had always tried to ignore everything to do with his sisters in the press and, aside from the news about the crash and Billy Payton's death, Jack hadn't seen any of the details around the case. He made a promise there and then to help Skylar however he could. He couldn't let her and her children suffer any more from what Rosalind had done. Was this why his father had added her name to the list? She'd had no information that could help him, just a familiar story of the wake of destruction left by his sisters. Maybe his father had seen some chance for redemption? That somehow if Jack could see them right, maybe it would expunge some of his father's culpability? Jack couldn't tell, but if he came through the next week alive, he would step up and help. So, that left only Josephine Paget. Jack looked at the battery indicator on the phone. Sixty percent should do it. He'd already tracked down her landline number, so now he crossed his fingers and hoped she'd be in.

Josephine Paget loved Bermuda - even on a grey Monday morning in February. She stood on the rear porch of her violently pink bungalow, coffee in hand, and looked at her lush, green garden and beyond to the green hill studded with the white rooves of Somerset Village. What wasn't to love? Her golden eyes took in the scene in a way that gave the impression she was seeing more than most. Even in a battered old pair of sliders and light green bathrobe she was striking, and although she was in her fifties, her deeply tanned skin showed few wrinkles. She stood around six feet tall with a solid build and her long, straight black hair neatly framed her kindly face. Although her surname came from one of the original English 'Adventurers' who invested in the Somers Isles Company, she had English, Portuguese, native American and African ancestors from her family's four-hundred-years living on the island. She had a deep, spiritual connection to Bermuda, which was clear as she padded about the tumbling mass of greenery in her garden. She carefully checked the various plants and herbs in her little patch of heaven and talked quietly to them in a husky voice blending West Indian, the south of England, and the Carolinas,

"Good morning, mistress elder, yes you are looking good. Will you give me some fruit this year? Only flowers? That will be fine, thank you. How about you, madam hibiscus? Lots of lovely flowers this year? Yes, that would be grand," then she bent down and ran her hand through some fine green herbs,

"Hello master yarrow, what visions will we see together? Glorious ones? How excellent! Ah, yes, my dear rue, I'm not forgetting you either…"

And so she went on, cooing over everything from her rosemary and sage to the lemon balm and bay, and seeming to hear their replies to her enquiries. Yes, all was good in her garden. This was how she started every day, talking to the island and filling up on its energy. She finally pottered back into the house, carrying with her various cuttings she'd taken as she'd gone round.

Her kitchen, like her bungalow and her garden, was small and full of stuff – little bottles of coloured tinctures, jars with odd-looking plants in them and sealed containers of coloured powders crowded the shelves between the window and the fridge. There was also a selection of strange oddments hung around the walls ranging from a brass talisman in the shape of an eye to a string of shark teeth and what looked like a mummified monkey's paw on a loop of leather. There was a pot on the stove gently bubbling away and on the worksurface there was a sieve, a wooden spoon and a glass bowl, waiting to strain whatever was in the pot. Josephine laid her selection of herbs on the wooden chopping board and contentedly sang to herself as she turned off the stove and sieved the concoction into the glass bowl,

"There's a part of the Sun in an apple,
There's a part of the Moon in a rose.
A part of the flaming Pleiades
In every leaf that grows."

She squeezed out the last of the dark brown juice from the bits of twig, leaf and bark, then put the pot in the sink and the contents of the sieve into the bin.

"I'll leave you to cool," she said and padded through the half-light of the sitting room. The blinds were still closed and the room was heavy with the aroma of incense, which had suffused every item of furniture and every colourful throw and cushion that adorned them.

Her size made the small bathroom appear even smaller as she disrobed, turned on the shower, pulled back the shower curtain and stepped over the rim of the bath to ease herself under the cascading water. Normally by this time, she'd have been on her little red Kawasaki scooter and enjoying the scent of the sea and the views across Great Sound as she puttered her way to work at the National Museum of Bermuda. It was at the furthest tip of the north side of Ireland Island and, if ever work was getting difficult, all she had to do was look out of her office window at the vast ocean to calm herself and re-charge. But this morning, she had decided to take the day off. The thought had come to her on Thursday of last week. She had been writing an article about Bermuda for an English magazine when the thought had popped into her head that Monday would be an important day to have to herself. And, as she had long ago learned to listen when the world spoke to her, she had immediately asked her boss for the day. In low season, this was no problem. As she stood under the warm water, she gently explored her feelings. Should she go out, or stay in? Stay in. Going out would be wrong. No, she would stay, get some things done and wait. For what? Fate, of course. Oleander! The word appeared out of nowhere. What was her supply of oleander like? She thought it was good, but she would check. Hmmm… oleander – powerful and dangerous. The feeling rose up within her that something evil was coming. Not specifically for her, but coming… and more importantly, that this evil was coming home.

When the phone started ringing just after eleven-o-clock, Josephine was on the sofa next to it, reading a book about the uses of plants. She hardly batted an eyelid when it rang and she languidly picked it up,

"Good morning?"

"Oh, er, hi, is this Josephine Paget?" said the voice of an English man from far away.

"Speaking. And who might you be?"

"My name is Jack Kidd. I'm very sorry to bother you, but I was given your name by my father, who asked me to contact you..."

"And what was his name?"

"David. David Kidd. Did you know him?"

"No, I can't say that rings a bell. How can I help you?" even as she asked the question, she wasn't sure that the caller knew the answer.

"Um..." in the steamed up little car in a mountain town in Italy, Jack desperately thought of what he could say. He couldn't just come out and tell her what was happening – she'd slam the phone down on him. How could he get a handle on this?

"Er... if you don't mind my asking, what is it that you do?"

"No, I don't mind. I'm a historian, working at the museum," she said with a smile. She could sense a great need in this man.

"I see..." Jack mused – maybe she might have some historical context? Perhaps there were records that could shed light on what he should do next. But how to put it?

"I suppose you know a lot about shipwrecks?"

"We have had a lot of 'em over the years," she said, but she suspected that this was not what he needed her for. He needed her for something that he couldn't talk about. She decided to move the conversation sideways,

"I do have another line of work..."

"Oh yes, what's that?"

"I'm a witch."

Silence. Josephine held her tongue. She could almost hear the man thinking. Finally, he said,

"Well, I guess that's why my father wanted me to contact you. You see, I have a... supernatural problem. I wonder whether you might be able to help me?"

Jack talked and Josephine listened, only interjecting to let him know that she was still on the line. As he told her the tale of his sisters when they were young, the storm, the notion that they had been possessed by sirens and the trail of lust and destruction the creatures had left, Josephine nodded along. To her, it all sounded perfectly reasonable. The sea spirits had haunted the islands long before men had arrived. She herself had heard them singing, their voices carried within the howling winds of the worst storms. And these two had found a way to get out and have some fun. Josephine was impressed. She didn't know that sirens could possess the bodies of the living. Fascinating! As a woman, the sirens had never bothered her and very few people knew about them. Advertising their existence wouldn't exactly help with the tourist trade, so everyone who was in the know kept their mouths firmly shut. And if the occasional person was lost to the sea during a storm, everyone put it down to the dangers of rough waters. No sirens to see here – move along. Just another mystery of the Bermuda Triangle.

Josephine was especially interested when Jack talked about the porpoise necklace.

"I would love to see it sometime," she said with the covetous interest of the connoisseur.

"Of course," said Jack.

"But how did you come by it? You don't find powerful objects like that in tourist stores."

"No, it came to me from my mother's side – the Hicks family. They have long ties to Bermuda."

"Oho!" Josephine exclaimed with a joyous look on her face, "In my circles your family is famous!"

"Really?"

"Sure! The Hicks women were blessed with the Power. Some say that if it hadn't of been for Goody Hicks, the whole colony would'a been lost in the sixteen fifties. Wow! I gotta see me that necklace! But first, you gotta banish some sirens back to the sea. And that ain't easy!" said Josephine as she stared seriously into the middle distance.

"Can't I kill them? I read something about how you can kill them using a bronze dagger and the blood of one of their victims," said Jack.

"That don't kill them. They're immortal. Only another immortal can totally destroy them. No, the best you can hope for is to force them back into the sea. If the blood is fresh and the spell is strong, then you could banish them for maybe a century. Long enough to really anger them, but allow you to die in peace before they can wreak their vengeance. The problem is getting the blood," Josephine looked downcast. That was the key. Without it, nothing could be done.

"Is a pint enough?" asked Jack hopefully.

"A pint! Yes, that would be enough to perform all manner of spells, but how are you going to get it to Bermuda?"

"It's already there."

Now Josephine really sat up and took notice.

"Where?" she demanded.

"Do you know the George the Second medical centre, 53 Point Finger Road?"

"Yes. If you live here long enough, you get to know pretty much everywhere. It's over in the parish that bears my name."

Jack thought for a moment and said,

"I can call them today and tell them that you're coming to collect it. If you're interested. Obviously, I'll pay you for your time and expertise."

"Thank you kindly," said Josephine, smiling. Although she was happy to pit her skills against the sirens, getting paid for it would be even better.

"So, you're in?" asked Jack.

"I am indeed. And from the sounds of it, you're gonna need all the help you can get."

"My sisters are only the half of it. Each of them has a security team that's under their spell and those men are killers. Once they know I'm in Bermuda, it'll be very difficult to hide from them."

"Don't you worry," Josephine replied with a smile, "With a pint of fresh blood, there are a number of protective spells I can perform to disrupt their enchantments. Where will you be staying?"

"Cliff House. It's on The Drive in Warwick."

"I'll need to be able to get in there, too."

"No problem. I can phone the housekeeper and tell her you're coming to collect the keys."

"Good. So, when are you coming?"

"As soon as I can, but it's already after six here in Italy, so I doubt I'll make the last flight to London today. If I can catch an early flight tomorrow and pick up a connecting flight, I might just get to you by early evening tomorrow. How would that work for you?"

"I'd have to get moving, but I can get everything ready by tomorrow evening."

"Where are you going to find a bronze dagger?" Jack asked, surprised by her confidence.

"I'm a witch with lots of good connections on an island with a strong community of witches. You'd be amazed what I can lay hands on."

"Wow... okay. Now, the other problem is that they seem to know exactly where I'm going. They followed me to Italy and the only person who knew was my wife – do sirens have E.S.P.?"

"Not to my knowledge."

"Well, either way, they seem to know where I'm going. I don't want to put you in any danger, so how can we do all this without meeting in person?"

"It's all right. I don't need to see you," Josephine replied – she was enjoying this, "I simply need access to the house. I can lay protections on it, so that when you enter it, you'll be totally safe from the sirens and anyone they've bewitched."

"Seriously?" Jack didn't sound convinced.

"Like I say, a whole pint of blood goes a very long way. I can make some mighty powerful spells with that. They won't know what hit 'em. But..."

Yes, there would be a 'but', thought Jack.

"When you get to Bermuda, you go straight to the house and get in quick. Until you're there, you're vulnerable," said Josephine and her tone left Jack with no doubts about the level of danger he was in.

"Now here's another complication," Josephine said, "It's much easier to banish them if you're close to where they came from..."

"That's okay, I know the exact spot."

"That's not the complicated bit,"

"Oh," said Jack, who now felt a bit stupid.

"What's complicated is that the closer they are to their lair, the more powerful they become. You've gotta remember that they're spirits of the sea and they can control the creatures of the sea and even the sea itself. So, when you face off against them, it will be when they are at their most powerful. What sort of a man are you?"

"I... um, I don't know what you mean," said Jack in confusion.

"Are you a ninety-pound weakling, fat, unfit, ripped, strong – what?"

"Oh, I see... I'm about six feet tall and weigh two-twenty. I'm fit and I wrestle as one of my sports."

"That's good. You'll need all that. What you're facing is an ancient evil more powerful than you can imagine. They ain't gonna go quietly and they're gonna do anything and everything to keep the bodies they've stolen. They're gonna play dirty and you gotta be willing to get right into the gutter with 'em."

"Don't worry. I've got a few tricks up my sleeve."

"Good! Then we are ready to go. You call the medical centre and tell 'em I'm coming for the blood, then I'll get to work," Josephine said briskly.

"There is one thing we haven't discussed," said Jack tentatively, "How much?"

"Yes, good question. I'll charge for my time and I'll need to cover the cost of the bronze daggers..."

"Daggers?" Jack repeated.

"Yes, you'll be wanting more than one. What if you banish one of the sirens but lose the dagger in the struggle? You don't want the other siren running around the place, now do you?"

"Fair enough."

"I'd say I need five thousand dollars in my bank account as soon as possible. And if everything goes according to plan, then I leave any discretionary payments to your good judgement after the fact," said Josephine with a smile in her voice.

"Sounds good to me. What are your bank details?"

Chapter Thirty-Three

The Zurich Sanction

Aristide Favre knew, as he drove like the devil towards Zurich, that he had big shoes to fill. Gianfranco Cacciatori had been a legend – tough, popular with the other men and the only one who had been able to satisfy the mistress for more than six hours. And yet, by tomorrow, he would be nothing more than dogshit to be bagged and binned. The mistress was harsh and part of Aristide was terrified. This was good. That terror would keep him focussed and ensure that the next time he saw the mistress, she would reward him with pleasure. Ah, and the pleasure she gave was indescribable! Aristide's desire for more of that would also drive him to succeed. After today, *he* would be the one riding in the Ferrari alongside her. *He* would be first in line to serve her sexual needs. All he had to do was complete one task...

"Think of it as a test," Veronica had said as they had lain in her bed together after two strenuous hours of lovemaking,

"Pass, and you will have everything you want – money, cars, houses... this..." and she had thrown off the sheet to reveal her luscious curves, which she indicated with a movement of her hand like a salesman presenting a Rolls Royce to a prospective customer.

"Fail, and..." Veronica stared at him and her eyes were venomous,

"Don't fail. You won't enjoy it."

"Command me," Aristide had said and she had smiled at his choice of words, yes she could work with this one – that was just the attitude she liked,

"Follow Jack Kidd. Interrogate him. Find out who else is on the list my father gave him, then kill him."

"I shall do it."

"Good. I'm sick of that little shit ruining things," and then Aristide had witnessed the terrible side of the mistress as her anger bristled and her eyes flashed with murder,

"And I know that Rosalind has a plan, but she doesn't control me," and her voice had risen like the wind across a raging sea,

"No one controls me! I am beyond Nature. I am the spirit of the sea. I break ships, I destroy the flimsy harbours that men build, I rise up and ravage the land, I swallow rocks and eat cliffs until they collapse. I am the roaring waves, I am the black deeps, I am irresistible!"

And then she had turned her furious eyes to Aristide, who was filled with a mixture of fear and desire for her power.

"Do-not-fail."

The resolute set of Aristide's face as he drove along the shore of the Zurichsee proved that he had no intention of failing. Of Veronica's guards, he was the least pretty. His heavy, almost Neanderthal, brow gave onto a wide face, which had been battered by ten years of rugby, but his dimpled chin and deep brown eyes softened his features and that had been enough to get him on the team. He was now, after the passing of Gianfranco, the cleverest of Veronica's men and he was calculating how best to do the job. As he saw it, he had two advantages: one, his victim didn't know he was coming; and two, the Glock-17 holstered under his jacket. Coupled with the suppressor in the glove compartment, that would be enough to get all the information he needed, then finish the man off quietly. To avoid unfortunate problems at the border, he'd travelled 'clean' from Italy and picked up the firearm from a contact in Switzerland on the way. All very clean, all very simple and no way of tracing the gun. Best of all, the tracker still seemed to be working and his target had now been stopped near Zurich airport for an hour. It looked like he'd gone to a hotel for the night. That would work.

Half an hour later, Aristide wobbled into the foyer of the plush hotel looking every inch like a wealthy businessman who's had far too much wine on his expense account. He weaved his way up to the front desk where a young, bright-eyed man was on duty.

"Sssprechen sie Englisch?" Aristide slurred in his best impression of a drunk Englishman mangling German.

"Yes, sir, how can I be of help?" the young man replied.

"Ah, good, thank you. Um... I've been a bit shilly," Aristide bumbled, "I'm shtaying in thish hotel and I've forgotten my room number."

"Not a problem, sir, that happens more often than you'd imagine," the young man smiled,

"What is your name?"

"J. Kidd – with two d's," and Aristide gestured with two fingers.

"Yes, thank you Mister Kidd, you are in room 307. Take the elevator to the third floor and it's along on the right."

"Thanksh, mate!" Aristide said loudly and he could almost feel the young man cringe. Then, apparently taking infinite pains to walk upright and in a straight line, Aristide made his way to the elevator and pressed the call button. He turned and winked at the young man when the elevator arrived, got in and waved. The young man waved back embarrassedly as the elevator doors closed.

Aristide shook off the fake drunkenness and put his game face on. It didn't matter that the receptionist had seen him. By the time they found the body, he'd be out of the country and long gone. He turned away from the camera in the ceiling of the elevator and carefully took out his Glock, screwed on the suppressor and pulled back the slider to cock it. He held it under his jacket as the elevator doors opened and he stepped out into the heavily carpeted corridor. It was almost midnight and silent as he moved quickly and quietly to room 307. He checked around – no one – then took out something that looked like a credit card attached to a small electronic device. He put the card into the electronic lock of the door and after a brief delay, it clicked. There was nothing he could do about the noise, so from here on in, speed would be his friend. He opened the door and was swiftly through and moving down the six feet of narrow space between a wall on his left and a floor to ceiling wardrobe on his right before the bedroom opened out. He held his gun with the double-handed grip so beloved of cop shows, his nimble feet moving fast. In the dim light he could see the end of the bed. It looked empty and the sheets were thrown back. A shaft of light, presumably from the bathroom over in the far corner of the room, cut across the bed from the left and he could hear the sound of a shower running. Good, that would make things easier. Naked people were always more compliant. Just as he got to the point where the room widened, his left foot tangled in something and his momentum sent him sprawling forward. With his two hands holding the gun ahead of him, he wasn't able to save himself and he face planted with his arms outstretched. Before he knew what has happening, all the breath was knocked out of him with a pained grunt as someone big landed on him with a knee either side of his spine. The dull cracking and starburst of pain in his chest registered as broken ribs, but worse than that, the impact had forced the gun from his hand and it was now a couple of inches out of reach. A powerful arm was around his neck in an instant and the well-practised choke hold stopped him from getting any breath back in. He scrabbled for the gun, but the big man pulled him back and away. Aristide tried to get a hand back to claw at the eyes, but couldn't reach anything but shoulder. His lungs were screaming and his head was pounding as he tried to buck the other man off, but it only allowed the man to pull him over backwards and lock his legs around his torso. Finally, desperate panic took him as every cell in his body starved of oxygen and then he felt himself falling to oblivion.

When the man went limp, Jack wasn't sure what to do. Keep the pressure and finish the job, or let him live? But what if he was faking? No. This guy was out. He could feel it. Although he had decided he would happily kill any of Veronica's men that got in his way, this would be wrong. He released his grip and scrambled over to the gun, which he trained on the man. Jack stood there panting from fear and exertion and tried to bring calm to his breathing. Fright sweat had soaked his armpits and his head was already wet with it. His legs were feeling horribly wonky and as he looked down at his hand holding the gun, it felt like he was seeing through someone else's eyes. It didn't seem connected to him. Christ! This feeling was horrible! He felt sick to his stomach. Fighting for your life was nothing like wrestling down at the gym. That only trained your muscles and reflexes. It couldn't train you for this sickening feeling. Then, as his breathing came under his control, he felt anger rising again. What the hell was wrong with these people that they should be willing to kill the innocent? And for what? What could Veronica and Rosalind possibly give them that would be worth that? He checked the gun – cocked with a round in the chamber and the safety off. Jack then levelled the gun at the man's torso. It would be so easy to finish him... but no. The rational side of his brain was running through the scenarios of the body being discovered by the cleaners and his being picked up on suspicion of murder on landing in London. And there was another voice inside him, telling him that none of this was the other man's fault, that he'd been bewitched just like Jack's father, that under the spell of these devils, he had no choice in what he did. Jack relaxed his aim.

Okay, so the bloke was unconscious and disarmed. Now came the tricky bit – safely restraining him. Jack went to the bed where he'd left the belt of the complementary bathrobe and approached the man, keeping the gun trained on his torso. He put the gun to his head and heaved him over so he was face down, then quickly moved down to his feet. He placed the gun on the floor and tied the man's ankles together tightly with the towelling belt, then picked the gun back up and went to the head. With the gun held to the man's temple, Jack patted the man down, found a knife in his waistband and his phone in his jacket pocket, then he got away fast and sat on the edge of the bed panting and watching.

The restraint was naive at best, but between that and the gun, it should give him all the advantage he needed. Jack heaved a sigh and sat in the gloom with only the running shower breaking the silence. He ought to turn it off. It had been running constantly for over an hour as he had waited in the wardrobe and he felt guilty about the waste of water. But it had been worth it. The man had been concentrating on the thought of Jack being in the shower, rather than looking for the tripwire in the semi-darkness. Well, maybe 'tripwire' was a bit grand. It was half a dozen of the metal clothes hangers from the wardrobe, straightened out and twisted together, then fastened to the radiator pipe at one end and the leg of the inbuilt desk 'for the executive' at the other. Once he'd set it all up, Jack had drunk two cans of Red Bull and waited, wide awake in the wardrobe with enough of a crack open at the end of the sliding door so that he could see the tripwire. When the man had entered the room, Jack was sure that he would be able to hear the drum solo his heart was thrashing out in his chest. And then, thankfully, the man had moved quickly past him and the tripwire did the rest. The moment the man had started to fall, Jack had wrenched back the wardrobe door and leapt, knees first, onto his back.

He watched the unconscious man and listened to the shower. Between the Red Bull and the sound of running water, he was starting to need to pee. No, he had to switch off the shower even though leaving his vantage point over the man might be a risk. He walked backwards across the room to the bathroom, keeping the gun trained on the prone man. Fortunately, the shower cubicle was right by the bathroom door, so he was able to reach inside to turn off the water without losing sight of the man. That was better. Jack went back to the bed and sat down with the handle of the gun resting on his knee and the uncompromising, black eye of the suppressor watching the man on the floor. Jack looked him over and wondered what it would be like when he came to. A shiver ran down his spine. He hated this nightmare he'd been dragged into. He had to be sure he could get to Bermuda safely without another one of these goons coming out of the woodwork. He needed to know how they were tracking him. But if he wouldn't talk, what then? Torture it out of him? Did Jack have the stomach for that? The lives of his family were at stake. He would do whatever needed to be done. But what would that be? The man looked tough. It would take more than a simple roughing up to get him to talk. He could kneecap him. Maybe that would work? How much noise would the gun make even with the suppressor? As part of his road to becoming an American, Jack had taken some shooting lessons and was familiar with the racket even small pistols could make in an enclosed space. Could he get away with firing the Glock without hotel security descending on him? As his conscious mind, his slow thinking brain, turned the problem over and over, another part of his mind started tugging at him. Excuse me, sorry to bother you... excuse me, there's something you need to see... Excuse me – you do realise he's awake, don't you?

Yes, almost imperceptibly, a change had come over the man lying face down on the floor, a rigidity, a sense that the body was consciously being held to look unconscious.

"Are you all right?" Jack asked and immediately regretted it. What a stupid question! Now any fear that his assailant might have had, would have dissipated. Mean people who torture others are probably never polite.

"I know you're awake, so you'd may as well sit up. Although I ought to warn you that I have your gun aimed at the middle of your spine and I'm a pretty good shot. Any sudden moves and I will shoot."

What was all this polite blather? Come on, Jack, play the tough guy! Was it any wonder this prattling was getting no reaction?

"Okay, fine," he said, trying to sound rougher, "Stay there like that, but know this – between keeping you alive and protecting my family, my family always wins. I won't hesitate to kill you."

Still no reaction. Bloody hell! Now what? Jack allowed the minutes to pass. He was comfortable lounging on the bed. The bloke on the floor would be far less comfy. That was certainly in his favour, although there was a joker in the pack – Red Bull. Those two cans were being vigorously dealt with by his kidneys and now, with every passing minute, the need to take a leak was getting stronger and more insistent.

Here was a dilemma. On the one hand, he knew that the man was awake and waiting for any moment of weakness to make his move, and on the other hand, Jack didn't want to piss himself. Plus, the longer he left it and the more desperate he got, the more likely he was to make a mistake. He wondered whether this ever happened to other would-be torturers. It was ridiculous. At least, on the bright side, he didn't need a dump, because that was a major event, not to be trifled with. He looked around and spotted the bin under the desk. It was lined with a plastic bag – that would do. It was unlikely he was ever going to come back to the hotel, so who cared? He carefully got up from the bed and walked backwards to the desk, ensuring the gun stayed pointed at the man. Without taking his eyes off him, he fished around with his left foot under the desk for the bin. Yes, there it was. He eased it out, then bent down and picked it up to take it closer to the man – all without breaking his gaze. He put it down carefully, slowly unzipped his fly with his left hand, which felt a bit weird, reached in for the old fella and finally let go.

The moment the first drops hit the inside of the bin, Aristide Favre flipped himself over with the ease of a man who did advanced calisthenics. His intention was to leap at the other man, but that intention disappeared the moment he looked up into the black hole that was the end of the suppressor. He pulled focus to the face of the man behind the gun and could see that there was no way he could try anything without getting shot. Aristide sat and tried not to look at the part of the view that involved the man's dick pissing into the hotel bin.

"Sorry you had to see that," said Jack with a couple of shakes before he put it away,

"And thanks for not trying anything while I was pissing, because I'd have shot you... a lot. Now," and Jack sat back on the bed, pointing the gun at the belly of the man who was now sitting up,

"We need to talk."

"Fuck you!" Aristide spat.

"I'm going to cut to the chase – how did you track me here?"

Aristide gave him a bored look.

"Please answer the question."

Aristide looked deeply unimpressed.

Jack sighed,

"Look, I don't want to torture you. I've never done it before. It'll be messy and needlessly unpleasant. But I will."

"Will you?"

"Yes,"

"You sound to me," said Aristide in his French-Italian accent, "Like a man trying to convince himself of what he's about to do. I don't fear that man. And if I don't fear him, I won't talk to him."

Annoyingly, Jack thought that it was a good point. He needed another tack.

"You know who I am? You know my sister?"

"Know her? I was fucking her four hours ago," but Aristide was disappointed when Jack gave no reaction to this.

"Good for you. So, you realise that she's not human and that you were being fucked by a demon of the sea? She'd kill you as soon as look at you."

And there it was, the faintest flicker in his eyes that there was truth in what he'd said.

"I suppose that last bloke who failed to capture me was told to do better next time and let off with a warning?"

Aristide's eyes were seeing the mutilated corpse of Gianfranco lying on the table in the big kitchen of the villa, while Ivan broke out the butcher's knives.

Again, Jack could see the flicker.

"Yeah, thought so. Tell me how you tracked me here, or I'll make sure you are very much alive when Veronica finds you."

"I'll take my chances," Aristide looked at Jack with hatred.

Jack realised that this was going nowhere and that, even with the gun, he was about as threatening as a soggy sponge cake. He needed to change tack... again. Then a thought flashed into his mind.

"How much is she paying you?"

"Plenty."

"I can double it. I came into millions last week. And, just as a sweetener, I can give you something right now," and his hand went to his neck. He pulled the porpoise necklace out of his shirt and eased it over his head,

"This is a solid jade porpoise made in the sixteen hundreds. It's worth twenty thousand pounds. Take a look," and he tossed the necklace over.

Aristide caught the necklace out of the air and it was like being plunged headfirst into a barrel of cold water. The sudden shock made him gasp and he had to prop himself up with one hand, while the other gripped the porpoise. Now he could see clearly and all the violence and debauchery of the last two years were revealed for the evil that they were. He saw the cowering family of the journalist Hans Muller as he and three other men had hanged him. He remembered the screams and sobbing of the wife and children as the journalist's legs had kicked out their last. The looks of terror on their faces as he, Aristide Favre, had turned his gun on them. On the seven-year-old girl with the gap in her front teeth and her golden hair in a frizz of curls. On the four-year-old boy with the face, red from crying and screaming for his papa. He relived the way the girl had been thrown backwards by the shot to the chest and how the wife had shielded her son with her body as he had fired round after round into her, then his pulling her aside to fire the last round into the boy's head, and his face blowing out to the side.

"What have I done?" he choked, looking up at Jack.

"I don't know," said Jack, who could see that the man was no longer under the spell,

"I don't want to know, either."

Now this man, this big bruiser, this killer who, moments earlier would have murdered him without a second thought, broke down into uncontrollable tears. Jack looked at him with pity. Was that what it had been like for his own father? Had he awoken from their spell to a flood of nightmarish memories, which had ultimately been too terrible for him to live with? Jack imagined what it must have been like for him to suddenly realise what he had been doing to his daughters, the two lights of his life. It would have been intolerable for any normal human being to cope with. The sheer weight of the horror would crush any loving father. And now Jack knew that his father's suicide proved that he had once been a good man, a good husband, a good father. For the first time he was filled with sorrow for his father. He caught his breath. He couldn't cry. Not here, not now in front of this stranger, who was going through his own torment.

Jack sat with the gun still aimed at the man as he wept for minute after minute, with the sobs finally subsiding. At last, Aristide mastered himself and looked to Jack,

"May I?" he indicated he wanted to get something out of his pocket. Jack nodded but stayed vigilant as Aristide pulled out a handkerchief and wiped his eyes, then blew his nose.

"Sorry," he said, "It's... I was... I couldn't..."

"I know. You've been bewitched. She has made you do things you never wanted to. Maybe things you would never dream of doing..." the man nodded, "But it's over now and I need information... what's your name?"

"Aristide."

"Okay, Aristide, I need information – can you help me?"

"Just ask. I will do anything to make up for the last two years," he said, but his voice broke as he realised that there was nothing he could do to atone for his actions, that the evil he had wrought could not be undone. He cried again, his great chest heaving in deep sobs. Again, he wiped away the tears and blew his nose.

"How did you find me?"

"There is a geo-locator in your suitcase. There is also one in your wife's."

"Okay, that's good. I was beginning to think my sisters could read my mind."

"Fuck – those things are your sisters!" Aristide said in astonishment. Now he understood what they were, this man's survival was almost miraculous.

"Yes. Growing up with them was really shit. What were your orders?"

"Find you, torture the names on your father's list out of you and then kill you."

Jack raised an eyebrow.

"The mistress... I mean that creature Veronica... decided on a change of plan. She was sick of being told what to do by Rosalind and she wanted you dead. She despises you."

"Well, the feeling is mutual. And Rosalind didn't know about this change of plan?"

"No."

"Just Veronica being reckless. Sounds about right. Vicious fucker!" then Jack turned his thoughts back to Aristide,

"So, they want to kill everyone on the list?"

Aristide nodded.

"It makes sense. Tie up all the loose ends. How did you get in here?"

Aristide motioned to his pocket,

"It's in here," he said and took out the device.

"Toss it over there, please."

Aristide threw the device over by the bedside table.

"Okay, I think our business here is done," said Jack briskly and, for a moment, Aristide thought he was about to be shot, then Jack added,

"I'm going to keep this," and he indicated the gun, "And your phone. Oh yes, is Veronica's number in this?"

"Yes."

"What's it under?"

"Mistress," just saying it out loud was a humiliation and reminded Aristide of the depths of shame to which he had fallen.

"And what's the code to access your phone?"

"Double zero, double zero, double zero. Yes, I know it's dumb," Aristide said in response to the look on Jack's face,

"But that's the code for all our phones. She insists on it so she can check up on us whenever she wants."

"Fair enough," said Jack as he entered the numbers. Yes, that worked. Now for the difficult goodbye.

"Can I have that back please?" he indicated the necklace with the barrel of the gun.

"But what if I go back to how I was?" Aristide looked distressed at the thought that he might lose his newly found freedom.

"No, once the spell is broken, you're out. Unless you meet her again," Jack said confidently, although he didn't know what would happen. All he knew was that he wanted the necklace back.

"Ok," and Aristide threw it back. Jack caught it and put it on.

"How do you feel?" he asked.

"Stupid," Aristide replied. Yes, the spell was still broken.

"Right, this is what we're going to do. I'm going to go to the far side of the bed. When I'm there, you can untie yourself and leave. If you try anything, I'll shoot you. Go out the door and get as far away from Veronica as you can. I'm going to keep this gun until I get on my plane. If I see you again, I'll kill you. Understand?"

"Yes."

"Well then," said Jack and he backed around the bed, keeping the gun on the man.

"Okay, go!"

Aristide easily got out of the towelling belt around his ankles – yes, naive at best – and stood up.

"Sorry," he said, then turned on his heel and walked quickly to the door, which closed heavily behind him. Jack stood with the gun aimed at the door for a full five minutes before going over and looking through the spyhole. The fish-eye view showed the corridor was empty. He breathed a sigh of relief and looked at his watch – a quarter past one. Only four and a half hours until he had to check in for his flight. There was no way he was going to risk sleeping. What if Veronica had sent a second man? He went to the mini-fridge and took out the last of his Red Bulls, opened it and necked it. In for a penny! This would keep him awake until he was on the plane to Bermuda and then he could sleep the sleep of the just. He walked over to the treacherous suitcase, opened it and took out a pair of underpants. He checked them over – no devices there. He would take those and the clothes he was wearing and leave the rest. If they could see that his locator wasn't moving, maybe that would give him some extra time.

After an hour lying on the bed watching the TV, Jack decided it was safe to un-cock the pistol and put the safety up. He set an alarm on his phone just in case he fell asleep, then lay back on the bed and was soon in a state halfway between waking and sleeping. He was fully aware of where he was and what was going on around him, but at the same time he felt disconnected and as if part of him was in another region altogether. He was drifting to other places outside the bounds of time and space. And then, out of nowhere, he was viewing a sort of cartoon landscape. Blocks of colour created an island with a figure standing on a hill. The figure had smeared edges as if they'd been drawn with charcoal and the artist had deliberately smudged their outline. A huge eye was looking down at the figure, but then turned its terrifying gaze on him! Jack woke with a start and damn near fell off the bed.

"Fuck!" he moaned, rubbing his hands over his face as if washing it. That dream was too vivid! It left him feeling sick inside, so he got up and went to the bathroom and drank some water. When he came back into the main room, he avoided the bed and instead perched on the chair. It was already half past three, so he only had about an hour before he'd leave. He busied himself with doing things. He took the gun and wiped it all over for fingerprints. Did that really work? He didn't know, but he did it anyway, then put the gun into the white plastic bag from the bathroom bin and took it back to the bed. He emptied the contents of the main bin into the loo and flushed it away, checked he had his passport and tickets, and washed his face in cold water. The time dragged until finally he could pick up the bag with the gun and go downstairs to check out. Twenty minutes later, he dropped the gun into one of the many public bins outside the airport and walked into the check-in zone feeling unburdened. Yes, there was a chance he might still have to face one of Veronica's thugs, but in the public space with its heavy security, he felt relatively safe.

By the time he landed at London City airport around nine-thirty, he had a clear plan in his mind. His connecting flight wasn't until four. As far as Veronica was concerned, he was still in Zurich, but just in case he'd been tailed, he wanted to get to the sanctuary of Heathrow airport as soon as possible and wait out the time there. He went straight from passport control to the cab rank,

"Heathrow, please," he said, bundling himself into the back. As they moved off, he breathed a sigh of relief. All this subterfuge and spy stuff was very stressful.

Naturally, the drive across London was slow and frighteningly expensive, but it was worth it to be able to get to Heathrow safely. Once he was in the terminal building with its security dogs and armed police, he felt able to unwind just a little. As always, Heathrow Terminal 5 was a bunfight, but at least he was unencumbered with luggage as he waded through the crowds. It was incredible to think that just three years earlier the place had been deserted because of the pandemic. How quickly people seemed to forget the fear of contagion. He still had a few hours to kill and the tiredness was starting to tell, but that was all right. He made his way to an oyster bar and had a square meal of champagne, caviar, smoked salmon and blinis. As he munched his way steadily through his outrageously priced lunch, he looked back on the day so far - God, what a crazy day! It was more like remembering a dream than actual events. He was particularly struck by the power of his necklace. Four hundred years old and it had dispelled Veronica's hold over that man in a flash. Goody Hicks must have been a woman of immense talent and power. For the first time, Jack felt that they might actually beat these devils. To see the witch's magic work close up like that had been incredible. It had been as if a switch had been flicked off in the man. It gave Jack great comfort to think that at that very moment, there was a witch casting spells for him in Bermuda. She would set a trap for the sirens that they would walk into blind. They had no idea who was on the list and, as far as he knew, no idea about the pint of his father's blood. All he had to do was lure them in. Oh yes, and kill them. There was that small detail. Jack's good mood lessened somewhat at the thought. He'd been lucky with the thug in the bedroom and even then he'd only made headway because of the necklace. When it came to a fight to the death with two immortal sea spirits, he'd need to be a lot more ruthless and more on the ball.

He desperately wanted another champagne to buoy his spirits, but that would be a mistake. Just in case there were people watching him and ready to pounce, he ought to keep his wits about him. He paid the bill – that certainly woke him up – and decided that the best thing to do was get some semblance of normality back into his life by window shopping. He enjoyed flaneuring around the high-end shops, watching the people as much as looking at the goods. At the whiskey shop, he allowed himself a wee dram of the Jura they were offering for free as a taster.

"What do you think, sir?" asked the middle-aged man behind the counter.

"Not bad," Jack replied, "Although I prefer the peatier Islay whiskies."

The assistant gave him a sour look as he realised that there'd be no sale. Jack decided to cheer him up,

"I'll tell you what, I'll take a bottle of the Lagavulin instead."

That did cheer the man up and he was smiling broadly as he took Jack's money and then waved him goodbye and a safe trip. It was nice to spread good cheer, but it would be even nicer to get rat arsed on Lagavulin to celebrate victory over the sirens.

And so, the afternoon passed easily but all the while, Jack knew there was something he had to do before he got on the plane. And it wasn't pleasant. He would have to call Veronica and make sure that she would come in person with Rosalind to Bermuda. He needed to leave it late enough that they couldn't get their thugs to the island before him. He waited until he was at the departure gate to make the call. He entered the pass code on Aristide's phone, then pressed 'Mistress' in the call list. Jack smiled – Veronica was arrogant and full of shit, and that would be her downfall. The phone had barely rung once, when Veronica's voice came sharply through the earpiece,

"Where the fuck are you?" she demanded.

"And hello to you, dearest," said Jack, grinning broadly.

"You're not Aristide. Who is this? How did you get his phone?"

"It's your darling brother and I'll give you three guesses how I got the phone of the man you sent to kill me."

The shrill explosion of swearing from the other end of the line made Jack move the phone away from his ear. Finally, Veronica calmed down enough to scream,

"I'm going to find you and I'm going to fucking kill you, you little shit!"

"You've roundly failed to kill me twice, so forgive me for not being intimidated," Jack said smoothly.

Another – inevitable - stream of expletives and graphic descriptions of precisely how she would kill him. Veronica was, at least, wonderfully predictable.

"Listen..." Jack began, but he'd caught her mid-threat,

"...Open up your stomach and force feed you your own guts, you queer little gay boy!"

Jack shook his head pityingly at that old gibe. Veronica and Rosalind had always accused him of being gay – presumably because their charms never worked on him, though at the time he thought they were simply being mean and rather un-PC.

"I want to call a truce!" Jack said quickly, before she could start off on another threat,

"I'm willing to sign over the house in Bermuda to you and Rosalind tomorrow, if you give me your word that you will leave me and my family alone and let us live in peace a long way away from you."

"Really?" Veronica sounded sly, "Maybe we could agree to that."

Jack thought she'd be a terrible poker player. She couldn't have made her intention to break the bargain more obvious if she'd gone 'Mwa-ha-ha-ha-haaaa!' at the end of the sentence.

"Great, because that's all I want. To live in peace. The past is the past."

"But you must know about us?" said Veronica.

"That you are sirens? Yes. That's why I don't want to fight you. You're far more powerful than any mortal. I would only lose. So, if you want the house in Bermuda, you can have it."

"That is a very sensible move, Jasper," said Veronica and Jack could almost hear the evil smile that was on her face.

"I'll be in Bermuda tonight…"

"How? You're still in Zurich. You won't be able to get a flight…"

"No, my suitcase with the tracker is in Zurich. I'm in London."

"Sneaky little fucker! God, why didn't Rosalind let me drown you when we had the chance?"

"You'll have to take that up with her. Just come to the house tomorrow and I'll sign the deeds over to you. You then need to sign a couple of documents admitting to the murders of me and my family in the event of our untimely deaths."

"What? Why would we do that?"

Jack rolled his eyes – how could an immortal be this stupid?

"That's your half of the bargain. You get the house and I get a signed confession that goes into the vault of a law firm I'm yet to decide on, so that you aren't tempted to bump us off. Leave us alone and everything will be fine. Kill us and you'll be up to your ears in arrest warrants. Deal?"

Silence down the line. Presumably, Veronica was working out that all they needed to do was kill him the moment he'd signed the document and then pick off his wife and son at their leisure.

"All right, it's a deal. See you in Bermuda on Wednesday you shit eating little fuck."

"You know, when all this is over, I think I'm going to miss these family moments," Jack said sweetly.

"Fuck you!" Veronica screamed, then the line went dead.

Chapter Thirty-Four

The Chase Begins...

At three in the afternoon the previous day, and half a world away, Piet Van Wyck and Johnny Sands, another of Rosalind's 'security team' were sitting in a grey Ford Edge with a view of the front entrance of the Southampton hospital where Annie's mother and son were recovering. Unlike Veronica, Rosalind didn't require her men to be attractive. Just as well for Johnny. He looked frightening. There was no particular feature of his face that could be pointed at as ugly – his eyes weren't 'too close together', his nose was average, his jawline and cheekbones were in good proportion and he had no visible scars – but there was an intensity and a nervous tension in the face that made it impossible to predict what he might do next. This was coupled with an indefinable aura of violence in the way he held himself, something that signalled that smashing a cup or shooting a puppy in the face carried the same emotional weight for Johnny Sands. In his hometown of Oak Harbor, Ohio, he'd never fitted in, but when he'd joined the 82nd Airborne, everything had clicked into place. He'd done well – although his officers recognised that he would never progress far up the ranks. He'd enjoyed the life... right up until the humiliation of Afghanistan in 2021. After that he'd got out and gone private. Now, here he was looking across at the hospital. Was he thinking of nothing, or was he thinking about walking in with an M-15 and slaughtering everyone? Impossible to tell.

His phone rang and he answered,

"Sands," he said. His voice was mid-range and edgy.

"Slight change of plan," it was Rosalind.

"Yes?"

Johnny listened intently as she spoke. The call lasted less than thirty seconds.

"Well?" Piet asked.

"Don't make a move on the target. Let her go about her business but keep her on a short leash and await further instructions."

"I like those orders," Piet smiled. He'd seen Annie the previous day and had thought about what he'd enjoy doing to her, "I'd be very happy keeping her on a short leash," he added and Johnny gave an amused sniff, "Skinny little bitch. Probably fucks like a spider monkey."

This made Johnny laugh out loud, then he said,

"If we get orders to terminate them, you can find out how far she'd go to save her son."

"I bet she'd do anything," said Piet and he ran his tongue across his dry lips as various scenes of what he would do to the begging, desperate woman played on the big screen of his mind's eye. Meanwhile, Johnny wondered what it would be like to kill a toddler. All too easy, he guessed. Just pick it up by the feet and swing it into a wall to dash its brains out. No. A marble or granite worktop would be better – that way you'd have gravity working with you. Yes, white marble would be best. A big swing and aim to catch the side of the head against the edge. That would be spectacular.

After hours of no action, pissing into bottles and desultory conversation about their favoured weapons, Piet sat forward and tapped Johnny on the arm,

"Looks like they're on the move," he said as Annie, Nancy and Harry came out of the front doors of the hospital, accompanied by two burly looking women. A white Jeep Grand Cherokee swung around in front of them and they all got inside. It drove off and Johnny gave it some room before following at a good distance.

"Looks like they're going back to granny's house," Johnny said as they worked their way across town in the direction of Shinnecock Hills.

"I wonder what granny would do to save her daughter and grandson. She looks in pretty good shape," Piet mused and again the cinema screen in his head flickered into life.

"Necrophilia, Piet? That's just nasty!" Johnny muttered, shaking his head.

"It's only necrophilia when they're dead. Given the right lubrication and encouragement," by which he imagined brute force at the end of a gun or knife, "A woman of any age can give you their greatest hits. This one's on her second husband, he's younger than her – you're not telling me they sit and play cards every night. I bet she's got some tricks up her sleeve."

"Yeah, along with a handkerchief, boiled sweets and diabetes meds," Johnny laughed. Even when laughing he looked terrifying.

"Seriously, I remember one time in Mozambique, a grandmother came to save her grandson. My God, that woman was incredible. I learned some shit that night."

"You're sick and you need help! Get help!" Johnny was still grinning, "So, what happened?"

"Oh, you're interested now? Like to watch do you?"

"Fuck, no! But you've drawn me into your sick little story, so I wanna know how it ends."

"How do you think it ends?"

Johnny gave Piet a sideways glance before replying,

"I reckon you fucked her every which way from Tuesday, shot her, then shot her son."

"Close, but no cigar. Yes, I fucked her over and over, then throttled her while I fucked her one last time. I don't recommend it. Very messy."

Johnny made a grimace of distaste,

"And the grandson?"

"I killed him in the local style – took a machete and hacked him up."

Johnny gave a look that said, 'Respect'. He wondered if there might be the opportunity for him to pick up a machete to try that out later in the mission.

Sure enough, their targets pulled into granny's driveway and disappeared behind the trees. Johnny pulled up a couple of hundred yards down the road.

"Let's see what they're up to," said Piet, pulling out his phone and opening an app linking him to the security cameras they'd set up around the property during the night. It had been relatively straightforward because, even though the house was a crime scene, the police already had their man in jail. Piet got the feed up just in time to see the white Jeep come to a halt in front of the house.

"There, look!" he said as Nancy got out of the Jeep and walked towards the house,

"Still very do-able."

Johnny looked at Nancy as she walked gracefully up the steps to the house and shook his head,

"Not for me. Anyway, I'd've thought their security team would be more your types – strong, put up a good struggle."

Piet looked at the two women who'd got out of the Jeep with Annie and her family. They were looking hard all around them for would-be attackers. No, they were a bit too beefy for him. He preferred women he could totally dominate.

"Too manly," he replied. He was also disappointed to see that they seemed to know what they were doing. While one guarded their backs, the other went into the house first. The driver had stayed put and was keeping the Jeep running. Personally, he might've kept the clients in the vehicle until he'd checked the house over, but otherwise, the women looked professional and tough.

"You'd better tell them that if they want us to go in, we'll need more men. Four more should do it," Piet preferred to have the numbers in his favour. After a couple of minutes, the bodyguard came out and indicated that everything was clear. She and the family went in, while the other went on a perimeter search of the outside of the house. The driver turned off the engine but sat, vigilant, in the Jeep. And then they were waiting again. Piet put the phone into a holder on the dash so they could both watch, and killed time flipping between the three cameras around the house. From the one set up on the summerhouse in back, they could see into the kitchen and the bedrooms. The view wasn't detailed, but they could see figures. Now one of them was in the middle of the upstairs bedrooms. It looked like granny moving to and fro quickly and efficiently.

"They're packing," Piet said.

"I'll call it in," and Johnny made the call.

On entering the kitchen, Annie had instinctively gone to make a cup of tea, but pulled back. No, she wouldn't have any tea in that house until she'd personally thrown it all out and started from scratch. Harry ran in to find her and she was glad to see him so full of beans. It was as if nothing had happened.

"Hey, little man, what're ya up to?"

"Running!" Harry declared as he circled the table with a serious look on his face and then headed back to the door.

"Where're you running to?"

"Running!" and with that he was gone, leaving nothing but the sound of steps disappearing into the distance.

"Kids!" Annie smiled at Beth, who was standing looking out the back window.

"Cute," Beth replied neutrally. She couldn't stand rug rats herself, but could see how they might be fun for breeders. The thought of having kids literally made her queasy. She couldn't stand the idea of losing control of her body to some alien implanted in her. She'd worked and sweated long and hard to get her body just the way she liked it. Why would she throw all that away? And besides, kids were expensive, ungrateful and ruined your social life. No, they were fine so long as they were other people's.

The sound of approaching footsteps heralded the return of the Running Man, and once more Harry jogged in, went around the table and headed out again. Beth gave him a quizzical look.

"He goes out of here, across the hall, into the dining room, around the table and back," Annie explained, "Don't worry, he'll tire himself out in ten minutes."

Beth smiled thinly. Expensive and moronic with it. Why did anyone have them?

Annie paced to get rid of some of her own nervous energy. They were about to set her plan in motion and she wasn't nervous per se, but had that restless energy she got before a difficult climb.

"I'd better change," she said, "Do you mind keeping an eye on him?" she indicated Harry, who was back and circling the table – in the other direction for variety.

Beth forced happiness,

"Sure. You go right ahead," inside she was thinking this might be a long few days.

"Great," said Annie and she went up to the spare room, where some clothes had been laid out – from sneakers and socks right up to a big black puffer jacket and a New York Jets cap. All fine although, as she pulled on the light blue jeans, she wished they were a darker colour.

"How do I look?" Nancy asked from the door. Annie turned and looked at her, dressed in unflattering brown cords, a chunky brown jumper and, inexplicably, a Montreal Canadiens cap.

"You'll do for a day or two. Got your bags ready?"

"Yep. All ready to go," she tried to sound upbeat, but she was clearly tense.

"It'll be all right," Annie said, going over to her and giving her a hug,

"I promise. If I can get up and down Annapurna, this should be easy."

"Really?" Nancy looked into her face for reassurance.

"Yeah!" Annie smiled, "Annapurna's really dangerous. It used to have a thirty-two percent kill rate."

"What?" Nancy exclaimed and Annie immediately wished she'd kept her big mouth shut,

"You never told me that before you went!"

"I didn't want to worry you needlessly."

"A one in three kill rate is not needless worrying," Nancy said crossly.

"But I was fine. And this'll be fine, too," Annie soothed, running her hands up and down her mom's arms,

"Now, come on, if you're ready, let's get going. I wanna get to Newhaven by seven," she said, closing the subject and shooing her mom out of the room. Annie took one backwards glance – yes, she had everything. The time had come to take the plunge.

About forty-five minutes later, Piet and Johnny watched Annie emerge from the house carrying the kid in one hand and a black sports bag in the other. She went over to the big campervan, opened it up and strapped the kid into his seat.

"Looks like they're about to move," Piet said after activating his mic.

"Car two, copy that," a voice crackled through the earpieces Piet and Johnny were wearing. The voice belonged to Florian, a German mercenary who had, almost inevitably, spent a lot of time in Africa before discovering that working as security for the very rich was more fun and better paid.

"Car three, copy that," said a voice with a Southern drawl. That would be Brooks – a big, vicious ex-SWAT specialist from Birmingham, Alabama.

Back at the house, granny was coming out carrying a holdall. Soon she'd loaded it into the back of the camper and got in, followed by Beth, who got into the front seat next to Annie. The other bodyguard got back into the Jeep.

"Okay, so we have the granny, mother and kid with one bodyguard in the cream Storyteller Overland Beast, followed by a white Jeep with two more bodyguards. Assume they've all got handguns. The one in the camper has hers holstered on her hip. We'll take point."

Johnny started the engine. About three hundred yards down the road, a dark green Dodge Ram revved into life. About three hundred yards behind that, a black Chevrolet Impala gave a growl and the wheels turned, ready to move away. Half a minute later, the Beast and the Jeep pulled out of the driveway and headed for the Southampton bypass. They turned left and Johnny followed them at a reasonable distance. Soon they had cleared the Shinnecock canal, driving into the gathering gloom of another dull late February afternoon.

"How do you cope with this bloody climate?" Piet complained, "It's so cold and grey."

"Ya get used to it," Johnny replied.

"I couldn't. I'm glad She doesn't spend all her time over here."

"Just be glad that she and her new husband aren't going to live in Sweden. That'll give you a whole new definition of cold and dark."

"Come on, man, it can't be any worse than Switzerland."

"No, it is, believe me!" Johnny said, remembering the November he'd just spent in Karlstad, Sweden, while Rosalind had been sealing the deal with her prince. Cold, cold, and more cold, with a side order of dank.

"They grow grapes in Switzerland. You know what they grow in Sweden?"

"What?"

"Reindeer and herring."

Piet laughed.

"Anyway, she's always jetting off to Dubai, Singapore, Rio. Anywhere there's some action. Half the time you'll be sweating through your shirt before breakfast."

"Good, 'cos this grey, cold bullshit's getting me down," said Piet, who then settled back to keep an eye on their quarry. At least they had two big vehicles. It was hard to miss them.

Johnny was used to the weather. His old home in Ohio in winter was about as dull as you could get. He guessed that Piet wouldn't be able to make it through one of those without putting his Mossberg into his mouth and blowing the back of his head off. Folks from hot countries were weird. The Afghans had been totally nuts. Even the ones on their side had been flaky. No, Johnny preferred northerners. But Piet could be funny and maybe he'd change the longer he worked for Her. He knew *he* had changed. Before he'd met Her, his previous clients hadn't meant anything to him. Sure, he'd've taken a bullet for them, but purely out of professional duty. With Her it was different. He *needed* to protect Her and he would do anything in his power to do it. With other women, sex had only ever been functional. An occasional itch he'd needed to scratch, but when She had beckoned him into her room one night after he'd been working for her about a month, it had been incredible. New worlds had opened up for him. After that, She could have asked him to slit his own throat and he'd have done it without question. She was different to her sister. Johnny had talked to a couple of Veronica's guards and they'd said half their time was spent fucking her. Rosalind was much more controlled. She would only have one or two of her guards a week. That made it special. Made Her special. She was his goddess, the limit of his universe, and if she wanted the women and child in the campervan dead, then dead he would make them.

Behind the wheel of the Beast, Annie was driving sensibly.

"Anyone following us?"

"Hard to tell," Beth replied, looking at an iPad which was running a live feed from the camera they'd fitted to the back of the Beast earlier that day.

"Give it twenty minutes and we should know."

Annie wanted to put her foot down and get her mom and son as far away from danger as she could, but that wasn't part of the plan. She was going to lead anyone following them on a merry old trip to give Jack the time he'd require to do what needed to be done. The more of Rosalind and Veronica's men they could tie up, the better. Also, she felt pretty safe in the Beast, especially with her escort. She looked in her mirror and there was the white Jeep keeping pace behind them. Beth's phone rang,

"Yup?" a pause and Beth's face clouded, "Okay. See if you can spot any more," and she rang off.

"Well?" Annie asked tersely.

"We got company. A grey Ford SUV," Beth replied and she looked hard at the iPad, "Can't see 'em from here. They're good. Without Amy in the Jeep, we wouldn't know we were being followed."

"So, is this bad or good?" Nancy asked. She was worried but trying not to show it in front of Harry.

"Kinda both," said Beth, "It's not good to be followed, but it's good to know about it when it happens. Means we can be prepared."

For what? Nancy suddenly had a queasy feeling in her gut. This was real. The danger was real. They were being followed by people working for sirens who'd already tried to kill her daughter. She felt like her head was too small for all the thoughts and feelings swirling around inside it. She'd agreed to Annie's plan, but now they were doing it, she wasn't so sure. What if their pursuers decided to attack them? What could she do to protect her daughter and grandson? Being honest, very little. Wouldn't it be safer to get away? For Annie to put her foot to the floor and lose whoever was following them? She thought about Doctor Bob. Her lovely Doctor Bob, who wouldn't say boo to a goose. Somehow, they'd turned him into a murderous psycho. What were the men (and they were almost certainly men) following them like? She doubted they were originally Sunday School teachers. If they were tough before they started working for the sirens, how much more dangerous might they be now? Nancy shook her head and looked at the floor. God, what had they fallen into?

"Mom, stop it!" said Annie.

"Stop what?" Nancy asked.

"Worrying!"

"I wasn't..." Nancy began.

"I can almost hear you worrying," Annie interrupted, keeping her eyes on the road ahead.

"I... all right – yes, I was."

"There's no need," Beth interjected, "You leave all that to us. That's why we're here."

Despite the reassurance, Nancy couldn't help feeling the tension rise as they ate up the miles on the road. The evening thickened around them until it became dark. Now all they could see were the lights of other cars. It was as if the world beyond the road didn't exist. Between the darkness and the hypnotic lights on the highway, Harry started to nod. That was good. Nancy thought it would be better if he slept. They turned off the Expressway and onto the Cross Island Parkway, heading north with Queens on their left. Beth's phone burst into life. Nancy looked at her anxiously as she took the call,

"Yup?"

The person at the other end spoke, but Nancy couldn't tell whether the news was good or bad from Beth's expression.

"Ok. Keep checking. There may be more of them," and she rang off.

"That grey Ford kept heading straight when we turned off."

"We lost them?' Nancy asked brightly.

"Maybe," said Beth, "More likely they've got another car tailing us and they've switched out to make us feel like we're safe. That's what I'd do."

"Oh..." Nancy was less than reassured.

"We want them to follow us," said Annie.

"I know, it's just... it's not very nice being the bait," Nancy replied.

Annie looked over to Beth in the front and rolled her eyes. Beth smiled.

"I saw that, young lady!" Nancy said sternly.

"What?" asked Annie, trying to sound innocent.

"That look you gave Beth."

Annie knew she'd been caught and didn't argue it,

"I'm sorry. But you really don't need to fuss."

"I can't help it. I'm not used to this crap," Nancy said testily.

She looked out through the front window and found no cheer from the sight of the vast blackness of Little Neck Bay on their right. Soon they were on the slip road to Throgs Neck Bridge, then they would peel off towards Eastchester and New Rochelle. Nancy didn't like the way the lights on the bridge seemed to wash out the colours of everything and she was glad when they were off it. She wondered how Annie was staying so calm. Then she had a moment's revelation. She didn't really know what her daughter's life was like at all. Yes, Annie had told her stories of climbing mountains, but Nancy had no idea what it was really like. How dangerous it was. Now she understood. Annie had been living with the danger of sudden death for years. For her, it was an occupational hazard. What Nancy found unbearably tense was like another day at the office for her daughter. She looked at Annie's profile. She was magnificent! So focussed, so strong. Nancy felt pride spread through her. She felt so lucky that in spite of growing up with parents who were growing apart, Annie had created her own strong personality. Nancy couldn't take credit for it. She didn't believe in reflected glory. She was simply glad, especially now, that her daughter was such a badass. Whether they were being followed or not, she felt safer knowing Annie was at the wheel.

Johnny Sands picked up the pace as soon as he'd watched the Jeep and the camper van take the sliproad to the Cross Island Parkway. He and Piet would leave Florian to take point while they hurried along to the Clearview Expressway and took it up to the bridge. Then they would fall into third place in their little convoy until it finally came round to their turn to take point again. The traffic was typical for a Monday evening and they worked their way through, keeping in touch with Florian and Brooks in the other cars.

"Do you think we've thrown them off the scent?" Piet asked.

"Only if their protection team are amateurs," Johnny replied,

"But I reckon at night with three cars on 'em, it's gonna be hard for 'em to make all three of us."

"Pity the tracker is stationary in her apartment. That would've made this easier."

"Yeah, but there wouldn't be any fun in the chase," Johnny said, clearly relishing the situation.

"I don't believe the chase is better than the catch," Piet replied flatly.

Yeah, that sounded about right. Johnny was beginning to think that Piet wasn't much fun – a feeling confirmed when Piet filled another bottle with piss as they drove along. How much could one man piss?

"Sorry, mate," said Piet, "Too much coffee earlier."

"Could be worse. I was working with a former British Royal Marine last year – that guy was an animal! Do almost anything for a bet. I watched that dirty son of a bitch take a shit onto a piece of bread, fold it over and eat it."

"A shit sandwich?" even Piet was disgusted.

"A shit fuckin' sandwich. Crazy motherfucker ate it with a fuckin' smile on his face."

"Fuck!"

"Worst part was, four of us then had to get into a truck with this guy and drive for three hours.

"No way!"

"Oh yeah! Stank like shit every time he opened his mouth."

At this, Piet started laughing,

"How much did he win?" he asked.

"Ten bucks."

"Ten bucks! Nah, you're having me on, man."

"As God is my witness – ten bucks to eat a shit sandwich. So please, piss away. That don't bother me," and now Johnny laughed.

"Those Royal Marines are fucking nuts, eh?" Piet chuckled.

"Yup. But good in a firefight."

Soon they had re-joined the strung-out convoy, which was following the I95 towards Stamford. How far would they go tonight? Johnny hoped it wouldn't be too much more. He was tired of sitting in the car. He needed to move. He reckoned they wouldn't be able to go too far, because they were hampered by having a young kid with them. A young kid and an old lady. He was very glad he was on the offensive team for this play. He'd hate to have to defend a kid and an old person. They would always slow you down, complain, make noise and divert your attention from the job in hand. He might even have pitied the protection team, if he'd ever felt real pity in his life.

"Well, there goes Stamford," said Piet as they motored on past the various off ramps for the town and continued their drive into the night.

"I hope they're not going to Canada," said Johnny, "I hate Canada."

"Nah. What will they do with their pistols? They'll stay south of the border. Probably try to hide away up in Maine or Vermont."

"Great," said Johnny sarcastically, "Trees – that's all we fuckin' need!"

Less than an hour later, Brooks' voice came through their earpieces,

"Okay, look alive! They're coming off at exit forty-six. Repeat exit four-six."

"Copy that," Piet replied.

"Finally!" Johnny groaned.

"Turning right into Long Wharf Drive," Brooks said, then a pause,

"Coming back under the I-ninety-five... turning right into Sargent Drive..." another pause,

"Okay, they're pulling into the Mobil gas station. We'll keep eyes on 'em. Come off the ninety-five and await further instructions."

Piet and Florian both copied back, and in a few minutes, Johnny was pulling off the interstate and finding himself somewhere to wait.

"Looks like granny, followed by the daughter, who's carrying the kid. They're going to the restrooms," Brooks said.

"Lucky them!" said Piet, opening the door so he could empty his piss bottle on the road.

"Their guard has stayed in the camper van. One of the guards from the Jeep has followed the family to the restrooms," Brooks continued.

"I wonder which way they'll go – stay on the ninety-five and head for Boston, or take the ninety-one for Hartford?" Johnny thought out loud.

"Want to put some money on it?"

"Sure," said Johnny. This was more like it – a bit of action,

"Fifty says they're going for Boston," he declared.

"You're on!" said Piet.

They shook on it.

About ten minutes later, Brooks' voice crackled through the night again,

"They're coming back out. Granny's still wearing that Montreal Canadiens hat. Jesus, some people are born dumb. So, here we got granny, the mom and she's carrying the kid again. Security following them out. Okay, they're all back in their vehicles. Get ready to roll..."

Johnny started the car.

"Yeah, we're coming out of the Mobil station now, Heading back to the ninety-five."

"Ha! Told ya!" Johnny cried.

"That doesn't mean anything. You've got to get back on the ninety-five before you can take the ninety-one," said Piet calmly.

"Crap!" Johnny cursed and turned the car around to follow Brooks.

"Back on the ninety-five," said Brooks.

"Now we'll see," said Piet, "The junction's coming right up."

"Okay, they are heading for the ninety-one. Repeat nine-one," said Brooks firmly.

"You owe me fifty bucks," Piet said smugly.

"Yeah, yeah!" Johnny griped, "Jees! You can never trust women!"

"Hey, look on the bright side – at least losing this bet doesn't make the car stink of shit sandwiches."

Johnny had to laugh and the rest of the journey was spent in good humour. This was made even better when their quarry pulled into a motel outside Springfield about an hour later. Finally, they'd be able to get out of the car, get some sleep and a wash and be ready for whatever tomorrow might bring.

"They're at the Sleepy Pines motel on East Columbus Avenue. Take exit 4. You can't miss it," Brooks drawled, "We'll take first watch. Find somewhere good and get us a room, ya'll."

"Copy that," said Piet, "We'll take first relief. See you in three hours."

"Sounds good to me. Brooks out."

Chapter Thirty-Five

Monday On The Isle Of Devils

"So much to do, so little time!" Josephine Paget exclaimed as she put the phone down after her call with Jack Kidd. It was nearly midday.

"Please be in, Fred," she said, picking up the phone again and dialling the number of the man in Bermuda most likely to be able to help her. After fifteen rings, she was about to give up, but then,

"Hello, Josephine," said a man's voice with a trace of amusement.

"How did you know it was me, Fred?" had he divined it somehow?

"You're the only person I know who keeps on the line after ten rings."

Josephine laughed, but there was tension in it,

"Listen, Fred, I need something. Two things, in fact."

"What've you run out of? If you're wanting yew, I ain't got any," he said seriously. He could tell something was wrong.

"No, I got plenty. And I'm gonna need it, too. What I need from you are two bronze daggers. Sharp ones."

Josephine had expected silence after this request and silence there was.

"You in trouble?" Fred asked finally.

"Not me personally, but there's trouble coming. I can't explain it now, because I don't have much time. Can you help me?"

"Yes, of course. I can sharpen them up right now and have 'em ready for you within the hour," Fred replied. He wanted to know more, but knew

Josephine well enough that if she wasn't giving much away, there was a very good reason.

"You're a life saver, Fred. Truly a life saver. I'll see you in about an hour," Josephine was about to ring off, but then decided she had to warn him,

"Hey, listen, you wearing your turtle amulet?"

"No, wh…"

"Go put it on right now. I'll hold."

Fred didn't even reply. There was a pause of about a minute, then Fred's panting voice came back on the line,

"Sorry, it was upstairs by the bed."

"You got it on?" Josephine's voice was thin with tension.

"Yes," Fred replied, still regaining his breath.

"Good. We got sirens."

"We've always got sirens," Fred sounded relieved. Sirens, he could handle.

"Not like these. These ones have possessed humans."

"What? But that's impossible!"

"That's what I thought. But it's true. These two have been living it up in their human bodies for over twenty years and they're coming back in the next day or two. I think I've got it under control, but you need to tell Andy, Shamarh, Josh, Roston and Devon to wear their protections."

"I'll WhatsApp them. Do you want me to give them details?"

"No, the less they know, the safer they'll be."

"This is incredible!" Fred said in confusion, "How in hell did they possess humans?"

"I don't know, but you wanna hear something really crazy?"

"Yes!"

"They've possessed female descendants of Goody Hicks."

That stunned him into silence! Josephine could almost hear the cogs whirring in Fred's brain. Finally, he said,

"This is huge, Josy. You sure you can handle this on your own? Just say the word and the women in the coven will have your back."

"It's okay, I got help. There's a man – also a descendant of Goody – and he's got to do the deed. And get this… he *survived* growing up with 'em."

Fred made an inarticulate noise somewhere between shock and disbelief.

"And he's coming wearing a protection made by Goody's own hands."

Another inarticulate noise from down the phone.

"You alright, Fred? You ain't gone and pissed yourself?"

"Almost!" Fred replied, excitedly, "An artifact made by Goody Hicks! I want to see that!"

"Just wait your turn and if you're a good boy, I'll see what I can do," Josephine laughed. Fred did too, but then he became deadly serious,

"You just take care of yourself, Josy. You never know who or what else might be watching this little show of yours."

"Don't worry, I will. See you in an hour."

"Good luck!" and Fred hung up.

Josephine's face clouded as she put the phone down. Fred was an old, wise and insightful witch, and he was right. There were plenty of other beings to worry about in the waters off Bermuda. The kind that could drag ships under the waves, pluck a squadron of planes from the sky, or conjure phantom ships to lure the unwary to disaster. She would have to be very careful indeed. Maybe there was more at stake than just Jack Kidd's life? Maybe this was the start of something bigger? Josephine stood up, shook herself and breathed away her negative thoughts. She would go out, get the tools to do the job at hand, cast the strongest protection spells the island had ever seen and enable a man to prevail against evil.

"Just another Monday morning in paradise!" she said to herself and went out to the garage, pulled out her scooter and fired it up. It wasn't quite a broomstick, but it was by far and away the best form of transport for a Bermudian witch on a mission. It was still overcast, but the clouds were thinning. No rain in the foreseeable future. Okay, that was a bonus. Josephine hated biking in the rain. She pulled out of her drive, headed up the hill between high green hedges and turned left onto Somerset Road. As she puttered along, she wished that there was a way of keeping inland, away from the water, but Somerset Island narrowed before it came to the bridge over to the main island, so she had no choice but to skirt the shoreline. As she approached the end of Ely's Harbour, she kept one eye on the water. The scene was as picturesque as ever. Calm and blue, as if there was nothing out there that might be watching her, waiting for its chance to intercept her before she could start weaving her magick. She stayed tense all the way around the end of the harbour and didn't settle until she was halfway up the hill that climbed inland.

Now she had perfectly manicured gardens above the wall to her left and a scrubby semi-tropical chaos on her right, forming a barrier between her and the sea. Maybe she was worrying needlessly? How could anything out there know what she'd been doing that morning? The unknown forces of the deep were powerful, but they couldn't read minds or bug telephones. No, she should be safe until she began her spells. Then, her magick would be like a beacon for all spirits to see – angel and devil alike. They would all be able to see that she was working. Most would ignore her. Spirits usually had better things to do than fuss over a single witch casting a spell – unless they were weaving a conjuring spell. That usually got the attention of a lot of them. Usually pissed them off, too. Reminded them that even though they were immortal, that some mortals had the power to summon them against their will. And that included Lucifer himself. Not that she'd ever tried anything like that. She liked a quiet life and didn't fancy marking her card with a powerful spirit from beyond. But when she weaved her spells later, it would become clear that she was attempting to bind water spirits. And that would attract the attention of a lot of interested parties in the sea around the island. Once the spells were cast, she would have to watch her step.

Even though she had reasoned that she was safe for now, she couldn't help but shiver as she approached the Somerset Bridge. Again, the water looked calm and the bridge was barely a chain in length, but she couldn't help but hold her breath and gun her engine. She zipped over the bridge without a problem and up the hill where the road ran – as so many Bermudian roads do – between high walls topped with lush hedges. That made her feel safer, like she was being protected by the earth itself and hidden from the sight of the creatures of the sea. Of course, it didn't last and soon she was skirting the edge of Great Sound again. It had brightened and the sun peeking through the clouds glittered off the water. The light breeze carried the scents of the island - sea, succulent sub-tropical plants, pines, cedar and, less romantically, scooter exhaust. But that, too, was a smell of Bermuda. She put-putted her way back inland and was cocooned again by high, lush hedges until, about twenty minutes later she arrived at her first destination – Cliff House.

The entrance to the private beach development wasn't exactly grand. The surface of the five-car parking area was pockmarked and the road leading up from it to the stately looking houses on the hillside wasn't much better. There were no big gates to try to scale, as the entrance was open to the road and the far side of the little parking area had been left as a jungle – a cheap way of keeping people from being nosy. Josephine turned the scooter up the little private road and in half a minute was pulling up outside Cliff House, where a reception committee awaited her. Standing outside were what she presumed were the gardener and the housekeeper. They appeared to be a couple in their late sixties and for all Josephine could tell, they'd been standing outside the house waiting for her their whole lives.

"Josephine Paget?" asked the somewhat round woman with a smiling face as Josephine got off the scooter and approached them.

"Yes, I've come to..."

"They're right here," said the woman, handing her a set of keys,

"Mister Jasper said you have no time to waste, otherwise I'd invite you in for some tea. Maybe we can catch up later?"

"Thanks, that would be great," Josephine nodded as she took the keys.

"I'm Mary and this is my husband, Joe."

"Pleased to meet you," said Joe, leaning forward to shake Josephine's hand.

"You, too," said Josephine.

"If you need us for anything to do with the house, give us a call on this number," Mary said, handing over a piece of paper with a phone number on it.

"Thanks... Er, I guess I'd better go. Got a lot to do," Josephine said, backing towards the scooter. Mary and Joe waved to her as she got on and fired it up. Then, with a wave, she set off back down the little road. As Josephine looked in one of her mirrors, she could see the pair still standing there watching her go. Kinda odd couple. But at least Mister Kidd had been as good as his word and prepared the way for her. If this kept up, she might be able to get everything done in time.

Ten minutes later, she took a left turn into Point Finger Road. After about a hundred yards she pulled into the drive of the George the Second medical centre. It was a white, two storey house in the colonial style and she was able to park next to the front steps. She went into the neat reception area with its brilliant white walls and approached the female receptionist who was dressed in a white nurse's uniform and cap. Could she really be a nurse? Seemed like a waste of talent to have a qualified nurse on reception. It was probably some hokum on the company's part to give the impression of clinical professionalism from the moment people entered. The receptionist looked up with a smile and before Josephine could speak, she said,

"Josephine Paget?"

"Er... yes," Josephine was caught off guard.

"We've been expecting you. Come to pick up the package for Mister Kidd, I presume?"

"Yes, that's right."

"He told us to expect you within the hour," the receptionist smiled, then pressed an intercom button and said,

"Jimmy, could you please bring out Mister Kidd's package," then she smiled at Josephine again,

"If I could just check your ID?"

"Sure," Josephine replied and showed her driver's licence.

"Thanks. It won't be a minute."

They waited in a friendly silence for about thirty seconds. Josephine was impressed – this Jack Kidd was certainly efficient. That was good. It meant that he was taking the situation with the deadly seriousness it required.

A door behind the receptionist opened and a man in a white coat emerged carrying a sealed polystyrene box.

"Here you go, Lil," he said, handing the box to the receptionist and smiling at both women before disappearing back through the door.

"And here *you* go, Ms Paget," said the receptionist, handing the box across the desk.

"Is there anything to sign?"

"No, all the paperwork is in order. Mister Kidd impressed the urgent nature of your business to us."

"Thanks," said Josephine, relieved not to have to fill out endless forms.

"We hope that you and Mister Kidd have found our service satisfactory and look forward to working with you again," she said with the sing-song timbre of an oft-repeated phrase that's started to lose its meaning.

"Thank you, I'm sure we will," Josephine said, taking the box.

Then she was off again, with her precious cargo safely stowed in the travel box on the back of the scooter. Now to get over to Fred's, pick up the daggers and get home asap. Fortunately, Fred lived on her route home over in Hog Bay, so she wouldn't waste any more time. Hog Bay... that got Josephine thinking. There was something about Hog Bay she couldn't quite put her finger on and it drove her mad all the way to Fred's quirky little yellow house with its square turret above the front door. Josephine pulled up in the drive and took the polystyrene box with her to the door. She was just about to knock when Fred opened it. He was shorter than her, dark and very slim, with a nervous energy as if he'd drunk a pint of espresso,

"Josy! Come in, come in!" he cried and he ushered her into the house, the inside of which was not unlike Josephine's own. There was the smell of incense and an array of oddments on the shelves and walls. A deep red rug covered most of the dark wooden floor of the sitting room and he indicated for Josephine to sit on one of the two leather sofas. She did so and he sat down on the sofa opposite with a coffee table between them on which Josephine placed the box.

"So, what's in the box?" asked Fred.

Josephine hesitated. Should she tell him? What if it endangered him? But hadn't she already done that by dragging him into it? She couldn't very well make him risk his life without even knowing what was going on,

"A pint of blood from one of the sirens' victims. To be precise, from the father of the girls they've possessed."

Fred's old, deeply lined face set in wonder. He knew the significance of that.

"Wow!" he said, leaning forward with his elbows on his knees and his wrinkled hands held almost in prayer in front of his face,

"So, you're gonna send 'em back to the sea?"

"That's the plan. You got the daggers?"

"Oh yeah, yeah, right here..." and he leapt up, almost ran into the kitchen and came straight back out with a black cloth bundle. He laid it on the table and pulled the cloth aside to reveal the two daggers, the handles and blades of which were bronze.

"Oh yes, they're just the ticket," Josephine said, looking at them glint in the light, "They look good and sharp, too."

"They are," said Fred proudly, "One thing, though – one of them isn't a dagger. It's the removable tip of a spear. That won't be a problem will it?"

"Not at all... in fact," and a gleam came into her eye, "Do you have the shaft of the spear?"

"Yes."

"Can I have that, too?"

"No problem," and he was up again and almost bounding into the study, returning moments later with a six-foot spear shaft in his hand. One end was encased in bronze.

"See, you just take the dagger and click it into place," Fred demonstrated and Josephine noticed that there were two spring-loaded pins in the top of the spear that fixed into the dagger's hollow hilt.

"It's kinda fiddly to get it off again and you need a good grip, but..." and he grunted as he unclipped the dagger, "You've probably got a stronger grip than me, Josy, so it shouldn't give you much trouble."

"It's perfect!" she said in delight, "Can you drop it round to this address later?" and she took out a small pad and the nub of a pencil from her pocket and wrote the address of Jack's house on it,

"Just leave it by the front door and I'll text the housekeeper to take it inside."

"I'll bring it about five."

"Great," she said as Fred placed the dagger back on the cloth and wrapped it up, while she quickly texted Mary about the delivery.

Fred looked at her and he was excited as he said,

"I think I might know why the sirens were able to possess those girls."

"Spill," said Josephine, putting her phone away and leaning forward so they were close across the coffee table.

"I had a look in our secret history," he said, indicating a rough, leather-covered folder on the table,

"Says Goody Hicks was murdered – right around here in what's now Hog Bay Park,"

That was it! Josephine had known there was a connection to Hog Bay.

"But what's interesting for us," Fred continued, "Is she wasn't simply killed. She was eaten,"

Josephine's eyes widened.

"They found her skeleton picked clean and staked out on top of a pentagram drawn on the ground. The authorities at the time only identified her by her clothes and a couple of personal items that'd been left nearby. They assumed she was a witch and she'd tried a conjuring spell that had gone wrong and she'd been devoured by whatever demon she'd summoned."

Josephine snorted in derision at this – as if Goody would be so foolish!

"I know," Fred nodded, "They were idiots. But here's the thing – what if your sirens were the ones that killed and ate her? What if, by consuming her, they gained some of her power? They might not have realised it, because it took 'em about four hundred years to use this power, but it might explain how they were able to possess the bodies of those two girls."

"There's a lot of 'what ifs' there, Fred..." Josephine began,

"I know, I know," he admitted,

"But," she continued, "It does explain a lot. Sirens haven't done this before. If they had, we'd know. And it's too much of a coincidence that the only people they've ever possessed just happen to be Goody's descendants. But now, finally, Goody Hicks could have her revenge on them through their brother."

"He must have The Power," Fred smiled.

"What makes you say that?"

"You said he survived growing up with them?"

"Yeah."

"How did he manage that? Luck?"

Josephine shook her head – that was unlikely.

"And once he came to sexual maturity, they should've been able to bend him to their will," Fred declared, "Yet clearly they haven't. What kept him safe? I think he could be like John Middleton."

Josephine nodded,

"So, you think he's an unwitting witch, like John Middleton?"

"Exactly!" Fred cried, "I reckon he was born with The Power and has been using it to protect himself without even knowing it. And if he now has a resistance charm against the sirens made by Goody herself, then he could be more than a match for 'em. Are you going to meet him?"

"Not 'til after. He said he didn't want to put me in danger, which shows he has no knowledge of the Craft, because my spells will put me in plenty of danger," Josephine sighed,

"And, speaking of, I've gotta go. Gotta cleanse myself first and then I've got a lot of magick to perform."

Josephine got up and Fred followed suit. She took the daggers in their wrapping and her container of blood and put them into the travel box on the scooter. She turned to Fred and gave him a warm hug,

"Thanks, Fred."

"No problem," he replied as she enveloped him, "But I really wanna meet this guy when it's all over – see if my theory's right."

"Sure thing," she said, pulling on her helmet and starting up the scooter.

"Stay safe!" Fred shouted over the rattle of the motor and then Josephine pulled away.

Fred watched her up the hill until she disappeared over the crest. Brave woman! She knew the risks of what she was about to do. Well, whatever she said about not wanting to endanger anyone else, he felt the women of the coven needed to know something. He'd WhatsApp them, too, and tell them to send good, strong vibes to Josephine because she was doing something important - and that they should be ready to help if needed. He and the other men would have to make themselves scarce and sit this one out. They were too vulnerable to the sirens' powers. And if the sirens' natural powers were somehow mixed up with Goody Hicks' familial magickal abilities, who knew what the sirens might be capable of? Fred looked carefully to north, south, east and west – it all seemed very normal. The calm before the storm? He hurried into his house and bolted the door behind him.

Riding back home, Josephine suddenly felt vulnerable. She now had everything she needed to send the sirens back to the deeps and until she got home, she was an easy target. She wasn't expecting anything crazy, like a great wave coming out of nowhere to sweep her off the bridge as she crossed, but interested parties might be able to control the other people on the road. Maybe the driver of that fruit truck coming towards her down the narrow road with its high hedges? Or the taxi driver coming up behind her? All it would take would be a slight swerve or a dab on the gas instead of the brakes and either vehicle could take her out and her death could be put down to yet another accident on the island's infamous roads. Forget the Bermuda triangle – if you wanted to dice with disaster, you could simply get on a scooter and drive around the island a while. Sometimes riding around on an ordinary day gave her the collywobbles. She'd have moments, especially when riding with a high wall right by her elbow on a narrow road, when the image of her crashing would pop into her head. The hard stone tearing the flesh off her elbow as she scraped along the wall; the front wheel skittering first one way, then the other before she lost control and it turned sideways to send her hurtling over the handlebars; and then her smacking into the asphalt face-first in a bloody mess of shattered bones. She shuddered at the thought of it and made very sure she was riding as safely as she could, taking extra care about oncoming vehicles and anyone behind her.

She laughed in relief as she finally pulled up in front of her garage and she was off the scooter and opening up the door in a flash. Once the scooter was parked, the blood in its thick plastic bag safely stored in the fridge and the daggers on the living room table, she grabbed a faggot of sage and cedar. First, she would cleanse the house, then herself and only after that would she be able to start the real work. She breathed deeply to bring herself fully into the moment, then lit the faggot with a long match and methodically set to work. She slowly walked around each room, wafting the fragrant smoke so that it could break up any negative energies, gently allowing pure energy to flow freely throughout the house. That was the way. As she went, she repeated an incantation. She concentrated her mind on the power of every word and made each one the centre of her universe as she said it. She bound the world to each word as she spoke it, changing the reality of her home with the power of her words and the cleansing forces of sage and cedar.

When she finished, she started to run a bath. While it was running, she locked every door and window. She returned to the bath with a small bottle of myrrh oil, poured some in and stirred it, then stripped and got in. Josephine closed her eyes and cleared her mind, allowing the heady scent of the myrrh to take up all her conscious thought. Her tension dissipated, all her worries about the rituals ahead melted and she was left floating in the endless universe as her energies balanced. Calm, neutral, without ego, an indivisible aspect of the universal flow of energy with no beginning and no end. Space and time lost their meaning as she became one with the universal rhythm, one with everything.

Half an hour later, she emerged from her bedroom in nothing more than a loose white cotton robe and walked through to the kitchen, where she put a small iron cauldron onto the stove. She pulled a leather-bound book from the shelf and opened it to the page she needed, then fetched the daggers from the sitting room. Now she needed to gather her ingredients: saltpetre, rue, crushed seashells, ground yew, rosemary, crushed Bermuda coral, rowan, oleander and the bag of blood from the fridge. The rue and rosemary had been carefully harvested with her boline, a beautiful, curved copper knife, and she put them into the cauldron in which she had started heating some water. She quickly consulted the book and repeated the words written there, then added a whole, dried oleander flower, whose power was enhanced with more words read aloud from the book. Yes, she could feel the energy building now. It was as if she were standing atop a barren hill, holding a flaming torch and ready to light a beacon on a six-foot-high black marble column. Anyone in the great beyond would be able to see the flame in her hand, but as yet they would not be able to descry the object of her spell. Soon that would change. Yew went in next, followed by saltpetre, and the water fizzed as she spoke the words of power. Now the feeling in the house changed. The universe around was crushing it and the air had become denser, oppressive.

Josephine took a deep breath, her lungs having to work harder to draw the air in. Yes, this was where her strength and stamina would come in. The Oleander leaves floated on the surface of the bubbling mixture when she put them in and said the words as written in the book. Then she took the rowan stick and snapped it. In the heavy, still air it was a thunderclap and, as she threw the two halves into the cauldron and read the incantation, she knew that she had announced herself in no uncertain terms. Things would be watching her now and many of them would be malevolent. Now it was time to come clean and state her intent. She poured the crushed seashells in, speaking the words of the spell clearly in spite of the difficulty she now had in breathing. The watchers in the beyond would be able to see what creatures would be bound by the spell. Some would now be getting angry. The crushed Bermuda coral followed and Josephine was sweating as she gasped out the words. Now the world beyond could see the nature of the spell and the temporal location of its caster. She turned and walked with heavy limbs to the worksurface where the bag of blood lay. She picked it up – it felt like a fifty-pound weight in her hand! She struggled with it to the cauldron and held it above the heat, taking her sharp-tipped boline and puncturing a hole near the top. Now she poured some blood into the cauldron, slowly speaking the words of power, blinking sweat out of her eyes and struggling to hold the blood bag as her body wilted in the stifling, heavy air, thickening with every passing second as the universe crushed down onto the house.

Gasping, Josephine poured out half the blood and stopped. She carefully placed the bag upright into a glass jug and put it in the fridge, then put her boline onto the worktop. She took the two daggers and placed the blades into the potion, then turned the heat off under the cauldron. She shook her head. She was losing focus and the fringes of her vision were going grey. Come on! Dig deep! She forced herself to breathe and spoke the incantation slowly, lingering on each word to ensure their power suffused the blades with magick. As the last word left her lips, she staggered back and had to steady herself on the worktop. Now for the penultimate act. Her hand reached for the iron handbell next to the chopping board. She picked it up and then, with every last iota of strength, she rang the bell. In the kitchen, the bell – barely bigger than her fist – rang loud and clear. In the world beyond, it clanged like the crack of doom and the force of its peel reverberated through existence, sending a wave through the earth and the beyond.

At once, Josephine could feel a wind rising in the house and as she looked, the edges of things seemed to be blurred, as if the force of the wind was so strong it was blowing matter from the objects around her. She braced herself into the wind and could see the edges of her own arms and legs were blurry and smearing away with the swirling air. There was a great creaking and groaning from the wood in the house – it was struggling to contain the sudden flow of air. Suddenly, a small jar blew off a shelf, shattering the kitchen window. And now the house was a depressurising plane as everything was sucked towards the broken window. Cereal packets, bowls, house plants, ornaments, colourful cushions, a maelstrom of the material things she'd picked up in her lifetime swirled past her and out the window as she clung onto the cooker for dear life. The only things not affected were the cauldron, the daggers, the blood and the spell book. Then came a deep, terrifying crack and the whole house moved. Josephine looked around her in terror and realised that the walls and ceiling were starting to shift. Suddenly, with a final scream of tearing wood and metal, the entire house around her was ripped out of the ground and sucked into the void. All that was left was the cooker and the work surface with the items essential to the spell, and Josephine leaning with all her might against the howling wind.

But it wasn't only her house that was gone. All the houses were gone. All reality was gone. She was on the side of a hill, just as she had been when her house was there, but there was nothing around her but a golden yellow island, set in a pitch-black ocean under a blood red sky. She looked and saw that the shape and undulations of the yellow island around her were those of Bermuda, but she was the only living thing there. She stood, struggling to hold her own as more of her body was blurred and swept away by the screaming hurricane in the landscape of insanity. And then she looked up into the sky and the sight made her bladder release. There, instead of the sun, was a giant eye. It was a horribly human eye with a violet iris, looking all around, looking to find... and then it stopped and stared unblinking down at Josephine from the bloody sky. And now she could see the hate and the rage in the great eye. She had lit her beacon of magick and a terrible, malevolent spirit had come like a moth towards it. Josephine was starting to disappear. She could feel herself dispersing into the wind. She had one last thing to say. One last phrase of power to complete the spell. She tried to take a deep breath, but it was almost impossible. Why should it be so difficult to breathe when the wind was blowing so hard? She concentrated every ounce of her being into staring at the text on the page and, with the last of her strength, shouted the words into the wind. Then... darkness.

Chapter Thirty-Six

The Daughters Of Satan

Josephine Paget awoke with a start. She was lying, cold and aching on the kitchen floor. It was wet. She didn't need to think hard to know why. Her nose crinkled in disgust. She got unsteadily to her feet and looked around. It was just her same old kitchen in her same old house. Nothing had been blown away into an alternate reality, but it was now dark outside. Thankfully, it was a Bermudian darkness, sprinkled with the warm lights of cosy houses. She let out a sigh. Boy, that spell was a doozy! She looked at the clock – half past ten. She must've been out nearly four hours. She felt drained and needed food, but first she had to get out of her robe and mop the floor. Wait. Some instinct told her that she needed to get out as soon as possible. Get out of the house and over to Jack's place. Forget the food, forget the floor, just take what she needed and go! She knew to heed these feelings and she pulled off the robe where she stood and dropped it onto the wet floor. That would have to do. In a moment she was in the shower washing the lower half of her body and then she was towelling down as she went to the bedroom. Fortunately, she had another robe like the other and she got it on in a flash. It took her less than five minutes to gather everything she'd need for the other spells. Now she had to call a cab. She didn't trust herself on the roads at night on her scooter – at least not after an experience like the one she'd just had. She dialled the number,

"Hi, Cool Cabs," came a warm, friendly man's voice.

"Hi, I need a cab to pick me up from Bob's Valley Lane."

"Sure thing. What number?"

"Twenty-six B."

"Okay, we can be there in ten minutes."

"Thanks. Oh, yeah, do you have any female drivers? I'd prefer a female driver, please?"

"We got one tonight, but Donna's on a job right now. Can you wait?"

Josephine looked anxiously around her – could she?

"I guess."

"Okay, then Donna should be with you in half an hour," said the warm voice in a deep, relaxed tone.

"Thanks," said Josephine and her relief was palpable.

"But it'll take more than a lady taxi driver to save your sorry ass."

"What?"

The voice came back higher and nasty, with a rasping, metallic tone,

"We know where you are and we're coming for you, witch!"

Josephine stood, petrified.

"We'll cut off your head and gorge on your eyes!" came a chorus of rasping voices down the phone line, "We'll fist your ass and shit in your mouth, you dirty bitch. We'll drown you in your own blood and skullfuck your eye sockets!" the voices squealed.

"Shut up! You're not real. Shut up!" Josephine screamed.

"Hey, hey, calm down, lady," came the laid-back voice of the taxi dispatcher.

"What? I'm sorry... it's just..."

"No, I'm sorry. If you're gonna be abusive, we can't take your business. You have a safe evening," and he was gone.

"Shit!" Josephine said with venom.

Suddenly, all the tension came out and she started to sob uncontrollably. What had she done? Her spell had been powerful – with the blood of the sirens' victim, of course it had been – and now it had attracted the attention of... of what? Of evil. She suddenly realised that she'd been a fool to agree to Jack's request. She was hopelessly out of her depth and struggling against a rip tide that would deliver her into the hands of creatures of unimaginable power and savagery. They knew exactly where she was – anything from the great beyond that cared to look could see what she'd done – and they knew that the spell must have weakened her. They would come in numbers and quickly overwhelm her. Then her fate would be that of Goody Hicks – torn to pieces and a feast for malevolent demons. What could she do? What could she do? What could she...

The bang on the door made her leap straight up in the air like a startled cat. She instinctively backed away, clutching her amulet of protection. More banging on the door. Could she get out the back? She turned and cried out in horror at the twisted face leering in through the glass of the back door.

"Josy? Josy! You all right in there?" it was a woman's voice coming from the front door. Josephine turned and looked at the front door, then looked back at the rear door,

"Josy, let us in, we're here for you," said the woman standing at the back door, peering in through the glass.

"Patty?" Josephine gasped, recognising the face of one of her friends from the coven.

She rushed to the door and opened it, practically flinging herself into the arms of the big woman standing on the step,

"Patty, thank God! I think I went too far," and suddenly, she was sobbing again.

The person at the front hammered on the door again,

"Josy?"

"It's okay, Becca!" Patsy called and then she comforted Josephine, stroking her hair,

"It's all right, darling, we're here for you now. Everything's okay."

A moment later a small, spare woman with long, beaded hair appeared at the back door,

"Come on," said Becca, "We don't have time to lose. You know they're coming."

"I'll take her to the car, you get her things. Josy!" said Patty firmly, "Is everything you need right there?"

"What? Yes," she said, sniffing and wiping away tears, "Bring everything on the living room table," and then Patty was leading her around the side of the house to the waiting car where an older, white-haired woman named Denise was at the wheel with the engine running.

"Come on!" she urged through the open window as she revved the engine, "Shift your ass, or your ass is grass!"

Patty and Josephine bundled into the back of the car and slammed the door.

"Come on, come on!" Denise said impatiently as she looked to the skies with concern, "We don't want to get caught half-way there!"

Finally, after what seemed like an age, but was really only about thirty seconds, Becca appeared from the side of the house carrying a pile of stuff. Denise leaned across and opened the passenger door,

"Get in!" she snapped.

"Okay! This ain't easy, y'know – I've got the shortest arms," and then she was in.

"You sure you got everything?" Patty said sternly.

"Yes,"

"'Cos you'll be the one coming back here if you forgot something."

"I didn't!" said Becca with surety, "Let's go!"

"Finally!" Denise cried and she put her foot to the floor and the car pulled away with a screech of tyres.

She drove quickly up the hill and as they took the turn onto Somerset Road all the ladies were thrown across the car.

"All right, calm down, Denise. We wanna get there in one piece!" shouted Patty.

"Sorry," said Denise, "I'm over-excited," and she brought her speed down as she drove them towards the main island.

Josephine was awash with emotions ranging from relief to utter bewilderment,

"How come you're all here? I told Fred not to get you involved."

"He didn't," said Becca, turning in her seat to look back at Josephine, "You did."

"Me?"

"Yes," the other three all said at once.

"When?"

"'Bout four hours ago," said Denise, but keeping her eyes firmly fixed on the road ahead.

Josephine shook her head,

"I don't remember."

"You're lucky!" Patty cried, "I'm never gonna forget! There I was, minding my own business chopping peppers for the dinner, when Bam! Suddenly I'm in a waking dream and there's you and me and Becca and Denise all standing on this golden hill..."

"And we were all having bits of us blown away in the wind..." Becca interjected.

"Hey, who's telling this story?"

"Sorry,"

"Anyway, so there we were on the golden hill..."

"Don't forget the eye. Goddam eye! I swear I nearly had a heart attack!"

"Yes, and there was a horrifying eye looking down at us, and you told us what you'd done and that they'd soon be coming for you, and that there were things we had to do."

This was all incredible and Josephine started to giggle in tense joy.

"So, you told us to go to a house over in Warwick – great place, by the way – and that we had to combine our power to put a spell of protection on the place. And then to come and get you as soon as we'd finished. And then just as suddenly as it began, it was over and I was back in my kitchen."

"We dropped everything and did what you asked and now here we are," added Becca, beaming at Josephine.

"Yeah, here we are – the targets of God knows what from the spirit world," Denise smiled ironically.

"I'm sorry. I shouldn't'a got you involved, but that spell really took it outta me. If you hadn't come when you did..." Josephine didn't like to think about what might have happened.

"Hey, don't worry! We're sisters, right?" Patty said.

"Right!" chorused Becca and Denise.

"And we're not going to be pushed around by demons, devils or sirens, right?"

"Right!" they chorused again, though Denise quickly added,

"Yeah, but let's not shout about it too much before we get to safety. I'm too young to die."

The others all gave her a '*you're* too young to die?' look. They all knew she was over seventy, though they weren't sure how much over.

"Ah, you know what I mean," Denise chuntered, "While I'm still getting it regular, I'm too young to die."

"Goddam it, Denise! Now I've thought of you and Marlon doing it," Becca complained.

Even though Marlon was a good fifteen years younger than Denise, that still put him somewhere in his sixties. So, while Becca was happy for them to have as much sex as they liked, she just didn't want to imagine that many wrinkles writhing around. Becca was the youngest and prettiest of them, and was still of an age where people are less forgiving of those whose bodies have a lot of city miles on them.

"No one's gonna die tonight," said Patty vehemently, although had any of them been paying better attention, they'd have realised that the strength of her feeling on the matter clearly pointed to her own fear that one or more of them could very well die that night.

"That's the plan, anyways," Denise agreed, "Now, keep 'em peeled – we're about to go over the bridge."

They all fell silent for a moment and then Becca started muttering an incantation as they came down the hill to the bridge. The road ahead was clear and Denise was sorely tempted to put her foot down and get over it as quickly as possible, but a sudden,

"Don't go fast! That's what they'll hope you'll do," from Josephine stopped her. It saved their lives. Out of nowhere, a motorbike came hurtling across from the other side of the bridge in the middle of the road. It then roared harmlessly past them.

"But if I'd been speeding across the bridge..." Denise began, "He'd've either hit us right in front, or I'd've swerved to miss him and landed us all in the drink."

"Remember, they can use other people to get to us," Josephine said, and again all four of them were vigilant as they drove on through the dark.

The next fifteen minutes were tense, but there were no other scares and it was with infinite relief that Denise pulled the car up outside Cliff House.

"Gimme the keys," said Becca and a couple of moments later she was over at the door and opening it up,

"Okay, c'mon!" she called and Patty ran alongside Josephine like a Presidential bodyguard as they made a dash to the house. With the two of them safely inside, Becca ran back to the car to bring in all of Josephine's kit and Denise hobbled in after her.

"You okay?" asked Josephine.

"Yeah, fine. It's my goddam hip. There's this one position I do with Marlon that feels great at the time, but the payback's a bitch and driving makes it worse," said Denise, who smiled when she caught the look of horror on Becca's face. One day she'd learn.

"But we're here and we're safe!" exclaimed Patty, "In my book, that's a score for us," and she locked the front door.

As they stood in the large entrance hall, Josephine looked at the three of them and held out her arms,

"Come on, bring it in!" she said and the four of them hugged. Josephine's tears came again as she said,

"Thanks, girls. You saved my life tonight. I couldn'a done it without you."

"Anything to help," said Patty and they hugged each other even tighter. Now they could feel something. Yes, a warm feeling of collective strength rising up through them from the ground and passing one to another until the whole group was pulsing with energy.

"Now, food!" said Becca, as she broke the circle, "I've got Hoppin' John, boiled eggs and a big salad ready to go, c'mon" and she led the way into the spacious kitchen with its dark red tiled floor and natural wood surfaces.

Once the food was ready, they decided to stay in the cosy kitchen and just eat around the table. It was the sort of kitchen that you could imagine relaxing in to wile away cooler evenings playing cards. The Hoppin' John, a mixture of rice, black-eye peas, smoky bacon, onions, thyme, garlic and chorizo was delicious and fortifying.

"That sausage has some kick!" Patty said in appreciation, "Where'd you get it?"

"Over at Sammy's in Tucker's Town," Becca replied, "He gets it imported from southern Portugal, but it's what you do with it that makes the difference. I score it and then flame it in an assador with Black Seal before adding it to the rice."

It was that attention to detail that made Becca's love potions such a hit.

"I'm gonna have some more," said Josephine, helping herself from the pot on the stove. She was feeling much better already, but knew that she needed more sleep before trying to perform the special protective spells that would make the house and grounds impossible for the sirens or their thugs to enter.

"What now?" asked Denise.

"Josy's gonna sleep and we'll keep watch," said Patty.

"Are you sure you're okay with that?" Josephine asked looking sheepishly at her friends.

"Of course!" Becca cried, and the others all agreed.

"One for all and all for one!" said Denise.

"Whatever they try and throw at us, we'll give it back to them double!" Patty said firmly. Again, if the others had been more attuned, they'd have realised that her conviction was covering her concern that maybe they were outgunned.

"You're the best!" said Josephine, looking each of them in the eye in turn. She felt the love and the trust they all had for each-other and knew that she'd be safe with them.

Once they were done eating, Becca put some coffee on and Patty prepared the sofa for Josephine to sleep on. Even though the house had five perfectly good upstairs bedrooms, Patty was adamant that the living room would be the best place for Josephine to sleep,

"Out of sight means 'in danger' in my book," she said in response to Denise's question about why they weren't using one of the bedrooms.

"This way, if they want to get to her, they've got to literally come through us," Patty added.

"That's what worries me," Denise replied, but before Patty could argue the point – and boy, was she good at arguing – Denise continued,

"But I get it. This way they can't sneak in and get to her while we're down here thinking we're doing a good job."

"Exactly. Come on, Josy, you look beat," Patty said, leading a yawning Josephine to the nest of pillows and blankets on the big sofa.

"Okay, Becca will stay in here with you, Denise will be on roaming patrol through the house and I will be guarding the front. We'll swap round every three hours."

"Thanks," said Josephine as she snuggled into the pillows, then she remembered,

"Oh yeah, did any of you notice a spear shaft by the front door when you came?"

"Yeah, we brought it in. It's propped in the hall. Is it yours?"

"Fred lent it me. I'm gonna need it in the morning."

"Okay, well it's safe. Now, c'mon, get your head down," said Patty, lighting a couple of candles and turning off the main light, so Josephine would be able to sleep.

In the event, Patty could have turned on all the lights, played AC/DC through the stereo and marched around shouting, because Josephine was out within seconds of her head hitting the pillow. Patty went out quietly to have a quick conference in the hall with Denise and Becca.

"So, we're agreed that if any of us gets in trouble, we'll call the others?" Patty said.

Denise and Becca nodded.

"Hold hands," said Becca and the others did so without question, making a circle as they stood in the hall. They looked into each-other's eyes and could feel energy coursing between them. Yes, this was good. They were strong. They could do this. They didn't need words or an incantation. They were one. After a few minutes, they stepped apart. Denise drew her athame from a pocket and weighed the ceremonial knife in her hand.

"Be my strength," she said to it.

Patty had a small willow wood wand and took it from her bag by the door. Denise gave her a look.

"I've never got on with an athame. This is what I use for all my spells," she said.

"Good thing about the athame is, if you can't channel your magic through it, at least you can have their eye out with it," Denise smiled.

Then Becca went to her pile of things in the corner and opened a long, cloth covering to reveal a sword.

"I think I win," she said, holding the glinting blade up for the others to see.

"Size isn't everything," Patty observed sourly.

"I used to say that, too," said Denise, "Then I met Marlon..."

Patty laughed and shook her head,

"You're worse than a teenage boy! Now, let's go. We've got work to do."

As she went to join Josephine in the living room, Becca didn't even mind Denise's remark about Marlon – just the vague thought of those two getting it on had woken her up more effectively than a bucket of iced water.

It's not easy to stay focussed while keeping watch in the night. The mind naturally wanders and the deeper you get into the silent hours, the easier it is for sleep to steal away with you. The first shift until two-thirty went by without incident. The three women were still very much awake from the coffee and they were all used to late nights. After a quick conference in the kitchen over another cup of coffee, the three of them went to their new tasks – Patty in with Josephine, Becca on roaming patrol and Denise at the front. Again, there was little incident, but between three and four, the time began to drag and tiredness was setting in. Becca had climbed the wide, curving staircase, which opened into the upstairs hall, from which you could look down on the entrance hall below. To the left were three bedrooms and one bathroom and to the right were two bedrooms and two bathrooms. She had decided to go left down the well-lit hall and had just checked the two furthest bedrooms, when the carriage clock on the living room mantlepiece chimed four. It was a cheery, light sound and when the house was full, the sound of it barely carried upstairs, but on a still night like that, she could hear it clearly. She walked up the hall to the bathroom and third bedroom. She opened the bathroom door and switched on the light. All clear. Nothing to see here. Becca crossed the hall to the other bedroom. She flicked on the light and the empty room stared back at her. Yes, all fine. She turned off the light and was closing the door when she heard something. Instantly, her heartbeat leapt and her breath shortened. There was a skittering sound, like little claws on the hardwood floor – a mouse? A rat? She reached back in and flicked the switch. Was there a flash of movement behind the bed? Becca gulped and dashed quickly into the room around the foot of the bed. Nothing. She uncoiled from the pose she held with the sword, ready to swat anything in sight. She stood and listened to the silence which now seemed to weigh heavy on the house. There! Skittering behind the head of the bed, running away along the skirting board.

Becca ran round the bed. Nothing again. Where could it be? There seemed to be no place to hide in the room. It was about fifteen feet square and sparsely furnished with nothing more than a king size bed with plain pine bedside tables on either side, and a wooden clothes horse in the far corner. Most of the rest of the far wall was taken up with the window that looked out onto the drive. The wall opposite the bed was floor to ceiling fitted wardrobes, while the wall with the bedroom door was bare aside from a full-length mirror. It was a typical guest room - functional and without much character. But where a mouse or rat might hide in there, Becca couldn't imagine. Well, almost. There was one place. Under the bed. Becca didn't like this. She had visions of bending down to look, only to see a blur of hair and teeth as some enormous rat leapt at her face. What to do? She had to look, but she didn't want to commit herself. She stood as far from the bed as possible and, using the tip of the sword, gingerly lifted the low-hanging valance. Her mouth had dried out and her heart was beating wildly as she lifted and peered underneath the bed. Nothi...

Bang! The door of the room slammed behind her and she swivelled around in alarm. She was across to the door in an instant, turning the handle,

"Oh shit!" she swore as the handle turned but the door wouldn't budge.

This wasn't normal. It wasn't a windy night and the bedroom window was closed, so there was no through draught that could have caught the door. Becca banged on the door,

"Denise! Denise! They're here! They've locked me in the bedroom. Denise!"

Then her hair stood on end as she heard the clear sound of claws on wood from behind her. Big claws. Accompanied by the breathing of something large. She didn't want to think about what might be there, but she was damned if it was going to jump her without a fight. She turned, sword at the ready to fend off some huge, filthy rodent, but there was nothing to be seen. What the hell? She was sure she could hear it. She walked over to the bed and, using the flat of her sword, smacked all over the bedclothes, just in case there was something in there. Still nothing. She turned. And stopped.

She was opposite the mirror and although her reflection was normal, the room in the reflection was nothing like the one she was standing in. It was a dark dungeon with stone walls and flaming torches set into the walls for light, and there, looming up behind her reflection was a gigantic rat. It was sitting up on its haunches and baring a viciously sharp set of teeth. Becca turned. In her room there was nothing behind her. She turned back to the mirror. The dungeon and rat were still there, with her looking scared and confused. Then her reflection winked. Becca's breath caught in her throat.

"En garde!" her reflection cried and, before Becca could move, her reflection had leapt out of the mirror and was swinging at her with the sword. The clang of metal on metal in the bare room was harsh and Becca winced at the loudness of it. Her reflection – or whatever this creature was – swung again, trying to bring the sword down onto the top of her head. Becca parried just in time and the blade clanged off to the side. Fortunately, Becca had been practising various moves she'd seen on YouTube with the sword and she stepped neatly away from the bed and swung the sword at her reflection's midriff. Her reflection parried it and now they stood facing each other, blades up and ready to attack or defend.

"I'm going to stick you, witch!" shouted the reflection in a voice that seemed simultaneously speeded up and slowed down,

"I'm going to cut you open from your mouth to your cunt!"

The speed of its thrust almost skewered Becca and her parry deflected the blade so that it grazed her left shoulder in a burst of hot pain.

"Fuck you!" Becca screamed, as much as a reaction to the pain, but now her reflection, twisting her usually pretty face into pure hate, came at her with a combination of thrusts and blows. With her shoulder burning, Becca fended off the assault, but couldn't get in any hits of her own. Now her reflection went for a side swipe to take off her head. Becca stopped it and held off the blade, which slid down hers so that they were now locked at their cross guards and face to face, framed by the blades. She was staring into the face of evil and it was her own. She was full of fear and full of doubt as to her next move. She didn't know how to sword fight! Swishing about a bit to YouTube videos was great, but this was the real deal. And as these thoughts flashed through her mind, she could feel her reflection growing in strength, pushing her back. She tried to hold her ground, but the reflection was too strong as it slowly pushed her back towards the mirror. Becca felt her back foot butt up against the wall and she was enveloped in the dank smell of mould and damp and the unmistakeable musky odour of rat. Fuck! The reflection was trying to push her through into the mirror world. Becca panicked and tried to struggle, but she was being pushed back into the wall and could feel herself teetering toward the tipping point where she would fall back against the mirror.

Then she realised she'd been doing it all wrong. She'd been trying to fight as if the sword was just a sword. But it wasn't - it was the conduit for her power. And now, just as she felt her legs weakening and her shoulder about to touch the mirror, she concentrated every ounce of her spiritual strength and said,

"No darkness may enter this protected space. Unwanted spirit depart!"

And although her reflection laughed and snapped its teeth at her, Becca felt the power shift and her weight come away from the wall,

"No darkness may enter this protected space. Unwanted spirit depart!" she cried and she pushed the reflection a full step back, despite its fury. Becca breathed deeply, drawing up her power and focusing it into the sword as she screamed the words into the face of the creature,

"No darkness may enter this protected space. Unwanted spirit depart!"

The sound of her command crashed against the walls of the room, which seemed to expand like rubber to absorb the sudden release of power. At the same instant, Becca pushed her reflection backwards and slashed, cutting off the hand that held the sword. The reflection squealed in agony and clutched at the spurting stump of its wrist, but Becca gave it no time to regroup and stabbed and slashed at it. Her reflection swayed and dodged, but Becca had turned it around so that its back was to the mirror. The rat in the dungeon in the mirror was squealing angrily and preparing to leap through into the real world, when Becca, with a cry of fury, and focussing all her intent, thrust the sword deep into her reflection's solar plexus. Her reflection coughed a spray of blood. Becca gathered herself and gave the sword, still skewering the evil replica of her, an extra push, just as the rat made its leap forward at her. The tip of the sword pushed clean through and shattered the glass of the mirror. In an instant, the dungeon, giant rat and nightmare doppelgänger were sucked down into the centre of the mirror and disappeared into a vanishing point of nothingness as all the glass of the mirror cascaded to the floor.

At the same moment, the bedroom door flew open. Becca ran out into the hall. She knew that she wasn't the only one being attacked, that whatever evil was out there would be assaulting them all at once. Now she had beaten her demon, she could help the others. She was down the stairs in seconds and, as she bounded into the hall, she could see Denise at the entrance to the utility room, sitting astride Marlon and stabbing him repeatedly with her athame, screaming

"Die you motherfucking shit-eating demon!" as sprays of grey-green blood spurted out of Marlon's jerking body.

"Use your banishing spell!" Becca shouted, as she ran past and into the living room.

"Thanks!" Denise, called back and then, still stabbing away, she shouted,

"No darkness may enter this protected space. Unwanted spirit depart!"

As Becca skidded into the living room, the screams of the demon from the hall seemed muffled, as if she'd slipped into another, adjacent reality. It was still in the sitting room. Too still. Josy was asleep on the couch, but the rest of the room was empty.

"Patty?" Becca called, but it was as if she was shouting into a pillow. Her words couldn't carry. Then she saw that the door to the patio was open. Shit! Patty had gone outside! Why the hell? Becca went straight for the door and as she looked out, she immediately understood. Away, to the side of the patio stood a boy of about five. Becca recognised him as Patty's son, James. Patty herself was kneeling in front of him, weeping and saying how sorry she was.

"You should be sorry," said James with a tinge of metal in his young voice, "First you let me drown and now you won't even ask me in so I can warm myself."

"I'm sorry," Patty gasped, "So, so sorry. I only turned away for a minute and then you were gone."

"But will you let me in?" the boy insisted, and Becca could see the smile twisting on his lips as Patty bowed. She was about to do it, to say the words that would unmake the protections around the house. Becca sprinted forwards with barely a sound and, as Patty opened her mouth to speak, Becca brought the blade of the sword down with all her might across the head of the little boy. It made a sound like a machete cutting into a green coconut as the blade stuck deep in his skull. Patty froze, staring. Blood ran down the sides of the boy's cheeks. His eyes turned upwards as if trying to see what had happened. Becca stood with both hands firmly grasping the hilt,

"No darkness may enter this protected space. Unwanted spirit depart!" she bellowed.

"Fucking bitch! I'll tear the skin off your back!" the boy screamed, unable to turn his head to look at Becca standing to the side.

"Becca, what have you done?" Patty sobbed, "You've killed James…"

"That ain't James," shouted Denise, coming out of the house and joining them. She was covered in stinking gore and still brandishing her athame.

"It's one of *them*!" said Becca.

"What?"

"It's some fucking demon and we're gonna have to send it back to whatever shithole it came from," Denise said, spitting grey-green gunk,

"C'mon! Take your wand and stab the little fucker in the eye."

"Fuck you, witch! I'll spend eternity ripping you open and eating your guts."

Denise's reply was wordless. She simply stepped up and thrust her knife into his throat. The boy made a gurgling noise as he tried to speak, but couldn't.

"Not such a chatty Kathy now, are ya?" Denise smiled.

"Come on, Patty. Do it!" Becca said.

Patty looked at her two friends – one with a sword stuck in her son's head and the other with a knife in his throat. Then she looked at the boy, who was trying to snarl and wriggle away even as blood gushed from this throat. That couldn't happen. That wasn't real. He wasn't a real boy. And he certainly wasn't her son. She pulled her wand from her pocket and pushed it into his right eye with all her strength. The boy tried to scream as his eyeball drained down his face, but all that came out was a gargling shower of blood,

"No darkness may enter this protected space. Unwanted spirit depart!" the three women shouted together.

There was an unbearably loud rushing sound, the sudden agony of being sucked through a hole in space and a horrible screaming wail. Then the three of them were standing in the living room as clean, fresh and unharmed as if nothing had happened.

Chapter Thirty-Seven

Objects In The Rear-View Mirror

T he night wasn't nearly so eventful for Piet van Wyk and Johnny Sands. Dull, tiresome, uncomfortable at times, yes – eventful, no. They'd found a pretty good motel less than half a mile away from the Sleepy Pines motel where Annie, Nancy, Harry and their security team had bedded down for the night. The two men had napped for a couple of hours, before heading over to take their three-hour shift watching the doors of the motel rooms their targets were staying in. Rather than both of them losing sleep, they split the vigil in half, so that each could get another hour-and-a-half of shut-eye. The work was dull, but Piet felt it was all worth it - if it made Rosalind happy. At the end of their shift, they headed back to their hotel for some more sleep, leaving Florian and Gus to take the final shift watching the motel. As usual, during the handover, Florian did all the talking while Gus hung back, apparently not paying attention. Piet didn't like Gus, and he was glad to leave Florian and his fat partner to it.

Gus wasn't like the others in Rosalind's security team, who were all either ex-police or ex-military. Gus was nothing more than a big former nightclub bouncer from some Texas shithole with a vicious streak as wide as his fat gut. Piet couldn't understand why Rosalind kept him on the team – he'd be useless in any situations that required fast movement or prolonged running (or any running), and his gun skills were amateurish at best. He'd probably make a good human shield. Maybe that was it? Of course, what Piet didn't know was that Rosalind hadn't hired Gus for his protection skills. Instead, he filled a very particular need that few men had the imagination or skills for. Gus was a colossal pervert. His speciality was using a selection of home-made tools and devices to restrain, dominate and sexually violate. Men, women or anything in between, Gus didn't care so long as he could dominate and inflict painful pleasure. There were times when Rosalind craved total powerlessness and Gus was the man to do it. And, yes, she had calculated that if the need ever arose, he would make an excellent human shield.

As he and Florian sat in their usual silence outside the Sleepy Pines, Gus was thinking about what he could do to the women inside. It made the brutal daydreams of Piet and Johnny seem like a kiddies' tea party. Around seven-thirty in the morning, the door of one of the rooms opened and a couple of the security team came out. They got in their car and drove over to the diner about three hundred yards down the road. After half an hour, they returned and emerged from the white Jeep with arms laden with brown paper bags. They knocked on the door to Annie's room. It was opened by Beth and the two with the food entered.

"All right, time to get ready," said Florian. Gus grunted in reply and his doughy face joggled minutely from the movement.

"They're having breakfast in their room. Be ready to roll in the next half hour."

"Car one, copy," Johnny's voice crackled in the car.

"Car three, copy that," came Brooks' voice.

"Car one, can you pick us up some breakfast while car three takes the lead?" Florian asked.

"Sure thing. What're you wanting?"

Florian looked over at Gus.

"Four blueberry muffins. Large coffee. White, five sugars. Thassit," Gus replied.

Florian nodded, then relayed that order to Johnny,

"And for me, whatever mixed fruit bowl they're doing. Plain yoghurt. Sliced ham, sliced cheese. Large black coffee. Thanks. See you in thirty minutes."

"Got it. Car one out."

It was about thirty minutes later when the small group emerged from their motel rooms and walked out to their vehicles. Watching them at a distance, Ed Brooks and his partner Kyle Williams made the Chevvy Impala look hilariously small. Both men were about six foot four and looked like they could deadlift eight hundred pounds with little trouble. Williams – no one ever called him Kyle, even his girlfriends – was a former US Marine and he, like Brooks, hailed from Alabama, although his hometown was Tuscaloosa. He was black, Brooks was white and that suited them both just fine. They were Alabamans first and foremost and trusted each other totally. In the watery February sun, Annie's flowing red hair shone from beneath her New York Jets cap as she carried the kid to the campervan.

"Lazy little snot," Williams observed, "She's gonna spoil that kid."

Brooks nodded along as Williams continued,

"When I was his age, I was runnin' every which way. My momma couldn'a hardly keep up. Northern kids are wrapped in cotton wool."

"Yup!" Brooks couldn't fault what his partner was saying, then he picked up the mic,

"Here we go, pullin' out now."

It was back onto the '91 and heading north. Within an hour, they were out of Massachusetts and driving past Battleboro, Vermont. Crossing the West River, Williams looked south at the view of hills muscling up from the river valley. It was good to see the lie of the land. Most of the journey had only offered them panoramas of sorry, winter-bare trees which, despite their barren starkness, still managed to block out any views of the landscape. Their targets stopped at a gas station and Williams watched as Annie carried the boy to the restrooms.

"Goddam, she oughtta put that boy down!" he said with genuine anger, "Where's he gonna get in life if he don't use his legs? She's spoilin' that boy."

"You can tell her that if'n we get the order to engage," said Brooks, smiling.

"I will."

"Maybe they got him on some motion sickness drugs for the journey? Keep him sleepy," Brooks mused.

"Could be. Or she's just a straight-out bad mom."

Annie reappeared, carrying the boy again.

"Je-sus!" Williams exploded, "If we wasn't under orders, I'd march right over there an' give 'er whatf'r right now. Right Goddam now!"

"Save it for when we gotta deal with their security. Hold onto that feelin' an' take it out on one'a them."

"And the mom," Williams added.

"From what Johnny and Gus was sayin' earlier, you're gonna have to get your parenting advice in lickety-split, 'cos a few of the boys wanna go some rounds with her."

"Don't you worry, I'll have my say, then they can do what they want with her... okay, here we go again..."

***

Unbeknownst to the men, as they were pulling out to follow the camper-van and Jeep north, Jack was calling Veronica from the airport in England to drop the bombshell that he wanted a meeting with her and Rosalind. At that very moment, Rosalind was in the elegant sitting room of the East Hampton holiday home of a prominent Senator, sipping a strong coffee and looking out across the Atlantic. She had spent the night in a very enjoyable meeting with the Senator, whose wife was currently in India on a goodwill trip. Rosalind was blissfully unaware that while she had been face-sitting someone else's husband, a witch in Bermuda had been casting spells that could be her undoing, and that her brother had totally outmanoeuvred her sister. On the latter point, she was not going to remain in the dark for much longer. Her phone buzzed next to her.

"Sister, how delightful," she said, taking the call.

"We don't have time for pleasantries, sister," came Veronica's voice down the line, "That little fuck Jasper has given me the slip."

Rosalind shifted position minutely at the news,

"That's rather unfortunate," she replied, icily. Why couldn't her sister do that one simple task?

"Maybe not. He says he wants a truce and that he'll sign the Bermuda house over to us if we promise not to kill him or his family..."

"Idiot! Of course we'll kill him and his family," Rosalind laughed and the sound clattered like a silver tray being dropped onto the hard oak parquet floor.

"I know, but he wants us to sign an affidavit admitting we've killed him, which will go to his lawyers and then be produced in the event of any nasty accidents."

"Sneaky little fucker!" Rosalind's face twisted into an unpleasant shape.

"That's what I said," Veronica replied, "He'll be in Bermuda today. Can you get over there and head him off?"

Rosalind looked at her watch – ten past ten in the morning. Could she gather her men and get over there today?

"No."

"Fuck!"

"Calm down," Rosalind said coolly, "I've got all but four of my personal team tracking his bitch. I can take care of her with a phone call at any time. Apparently, she's trying to hide in Vermont, or some nonsense..."

Veronica shrieked with laughter.

"Yes, pathetic, isn't it?" Rosalind said, "Does she really think she can get away from us? What a fool! And meanwhile, Jack will be in Bermuda on his own. What can he do? Nothing! So, we pool our resources and go after him together. Agreed?"

"Agreed. I can catch a flight to New York in two hours and be with you for a late supper."

"I'll be at my usual hotel."

"The one on Fifth?"

"Yes."

"Very nice. One annoyance. I'm two men down."

"How careless of you. Not Gianfranco, I hope?"

"Yes, I had to sever all ties with him," Veronica said archly.

"Pity. I always rather liked him. Zesty."

"To the end… but the fact remains that I can only bring six."

"With my four, I think that's more than enough to deal with our snotty younger brother. Now, let's not waste any more time. Get yourself to New York and then we can go home."

"See you tonight."

***

Piet and Johnny were the lead car tracking Annie when the call from Rosalind came an hour later.

"It's me. What's going on?" Rosalind demanded.

"We're following Mr Kidd's wife and boy. They're on the I-91 heading north from Windsor."

"Where the hell is that?"

"About halfway up Vermont."

"Right. Do they know you're there?"

"They have a security team and they wouldn't be doing their job if they didn't suspect, but as far as we can tell, they haven't made us for definite. They're driving real easy."

"Good. Keep on them. I've had a change of plan. I'll be taking the rest of the team to Bermuda tomorrow. If things go as I hope, we'll require full termination of all parties, regardless of age. Yes?" Rosalind's voice was hard and commanding.

"Yes," Johnny replied with no hint of anything but total devotion.

"The go code will be a text message. The minute you receive a smiley face from me or my sister, execute my orders. Understand?"

"Yes."

"Good. And if you can bring me back some genuine Vermont maple syrup," Rosalind's voice had become warm and silky,

"I'll give you a very personal bonus, Johnny."

"Thank you. I look forward to that," he replied with a smile.

"Look out for my text," and Rosalind was gone.

Piet gave Johnny a sideways glance.

"Well?"

Johnny explained the situation first to Piet and then to the others over the radio as pursuers and pursued motored in a stately procession up to McIndoe Falls. Here, Annie and her crew pulled into a gas station. It was more or less lunchtime. Piet envied them. They didn't keep having to piss into bottles. Again, he and Johnny watched from a distance as the two women and the child (being carried, as per usual) along with two of their security detail went into the restrooms. Then they were back in the safety of the campervan, while one of the security team went into the gas station to pay for gas and get snacks.

"Son of a bitch!" Piet said suddenly, as the burliest of the women emerged with the snacks, "You know why they're not stopping for real food?"

"Why?"

"'Cos that bloody camper's got it's own fridge, it's own stove and a big area inside to relax. They must've stocked up before they left. And it's no wonder that kid doesn't need to run around. He's probably been playing in the back all the way."

"Lucky kid," Johnny replied.

"Yeah, while we sit here getting cramp. I tell you, when She sends that smiley face, they'll wish they'd never been born."

After the lunch stop and when they were back on the road, the mood in Piet and Johnny's car didn't improve. The bitches were still heading north and Johnny was gloomily contemplating the prospect of crossing into Quebec. He hated Quebec with a passion! Far from enjoying the joie de vivre of the French Canadians, he despised them. Why couldn't they speak English, like everyone else? Why did they have to eat weird stuff? Poutine... what-the-fuck? Why did any of them give two shits about hockey? It must've been thirty years since a Canadian team last won the Stanley Cup, but they always strutted around like they were the only country that played the sport. They didn't have decent guns, they were too fucking polite and, oh yeah, you never knew when someone was going to talk to you in fucking French! For Johnny, that was the worst bit. It always made him feel stupid and awkward and those were two things he hated. So, as the journey progressed and they ticked off the towns as they inexorably headed north – St Johnsbury, Lyndonville, Orleans – Johnny became more twitchy. Then suddenly, thankfully, the women turned off the I-91 and took the road west to Newport.

"Take exit twenty-seven," he said cheerily into his mic and the other cars acknowledged the new route.

Soon they were crossing the bridge over the southern tip of Lake Memphremagog. Johnny was glad they weren't going into Canada, but this was tempered by the change in roads. They weren't on the busy interstate any more, where they could hide amongst the other cars. They were on a single lane road and they were going to have to keep well back. This meant there was the possibility that their quarry could turn off the road without them seeing. They would now have to be very careful and collaborate closely with the men in the other two cars. If they lost the women, the consequences would be grave. Johnny puffed out his cheeks and settled back in his seat – it was going to be a difficult afternoon.

***

"You all right?" Annie's sharp eyes searched Nancy's face for signs of fear and fatigue. Her mother seemed to be bearing up.

"I'm fine. Just tired from all the driving. It's funny, you wouldn't think being driven around by other people would make you tired, but it does," Nancy said and now Annie could feel her weariness. Maybe this hadn't been such a good idea...

"It's sitting in the same position and not stretching enough," Annie replied, "That's the first thing you should do on arrival – have a good stretch. Do you think Harry's okay?"

"He's fine," Nancy smiled, looking over at him staring into the iPad, "He's got cartoons to watch and toys to play with. Right now, I'd say he's pretty happy, but he'll probably run around like crazy when we get there."

"So, you don't think we're emotionally scarring him?"

"Nah! Anyway, kids hardly remember anything before the age of five, so he'll be fine."

"Spoken like a true Baby Boomer!" Annie laughed.

"You millennials have no respect!" Nancy replied.

"But seriously, you're okay?"

"Yes. Nervous, but okay."

***

In East Hampton, Rosalind had left the house and walked down to the beach after briefing her men at eleven. There was a fresh breeze and broken clouds were riding across the sun. The sea was full of vigour, as if it was winding itself up to become tempestuous. Rosalind had kicked her shoes off at the gate of the garden, which led out to the beach, and now she allowed the fingertips of the waves to caress her bare feet. Oh yes, that was good. She loved the sea. She was the offspring of a water god, after all. But she didn't want to be forced to return to it. She was having too much fun! Her face took on a look of pure malevolence as she thought about her 'brother'. How much of a threat did he truly pose? Should she go back to the house and make the Senator and his security detail watch over her human form, while she emerged as her true self and flew to Bermuda now? With the help of the wind, she could be there in eight or nine hours. Then she could lie in wait for Jasper and kill him when he arrived at the house. She could fly straight back, repossess Rosalind's body and show the Senator and his men how grateful she was. That was risky. More risky than waiting until tomorrow and facing Jasper in numbers? She couldn't tell. She knew the significance of the blood, that it could be used to send her back to the sea, but what would Jasper know about all that? He'd only found out about the blood a handful of days ago. He hadn't had the time to learn what to do. And anyway, he didn't have magical knowledge or skills. No. She would play it safe. She'd go back to the house, fuck every last ounce of power out of the Senator and then leave for New York. Then, after a night gathering more strength with her sister, they would go to Bermuda and end this once and for all...

But on the other hand, ending it quickly by catching them on the hop was very tempting...

Chapter Thirty-Eight

Witch's Brew

Josephine woke around eight and looked out through the patio doors at the garden with its pool looking beautiful under sunny skies.

"Good sleep?" Becca asked from the easy chair in the corner where she'd stationed herself.

"Great," Josephine yawned, "How was your night?"

"Fairly eventful," said Becca.

"Bloody horrible!" cried Denise, as she came in from the hall.

"What? Why?" Josephine looked perturbed.

"I thought we agreed not to say anything," Becca growled.

"Yeah, but now I'm agreeing to disagree. She needs to know, or she won't understand the power of the forces she's pissed off," Denise replied.

"Okay, tell me everything," said Josephine, swinging her legs over the edge of the sofa.

Becca and Denise told her what had happened, with Denise using more curse words than Becca felt were strictly necessary. At the end, Josephine said,

"Poor Patty! That must've been terrible for her. Where is she now?"

"In the kitchen fixing up some breakfast. She's a trooper. She'll be okay," said Denise.

Josephine got up and walked to the kitchen, where she went straight over to Patty and gave her the biggest hug she could muster.

"Thanks," Josephine said, looking into Patty's bloodshot eyes.

"It's okay. Nothing you wouldn't do for any of us," Patty replied, trying to bluster her emotions away.

"I heard how they tried to get to you – that's cruel and I'm sorry you had to go through it.'

"What can ya do? Demons…" said Patty, then she and Josephine laughed until the laughter turned to the inevitable tears, but it was okay. They were the sort of tears that cleanse and wash away negative emotions. By the time they were wiping the tears away, they were both feeling much better.

"So, what now?" Patty asked.

"First we have breakfast and then the three of you need to go."

"What? After all we went through last night?" exclaimed Denise, who had come to the door, followed by Becca.

"Yes, it isn't safe for you here any more."

"Any more?" Denise couldn't believe her ears, "It wasn't safe last night, either, but you didn't see us running away!"

"No, you didn't, but you weren't the only ones who were busy last night," said Josephine as the three other women looked at her,

"I travelled in the astral plane last night. I was shown things that haven't happened yet – some may never happen. Some of the visions were very clear that if you stay with me today, you will all die."

"*Some* of the visions?" Denise cried, "You mean you saw more than one vision of all of us getting killed?"

"Yes," Josephine replied simply.

"How?" asked Becca, "Maybe if you tell us, it won't happen."

"If I go into the details, that will start us on a path to destruction. On at least one path, I tell you why, but you don't believe me at all, Denise," Josephine said, looking Denise in the eye.

"Sounds like the kind of crap I would come out with," Denise admitted.

"And it all goes wrong from there. Trust is the only way you survive. You gotta trust me."

"We do," said Becca, but now her tone became urgent,

"But how can you trust the vision? Who was your astral guide? What if it was one of those things we were fighting off in the night? They can be very persuasive."

"My guide was Goody Hicks."

The three women stood and stared at Josephine.

"How d'you know it was her?" Patty asked.

"She told me things that only she could know. Things about her life, things about her death. Mostly she showed me the sirens, what they are, where they came from, their power. But that's all I can say. You gotta trust me when I say you gotta leave for your own sakes. Your work here is done."

None of the others looked happy about it. Denise seemed to be sucking on a lemon, Becca had the demeanour of a betrayed lover, and Patty looked like someone had just kicked her puppy in the face.

"Can we at least have breakfast?" Patty asked.

"Sure," Josephine smiled, "Pour the coffee and let's eat."

Half an hour later, the four women said their goodbyes with hugs and a few tears.

"But don't you think we're out of the game," said Patty firmly, "We'll be supporting you from a distance."

"Thanks," said Josephine, "I can't say how much you all mean to me. What you have done..." and she trailed off as tears came again.

"C'mon, let's go!" Denise exclaimed, "Otherwise we'll still be here crying when they arrive and then we'll all be fucked."

Josephine laughed and waved them away as they got into Denise's car and drove off.

"Okay, Josy, you gotta get movin'!" she said to herself as she bustled into the house and got her copper-bladed boline, a pair of rubber gloves, a clear plastic sandwich bag and a cotton sack. Then she walked down the steep path, which wended its way through low aloes, seaside goldenrod, prickly pear and sea ox-eyes to the crescent of pink sand below. The wind was picking up and it was cool against her face, enveloping her in the scents of the sea. Josephine looked out to the horizon and didn't like the way the clouds were building. Rain was coming. She had maybe an hour, but she thought that would be plenty of time, especially as the first item on her list was right there on the beach. It was a Portuguese Man O'War, whose stinging tentacles trailed about forty feet along the beach behind it. It looked like it had washed up in the night – perfect. She ignored the blueish gas-filled balloon of a sail of the creature that wasn't really a jellyfish, but a colony of different creatures all with their specialist roles. Instead, she put on the rubber gloves and followed the trailing tentacles to the end, where she used her boline to cut about six inches of stinging tentacle. She put it into the sandwich bag and placed it carefully into the canvas bag. Then she walked away, watching her step. The last thing she wanted was a half-covered bit of tentacle to sting her through her open-toed sandals. Men O'War could be a nuisance, as even tentacles that had been detached from the main body for a few days could badly hurt you. But this little clipping would certainly help to keep the sirens and their men out of the house!

Josephine walked over to the rocks where the girls had first been swept into the sea and started collecting seaweed, shells, a few mermaid's purses and other items most people would think of as little more than flotsam. As she went about it, she thought of the night before and of the things that Goody Hicks had shown her. Josephine had fallen asleep very quickly once she had snuggled down and it was as if a black veil had been drawn over her. Oblivion was deep and dreamless until,

"Josephine," the voice of an English woman said softly, "Josephine Paget, wake up."

And she had opened her eyes to see a kindly woman in a plain, white robe standing over her. She had long, dark hair and bright brown eyes. Although she didn't know the woman or how she had gotten into the house, Josephine wasn't afraid of her.

"Who are you?"

"Goody Hicks. I will be your guide. With my help, you will avoid the roads that lead to disaster. Come with me, we have so much to see..."

Josephine took her hand and rose from the couch. She knew that her body was still on the couch, but she knew that she mustn't look back at it. Goody led her out of the patio door and, as they stepped through, it was daylight outside and the sun shone down on them out of a blue sky.

"This is how it will be when you awaken – if your friends are strong enough to defend you. I'm afraid your spell has attracted a lot of attention."

"Don't worry. My friends are strong."

"Your faith in them will give them strength," said Goody, "Now, let me show you the paths of destruction."

And with that, the next two days unfolded around them. In the first scenario, the other witches stayed with her as she performed the protection spells around the house and grounds. Josephine watched as a version of herself took her athame, dipped into the powerful potion in the cauldron, and drew a magic circle around first the house and then the grounds. She was saying the incantations correctly as she went. All should have been fine. Then Goody took her to the far side of the house, where Patty inadvertently came out before the ring was sealed. Although she went back inside quickly, the damage had been done. Patty didn't mention it and Josephine thought the protection was in place. The scene fast forwarded to the next day. Men with guns came, with the two sirens behind them. The men were able to enter the house without a problem and they shot Jack repeatedly. He stood no chance. As he died, the sirens stood over him, taunting him, telling him that his wife and child would soon be joining him. And then suddenly, the scene switched back to the sunny morning.

This time, Becca stayed, while the other witches left. Although the magic circle was made perfectly, this time, Josephine had got one of the ingredients of the potion wrong, as Becca had chatted to her. The result for Jack was the same. Bullets slammed into his body, tearing his flesh, shattering bones, severing arteries. And again, as he choked out his last, bloody gasp, the sirens stood over him laughing and boasting about how his wife and son would be killed. And then they were back to the sunny morning. So it continued, like multiple re-takes of a film scene. In each one, something was different, but the results were always disastrous for Jack. In one, he was merely wounded by the men, allowing the sirens to drag him to the pool, where they drowned him. In another, he fought bravely, but the superior numbers of the men told in the end and they threw him over the cliff. He fell backwards onto the rocks below, breaking his back and shattering his skull. Then the sirens had gone down to feast on his flesh.

"Don't you have any to show me where he wins?" Josephine asked, after another horrific ending.

"That is not my task. I am here to show you only the things that will bring calamity. Not only here, but also in other places..."

When Goody said this, everything around them became blurred, as if the world was spinning, but they themselves were staying exactly where they were. Suddenly, they were in a ski resort, deep in the woods among the snowy trees. There was a large, luxurious cabin with an open door. Somewhere inside, a woman was screaming. They approached, even though Josephine didn't want to, and entered a scene of carnage. Three women – clearly some sort of security guards – lay dead in the large living area. Also dead was a big man with a machete in his hand. They followed the sound of the screams towards the back of the cabin. On the way, they passed a crumpled heap that looked like a small boy. They reached a games room in the back, where a woman with red hair had been secured naked and face down to the wooden floor. A number of dangerous-looking men were standing around, watching with greedy eyes as a big, fat man finished the incision he'd been making into the skin on the woman's back. Then he took out a pair of pliers, carefully gripped the flap of skin and started to pull it away as the woman's screams tore at their ears.

Thankfully, the world blurred again and they were back outside the house in Bermuda. Josephine was glad. The sky was clear and the sun was bright, and it cleansed her of the scene she had just witnessed.

"These are the paths to calamity," said Goody, "Now you have seen them, you can avoid them. Finally, look on these people and remember them."

Then, Jack, Annie, Nancy, Harry, Veronica, Rosalind and various members of their security teams stepped out one at a time from behind the house. They walked across the patio, stopped in the middle and looked at Josephine as Goody identified them and told her about them, their strengths and their weaknesses. Then, when each had had their turn, they walked around the other side of the house. It was like a bizarre beauty pageant.

"Remember them," Goody said, as the last of Veronica's security team disappeared, "It might save your life. Now, it is time for you to rest."

"Wait, I have so many questions!" Josephine exclaimed.

"You may ask me one," Goody replied.

"What was the spell you used to make the protective amulet that Jack wears and how did you imbue the amulet with the power?"

Goody smiled,

"That is the best question you could ask," then Goody beckoned Josephine to come closer and she whispered the instructions into her ear. The next thing Josephine knew, she was waking up.

Josephine smiled as she came out of her reverie. If she survived the next forty-eight hours, she would enjoy making protective amulets. She wondered whether she could make an industry of it. The thought of selling amulets to protect men from the evils of the sirens on Etsy and Amazon tickled her. However, that was for the future. First, she had to get back to the house and get cooking. She hurried back up the path. It was mid-morning by the time she'd laid out all her ingredients. She didn't know it, but it was about the same time that Annie and her group were leaving the gas station outside Battleboro, heading north. Josephine checked that she had everything and then stood breathing deeply and focussing her thoughts. She had to ground herself in the here and now to ensure that the complicated potion and spell could work. Then, as the rain started to fall outside, she began to work methodically, but quickly. She didn't want to be there by the time Jack was due to arrive, around eight that evening. She knew that if she was still there at that time, their cause would be lost.

Brewing the potion took about an hour and by the time she finished, Josephine was sweating. It had taken all her concentration to ensure that everything was perfect. Now she carried the small cauldron outside and placed it on the front porch. The rain had stopped and it was brighter, but broken clouds were riding across the sky on the strengthening winds. Josephine walked about ten yards from the front of the house and then, trying to keep that distance constant, she walked around the house. There were a couple of places where she had to brush past plants, but otherwise the circle would be fine for her needs. She went back to the porch, fetched the cauldron and placed it behind the edge of the circumference she'd just walked. She drew her athame and dipped it into the cauldron, speaking an incantation loudly and clearly. Then she bent down and began to trace a line on the ground with the tip of the knife. As she did so, she spoke the words of power, which would bind the universe to her will. Without taking the tip of the knife from the ground, she followed the course of her previous circumference, repeating the incantation all the way round. At the end, she completed the circle with her in it, clapped her hands loudly and made an invocation to the greater powers to give the circle the energy it needed.

She took the cauldron back to the porch, went inside the house and came out a few moments later with a small iron bell on a string, which she laid on the ground in front of the house. She dipped the athame in the cauldron and began a new circle just in front of where she'd placed the bell. As she drew the circle with the athame, she ensured that it touched each of the four corners of the house. This time, her incantations were different and this time they weren't in English. Any passers-by with a classical education would have recognised that she was speaking ancient Greek. Fortunately, there were no passers-by, because she cut a bizarre sight dragging the knife along the ground and speaking apparent gibberish. When she completed the circle, she rang the iron bell loudly. She knew that while the noise didn't carry far in the physical world, it would be reverberating in the beyond. Once the bell's tone had dissipated, she spoke the words of power. The circle was complete. Only incompetence on her part would allow the sirens to enter. Had she been incompetent? She didn't think so. She'd been careful. But what if she'd missed something? Or said something wrong? Suddenly, she was hit by a wave of self-doubt.

"I know…" she said to herself and, after she'd hung the bell on a hook by the front door, she hurried back into the house.

"Where would be best?" she said out loud, standing in the entrance hall and looking all around,

"Of course!" she said and went through to the living room. The large expanse of hardwood floor would be perfect. She put down the cauldron, then walked quickly to the kitchen to get what she'd need.

Back in the sitting room, she centred herself, then took a piece of chalk and, whispering an incantation, she drew a large pentagram around the cauldron in the middle of the room. Treading carefully, she then drew a circle around the pentagram, so that its corners touched the perimeter of the circle. She carefully placed a violet seasnail shell in the section between the pentagram and the circle on the eastern side of it. Then came a mermaid's purse, which took up the corresponding space to the west. She drew the athame and, with a clear, forceful incantation, she dipped it into the cauldron and traced around the outside of the chalk circle with the tip of the blade. She made a final incantation, raising her arms heavenwards, then clapped her hands loudly and stepped out of the circle.

"Get through that, bitches!" she said with a satisfied smile, then she went to the kitchen and cleared up. Even if she'd made a mistake in the other spells, that last one would certainly protect him – although she hoped it wouldn't come to that. It had been a good morning's work and she still had about six hours to clear up and get out before Jack arrived.

When Josephine had finished clearing her things and collected them by the door, ready for her to be picked up by a cab, she went into the study. It was a book-lined oasis at the back of the house, just off the sitting room. Before she left, she needed to leave Jack some instructions on what she had done and what to do in the event that he needed to use the final protective circle. She sat at the big, traditional wooden desk and started to write. It took her a few minutes and she must have been concentrating hard, because she didn't hear the person enter the house, but suddenly the hairs on her neck rose as she realised she was not alone. She gently put the pencil down and looked around for anything she could use as a weapon, because – of course! – her boline and athame were in the front hall and the two daggers were in the sitting room. She quietly got out from behind the chair and crept to the door. Her heart was racing and, after the spiritual exertions of the day and the previous night, her limbs felt weak. There was nothing of any use in the room. Should she use the Shorter Oxford English Dictionary to try to batter them? She stood behind the door, breathing as quietly as she could and listening hard.

Dammit! Whoever it was had come into the sitting room. That was the end of Josephine's plan to grab one of the knives! She looked over her shoulder at the window. Could she get out through it quietly and escape? Unlikely. She was a big woman and it was a small side-window with various pieces of glassware on the sill. Maybe the intruder would go to another room and she could get away through the patio doors? She stood there barely daring to breathe. Who could it be? Then she heard the unmistakable sound of one of the daggers being picked up from the table. Josephine had no choice. She gently slid one of the large dictionary volumes out of the shelf. It was certainly heavy enough to inflict some sort of damage, but who the hell brings a dictionary to a knife fight? Josephine's stomach tightened unpleasantly as she more felt than heard the person approach the study door. She raised the dictionary above her head, ready to defend herself. Suddenly the door was kicked open and she was faced with the dagger. Josephine looked with bulging eyes and breathed,

"How did you get here?"

Chapter Thirty-Nine

Bermuda Triangulation

U p front in the Beast, Beth sat forward in sudden tension,

"I can't see any specific vehicle, but I'm sure we're being followed," Amy's taught voice crackled across the ether into Beth's earpiece.

"Yeah, I know what you mean," she replied. She'd also had a sense of not being alone - even after the car that had apparently been following them had gone in a different direction back in New York the previous afternoon,

"One of you are just gonna have to keep your eyes on the road behind. We're off the highway, so it's harder for them than it is for us. Right now, we stick to plan A – get to the ski lodge, secure the perimeter and bed down for the night. If you see anything you think's suspicious, then we change to plan B."

"Got it, out."

Beth settled back into her seat in the front of the Beast with a pensive look. As they drove from Newport towards Troy, the view was typical 'Vermont' – neat rural houses, some with colourfully painted outbuildings, trees and woodland, and there lurking above them, the hills where the trees still held their snow. Beth wondered, not for the first time, whether the plan to get out of the city had been correct. Out in the boonies there seemed to be more places to disappear, but with fewer people, any newcomers stood out and yokels did so love to gossip – even to strangers asking questions. She felt like they were potentially exposed and she didn't like it. But this was Annie's favoured plan and it was Beth's job to protect the two women and the boy at all costs. Beth shot a glance at the driver, noting her taut jaw, framed by flaming hair as she concentrated on the road ahead. Could this really work?

In the lead car, Florian and Gus had the most straightforward job – ghost along in the far background, but staying on the main road and just hurrying every now and again to see if their quarry was up ahead, then falling back. If they weren't able to spot the target, then the other two cars were to check any of the side roads since the last sighting. This wasn't necessary for the first few miles, until a point where there was a right turn just where the road swung left.

"Car one, take the 105 West. See if they've gone that way," said Gus.

"Copy that," Johnny replied and when the right turn came, he took it and stepped on the gas.

About two minutes later, Gus's voice crackled through the radio again,

"Car three, take the left turn to Coventry. We'll take the right turn to Troy."

"Copy that," Brooks replied and when they got to the turn about a minute later, Williams put his foot down to make up lost time. The road to Coventry was desolate and haunted by leafless trees that miserably watched them speed past. Soon they came to a stretch where they could see the best part of a mile ahead, but the road was empty.

"This road's a dud," said Brooks, bluntly.

"Yup, but we gotta look anyways," Williams replied, pressing the accelerator into the carpet.

About two minutes later, Gus came through again,

"This is car two - we got 'em. They're on the road to Troy. Where're you boys at?"

"Car one, we're most of the way to North Troy."

"Car three, we'll be in Coventry in about two minutes."

"Okay, give me a minute," said Gus and the radios went quiet while he took a look at a map he'd bought from a gas station earlier. He hated sat navs, because he felt they didn't give him the wider perspective on the situation that he needed. He took a long, good look at the map and then picked up the mic again,

"Okay, I got an idea. When they get to Troy, they've got the choice: right towards North Troy or left towards Lowell. Car one, you open up the taps and get yourselves to North Troy, then take a left towards Troy. That way you'll be able to spot 'em if they come your way."

"Copy that," said Johnny.

"Car three, you're gonna have to shift your gears and drive like the devil round to Lowell. Take a right on the one hundred and if they come your way, you'll see them. We'll try to keep them in sight."

"Car three copy," said Brooks, and Williams did exactly as ordered, pushing the Impala at every opportunity. The road out of Coventry didn't give him much to play with, but after he'd turned right onto the fifty-eight, the road became a smooth-riding driver's heaven. There was next to no traffic and he was able to shift. Soon they were doing a hundred through open countryside and then through woodland.

"We're gonna get there easy," Williams said, and Brooks replied,

"There ain't no way in hell that camper's gonna be tearing up the highway like this!"

And that's how the afternoon played out, with the three cars triangulating around the camper and the Jeep. At no point were Amy or Beth able to spot anyone following them, but they were always being corralled at distance by the chasing team. And even though Beth took a circuitous route to their final destination of a hired ski cabin in the woods outside Smuggler's Notch, within half an hour of their arrival, their pursuers were positioned in the forest and staking them out. Aside from Gus, all the men were well versed in covert ops and the discomfort and deprivations of staying hidden while observing targets. First shift fell to Willams and Florian, who hunkered themselves down so that Williams had eyes on the front and Florian was covering the back. Fortunately, the men had packed to cope with a range of eventualities. So, having changed into thermals and camouflage gear, they were able to hide themselves in the scraggy winter forest with its dusting of snow. They watched the comings and goings as the women sorted themselves out. Occasionally, one or two would come out for a perimeter check, but they were clearly oblivious to the fact that they were being watched. Florian watched as the redhead and the granny busied themselves in the kitchen, but there was no sign of the snotty kid.

While they were out freezing their nuts off, the others went to the local store for supplies. Johnny found a hardware store and came out grinning with his newly acquired machete.

"I'm gonna live the dream," he said to Piet as he put it into the back of the car.

"Good thing you've got a change of clothes," the big South African replied, "After you set to work with that, you're gonna need them," he winked, as they got in the car and drove to the only local motel with rooms available.

As the ski season was in full-swing, they'd only been able to get two rooms, but that had to do. One was a family room, which Johnny and Piet were sharing with Brooks and Gus. Piet wasn't thrilled about this, but even he had to admit he was interested in what Gus was doing when they got back to the room. They came into the main section of the bedroom to find that Gus had opened up a well laid out set of tools onto the double bed. Brooks was sitting in a chair in the corner, watching with a cruel smile on his face.

"What's this?" asked Piet, putting a couple of bags of food on the shelf by the door.

"Ole' Gus, here, is showing me some of his toys."

Piet looked at the shining array of stainless-steel tools. Amongst them were the usual claw hammer, screw driver, an awl, pliers, mole grips and so on, but there were other, more intriguing items,

"Is that a speculum?" he asked.

"Yup," grunted Gus.

"What sort of corkscrew is that?" he asked, pointing at a steel implement with a simple bar for a handle, and a long, thin shaft ending in an alarmingly sharp looking screw.

"Doyen myoma screw," Gus replied, but continued when he saw the blank look on Piet's face, "Usually, they're used to extract fibromas from the uterine cavity. See the sharp tip?"

Piet nodded,

"That's designed to pierce through uterine tissue. I use it to extract screams."

"Anyone ever told you you're a sick fucker?" Piet asked seriously.

"Yeah," Gus smiled.

***

When Jack got on the plane in London, the local time was four in the afternoon on Tuesday the twenty-first of February. But as he flew west across the Atlantic, even though the flight took seven hours, it was only a quarter to eight on Tuesday evening when he stepped out of the Arrivals area of L.F. Wade International airport in Bermuda. Jack didn't know it, but at pretty much the same moment he was looking for a cab, Piet, Johnny and Brooks were looking over the tools that Gus was intending to use to torture Annie to death. Given the fact that Jack's nerves were already fraying around the edges, it was just as well that he had no idea what was going on in Vermont. He went to the head of the cab rank and said,

"Hi, I'm going to The Drive over in Warwick?"

"Hop in," said the driver with a warm smile. He was always happy to get fares in the depths of winter.

Jack did as requested and settled himself in the back.

As they drove across the island, there wasn't much to see in the darkness. Jack could feel that there were vast expanses of ocean beyond the warm lights of the houses, but under cloudy skies with no moon, there was nothing to see but a great darkness beyond. To be honest, exhaustion was finally getting the better of him. He'd hoped to get some sleep on the flight, but instead he had fretted away the hours. Had Josephine been able to do what was necessary? Would everything be ready for him when he arrived? Could Rosalind and some of her men have got to the island before him? How safe would he be in the house? How were Annie and Harry? He'd had no word since Monday and he was rightly worried. He didn't even know where they were. Was the plan working, or had it gone to rat shit like everything else? Now, as he sat in the back of the cab, tiredness fought for control of him against the ball of tension in his stomach. Just knowing he was back where it had all started raised the stakes. Somewhere in the dark ocean, just beyond the houses and the merry lights of a holiday island, there were evils that few visitors could guess at. Jack found it oppressive. What he needed was a stiff drink and a long sleep. He didn't want to break into the Lagavulin until they had won (if they won!), but if there was nothing in the house, he was sorely tempted to have a large one anyway.

It didn't take long to get to Cliff House and when he'd paid the cab and watched it drive away, he turned and looked at the house. There were lights next to the paths of the beach complex and the front porch light was on, so it was easy to get a good view of the place. He wished he could remember it from his youth, but he couldn't. Looking at it for what was effectively the first time, he thought it was lovely. Then he realised that for all he knew, there were men waiting inside to kill him. He drew a long breath and pulled the key from his pocket as he walked to the door. He readied himself for whatever might be inside and opened the door. The large hall was dark, but a light in the room beyond illuminated it enough for Jack to see the hall was empty. Jack hesitated. Should he call out 'hello'? This was really unpleasant. His heart was fluttering and he didn't know what to do. He decided the best thing was to put his shoulders back, his chest out and meet whatever might be there head on. He walked with firm steps into the room with the light and found a large, elegant sitting room. No one was there, but there was a weird pentagram with stuff in it on the floor, and on the coffee table there was a bronze dagger. Jack took the dagger and weighed it in his hand. It felt good. But when the time came, would he be able to use it? Yes! His hand gripped the hilt hard. Tomorrow, he would take great pleasure in burying the blade up to the hilt into each of his 'sisters'.

Jack looked around. What to do? He decided to familiarise himself with the layout of the house – and at the same time assure himself that he was, indeed, alone. There was an open door on the far side of the room. He'd start in there. Keeping the dagger in his hand, he walked over and could see that it was a study even before he turned on the light. He flicked the switch and entered. Yes, it was a neat, comfortable study with plenty of books.

Jack had a look at them. Yes, lots of books about the sea. Those would be his grandfather's. He vaguely scanned the rest of the room and was just about to leave, when something he'd seen tugged at him. There was a note on the desk, with a pencil placed next to it.

Jack picked up the note and read it:

Dear Jack,

I hope you had a good flight over. Everything is prepared. I cast spells of protection around the house and in it, too. They should stop your sisters and their men from entering. If they don't work, get into the circle on the floor. You will be safe there. If they get into the house, stand in this circle and don't leave for any reason. They won't be able to touch you or harm you in any way. Don't move the shell or mermaid's purse out of the circle! Here are the daggers. They have the power to return your sisters to the sea. I did 2, just in case one gets knocked out of your hand when you face them. The second dagger can fit onto the spear shaft in the hall behind the front door. This will be useful if you need to keep them at bay. Remember, be careful! The closer they are to the sea, the more powerful they become. I will stay away, but will put all my force into helping you at a distance.

Good luck!

Josephine.

P.S. There is plenty of food in the

And that was it. Jack looked around the room. An unfinished note and, more importantly, only one dagger! What the hell? Instantly his senses sharpened. If there were supposed to be two daggers, who had the other one? And what if they were in the bloody house?

"Shit!" Jack swore under his breath. Right, he'd have to undertake a sweep of the house. On the plus side, at least he had a weapon, but overall, he didn't like this! He went quietly back into the living room and carefully checked behind chairs, under the sofa, under all the cushions (just in case the dagger had slipped down there as things do) and finally ensured that the door onto the patio was locked. Satisfied that the room was clear, he stalked across to the door opposite the study. He listened hard, took a breath, then quickly opened the door and reached for the light switch. The light revealed a good-sized dining room with nice looking 19th century colonial furniture. On the far side of the room was a long sideboard, pride of place in the middle of which was a drinks tray with various bottles of spirits on it. Finally, a stroke of luck! Jack eyed up the bottle of Gosling's Black Seal rum. Yes, he'd be having an appointment with that later. All this aside, there was no dagger to be seen and nowhere to hide in the dining room. He walked over to the open door on the other side of the room. From the looks of it, the kitchen was beyond.

When Jack turned on the light, he could see that he was right. Again, there was nowhere to hide and no dagger to be seen, but he had a good look round while listening hard for the presence of other people. He checked the room off the kitchen – a utility room. Again, nothing. He went back into the sitting room. Now for the front hall and upstairs. God, there was another whole storey to check, constantly wondering if someone was about to pounce on him with the other dagger!

"Fuck this shit!" Jack barked angrily. He hurried out into the hall and turned on the lights. Empty. More importantly, there was no spear shaft behind the front door. Shit! Could he be about to face someone armed with a spear? He felt his anger rise. He looked up the stairs and played with the various light switches until the lights in the upstairs hall went on.

"Right, you fuckers!" he bellowed, taking the stairs two at a time, so that he was in the upstairs hall in about three seconds. He looked to left and right, made a quick decision and darted right, practically throwing the doors open as he searched for whoever had the other dagger. They were all empty. As he came out of the last of the rooms at the far-right end of the corridor, he had a slightly unhinged look on his face. He strode down the hall with the dagger held firmly in his right hand,

"Here I come, ready or not!"

He threw open the first door – a bathroom. Then he went to the next room and barged in. When he turned on the light, he could see the good-sized bedroom had clearly seen some action, as the floor was covered in broken mirror glass. He looked under the bed and then went to the far side. Nothing. But what about the wall of cupboards? Someone could be hiding behind any of those doors. With the dagger at the ready, he went along the line of doors, opening each one quickly and simultaneously thrusting into them with the dagger. If anyone was hiding, Jack wanted to get the first thrust in. He was about to open another door, when he noticed something move out of the corner of his eye. On the floor, the broken pieces of the mirror were moving! Jack stepped away from the cupboard and turned to face the moving glass. What was this? Fear gripped his stomach. This couldn't be! But then neither could the Gigiat, and he'd experienced that. He gulped. The glass was moving, reforming. Yes, it was insane, yes, it was against the laws of physics, but it was happening, so he'd better get his shit together and deal with it. Jack swallowed his fear and planted his feet, ready to take on whatever might appear.

In an instant, the glass flew back into place in the frame of the mirror, but instead of reflecting the room, it was a window into some sort of dungeon. In the background, bent over what looked like a dead body, there was a crooked mockery of a man. It was thin and sinewy, with rotting clothes hanging from its limbs and long, thin hair down to its shoulders, shrouding its face. Jack watched in terror-struck fascination as the thing twisted off the forearm of the body with a sickening crunch of tearing tendons and bone. It seemed satisfied, but then it became suddenly still. It knew! It knew Jack was there and that he was watching. As Jack's stomach crawled with fear, it slowly turned its face towards him and he saw that it was the diseased and decayed face of his father. The eyes, always so full of loathing for his son, seemed to be even more filled with hate than before. In fact, the left seemed to be overflowing with hate, as a sluggish black liquid oozed from it and ran slowly down his face.

"Hello Jacky-boy!" he said, turning full on towards Jack and starting to shuffle towards him,

"So glad you could make it. Now you can finally join your sisters – your real sisters. They've been here all along. We've been feasting on their pain and their fear every day since they were taken. I'm here now, too. This is my true form. Like it?"

Jack said nothing.

"We were going to let the sirens kill you, but now you're here, I'm going to kill you instead," and now he gained pace as he screamed,

"I'm coming for you, Jacky-boy! I'm coming to tear your throat out!"

He was running full tilt now and leaping forward to dive through the mirror and onto his son, when suddenly Jack lost his temper. In his whole life, he'd never truly lost it, but he felt all shackles of politeness, sense and reason fall from him. The power of his anger flowed from his feet and coursed through him, jamming in his throat until he unleashed it in a roar,

"No darkness may enter this protected space. Unwanted spirit depart!"

His father had been halfway out of the mirror, hands clawing towards his son when Jack screamed the incantation. He was held instantly in mid-air as if time had stopped and, although the hate was still in his eyes, he was totally unable to move. Jack approached and put his face right up to the face of the thing that looked like his father. The stench of decay was nauseating, but Jack ignored it. He looked long and hard into the creature's hate-filled eyes,

"Fuck you!" Jack yelled into the creature's face, stabbing the dagger fully into its oozing left eye. It popped spectacularly and that sparked a frenzy in Jack. He stabbed the face over and over again, screaming "Fuck you!" with every blow, into which he put all the anger from every beating his father had ever given him. Moments flashed into his mind as he raged – that time his father had punched him in the side of the head at breakfast for making too much noise when eating, or the snooker cue he broke across his son's back – and with each memory came another stab of the dagger until the face was little more than an unidentifiable pulp. Then, focussing a power he didn't understand, he held out his left hand as if gripping an apple and squeezed. Before his eyes, the creature from the mirror and the entire world behind it crushed into itself like so much crumpling paper. By the time Jack had completely closed his fist, the inside of the mirror was gone, leaving blank wall behind.

Jack opened his hand and tore the frame of the mirror off the wall. With a torrent of swearing, cursing every evil in existence, Jack stormed down the stairs and opened the front door. He snapped the frame of the mirror as if it were matchsticks and threw the pieces far beyond the boundary of Josephine's magick.

"I am here now!" Jack growled, "This place is mine. Stay out! And if any of you wants a piece of me, I'll fuck you up!" then he went back in, slamming the door behind him. Still full of some sacred fire that was beyond his knowledge, he marched straight into the dining room, took the bottle of rum and filled a glass with it.

"Fuck you all," he said raising the glass to whatever invisible entities might be watching him, before drinking half of the glass in one gulp. The shock of the alcohol brought him to his senses and suddenly he was feeling wobbly from the surge of adrenalin. At the same time, he was confused, but strangely elated.

"What was that about?" he said out loud. Something very strange had just happened and he didn't understand it. What had he shouted to stop his father coming out of the mirror? He couldn't remember and he had no idea where the words had come from. All he knew was that it had felt right. It had felt as if something he'd been holding back his entire life had been released. And now he felt as if there was a power inside him. With it, he felt he could take on anything.

He sipped contemplatively at the rum and realised that he was very hungry. Josephine's note had been right about the fridge – it was very well stocked. Later, as he sat at the kitchen table eating a couple of ham sandwiches washed down with more rum, he wondered about what might have happened to the other dagger. That was a mystery and worrying, but he was on his own. He didn't want to put Josephine in any danger – not realising that he'd put her in danger ever since he'd phoned her up – so he wouldn't call her to find out about the dagger. He would have to muddle through with what he had and stay on guard in case the person who had taken the dagger returned. He was also perplexed about the mirror. Had it been an illusion, or had it been a window onto another, darker reality? All he did know was that it had felt phenomenal to get rid of all the anger he'd felt towards his father. Having said that, whatever the thing had been that he'd assaulted, he was sure it was not David Kidd. His instincts told him that it was a creature from another part of existence. Some sort of demon? Possibly. He had no intellectual knowledge of such things, but being there, in Bermuda, it was as if a long dormant part of his being had awakened. He was a direct descendant of a witch, whose power had been closely connected with the island and suddenly, he felt instinctually what he should or shouldn't be doing. It was exciting, but at the same time, somewhat scary. What did he know about demons and alternate realities held in mirrors? Nothing. And yet now, he felt he could not only curse them to hell, but actually send them there. He shook his head – to think that two weeks earlier the only things he had to worry about were getting the designs right for his latest website and Harry's potty-training regime!

Jack went to bed early after ensuring that the house was locked up tight. In everything he did, he was listening to a new inner voice that seemed to have knowledge of things beyond sight. He was reassured that the house was safe, that there was no one else in it and that it was a place of peace. When it came to going to bed, he chose the room where the mirror had been. It was a statement of intent to the wider cosmos. It showed he wasn't frightened and that he could sleep peacefully even in a room where he had fought a creature from another dimension. Within moments of lying in the comfy bed, he fell into a deep and dreamless sleep.

Chapter Forty

The Calm Before...

As Jack was falling asleep, Veronica was arriving in New York like a winter storm. She was outraged at Jasper's effrontery and, worse, had a kernel of fear deep within her. The fear of being sent back to the sea, back to picking off those foolish enough to venture into stormy waters, back to the hunger in between. She hated Jasper for making her feel like that and her anger was terrible. As she sat fuming in the back of her limousine, the two guards who were with her found that her anger made her almost unbearably desirable. The flash of her eyes, as if she literally wanted to consume them, attracted them all the more. She herself needed to get as much power as possible before they went to Bermuda. She wanted to leave nothing to chance. She had to not only beat Jasper, but crush him into nothing, to make it as if he'd never existed. She had a team of strong men with her, but tonight that wouldn't be enough. On the journey she made a series of phone calls to men who would be perfect for her needs that night – a couple of champion boxers, the most brutal UFC fighter she knew, the drummer of a death metal band, three Mafia enforcers, a pitcher for the Yankees, a couple of hockey players, a tight end and a quarterback.

"Bobby! It's Veronica. Yes, I need you now. Tonight. You remember that place on Fifth? That's right, where you and Lamarr double-teamed me. I need you there at eleven. Bring Lamarr if he's available. Hmmm? Yes, I'll do that... and then I'll blow your mind. See you later. Don't be late," the last imperative was given as an order, not a request.

Walking into the vast, luxurious suite, the first thing that struck Veronica was the unmistakable smell of men having sex. The hot air was thick with it. Her eyes lit up as the mix of sweat and hormones enveloped her, teasing her senses and sparking a deep feeling of need within her. As she walked through the entrance area and into the vast, open-plan living space, she was treated to the sight of more than twenty men standing around naked in a circle, from the centre of which came the sound of an unquenchable desire for pleasure desperately trying to achieve satiety. Rosalind was in the centre of the circle, fucking like an alley cat. The man who had the pleasure was a famous financier and, as he took her hard from behind, he had a fistful of her hair, pulling back her head so that the veins stood out in her neck. Some might have thought it was reminiscent of the Roman Empress Messalina and her attempt to screw all the sailors on a ship in port. For Veronica, it took her back to their time when they lived on the islands near the Amalfi coast. A full ship of sailors had run onto their rocks and the sisters had pulled them all safely from the sea. Fifty men all to themselves. She and her sister took them all in an orgy of pleasure, making them keep going night and day without food until they were husks. Together, the sisters had been able to make the men hungry for only one thing – them - and Veronica remembered the hollow look of their eyes as they spent all their strength pleasing them. They took all the life power from each and every man, leaving them where they fell when their hearts finally gave out. And once they were all dead, she and her sister had feasted on their remains. Messalina's feats were nothing next to theirs – and besides, most of that had been made up by salacious gossips and then written down as 'fact' years later by men who'd never even known her.

And now, here they were again, feeding on men in a frenzy. They needed to get as much raw power out of the men as possible before they went to Bermuda. Veronica was slightly annoyed that Rosalind had a head start, but she'd have done the same thing had the tables been turned. She looked at her sister in action and her desire rose. Rosalind was grunting and wailing as the financier pounded her harder and harder.

"Ah, dear sister," Veronica said quietly to herself, "Always pretending to be so proper, but your darkness is even deeper than mine," and then she stripped off her clothes.

"You, you and you," she barked, causing three of the men in the circle to turn to her. They were in a daze, their eyes glassy with desire,

"Take me now," Veronica ordered and in a moment, three pairs of strong hands were carrying her to a sofa and the men began to take her together.

Tonight would be one to remember.

***

In Vermont, the night was long and cold. The men took it in shifts to watch the ski lodge. Except Gus. He was a big, clumsy man with no experience of surveillance, so the others decided they shouldn't risk their element of surprise by making him watch the house from the woods. He was very happy about this and slept well all night in spite of the comings and goings of the others. For their part, the women went to bed around eleven p.m. but every hour, one of them would appear and inspect the back and the front of the building. As Johnny lay in his surveillance position, watching the house through night-vision goggles, he was pleased that he'd had the foresight to bring a pocket hand warmer. The last thing he needed, if something kicked off, was to fumble his gun because of cold-stiffened fingers. Around him, the woods were still and he hardly dared move, because of the noise he'd make in the bed of leaves around him. Three a.m. came and with it an appearance by one of the guards and, as she opened the door, Johnny flipped the safety on his pistol. The woman who came out was the heaviest set one. Johnny thought she looked like the most experienced and wondered what her previous job had been. Rangers? Airborne? Whatever it was, she was thorough, methodical and efficient in her movements. As he watched her scan the forest from the back porch, he held his breath. Not a sound. Don't worry, there's nothing to see here. It's a forest in winter - cold and dull. Go back into the warm... annoyingly she took her time over her scan, so Johnny had to let out his breath with infinite slowness and breathe in slowly and quietly. Pain in the ass! That was enough to make him decide that if it came to it, she would be the first to feel the blade of his brand new machete. Finally, she went back inside and Johnny was able to relax minutely, although he stayed as still as a rock. The long night wore on.

***

Annie passed a fretful night, where oblivion only came to her in short snatches. She was scared - not for herself, her personal safety never really concerned her, but the safety of her son and her mother was a cause of great anxiety. Her plan had seemed like a good one on paper, but now it was in full-flow, she couldn't help but wonder if she'd made a mistake. Even with all the precautions she'd taken, what if the enemy had outflanked her? Also, she couldn't imagine what the morning might bring. She had no idea where Jack was, whether he was safe or even whether he'd made it to Bermuda. Too much was unknown for her liking. They were all too exposed! In the darkness and the stillness of the night, time dragged horribly until, sometime around five, sleep finally took her.

***

Patty, Denise and Becca stayed together all night. Unbeknownst to Josephine, after they'd left Cliff House, they'd headed straight to hers. The three of them had used what strength they had left to combine efforts in creating a circle of protection around the house. Then, they'd gone back to Patty's house in Hamilton where the three women slept most of the day. They got back to work around nine in the evening, preparing and casting a protection spell, before spending the night channelling their power to Josephine. It was around four, when Becca sat upright from a reverie and said,

"Can either of you feel Josy?"

The others gave her inquiring looks.

"I can't sense her. It's as if she's gone."

"I don't feel like anything's happened to her," Denise replied, "We'd feel if something happened to her, right?"

"Yeah," said Patty, though she didn't feel totally convinced. It was late, they were all tired from the previous night – they could easily have missed something,

"I don't feel like anything bad has happened, but Becca's right – I can't feel Josy's presence either," Patty added.

"Should we go over?" asked Becca.

"No," Patty said, "She was very clear – no contact until whatever needs to be done is done."

"But what if she needs us?" Becca insisted.

"We agreed to support her from a distance, and we've gotta stick to that."

"So, what do we do now?" asked Denise.

"I say, keep doing what we're doing. We channel our strength to her," Patty replied.

"But what's the point if she ain't there?" Denise didn't want to feel like a chump, channelling her strength to no one.

"We gotta have faith that she is there. Didn't she say we all gotta trust her if we're gonna get through this?" said Patty.

The other two nodded.

"Well then, this is the time for trust," Patty said.

The three women looked at each other, then joined hands to re-affirm their bonds and concentrate their thoughts on Josephine once more.

***

In the luxurious suite in the elegant building on Fifth Avenue around four-thirty in the morning, overexertion and arteriosclerosis finally got the better of a fat international financier. He was labouring on top of Vanessa, who had also taken a couple of other men in hand, when the inevitable heart attack began. She could feel him lose rhythm and then he slumped, pinning her under the best part of three hundred pounds of white, saggy flesh.

"Get him off me!" she gasped, and many willing hands set to the job of prizing the big, sweaty mound off her.

Rather than complaining, or taking time to get her breath back, Veronica worked fast,

"Get him into the kitchen onto the worktop," she ordered and the men did as they were told.

"Sister!" Veronica called, trying to look over the forest of naked men who were crowding around, "We've got a heart attack!"

Rosalind made a noise in reply that indicated that she'd registered what Veronica had said, but that she had her mouth full.

Veronica went swiftly into the kitchen, where six men had just managed to heave the fat financier onto the black marble worktop of the big island in the middle of the space.

"Leave us. Wait outside and be ready for me!" she ordered, and the men left at once.

A moment later, Rosalind entered. She was a dishevelled mess with mascara streaks down her face and drool, or possibly something else dripping from around her mouth. Yet she looked energised and her pale blue eyes were crackling with excitement.

"Oh Ralph!" she said, wiping whatever it was from her chin, "I always said you should go easy on the mayo!"

Ralph was moaning in pain – it was as if a golden lasso was tightening around his chest as he writhed.

Veronica opened a drawer and took out a serious looking knife,

"Heart or balls?" she asked.

"Balls every time," Rosalind smiled.

"Fair enough," said Veronica, "Although I do think there's nothing quite like a heart when it's still trying to pump."

"If you want to catch it pumping, you'd better be quick!" said Rosalind as she prized Ralph's legs apart.

Then they set to. Veronica pushed the blade deep into Ralph's torso, about two inches below his sternum, and sliced upwards. Then, with a strength gathered from the men that evening, she prized apart his sternum with a dreadful cracking. Ralph passed out instantly, which saved him from the sight of Rosalind's barracuda teeth flashing out to tear off his testicles. As blood spurt from the two wounds, Veronica grabbed his fibrillating heart, sliced it out and quickly put the end of it into her mouth. The feel of its last contraction on her tongue was overwhelmingly satisfying. Then she tore into the hot muscle and fat, while Rosalind darted in again to bite off what was left of Ralph's genitalia and then suck at the blood. Within two minutes, they were sharing his liver. Veronica cut it out, but before she could slice it into portions, Rosalind had started chewing on it greedily. Veronica didn't want to lose out, so she also went at it with her teeth. Now they were stood either side of the kitchen island tugging at Ralph's liver. A pair of hyenas, tussling over the entrails. They grunted and snuffled as the blood caught in their nostrils until, at last, their mouths met over the final morsel, which they tore in two and guzzled down. Their eyes met and an unspoken agreement passed between them. They immediately started licking the blood from each other's faces, lapping up what was left of the man on whom they had gorged. Then they parted and scraped off as much blood from themselves as they could, gulping it down.

"Do you think we might lose another one?" Veronica asked.

"Possibly," Rosalind replied. She'd thought that Teddy had been looking out of breath over the last hour.

"Let's make some room," said Veronica and together they shoved, pushed and heaved Ralph's bulk off the side of the island. Ralph Curtis, fund manager, multi-millionaire, philanthropist, Harvard graduate, a true mover and shaker landed on the floor with a wet slap. Just a piece of meat. Veronica and Rosalind left him without a backward glance. Both were naked and both still splattered with Ralph's rapidly drying blood. Veronica opened the kitchen door onto what could have been a scene from a zombie porn flick. All of the men were crowded around the door, quietly waiting for their mistresses' return. They parted as the pair came out of the kitchen and followed them through to the living area where Veronica went to one five-seater sofa and Rosalind went to the other. The men split themselves more or less evenly between the two. As half the group approached her, Veronica cried out,

"Come on, then! I'll take you all on!"

Then she was lost in a pile of naked, writhing flesh.

By six thirty in the morning, the suite was, for any normal person, a stinking, sweaty mess. For the Sirens, it was heavenly. Every breath was like drinking in a heady cocktail of pure 'man'. Upwards of fifty men had joined them during the night and three didn't make it out alive. Ralph, Teddy (another older man, who'd been a brilliant political strategist) and Joe, a slight, geeky man who controlled a range of social networks. Veronica had accidentally broken his neck while he'd been going down on her. All three were left mutilated in the kitchen. The alarm sounded on Rosalind's phone – the signal that they had twenty minutes before they needed to leave for their flight to Bermuda. Rosalind quickly finished who she was doing, then clapped her hands,

"Thank you, gentlemen, you may go now," and at their mistress' command, they dressed in silence and began to leave.

Veronica and Rosalind, meanwhile, hit the showers and twenty minutes later, they stepped into their limousine, looking perfectly turned out and as if they'd both had a good eight hours' sleep. In the back of the car, Rosalind called ahead to her connection in Bermuda,

"Darnel, we are on our way. Do you have the firearms and the vehicles for our teams?"

There was a pause as the man in Bermuda explained the situation to the woman for whom he would gladly step out in front of a bus.

"Excellent. We'll be landing at eleven thirty. I'm very pleased with you. I will reward you tonight," then she hung up.

"Feeling ready, sister?" Veronica asked, with the ghost of a wicked smile playing at the corners of her mouth.

"Oh yes, sister," she replied, "Jasper doesn't stand a chance. Although it might be worth having a couple of the passengers or cabin crew on the way."

"Better safe than sorry," Veronica smiled.

Yes, she was looking forward to this flight.

Chapter Forty-One

The Storm

Jack woke to the sound of rain on the roof. It was gentle and helped to ease him out of the arms of sleep. As he swung his legs out over the side of the bed, he felt energised and ready to face the day. It wasn't that he was looking forward to facing the sirens, but he was keen to get it over and done with. Once he was dressed and breakfasted, he thought about next moves. Although last night he hadn't dared to venture out of the house, this morning he had the sense that it would be a good idea. He left by the back door to get the lie of the land. The rain had stopped and the clouds were breaking up as he went down the path to the beach. He had the bronze dagger held in his belt and the feel of it at his side reassured him. He still had no idea where the other dagger was or who had it, so he made sure to keep his wits about him. He was wearing sand-coloured chinos and a blue polo shirt with comfy plimsolls and looked every inch the tourist. For the Bermudians, seventy degrees Fahrenheit probably had them reaching for their jumpers, but for him coming over from the freezing temperatures of the Italian alps, it was positively balmy.

His first view of the beach took his breath away. The sand really was pink! Not a gaudy pink, but that calm, sophisticated Bermuda pink. And the sea was a light teal, spotlighted by the rays of the sun breaking through the clouds. The air smelt fresh and clean in the light breeze and, as he got down to the sand, he realised that this was the first time he'd been on a beach in about fifteen years. Or was it more? It was funny, he couldn't actually remember the last time he'd stood on a beach. He looked out across the sea and puffed out his cheeks. Would he be sending evil back into its depths, or would his 'sisters' get the better of him and consign his soul to the deep? Looking to the right, he saw the infamous rocks where the thirty-year nightmare had begun. He walked over to them and clambered up. Wow! They were razor sharp! How had his dad and Katy Brewer survived being dashed against them? It was nigh-on miraculous. Jack walked across the rocks to look at the waves breaking against them. He knew, from a quick web check, that the tide was going out and that it would be at its lowest point around midday. The sea looked benign. The breaking waves didn't even seem to be all that interested in making a noise or showing off. He looked behind him up at the cliff that gave the house its name. It stood high above him, mostly covered in vegetation, but with patches of white rock standing out where the plants couldn't get a foothold. It all seemed so lovely. A picture-perfect island paradise. And yet...

Looking back at the water, Jack shivered. The child within him was screaming at him to run away from it. Flashing images came of all those times when they'd held him underwater, kicking and struggling. That horrible feeling that suddenly overtook him when his breath finally ran out and his lungs desperately wanted to gulp air, but couldn't without drowning him. The airless, bursting panic. Sometimes it had been as if he'd experienced it looking down at them from above, seeing his terrified face bulging under the water. And this was the place those two had come from. This was their home. Somewhere around here was their lair, from which they had called to his father to lure him and his children to the rocks and their destruction. Jack breathed deeply. He couldn't let such memories and feelings get in the way of what he had to do today. He deliberately stood at the edge of the waves, watching them as they came and went until the little boy within stopped shouting for him to run. Only when the voice was quiet did he walk away and head back to the house. He walked back up the path, then checked all around the outside of the house. Everything was beautifully tended and, come the summer, would be a riot of colour.

When he went back into the house, he debated whether to have another cup of coffee. He tried to gauge his stress level. It was certainly rising. As the minutes passed by, the tension was building. There was no risk of being sleepy when they arrived, and he figured that the coffee would only make him jittery. He needed to be rock steady. Now there was nothing to do but wait and he sat down on one of the sofas and looked out through the patio doors to the pool and beyond to the sea and sky. The minutes dragged their feet. There was a drawer in the wide coffee table in front of him and he decided to be nosy – anything to take his mind off the oppressive wait before the inevitable action. There was a big, leather-bound photograph album inside. He opened it and smiled. The first picture was a black and white of a chubby little boy sitting in the midst of a sandcastle. Underneath, it read:

Rufus, the King of the Castle. June 1933.

Of course, his grandfather had spent much of his youth, including the whole of the Second World War right there in Cliff House.

He looked through the old pictures and was intrigued by the way the gardens had changed. In his grandfather's time there hadn't been a pool and the area toward the cliff had been formally planted in the colonial style. The copse of trees further up the hill were much smaller then and there were no other houses on the estate. Presumably his grandfather's parents had sold bits off or leased plots out so that people could build their holiday homes around the original grand house. Jack preferred the way it was now. He never liked the idea of the splendid isolation that wealth brings. He liked to have neighbours to chat to. Then he turned the page and caught his breath. Suddenly all the photographs were colour and there was his mother. First as a girl, then as a young woman and finally as a mother herself – presumably with Rosalind in her arms. And there was the family growing before his eyes in the favourite snaps from holiday after holiday.

"My God!" Jack whispered, "They look so happy!"

It was incredible to him. He had never known his sisters or his parents being happy. His mother had had her moments, but Jack had always sensed her deep anguish. It had tinged everything when he'd known her. And yet here, in the pictures, he could see pure joy. The three, four and finally five of them looking carefree. All right, he himself didn't look carefree – he looked like a chubby baby – but the others were like people he'd never met. He could see the love his parents had for each other – that was unmistakable. And that love enveloped the children. The pictures of them all together captured the feeling that these were people who had fun! His sisters looked totally different. The way they looked struck him because he was, for the first time in his life, seeing his real sisters. There was none of the unworldliness that his sisters had when he knew them. These looked like two normal girls living a happy life. Sure, they were different to each other - Rosalind looked a bit more serious and Veronica clearly had a cheeky glint in her eye – but they both looked loved. That was it! Everyone in these photographs looked loved. That was the difference between the family he'd grown up in and the family he was looking at now. Once the sirens had taken his sisters, they had snuffed out the love and light in the family. Cuckoos in the nest, doing their best to push him and his mother out. And there was the last picture. The five of them with Katy Brewer just days before the 'accident'. Rosalind was laughing with Katy. Actually laughing like a normal person would. The camera had caught the moment perfectly. Something had just been said and Rosalind had been captured in the helpless paroxysm of laughter. What a golden moment!

And that was it. There were no more photographs in the album, because there were no more golden moments to capture. The rest of their lives had been tainted by evil. Jack could feel that there was something between the last couple of pages of the album. He turned to the place and, under words written in his grandfather's hand that read *'Where are my beautiful granddaughters?'*, two passports were stuck to the page. Jack carefully opened the first, to reveal a photograph of Rosalind aged twelve, next to her identity details. The photograph wasn't flattering, but she looked 'normal'. The other passport was Veronica's. She was aged ten when the photograph had been taken. His grandparents must have got hold of them after the passports ran out and put them here as keepsakes. This proved they had known something was wrong, but what could they have done? They couldn't have accused their granddaughters of being some sort of doppelgangers without sounding like total loonies. They hadn't even been able to tell Jack about their fears. All they could do was treasure the memories they had and ultimately save their grandson.

Jack felt a surge of overwhelming sadness. What torture must it have been for his grandparents to watch the sirens slowly but surely destroy their family. The only way they could have got through it was by supporting each other. They had suspected a truth they could never prove. Without each other to confirm the truth they felt, they would surely have gone insane. It explained a lot. What he'd noticed most when he'd gone to live with them, was their physical closeness. They would often hold hands, touch each other, hold each other. After witnessing his father hardly ever touching his mother, it had seemed strange, but now it made perfect sense. It had been more than affection, it had been their way of getting through the nightmare, of coping with the loss of their daughter and the dreadful change in their granddaughters and son-in-law. He wished he'd been old enough for them to have confided in him and share their burden. Maybe they would have, if they hadn't been killed in the 'accident', which he now knew was nothing less than cold blooded murder.

Jack sighed heavily, put the photo album back and checked his watch. Ten thirty. It would still be a while. He was just thinking about going to get a book on sailing out of the study, when a different thought popped into his head. It was the idea that it would be good if he went and stood in the magic circle on the floor. Since he had decided to follow his gut, he did just that. He stood outside it, regarding the pentagram, the shell and the other thing, which he presumed was the mermaid's purse. As someone who almost never went to the beach, he had no idea what the little black parcel was. Where should he stand? Slap dab in the middle? One foot on the top of the pentagram and the other at the bottom? He wasn't sure, but in the middle felt right, so he went with it. Stepping inside, he didn't feel anything particular. It wasn't like he'd expected to suddenly feel the power of magic flowing through him, but he kind of expected *something*. He couldn't help but feel disappointed. How long should he stand there? Should he try to clear his thoughts, or concentrate on visualising victory? Part of him felt a bit of a twit.

Jack checked his watch. Odd! It showed eleven fifteen, but he knew it had been half-ten when he'd stepped into the circle and he'd only been in there about a minute. He lifted the watch to his ear – yes, still ticking normally. Ah, his phone would have the right time... eleven twenty! What the hell? He looked back at his watch – eleven twenty-three. No, this was weird and getting out of hand. He looked back at the phone – eleven thirty. Was time really speeding up, or was the magic circle simply screwing with the electrics of his phone and watch? He looked over his shoulder – out in the back garden everything looked normal. It wasn't like the clouds were skimming quickly across the sky. No, it was all... and then he heard the sound of vehicles pulling up outside the house. From where he was standing, he could see out of the living room, across the front hall and through one of the narrow windows either side of the front door. Four boxy-looking black Mercedes G-wagons had pulled up in the drive and men were piling out. Armed men. Shit! And sure enough, there were Rosalind and Veronica. Jack wasn't sure what to do, but again his instinct told him to stay put. He decided that since he was so far down the road, he had to keep having faith in Josephine and his instincts. He stood still and watched.

As Rosalind stepped out of the car, she felt more powerful than she had in aeons. Yes, they were going to kill Jasper, eat him, kill his family and go back to living as they pleased.

"You men take the front – you take the back," she ordered, pointing out where she wanted the men to go. They split without a word, with two small groups going around each side of the house, while the third group approached the front of the house with pistols drawn. All of them had fitted suppressors to their guns. Their task was to kill quickly and quietly. Lorenzo Rossi was the most senior of Veronica's team and he was leading the group, softly moving towards the front door with guns raised. He was desperate to prove that he was more than a replacement for Gianfranco and Aristide. This was his chance to show the Mistress that he was the best and then he'd be able to have her every night. He would get into the house first, shoot this fucker and then go back to Veronica with his severed head in his...

As his foot passed over the line Josephine had drawn around the house using the blood of David Kidd, it was as if Lorenzo was waking from a dream. What the...? He was walking forward with his gun raised towards a house he didn't recognise. Where was this? What was he doing? He shook his head and looked around him. Who were these men? Why were they all armed? Why did they all look confused? Lorenzo stopped and lowered his gun. Suddenly he felt sick. He bent over with his hands on his knees. Everything was spinning. How did he get to this place? The last thing he remembered was going to a meeting for a job. Some high-class woman needed protection and he was going to organise security for her. That's right... he was an ex-cop who'd gone into private security because the money was better, and then he'd met... suddenly everything came flooding back.

"Oh my God!" he gasped as his knees buckled under the weight of bad memories. And, amidst the swirling mass of beatings, arson and murders - all done to prove himself to the woman - one memory replayed itself over and over until he wanted to tear out his own eyes in the hope of making it stop. It was him cutting the throat of an eight-year-old boy and standing back as the child had flailed around, trying to scream and clawing at the air until he finally collapsed. Why had he done that? How could he? That couldn't be *him*. It couldn't be! But why did he have that memory and why was it so vivid if he hadn't done it?

Around him, some of the other men seemed to be experiencing similar feelings of disconnection and disbelief at memories they had but couldn't identify with themselves.

"What are you doing?" a woman screamed and Lorenzo turned. The moment he looked at Veronica and saw those monstrous eyes and her imperious features raging with anger, he knew it was all true. Everything he was seeing in his head, he had done, right down to last night when he'd watched her break a man's neck and then suck out his eyeballs, swallowing each down with a nightmarish slurp. And then she had beckoned him to continue giving her the oral pleasure that had cost the man his life. And he had - even though her vagina had been oozing the semen of twenty other men. Then she'd roughly shoved him aside to make way for the next man. And he had waited patiently until he was called again to fuck her.

"Lorenzo! Get in there and kill him!" Veronica barked. What was happening?

Lorenzo stood and looked at her. He looked into the eyes of the devil, put his gun into his mouth and ended his pain.

"What the fuck?" Veronica screamed as the top of Lorenzo's head exploded, "Why did he...?" but she wasn't able to finish because the man who'd been standing next to Lorenzo roared,

"Die, you psycho bitch!" as he emptied his Glock into her.

The first shot caught Veronica in the right shoulder and twisted her round, so that shots two, three, four and five were easily able to thud into her left flank between her armpit and her hip. The force of the impacts sent her stumbling backwards and as she turned to try to stop herself, four more shots hit her in the back, sending her sprawling to the ground. Satisfied that he had rid the world of evil, the man who until thirty seconds earlier would have either died or killed for her, put the gun to the side of his head and blew his brains out with his last round.

"No!" Rosalind yelled, ducking behind the nearest car,

"It's magic!" she hissed, as she watched every man in the team stagger about trying to come to grips with floods of memories and emotions. She looked at Veronica, who was lying in a bloody heap beside her.

"That little shit must have found a witch to help him," Rosalind said angrily.

Three of the men had now dropped their guns and were walking towards the road in a daze. All they wanted to do was leave the island and put all their bad memories behind them.

"She's used our father's blood to undo our power. *That's* why we needed the list of names, Veronica!" she chided, "*That's* why we needed to find out where the blood was being kept! God, I should've done the job myself. Why did I trust you to do anything? Veronica?"

Her sister still lay motionless on the ground.

"Veronica!" Rosalind shouted and gave her sister a kick.

"Oh yes, blame me!" said Veronica bitterly, "Of course it's all *my* fault. It's always *my* fault," she said, easing herself onto her hands and knees.

"Yes, it *is* always your bloody fault," Rosalind growled.

"That idiot has ruined my Versace suit," Veronica complained, looking ruefully at the holes and blood stains.

"Did it hurt?" Rosalind asked.

"Yes."

"Good. Maybe if you hired your men for skills instead of looks, we wouldn't be in this mess."

"Oh really? Well, maybe if you went and fucked yourself, everyone would be happier!" Veronica replied and then she gave three deep coughs and spat the remnants of a bullet onto the asphalt.

"Getting some of these out is going to hurt," Veronica added.

"What are you?" asked one of the men, who had come over and was standing staring at them with his gun held loosely by his side.

Rosalind stood up to face him and thundered,

"We are the doom of men! Fall to your knees and pray to our beauty or die!"

"Fuck you!" he said, swinging his gun up to shoot her, but Rosalind was slippery quick. Before he'd had time to raise the pistol, she had darted forward and turned the gun back on him, placing her fingers around his and pumping two bullets into his chest at point blank range. As he fell backwards, she plucked the gun from his grasp.

The man's body had hardly collapsed when a couple of single 'clacks' came from the back of the house, where the other team of men had presumably also just crossed the line of the magic circle.

"Shit!" Rosalind swore. The unmistakable sound of suppressed gunfire told her she had two more men down and soon the rest would either be leaving or coming after her and her sister. She looked around and then caught sight of Jack through the narrow window next to the front door. He was standing staring at her like an idiot. Without hesitating, she aimed the pistol and fired. The first shot shattered the window and the rest of the shots in the magazine flew straight and true to their target.

Jack had watched the scene unfold in morbid fascination. He had worried for a moment as he'd seen the group of men converging on the patio door at the back of the house, but now two of them had shot themselves, one had deliberately walked off the cliff and the others were meandering away in a daze. He looked back towards the cars and that was when Rosalind had seen him. He stood, rooted to the spot as she fired at him and he flinched after the first shot broke the glass. He was a sitting duck, but he didn't want to move. He watched as Rosalind fired all the bullets in the gun at him. Behind him, the doorframe popped and spat as the bullets thudded into it. Jack looked down at himself - he was unharmed. Had the bullets gone round him? He looked back at Rosalind and their eyes met. Then he gave her a 'I dunno' shrug. That really made her angry and, even from a distance, he could see the lightning flashing in her eyes. She swore and threw the gun down.

"How the hell?" she yelled, "There's no way the witch can create a spell to stop bullets!"

And yet, there Jack was, gurning at her like a knuckle-dragging moron.

Of course, Rosalind was right. No witch had the power to stop bullets, otherwise war would have been a thing of the past. Josephine, with Goody's guidance, had been very clever. As soon as Jack had stepped into the magic circle, he'd been displaced from the temporal world's timeline. So, although his body seemed to be standing in the magic circle at eleven-forty, it wasn't. He had stepped into the magic circle at half-past-ten and, so far, he'd only been standing in it for about five minutes. His physical body was an hour and five minutes behind the world outside the circle. What Rosalind was seeing was Jack's astral form. And not even a pissed off siren can shoot an astral form.

"Come on! We're going to have to kill him the old-fashioned way," she cried, and marched towards the door. Veronica followed and, when she caught a glimpse of him through the window, he flicked her a V sign. Veronica's face contorted in anger,

"I'm going to snap those fingers off and shove them up your fucking nose!" she shouted, then Jack's sightline was obscured by the front door.

On the front drive, Rosalind was stepping carefully through the blood and brains as she approached the point where the spell had broken their control over the men. Veronica joined her.

"We need to be careful," Rosalind said, "I've never seen magic this powerful before. We don't know what it might do to us."

Veronica hung back, while Rosalind carefully put her foot forward.

"Anything?"

"No. Seems normal. Maybe I'm not there yet."

Rosalind stretched further,

"Still nothing," she said.

She made a full step forward and was sure she had crossed the invisible line.

"It's fine. Maybe all the witch could do was level the playing field by getting rid of our men," she said.

"Well, fuck the witch and fuck Jasper. Let's finish this!" said Veronica and together, they walked towards the door.

Their swagger and their confidence were their undoing. They weren't being careful, because they thought they had a handle on the situation. The result was that they walked face-first into the second protective circle. Instantly, they were gripped in an electric shock that enveloped them in pain like a thousand hot needles piercing them all over. Rosalind and Veronica staggered backwards, their unearthly screams shattering the morning as they clutched their faces.

"I'm blind! I'm fucking blind!" Veronica screeched as she fell to the floor, rolling in an attempt to get the all-encompassing pain to stop.

Rosalind made no reply as she vomited blood down herself, stumbling blindly with a hand outstretched. She should have stayed still. In her torment, she'd become disorientated and turned around. Instead of heading away from the magical shield, she was fumbling straight back towards it. The intensity of her scream as her hand met the invisible wall of the circle made the windscreen of the nearest car crack. Rosalind looked at her hand through puffed-up eyes. Her blurred vision registered bright red lines across her hand as if she'd been lashed with live electrical wires. She fell to the ground heavily, squealing and thrashing at the searing agony that wouldn't stop.

Jack took the opportunity to make a break for it. The moment he stepped out of the magic circle, his temporal form re-joined the flow of time. He'd known he couldn't stay in there forever. That would have only been a stand-off. What he wanted was to finish them, but he needed them closer to the sea. He went quickly to the front door and opened it. The sight filled him with revulsion and joy in equal measure. Both of his 'sisters' were still enduring agonies, making noises like tortured pigs. Their usually 'beautiful' faces covered in lines of scarlet welts and puffed up as if they were both suffering an allergic reaction.

"Does that sting more than nettles?" he said in a voice which sounded much more assured than he felt.

Rosalind couldn't respond, as she was jerking in new paroxysms, but Veronica turned her mangled face to him and screeched,

"I'll kill you!"

"You've got to catch me first. Last one to the beach is a rotten egg!" Jack cried gleefully and then he ran around the house, across the garden, past two dazed goons who'd dropped their guns and were making for the road, past the bodies of two more who'd shot themselves, and down the steps to the sand below.

Veronica channelled her strength and it took all her concentration to master the pain. After about a minute, she was able to get up and lurch her way over to Rosalind, who was still in her own private hell.

"Come on! We've got him right where we want him. The nearer we are to the sea, the faster we'll recover," Veronica said, trying to grasp Rosalind under the armpits and help her up. Rosalind thrashed herself free and started puking again – a hard stream of the blood she'd guzzled down so greedily from Ralph and the others the previous night. Veronica tottered back out of the way,

"All right, you do you. I'm going after him," and she weaved away clumsily towards the beach.

She was still in a great deal of pain that suffused every cell of her body, her mouth was dry and her head was feeling like it would explode, but as she tottered her way to the beach, she felt better with every step. She kicked off her four-inch Louboutins and now her steps quickened until she finally felt the pink sand under her feet. It was like a balm! Oh yes, that felt good. She ran straight to the surf and the moment the water touched her, the pain stopped. She stood in the waves and tipped her head back, luxuriating in the extreme pleasure of the lack of pain. After a few seconds of bliss, she snapped back into the moment. She had a little brother to kill and she was going to do it as slowly and painfully as possible.

From his vantage point on the rocks, Jack watched Veronica run into the waves and stand there. He could almost see the strength returning to her. He gripped the dagger in his right hand and held it down behind his leg so that she wouldn't be able to see it. Then she turned to him and in an instant, the sky clouded and strong winds blew in from the sea, unbalancing him while the sea became a mass of white foam and angry waves. Veronica visibly gathered herself and, with an alien scream, she leapt at him. She must have been thirty yards away, but her jump took her high into the air and the parabola landed her within two feet of him. Fortunately, Jack was a humble fighter. He always assumed that opponents were stronger than him, so he relied on speed and cunning to achieve victory, not brute strength. He was ready to sidestep her first lunge at him and as she went through the empty space where he'd been, he gave her a push to help her on her way. She sprawled horribly across the jagged rocks and grunted as the breath was knocked out of her. Jack backed off and worked his way around so that the cliff was at his back. He was very aware that Rosalind might turn up at any moment. Veronica got up and turned on him. Her face was torn up from hitting the rocks, but the grazes healed before Jack's eyes.

"You think you're so very clever, don't you?" said Veronica caustically,

"But you're not. You're a fool to challenge us here. The sea is our home. It's the source of our immortality. There's nothing you can do to us. Your strength is nothing."

"Really?" said Jack and he revealed the dagger, which he now held ready. Veronica flinched when she saw it.

"Yeah, that's right. It's been dipped in father's blood and a witch has cast a spell on it. One stab from this and it's goodbye, bitch!"

There was something about the way Jack said it that made anger flash up inside Veronica and, with her sea green eyes sparking, she struck at him. Again, his fighting skills were more than a match for her clumsy attack and he slipped her move and stepped in to deliver an elbow to her mouth. She was sent flying backwards and landed, dazed on her rump. Jack glanced quickly behind him to check he wasn't about to get blindsided by Rosalind, then moved in with much greater speed than his bulk suggested.

Veronica was still trying to get up when Jack caught her with a flying knee to the side of the head. The blow forced a shrill cry out of her and threw her over onto her face. Everything reeled. Jack should have pressed home his advantage and pinned her to the ground, then driven the dagger deep into her back, but for some reason he stopped. This mistake was all Veronica needed to recover herself and scramble out of his reach. She got up, looked into his face and laughed,

"Still so weak! The fat little gay boy with no killer instinct," she taunted as they began circling each other,

"Apparently, possessing your sisters, sleeping with your father and torturing you aren't enough reasons to make you go for the throat!"

Jack ignored the words and concentrated on Veronica's actions, but then she said something that drew his attention,

"I killed her, you know."

"Who?" Jack asked, not taking his eyes from hers.

"Your dear, sainted mother, of course."

"Bullshit. It was an accident. I saw it. You weren't even there," he said through gritted teeth.

Veronica laughed her soulless, clattering laugh and said,

"Why do you think she shouted my name before diving into the river?"

Jack said nothing,

"Because *I* was in the river, floating along the bottom, looking up at her. The last thing she ever did was try to save my life – stupid slut."

Oh yes! That hit home! She could see the anger flash across his face. She would taunt him some more and either force him into a false move or keep him occupied until Rosalind arrived.

"She dived down to grab me and take me to the surface, but I grabbed her! I held onto her and pulled her into the deeper water. How she struggled! I'll give her that – she was a strong swimmer. But when we're in water, we're unbeatable. So, I held onto her until her breath ran out – you should have seen the look on her face when she realised I was drowning her! It's one of my fondest memories."

Again, Jack's jaw tightened. Was that the sound of his teeth grinding? She could almost hear it over the sound of the waves on the rocks.

"Then I wedged her down under the mill, swam around, got back into my dry clothes and arrived on the scene. All very easy. Then we could finally have your father all to ourselves. And in gratitude for all the things we did to him – and we did so many things to him – he would make your life a misery. We suggested everything he ever did to you. Everything bad in your miserable little life is thanks to us. You're welcome."

Although Jack was burning with anger and a desire to avenge his mother and father, he was still in complete control of himself. So, when his face registered anger, it was premeditated. As Veronica had spoken, he'd watched her closely and she had given away her plan. He'd spotted the tiny movements of her eyes, looking out behind him for any sign of Rosalind. Yes, she was stalling. He'd have to end this fast!

"And then there's your wife," Veronica said, taking her phone out of her pocket,

"All I have to..."

Jack launched himself across the space between them, spinning around to deliver the dagger strike backhanded into her chest, but Veronica blocked the strike with both hands and held the arm firmly.

"Patheti..." she began, then realised the hand she'd blocked was empty.

Jack thrust the dagger, transferred from his right hand to his left as he was spinning, deep into Veronica's solar plexus. Her face crumpled in pain as the breath was forced out of her. Jack almost gagged – the breath stank of rotting shellfish. Suddenly, a thin, blue tentacle like thick wire shot out of the sea and wrapped around one of her wrists, wrenching it away from Jack's arm. He stepped back, pulling the dagger from her chest. A second blue tentacle whipped out of the sea and held her other wrist. In a moment, two more had secured her ankles as Veronica choked and screamed in pain. Watching in shock and confusion, Jack realised they looked exactly like Portuguese Man O'War tentacles. A final tentacle lashed out of the waves and darted down her throat as she held her head back, screaming. Now her entire body convulsed as a strange, muffled scream came from deep within her. The tentacle down Veronica's throat started to withdraw and Jack could see her chest expanding as if something might burst out of it, but then the shape inside moved upwards. Her throat began to bulge horribly and, as it moved up, her mouth opened wider and wider until he could hear the dull crack of her jaw dislocating. Then the screaming became clearer. High pitched, unnatural, more like a bird than a human and it was suddenly piercingly loud. Jack slapped his hands to his ears to protect them.

Then, from the grotesquely distended mouth, a face started to appear. It was a woman's face, twisted with fear, anger and hate, screaming words in a language Jack didn't understand. Now he could see the tentacle was wrapped around the woman's throat and it was pulling her out of Veronica. But when her shoulders appeared, they weren't the shoulders of a woman – they were those of a bird. A cormorant's shoulders, with black feathers, just as Giulia Mazzoni had described. And still the creature was being pulled out of Veronica, slowly but surely. At last its wings were free, but before it could flap and struggle, two more tentacles had whipped out of the sea to secure them.

Jack's eyes were seeing, but he was hardly believing as he knelt in pain because the screeches of the siren seemed about to split his eardrums. Finally and, Jack felt, most monstrous of all, the thin, scaly legs appeared with their taloned, webbed feet. These, too, were instantly secured by stinging tentacles from the sea. And now Jack could see the siren for what she was – a monster. An ugly, evil creature that could only spread death and despair. And this was the thing that all those men had desired! How many men? Thousands? Suddenly it turned its hate-filled gaze on him and screamed what he assumed were curses at him. Then, it was overcome with fear and seemed to be begging him. Begging him to make it all stop. Begging him to allow it to stay. But it was too late. Jack sensed it was all over and regained his presence of mind enough to put two fingers up at the hideous nightmare. And then it was dragged, screaming into the sea until the water closed over that devil's face.

There was a moment of absolute silence where even the waves were still, and then the sound of the sea and the shore washed around Jack once again. With the creature gone, the tentacles slid away from Veronica's body, which was still being held upright. Without them, her body stood straight for a moment and then collapsed onto the rocks. Jack scrambled over to it.

The jaw was gruesomely broken, but in spite of that, Veronica somehow looked better than she had when she'd been possessed. Gone were the cruelty, the arrogance and the vicious lines of malice. Jack was suddenly overcome with emotion. For the first time that he could remember, he was looking at his sister. This was what she could have been without that evil monster inside her. He ran the back of a finger across her soft brow. Her pure spirit shone through, even in death. He took her in his arms and held her, sobbing.

"I'm sorry! I'm so, so sorry," he whispered and he rocked her as he mourned Veronica, who had died right there thirty years earlier.

"Pitiful!"

Jack turned and put the knife up, ready to defend himself against Rosalind, who was standing twenty feet away. She had her phone in her hand.

"So, you sent my sister back to the sea?"

"Yes, and you're next," said Jack, letting Veronica down gently and getting to his feet.

"I don't think so. I think your wife and son will be next," Rosalind said with a victor's smile,

"When I send this text, the murder squad will go in and I've given my good friend Gus instructions to keep your wife alive for a very, very long time. He's forgotten more about torture than Torquemada ever knew."

"Fucker!"

"That's not the way to bargain for the lives of your wife and son. I guess you don't care about them after all. Bye bye, Annie!" and she sent the text.

Chapter Forty-Two

Annie Makes Her Stand

When the long, cold night was finally over, Piet had given Gus the job of watching the ski lodge while the rest of them got breakfast. Then, they would come in the cars and wait just down the road, ready to strike whenever the order came. Gus wasn't happy about it, but he had been able to sleep all night, so he couldn't complain. He had waited three hours in the cold in the hiding place Piet had set up in the night. It wasn't comfortable lying there on the ground in the leaves, but Gus had to admit that the South African had done a good job. He had an excellent view of the front of the building and the camouflage netting seemed to give him total invisibility. He'd watched as a guard had come out every hour, taken a good look around, then gone back in. At no point did it seem like they'd seen him. Then, at almost eleven, just when he was wondering what time he would be relieved, Johnny's voice came over the headset,

"Go! We have a go! With you in five. Gus, you protect our flanks and rear, then join us for the fun."

"Copy that," said Gus, and he shifted his bulk so that he could see what was happening, with his gun ready to shoot anything coming out of the lodge.

A few minutes later, the rest of the team came at speed and fanned out around the lodge, keeping low and using the natural blind spots of the building to allow them to get in close. They were all wearing gas masks.

When the men were all in place, one of them (Gus wasn't sure who – Johnny?) pulled a smoke grenade from his belt and threw it through a window. Seconds later the men would storm in.

***

"No!" Jack shouted, running forward as Rosalind sent the text.

Jack was quick, but Rosalind nonchalantly raised the Glock taken from one of the dead men and shot Jack through the right shoulder. He cried out, dropping the dagger and stumbling painfully onto the rocks. Rosalind gave a theatrical sigh and walked towards Jack, who was trying to regain the dagger.

"No, I don't think so," Rosalind said, kicking the dagger off the rocks and into the sea.

Jack looked up at her with nothing but hate in his eyes. The barrel of the gun looked back at him with nothing but darkness to offer. Rosalind kicked him in the face, sending him backwards. He lay still for a moment, looking up at a patch of blue in the broken clouds. Shit! Now he was well and truly fucked! Rosalind stood over him, pointing the gun at different parts of him as if deciding what to shoot next.

"No, that would be too easy," she mused, "You've caused me a lot of trouble, so I'm going to make this excruciating."

Rosalind then made a high-pitched squeak – like she was calling some pet animal - and stood over him, smiling a very unpleasant smile. After about half a minute, Jack became aware of a strange sort of clicking noise. Like the tips of lots of metal pens being tapped onto a hard surface. He raised his head slightly and his eyes widened at the sight of hundreds of land crabs scuttling across the rocks straight towards him.

In a few seconds, he was surrounded by the creatures, each of which was about the size of a man's hand. Most surrounded him, while some of them clambered onto him, using his clothes to haul themselves up. One had found his gunshot wound and was tentatively putting out a feeler to taste the blood around the wound. It was good! When could they get started?

The sound of their hard claws clicking on the rocks as they moved made Jack feel faintly queasy. And now he started to imagine what it might be like if they all began feeding. He didn't want to, but his mind immediately went there. He imagined they would start with all the softest things they could find – his eyeballs, for instance. They would start scratching and probing until they'd decided that this was good food, and then... And then the pain would begin. He wanted to get up, to run, but the hot pain in his shoulder and Rosalind standing over him with the gun stopped him from moving. One of the crabs had come to investigate his chest and neck. Jack looked down at it, looked into its beady black eyes. It was an alien creature and it saw him as nothing more than its next meal. Worst of all, Rosalind seemed to have them under her total control.

"And now it's time to say goodbye, Jasper," said Rosalind,

"Any last requests?"

Jasper was about to speak, when a woman's voice shouted,

"Die in hell!"

There was a dull 'thump' and Rosalind stumbled forward with a pained sigh. Jack looked up and in a patch of blue sky he saw the face of an angel, framed in tumbling copper-coloured hair.

Annie stood with her feet planted firmly on the rocks, gripping the bronze-tipped spear she had thrust into Rosalind's back. She pulled the spear out and Rosalind fell forwards, scattering the terrified land crabs, which scuttled every which way for safety. Rosalind was gasping for breath on all fours right next to Jack and frothy pink blood was coming from her mouth. Wincing from the pain in his shoulder, Jack shuffled himself away from her. He knew what was coming and didn't want to get caught up in it. Rosalind slumped to the ground and turned to look back at her attacker.

"That's what you get for trying to kill my family, you fucking bitch!" Annie snarled, moving in to stand over Rosalind with the tip of the spear at her throat. She very deliberately placed her foot on Rosalind's chest and pushed down, taking more pleasure than she should have from the way Rosalind's face twisted in anger, fear and pain,

"How..." Rosalind began, then coughed a spray of blood.

"You don't get an explanation, fucker!" and Annie pushed down hard on the tip of the spear, twisting it into Rosalind's throat. Blood spouted as Rosalind choked out her last and her eyes turned up in their sockets. Jack shuffled further away and said,

"You need to step back. It's about to get weird!"

Annie pulled out the spear tip and did as she was told. No sooner had she done so, than the first of the blue tentacles whipped out of the sea to grasp Rosalind's right wrist.

"What's that?" Annie gasped.

"It gets worse," said Jack, and he was right. This was an even more macabre sight than Veronica's exorcism. For, while Veronica had been upright and still alive, this time the tendrils had to manipulate Rosalind's corpse. Within moments, four of them had grasped her wrists and ankles, pulling her limbs this way and that like a broken marionette until she was finally standing upright. Only then did the final tentacle shoot down her throat and once it had found its target, that's when the muffled screams began.

This time, the creature within fought like fury against the pull of the Portuguese Man O'War tentacle, which Jack guessed had wrapped itself around the siren's throat. Annie watched with a horrified look on her face as the thing inside Rosalind was dragged out. Suddenly the tip of a black claw pierced through from the inside, just below the ribcage. The thing inside was clinging on with all its might. A second and then a third tentacle whipped out of the sea and slid down Rosalind's throat. The screaming got louder as the creature was dislodged and drawn inch by inch out of the woman it had possessed. Unlike with Veronica, where the process of dragging the siren out through her mouth had been gruesome but fairly straightforward, the horrible wound Annie had made in Rosalind's throat made everything harder. As the siren was pulled up into Rosalind's throat, the skin and the sinews around the wound stretched and split. And then Annie saw its face through the hole, screaming and spitting blood. Annie's stomach flipped and she could feel her gorge rising.

"Oh Christ!" she said, turning away as the siren wedged in Rosalind's throat, while screaming abuse at them in ancient Greek. The tentacles pulled harder and the hole in Rosalind's throat got bigger and bigger as the muscles and skin tore in a ragged line around her neck. The ugly legs and clawed feet of the siren were sticking out of the wide hole, scrabbling to grab hold of the flesh around Rosalind's collarbone. The tentacles gave a sudden yank and the siren was pulled up further, snapping Rosalind's jaw. Its head half came up through the broken mess that had been Rosalind's mouth, but now it was well and truly stuck.

Annie looked back at it to see that the tentacles were pulling Rosalind's head off with the siren wedged inside. Annie turned away again and was immediately sick. Only Jack saw the final moment when the sinews around the last of Rosalind's cervical vertebrae gave. The spinal cord stretched and then snapped. With the sudden break, Rosalind's head and neck, with the siren struggling inside, were yanked away into the sea before Jack could make a rude gesture or say something witty. Instead, he slumped back,

"Thank fuck that's over!"

***

When the smoke bomb bounced across the floor of the main living space of the ski lodge, the women inside were ready for it. They were all wearing gas masks and had taken different vantage points around the house so that every possible entrance was covered. They were all armed with suppressed MP5s and, as Beth lay on her stomach at the top of the open staircase on one side of the room, she had a perfect view of the front door. She ignored the smoke and concentrated on sound. The moment she heard the door kicked in, she would open fire. The women waited. This was weird. Their attackers should've come straight in, but nothing was happening as the smoke filled the room. Then came the unmistakeable sound of suppressed pistol fire. But none of it seemed to be aimed at the lodge.

"What the fuck's going on? Anyone got eyes on the outside?" Beth hissed into her headset.

There was a pause.

"Moving to a better position," it was the voice of Gillian, who had been posing as Annie for the last day-and-a-half,

"Holy shit!"

Then there was the sound of three more suppressed shots.

"Two dead out the front. Looks like they shot themselves. Those last three shots were a big fat guy taking out one of his associates. Wait, there's another one walking round the side of the house. Seems confused. He's dropped his gun..."

Again, the sound of three quick, suppressed shots.

"The fat guy's shot him! What the fuck? And now he's running... he's gone."

"What's happening out back?" Beth asked.

"Checking..." said Amy, who motioned to Megan, the team member who'd been posing as Nancy, to cover her back.

"Man down near the back door. Looks self-inflicted."

"Okay, I'm calling the cops," said Beth,

"But stay frosty – there might be others."

Gus was running for the first time in twenty years, his big belly bouncing left and right with each lumbering step. He didn't know exactly what had just happened, but he was going to get away as fast as he could. He'd been heading towards the ski lodge, when he'd suddenly come to his senses and not known where he was or what he was doing. Then the memories had flooded in. Of course! Rosalind! He remembered everything he'd done for her over the previous seven years and the images of torture, murder and depraved acts that even the most imaginative porn star would balk at had played out in his mind. Not a moment of it concerned him. What had concerned him was seeing Williams and Florian putting their guns to their heads and killing themselves. Then Brooks had started walking towards him, saying that they should turn themselves in, that what they'd done was wrong, and Gus had made a snap decision. Brooks had had to go, and when Piet had appeared from round back, Gus had finished the job and run. No one in the lodge would be able to identify him in his gas mask. At that distance, he was nothing more than a big man. And with everyone who could've ID'd him dead, in a country of big men, there was little chance he'd be found.

Finally, he made it back to the cars. Jesus! Another fifty yards and he'd've had a fucking coronary! Gus heaved himself, breathless, into the Dodge Ram and, sweating heavily, started it. Thank Christ he had the spare key. He'd go back to the motel and take everything he could that the other men had left behind. If he moved quickly, he'd be able to buy a lot with their credit cards before the banks knew their owners were all dead. He turned the vehicle and pulled away at a speed that would not raise suspicion. He smiled and wiped his arm across his face as he drove. Even better than the credit cards and other identifying documents like passports and drivers' licences that he was about to scoop, he knew where Florian kept his money stash and he'd copied the key to the safety deposit box. Yeah, old Gus was gonna come out of this just fine - and with a crowding host of awesome memories from the last seven years. He knew in his capacious gut that Rosalind was gone. What a pity. He doubted he'd find anyone else that filthy again.

***

Jack struggled to his feet. Aside from the hot, sharp pain in his shoulder, he felt okay-ish. He looked down at the bodies on the rocks. What a mess! It was hard to decide which was worse – Rosalind's headless corpse or Veronica's with its dreadful, broken mouth. He walked away towards his saviour.

"Annie?" he said.

"Right here, kiddo," she said, smiling, but then it vanished, "Holy shit! The bitch shot you! Are you okay?"

"I think so," Jack replied, wincing. Actually, talking was pretty painful. Annie appraised the wound,

"Looks like the bullet went straight through. Here," she said, taking off her shirt and folding it up into a makeshift pad, "Press this onto it as hard as you can. Last thing I need is you bleeding out on me."

"God, you're a sight for sore eyes. I'd kiss you if you didn't have sick on your chin," said Jack.

"Shit!" and Annie took a handkerchief out of her shorts and wiped around her mouth, "Better?"

"Yeah, but I'm still not going to kiss you."

"Even after I saved your life? Some thanks!"

"I don't care how sexy you look in your bra and shorts, or how grateful I should be – vomit's vomit and that's where I draw a line. But if you don't squeeze too tight, I could manage a hug."

Annie put her arms around him and held him lightly with her head on the side of his chest that wasn't shot.

"So, you're the one who took the other dagger," said Jack, looking at her with love and relief.

"Yeah, I ran into Josephine when I got to the house yesterday."

"Well, that explains that... would it have killed you two to leave a note?"

"Sorry, she wanted to get out fast and was insistent that I shouldn't contact you. She said something about what she'd seen in the... astral plane?" Annie looked to Jack for some kind of explanation, but he could only shrug, then winced in pain.

"We need to get that seen to."

"How?"

"What d'you mean 'how'? At the hospital," Annie said.

"Yeah, but how are we going to explain all this. We've got two bodies there – one of which doesn't have a frickin' head – a bloke further along who fell over the cliff and at least four men up there who've committed suicide. What are we going to say?"

"Crap! Maybe we should've thought of that before," said Annie, racking her brain. It hadn't occurred to her that if they won, there might be bodies.

"I don't think the 'they weren't really women, but sirens' is a very good legal defence. Shit! First we were going to die and now we're going to go to prison. That's just fucking peachy!" Jack said angrily. It wasn't fair. They'd won, but now they were in a whole different world of trouble.

"Er... there's something you oughtta see," said Annie, indicating something behind Jack, who swivelled round as quickly as he could, given the shoulder.

"Ah," he said, looking at the rocks. Aside from a few of the land crabs, making a square meal on spilt blood and scraps of sinew, the rocks were empty. Veronica and Rosalind's bodies were gone,

"I guess the sea took them," he ventured.

"Those tendril things must've dragged them in while we were hugging."

"Yeah..."

"D'you think we should move, just in case they come back for us?" Annie asked.

"Couldn't do any harm," said Jack and they started walking carefully across the rocks.

"That is really weird," Annie said, "But at least we won't have to explain the bodies to the authorities."

"Thank God! So, how are Harry and your mum?" Jack asked, walking carefully over the rocks.

"Good. Couped up in a luxury suite in an expensive hotel in Boston."

"Everything went according to plan?"

"Like clockwork. When we got to the gas station at Newport, mom and I went into the restrooms with Harry and gave our jackets and hats to the extra security team who were going to 'be' us. They waited for a while, then went out to the Beast carrying a Harry-sized doll, and drove off to Vermont, taking Rosalind's goons with them. Then I went to New York and flew here, while mom and Harry went with two more guards to Boston."

"And those idiots never suspected?"

"Apparently not..." then Annie's phone gave a chirrup. She pulled it out and looked at it as they made their way up the slope from the beach. She gave a long sigh of relief,

"Looks like when Rosalind died, her hold over her men was broken. They were going in for a direct assault, when they all stopped and started acting weird."

"Did some of them..." and Jack mimed shooting himself in the head with his good hand.

"Yeah, but one of them got away. Will that be a problem?" Annie asked with a worried look.

"I doubt it. He's hardly going to risk coming after us when nobody's paying him."

Jack heaved a painful sigh as the sound of wailing emergency vehicles drifted towards them from the direction of the house.

"Okay, big step down," said Annie, helping Jack down from the rocks. Jack swore as he jolted onto the sand.

"Sorry," Annie said.

"It's all ri..." but the words dried up in Jack's mouth.

"What is it?" Annie asked.

Jack pointed across the sand. There, sloshing their way out of the surf were two bedraggled girls.

"Holy shit – is that...?" Annie gasped.

"Yeah," was all Jack could say as they walked across to meet them,

"Rosalind? Veronica? Are you..." he struggled for the words and ended up simply asking,

"Are you all right?"

"We were swept off the rocks with our dad and Katy – are they okay?"

"Ummm..." Jack didn't know what to say or where to start.

"They got out fine," said Annie, stepping in. It was the truth, even if it was thirty years old, "But what about you? Are *you* all right?"

"I'm f-f-freezing!" Veronica stammered, her lips looking rather blue for Annie's liking.

"Come here," Annie said, opening her arms, "I'm nice and warm."

With the unquestioning innocence of a pre-teen, Veronica walked up to her and clung on tight, shivering. Annie made a noise like someone stepping into cold water and said,

"You're like a block of ice! Let's get you up to the house and get you a towel and a hot drink."

"You know our house?" asked Rosalind as they walked across the beach.

"Yes," Jack replied,

"We just arrived and we're going to be staying in the spare room. I know your parents," again, it was the truth, just not the whole truth.

"What's wrong with your shoulder?" Rosalind asked, looking at him shrewdly.

"I got hurt on the rocks. They're very sharp."

They were halfway up the path to the house, when a commanding voice shouted from above,

"Stop right there! Put the weapon down and raise your hands!"

They all looked up and stopped. A police officer in a bullet proof vest was pointing a pump action shotgun at them. Annie let the spear go and put up her hands. Jack raised one hand.

"My husband's been shot!" Annie called, "And these two girls have been swept off the rocks and need attention."

"Oh… Okay, walk slowly towards me. Hands where I can see 'em," said the officer, lowering the shotgun from his shoulder, and activating his walkie talkie,

"This is Simmonds, I've got a man here with a gunshot wound to the shoulder and two children requiring medical care," then to the group coming up the slope,

"You girls just follow me and keep lookin' straight ahead, okay?" and he led them around the side of the house towards the front.

Of course, the girls saw the bodies and started to panic,

"What's happened? Where are our parents? Are they all right?" Rosalind asked.

Jack couldn't think fast enough. His shoulder was throbbing horribly and his legs were starting to go,

"Um… it's… I…"

"They're safe," Annie said and strictly speaking it was true – nothing more could happen to them, even if it was because they were dead, "This was a terrorist attack, but it's over and your parents weren't here when it happened."

Rosalind gave her a look that said she didn't totally believe her, but the poor child was so cold and confused that she didn't have the strength to argue. Meanwhile, Veronica was an automaton, so cold that it was taking everything she had to put one foot in front of the other.

The front of the house was mayhem, with the four Mercedes blocking the drive, police cars, two ambulances and what looked like half the Bermuda Police Service crawling all over the place.

"Are those men dead...?"

"Yes," Jack said before Rosalind could finish, "But they were very bad men."

"Okay," Rosalind said, and then there was a swarm of medics around them, fussing, asking questions, putting thermal blankets around the girls and looking at Jack's shoulder. One team led the girls to one ambulance, while Jack was taken to the other. The police officer with the shotgun stayed with Jack and Annie, asking her questions while the paramedics tended to Jack's shoulder. Soon he was lying back in the ambulance with his shirt off, a dressing on his wound and an IV drip in his arm. Annie looked in on him,

"They're gonna take you to the hospital. They say you'll be fine, but they need to take a closer look. I've gotta go to police headquarters to give a statement," and then she lowered her voice, "What am I gonna say?"

"Tell them the truth," Jack replied. Annie looked at him in bewilderment,

"They'll lock me up as a crazy person!"

"No. Tell them to look in the cars. Rosalind and Veronica came straight from the airport, so one of them will have their passports in it. Now, the next bit's really important. In the coffee table in the living room, there's a photo album. At the back there are Veronica and Rosalind's old passports. That proves who they are. And it'll show the stamp from the last time they came. That's our evidence to show we're not crazy. Now, if you don't mind, I think I'm going to faint," then Jack slumped back into glorious oblivion.

Chapter Forty-Three

The Big Lie

Two days later, Jack found himself in a dull office in Police Headquarters outside Hamilton. He was in fresh clothes and his arm was in a sling. The pain was under control with happy pills and, all in all, he was in great shape after two good nights' sleep. The same could not be said for Chief Inspector Beresford, who was sitting across the desk from him. He was a big man with a face that looked like it was naturally cheery, but on that morning, it was anything but. 'Hassled' would be the best description of it. On the table were Rosalind and Veronica's old passports and the current passports, taken from their car. Each was in its own clear plastic evidence bag.

"So, you're backing up your wife's story about creatures from the sea possessing your sisters thirty years ago."

"Yes," Jack nodded.

"And that you were able to send them back to the sea by stabbing them with a..." at this point he read from Annie's witness statement, "A bronze dagger dipped in David Kidd's blood – David Kidd being your father?"

"Yes... although I think there was more to it than just the blood. I hired a witch to create the potion. You'd have to ask her what else was in it," Jack replied as if he was saying nothing out of the ordinary.

"Yeah... the witch – how could I forget?" Beresford said, passing an exasperated hand across his dark, bald head,

"And her name is?"

Jack paused,

"I don't want to get her into trouble."

"What possible trouble could she get into? All I've got is six men who've committed suicide, and four more with no ID, who're refusing to talk. Plus, two kids who, according to their passports," and he held one up at Jack, "Are in their forties, have been missing on the island for thirty years, who don't remember any of it, and want to know where their mom and dad are."

"They really can't remember anything?"

"No," but by God, Chief Inspector Beresford wished they did.

"Thank goodness. Are they okay? You can tell me, I'm their younger brother."

"And that's the other thing – you, the thirty-something guy, are the *younger* brother of the fourteen and twelve-year-olds!" Beresford rubbed his face hard with his right hand,

"Come on, help me out, here!"

"What can I say? What my wife and I have told you is the truth. I know it sounds crazy, but given the facts you're looking at, how can you expect anything other than a crazy explanation?"

Beresford hated the fact that Jack was making sense. Fucked up sense, but sense, nevertheless. He decided to park that line of questioning and change tack to some real data that he could trust,

"Okay, we know for a fact that your wife arrived in Bermuda on Tuesday the twenty first and that you arrived later that day. We also know that two women in their forties arrived on the island Wednesday morning, accompanied by ten men. The women are, according to public record, your sisters Rosalind and Veronica. As of now, those two women in their forties have disappeared and six of the men they arrived with have killed themselves. Do you dispute any of that?"

"No," Jack replied.

"Good," at least there was something solid he could build from, "So, where are the two women now?"

Jack opened his mouth to speak, but Beresford interjected,

"And before you say they were dragged into the sea by weird tentacles, I want you to know that we've trawled the site a dozen times and found nothing."

Unfortunately, Jack was filled with the urge to laugh. Not to laugh at the policeman and not to laugh because it was funny. He wanted laugh like a lunatic, to let go of the constraints of sanity and release his emotions in joyous, manic laughter. Laughing at the madness of it all was clearly the sanest thing to do but, of course, it was also the course of action that would most likely see him put into a strait jacket. After a pause, during which he buried the urge to laugh, Jack replied,

"Strictly speaking, I only saw the sirens - that had been possessing the bodies of my sisters - get dragged into the sea by tentacles. Portuguese Man O'War tentacles, by the way. The forty-year-old bodies they'd been possessing disappeared while I was hugging my wife. So, we've got no idea what actually happened to the bodies... Sorry?" Jack could see from the gathering thunder of Beresford's face that this wasn't the reply he'd been hoping for. So much for building up from the known facts!

"Great!" Beresford exploded, "Just great! Okay, here's a real simple question for you – what did *you* do when you arrived in Bermuda?"

"I took a taxi straight to the house – I'm sure you can check that with the cabby's records,"

Beresford already had, and it checked out,

"Then I made myself at home and waited for the creatures that had possessed my sisters to arrive."

Beresford sighed in annoyance,

"And you were doing so well! One whole sentence without a mythical creature in it. And your wife, what did *she* do?"

"I don't know. I haven't discussed it with her."

"So, she wasn't with you at Cliff House?"

"No. But I can't say for sure what my wife's been doing since last Sunday. That's when we parted ways in London. I'm guessing that when she landed in Bermuda she went to the house, found the witch still there doing whatever she was doing, and then they left together."

"And why would they do that, instead of waiting until you arrived?"

"I don't know. You'd have to ask the witch," Jack replied equably.

"The witch whose name neither you nor your wife will give us," Beresford said, barely controlling his anger.

"It depends – is she going to get into trouble? You know, if it wasn't for her, those monsters would still be possessing my sisters." Jack said.

The circular interrogation was driving him crazy, and Beresford was about to finally lose it when there was a knock at the door.

"Yes?" Beresford barked, grateful for the excuse to raise his voice.

The door opened and an immaculately neat Constable poked his head in,

"Sorry to disturb you, sir, but the Commissioner wants to see you."

Beresford's face fell, then he composed himself and turned,

"Thank you, Constable. Keep an eye on this guy, would you?"

"Yes sir."

Beresford scooped up the passports in their evidence bags, stood and headed for the door. As he got there, Jack began,

"I'm really..."

"No!" Beresford said firmly, raising a finger, "Don't you dare say you're sorry. I don't need sympathy from you," then he slammed the door.

Yes, that felt good! He walked down the long corridor to the barred door at the end, was allowed out by the guard and left the building. It was bright outside and the light shining off the low, pale buildings of Police Headquarters hurt his eyes. He shielded them with one hand. He walked across to the building that housed the Commissioner's office, went through security and within a minute was telling Lily, his PA, that he was expected.

Lily, a petite woman in her mid-fifties, knocked on the Commissioner's door and opened without waiting for a reply.

"Chief Inspector Beresford here for you, sir."

"Thanks, Lil," said the Commissioner, who was sitting behind his desk.

Chief Inspector Beresford was slightly thrown by the fact that one of the elegant leather chairs in front of the Commissioner's desk was occupied by the Governor of Bermuda. She stood as he entered and offered her hand, which he shook,

"Good to see you again, Chief Inspector, I don't think we've seen each other since last year's Cup Match."

"Er, no ma'am."

"Beresford," said the Commissioner.

"Sir," said Beresford, then the Governor indicated that they should all sit down.

"We were talking about this case of yours," said the Governor in a middle-class London accent.

"Would you care to bring the Governor up to speed?" the Commissioner prompted.

No, he certainly would not!

"Of course," Chief Inspector Beresford smiled and outlined the case that he hoped wasn't about to sink his career.

After about fifteen minutes, he had finished.

"That's all pretty crazy," the Governor said with a smile.

Beresford wondered why the hell was she smiling. Did she know something he didn't?

"The problem is, we've got no hard evidence," Beresford continued,

"The six dead men all committed suicide. The only question mark is the one who apparently shot himself in the chest. The four men we're holding are refusing to talk, the girls remember nothing, the couple are sticking to their insane story and the two women have vanished."

"Right... good..." the Governor said contemplatively.

Good? What the hell was 'good' about anything Beresford had just said? Suddenly, Beresford suspected there were wheels turning within wheels. Why would the Governor – the King's representative on the island - be interested in any of this? In the thick silence, the penny dropped. Beresford prepared for the inevitable cover-up.

"Nobody wants a scandal," the Governor began and she was right – a scandal in a tax-haven does no one any good, least of all the British Government or the City of London,

"And it seems that the two missing women are in danger of causing a scandal that could rock the foundations of a number of countries. Since they disappeared, I have been informed by MI6 that there have been forty-three high profile suicides around the world – including two British MPs and a United States Senator. Many of them have been reported as accidents. All the men involved were known to have had liaisons with the missing women. According to MI6, this is just the tip of the iceberg. The last thing anybody needs is a protracted investigation," and she looked very deliberately into Beresford's eyes. Yes, he understood – no investigation was desired at all.

"Therefore, this is how we're going to play it," the Governor continued, "The men were never here. Those who are dead will be buried a long way out to sea. Those who are alive will be on a plane to the USA in the next two hours. Our American cousins believe they will be a fount of information if given the correct... encouragement."

The silence understood the resonance of those well-chosen words,

"The children will be free to go with their brother and his wife. They are being given the chance to live in any country of their choosing with no questions asked, no visas required. Except England. Too many people there might recognise them. Otherwise, they will be able to come and go wherever and whenever they please on condition of the strictest confidentiality. And he will change his name, so that the gossip magazines don't bother him. They seem like sensible people. I think they'll want to put this behind them."

The Commissioner and Beresford both nodded.

"As to the missing women, they have been on a yachting trip to the Bahamas and will be listed as late at five-o-clock this afternoon. From tomorrow, a high-profile search and rescue operation will take place. Nothing will be found. Their yacht will have disappeared. Another victim of the mysterious Bermuda Triangle. The end. Understand?" she finished firmly.

"Absolutely, ma'am," said the Commissioner with a smile.

"Er... yes," said Beresford. Even he was shocked at the size of the 'big lie'.

"I only need one thing from you, Chief Inspector," the Governor said, and he looked back at her with as much eagerness as he could muster,

"I need the name of the witch who helped them. If we do, indeed, have a pair of sirens lurking out there in the depths, we need to know how to keep them in check."

"Of course. That... makes sense," he replied, even though he couldn't think of a world in which *any* of it made sense.

"Get me the name of the witch and the next time we meet, I won't be able to call you 'Chief Inspector'," she smiled at his quizzical look,

"I'll have to call you 'Superintendent'."

Chapter Forty-Four

The Way Of The Witch

By three-o-clock the following afternoon, all the deals had been done, papers signed and Josephine had come in to talk to the authorities and then gone on her way. Finally, Annie, Jack and the girls were free to go. The drive back from Police Headquarters to Cliff House was short and quiet. Jack, Annie, Rosalind and Veronica were seated comfortably in the back of the Governor's limo, but they didn't say a word, although Jack noticed that the girls were exchanging meaningful glances. For his part, Jack wasn't sure where to start. How was he going to tell these kids that their parents were dead? Christ! It made him feel sick to his stomach. It was one thing to sign the deal and become their legal guardian, but it was something else to get on and do it. Annie felt a similar weight of expectation. Could she be a mother to them? How would it affect her relationship with Harry? How would it affect Harry? Suddenly going from only child to third child might warp his whole life! But what choice did they have? Jack was the girls' only living relative... and what would they be like? What had happened to them was enough to screw anyone up. What if she and Jack were walking into a disaster? Well, they were where they were. All they could do was trust each other, be loving and do their best.

The car dropped them off at the end of the drive and they walked up the slope to the house, bringing the silence with them from the car. Jack gave Annie an encouraging smile when they got to the house. He opened the door and let them in, then said,

"Shall we go into the living room for a little chat?"

"Okay," said Rosalind quietly, while Veronica nodded.

Oh boy! This was going to be impossible!

"Do either of you want a drink?" Annie asked.

"I'd like some chocolate milk, please," said Veronica. It was more than she'd said in one go since they'd come out of the water.

"Sure thing," said Annie, smiling,

"How about you, darling?" she turned to Rosalind,

"May I have the same, please?"

"Of course," Annie smiled. Wow – they were the politest kids she'd ever met.

"Be with you in a minute," she said to Jack and he led them into the living room.

Standing by the window, wearing a colourful, flowing dress was Josephine. When they entered, she turned to them and Veronica gasped,

"It's you!"

"Ronnie!" Rosalind hissed and Veronica clapped a hand to her mouth.

"This is Josephine," Jack said, even though he himself had only met her the previous afternoon when she'd come into Police Headquarters,

"Do you know her?"

Veronica shook her head.

"It's all right," Josephine said in a soft tone to the girls, "You don't have to worry about them. They know."

"How?" Rosalind asked.

"Because we've all been fighting the monsters together," Josephine replied.

"You mean we can tell and they won't think we're crazy?" Veronica asked with wide eyes.

"It can't be much crazier than what we've been through," said Jack.

"We thought that if we told, they'd lock us up," said Rosalind, and Jack could see hope kindling in her eyes.

"Don't worry, no one's going to lock you up," said Jack as Annie arrived with the chocolate milk,

"Come on, drink up and tell us."

The girls sat on the sofa and drank some milk while Jack and Annie drew their chairs closer. Rosalind began with what she thought was most important,

"We know that our mum and dad are dead. Daddy came to us not long ago. He was very sorry for what had happened, but he told us you were coming to rescue us. Is that what you did?"

"Yes," Jack said hoarsely. He suddenly had a lump in his throat and had to control his emotions.

"We know mummy died too, but that was a long time ago..." said Veronica,

"Or, it seems like a long time. We were in a place without time, so it's hard to tell."

"Limbo," Josephine whispered, "That's where you been."

"Mummy was very sad when she visited us. She cried a lot, but I think it was good for her to see us before she went into the dark," said Rosalind.

"And then we saw Josephine and she told us you wouldn't be long," Veronica said.

"On the afternoon I met Annie," Josephine said, "We went back to my place and I took a draught made with yarrow to help me travel in the astral realm. I had to focus all my energy, but eventually I found these two."

"Those things that drowned us – did you kill them?" Rosalind asked.

"I'm afraid not," Jack admitted, "Apparently humans can't kill immortal beings."

"But he and Annie banished them to limbo for a long, long time. Your father helped me create some powerful magic and now they're wishin' they hadn't messed with us," said Josephine.

Both the girls smiled at this.

"So, you really are our little brother, Jasper?" Veronica asked,

"Yes," he said, "Do you want to have a hug?"

He'd hardly said the words when the two girls leapt on him in a flash. And then the tears came in a flood. All the unbearable feelings they'd had for so long cascaded from them. Jack was crying too – partly as a release from the last hellish week, partly out of relief, and partly in deep sadness at everything that had happened to his family since that day thirty years ago.

Annie and Josephine joined them, and Jack disappeared under them all. They held each other for a long time - survivors from a wreck, clinging to the board that has saved them right up until they're safe on a new shore.

Finally, they broke apart, wiping tears away. Annie went to the kitchen and brought back a roll of kitchen paper so they could all clean themselves up properly. Jack blew his nose loudly. Now that the ice was broken and they knew they could be themselves, the girls became more like the ones he'd seen in the family album. They'd had a long time to come to terms with their mother's death and seemed to be taking their father's as well as could be hoped. What filled Jack with hope as they talked was the excitement they had for whatever the future might bring. While twenty of his last thirty years had been filled with a lot of physical and emotional pain, theirs had been a void. Now they wanted to fill that with all the experiences they could. And ice cream.

Like all good parties, the five of them ended up in the kitchen, sitting around the table eating ice cream. With the tub of chocolate gone, half the strawberry and half the salted caramel, even Veronica finally had to call it quits.

"If I have any more, I'll be sick," she said, pushing her bowl and spoon away as if their proximity might tip her over the edge.

"It's a shame you grew up," said Rosalind looking at Jack, "We really enjoyed playing with you. You were so cute."

"Thanks," said Jack. He just couldn't get over how lovely they were - how very, very different to the girls he had grown up with.

"Well, you're in luck," said Annie, "'Cos we've got a little boy called Harry."

"Wow! That's brilliant!" Rosalind exclaimed.

"Where is he?" asked Veronica.

"In Boston with his grandmother."

"When can we see him?"

"As soon as we've got everything sorted out here."

"What does he look like?" Rosalind asked.

"A lot like Jack when he was little," Annie replied.

"Poor kid!" Jack interjected.

"Why do you call him Jack?" Rosalind asked Annie.

"Because that's the only name I've ever known him by."

Jack explained how the name came about.

"Should we call you Jack?" Veronica asked.

"Fine by me," he replied.

"You can call me Annie."

"And we'll call you Aunty Josephine," Rosalind said.

Josephine laughed,

"Yes, that works for me."

Once the girls had gone (reluctantly) to bed, Jack brought the bottle of Lagavulin to the kitchen table and opened it with great ceremony. He filled three glasses.

"We need a toast," he said,

"But I don't feel that 'To Victory' is right. They will come back eventually."

"How about 'New Beginnings'?" Annie suggested.

"Perfect! To New Beginnings!" Jack said, looking into their eyes as he clinked glasses with them.

They drank and Josephine crinkled her nose,

"That's strong stuff!"

"Sorry, it's an acquired taste – lots of iodine and peat in there," Jack said, "We've got some Black Seal if you prefer."

"No, I'll give this another whirl" said Josephine, pushing her empty glass towards Jack, who filled it. Josephine took a more considered sip,

"It's good."

"It's even better with some quality smoked salmon," said Jack.

"I'll bet!" Josephine laughed, then she allowed her smile to naturally dissipate and she looked at Jack seriously,

"Gimme your hands," she requested and he complied, "Oh yeah, you got it, all right. You got it strong!"

"What?" asked Annie with a worried look.

"Your husband has The Power. He has the potential to be a witch if he wants."

"Jack?" Annie exclaimed.

Josephine nodded.

"My Jack? Jack who spends his days drawing and making pretty pictures for websites?"

"One and the same. And I think you feel it, don't you, Jack?"

"Yes. I never did before coming to Bermuda, but now... something inside me has woken up. I had a very strange incident here on Tuesday night," he said and, in low tones that were almost a whisper, he described what had happened with the mirror.

As he spoke, the air seemed to thicken around them. He hadn't been able to tell Annie about it, but the fascination in her eyes reassured him that she didn't think he'd gone mad.

"I guess you didn't share that story with the police?" she said when he'd finished.

"As they say in England – not on your nelly," he answered.

"You see?" said Josephine brightly, "You got The Power! Even experienced witches would struggle to do what you did, and yet you did that on your first day of awakening. Incredible!" Josephine was impressed and, if she was being honest with herself, quite jealous,

"What you gonna do with it, Jack? That's the question."

"I don't know. What should I do?"

"Well, you've got yourself two choices. First, you can bury it. Ignore it completely and live wholeheartedly in the physical world. You will always have it, but it will wither and weaken, like a sad houseplant that's not being tended. You'll have a good life, but you might find there are moments when you feel a bit sad, like there's an empty space somewhere inside you. Second, you can work it, like you've worked those big muscles of yours," and she reached over and gave his left bicep a squeeze,

"Then you'll be strong in this world and the others. New universes will open up for you and you'll be able to live a truly fulfilled life."

"But if I take that road, isn't there a risk of more things like the mirror happening?" Jack asked.

"Ah, yes... that's the problem you've got. See, without meaning to, you've announced yourself to the world beyond. It is known what you are, and sometimes that's very attractive to the things that live beyond the physical world."

"So, Jack could be a target?" Annie asked.

"In a way, yes, but you can protect yourselves. We – I mean me and my coven – can provide you with amulets and other devices to protect you, your home and your family. Because these things from beyond are usually cowards. They don't go for the person with the most power. They'll get to you through your loved ones. That's one reason why kids and teenagers are most likely to be possessed – they're easier targets."

"Shit!" said Jack, "I thought this would be an end to it."

"And if Jack does nothing, then all of us still have targets painted on our backs, but he'd have no means of protecting us?" Annie asked.

"Yeah, pretty much."

"Bugger!" Jack said and took a shot of whisky.

"And I hate to ladle on more, but your sisters also have The Power. Not like you, but they got it. It's most likely the only reason they survived the possession. And now they've been in limbo, they'll be attracting attention, too," Josephine said regretfully.

"This gets better and better!" Annie couldn't hide her annoyance, "Sorry, Josy, that's not directed at you. It's those bitches. Even when they're gone, they're a pain in the ass," then another thought occurred to her,

"Oh Jeez – what about Harry? Could he have this Power, too?"

"Could be. You never know until you meet someone."

"Dammit. This Power sounds a lot like a curse," Annie didn't like the way her fun, active life looked like it was going to turn into some weird version of Harry Potter.

"No, no," Josephine's soothing voice had an immediate calming effect, "The Power and learning to use it doesn't take over everything. Look at me. Ninety percent of the time, I'm a historian with a respected job at the Museum. The other ten percent, I'm a witch. Each person strikes the balance that's right for them."

"Okay," Annie said, "I don't think you got much choice here, Kiddo. Be a sitting duck and hope everything leaves you alone, or build up your abilities so you can kick ass and take names. I know which I'd rather do."

Jack laughed,

"You sure you don't mind?"

"No... but if any of you calls me a muggle, you'll get a sock in the eye," Annie said, brandishing a fist.

All three of them laughed and Jack poured another round.

"Here's to taking a step into the great beyond," said Jack.

Once they'd touched glasses and drunk, Josephine took on a conspiratorial look and added,

"There is a big plus to all this, Annie – sex with witches is incredible. You're gonna love it!"

"Amen to that!" Annie cried, raising and then draining her glass before rapping it on the table, "Bar keep! Come on! No shirking!"

Jack laughed,

"You sure? This'll give you a killer hangover."

"Listen, Kiddo, I've drunk home-distilled Raksi in Nepal that could strip paint, now come on!"

Jack filled her glass.

"And I'm still gonna call you Kiddo, even though you're now Mister Hicks."

"Works for me," he said and picked up her left hand and kissed it.

"That reminds me," said Josephine, "Can I take a look at the charm that Goody made?"

"'Course," said Jack, taking off the necklace and handing it to her.

Josephine's eyes studied the little porpoise greedily.

"Yes... yes... Goody was a remarkable witch. The power in this is... it's like nothing I've ever seen."

"Goody?" Annie asked.

"Distant relative," Jack replied, "I'll tell you later."

"Wow!" Josephine exclaimed as she handed back the necklace, "I've got a high standard to try to emulate."

"You gonna make one?" asked Annie, who was beginning to get blurry from the Lagavulin.

"Me and the coven are gonna go into production. By the time the sirens come back, Bermuda will be ready for 'em."

"So, they will come back?"

"Yeah. And they ain't gonna be happy. See, what you gotta remember is, for immortals, two hundred years in limbo is like five minutes on the naughty step. That won't worry 'em. What'll hurt is knowing they've been bested by mere mortals like us. That'll rankle 'em good. They'll come back meaner'n ever, but they're gonna get a surprise."

Chapter Forty-Five

An Ending?

"Hurry up! You don't wanna be late for your first day!" Annie called from the bottom of the stairs.

"Coming!" chorused Rosalind and Veronica from their rooms two floors above.

Annie listened – yes, there it was, the rumble of stampeding feet.

"Okay, let's go! Let's go!" she urged waving them from the bottom of the stairs towards the open front door and the awaiting Ford Bronco.

"Hey, don't forget to kiss Harry," said Jack, carrying him into the hall from the kitchen. The girls stopped momentarily, gave him a kiss and fussed over him and then Annie ushered them out. They bundled into the car, which roared into life and Annie pulled away with a squeal of tyres.

"Such a child!" Jack muttered, shaking his head,

"Yes, your mommy is as much a child as you!" he said to Harry, who wriggled to be let down,

"And... away," Jack said as he put him on the ground, then Harry was off to make more mess on the sitting room floor.

Jack looked out at the neat, 'alpine' front garden and breathed in the air. Even with the Bronco's residue still hanging in the air, it beat the hell out of New York's pollution soup. Jack came back in and shut the front door.

Yes, a lot had changed since February. They had stayed in Cliff House for a month after it was all over. Nancy and Harry had joined them after a couple of days and he'd immediately taken to his new big sisters. They'd loved him to bits from first sight and were happy to tell Jack that Harry was even cuter and more fun than he'd been as a baby. Typical big sisters! They took a week to rest up, and then they'd thrown themselves into admin and planning. With the help of the Governor's office, they'd been able to neatly transfer control of the Mazzoni fashion empire to Giulia, who had been joyous,

"You are a beautiful man, Jack!" she'd almost shouted down the phone, "You are always welcome in Como,"

"Thanks, Giulia."

"You ski, yes?"

"Well, Annie and I snowboard."

"Okay, so keep New Year free. You come and stay at my place in Madesimo. It's a small resort, but it's fun and if the snow's good, there is off-piste to test the best. I do not accept 'no' as an answer!" and Jack had visualised the belligerent set of her face from the tone of her voice.

"Okay, it's a date!" Jack had laughed. Later, when he'd told Annie and the girls, they'd all been overjoyed.

Helping Skylar Judd had been more complicated. She'd been in a dark place and needed more than cash in the bank to help her. The effort they'd put into creating a support network around her was now paying dividends and in the last conversation he'd had with her, she'd sounded upbeat for the first time. Jack had high hopes that she would turn it all around. Sadly, the same couldn't be said for Mary Brewer. She'd been one of the sirens' last victims - as well as one of their first. She had apparently 'hanged herself', but Jack knew that wasn't her style. Maz would either have blown her head off with her shotgun or literally drowned herself in a bath of Famous Grouse. Style. That would've been Maz's way, not hanging herself from the bannisters with electric flex. She would have balked at the banality of it. Jack wished he could track down the killer, but there was nothing he could do. He couldn't return to England ever again and, frankly, was very happy not to. They would simply have to mourn Maz and wish her well in the next life. Another side of not being able to return to Britain was having to sell his grandparents' house. It made him sad, but it had to be done. England was now nothing more than memories and most of them were ones he had locked up tightly in boxes and stored in the deepest parts of his mind. After the admin was done, Jack had concentrated on learning how to control his Power. He had joined Josephine's coven and they had had some fun evenings. He'd got to know Patty, Becca, Denise and Fred very well. In fact, there'd been some moments when it had seemed that Patty and Denise were residents of Cliff House, they'd been over so much. It had been an exciting time – especially when Josephine had confirmed that Harry also had The Power. Again, Annie had threatened them with physical violence if the word 'muggle' was ever used to describe her. Then, there'd been the small matter of what to do next...

Jack wandered through their new house - a light, spacious modern-looking place that was barely five years old - picking up toys as he went and thinking about how they'd come to their decision. Without the financial need to work, Jack decided he would become the anchor parent, while continuing to draw, paint and develop as a witch. Jack smiled at the thought. If someone had told him on New Year's Day 2023 that by August, he'd give up work to concentrate on witchcraft, he'd have thought they were soft in the head. But that's what he was doing and his decision left Annie free to carry on with her career. A big positive was that because she'd never really been office-based, it gave them the chance to choose anywhere. They decided to stay in the States. For starters, that would make it easier to see Nancy and Doctor Bob. Yes, even though he'd drugged half the family and tried to kill Annie, they forgave him for the simple reason that, until Rosalind had bewitched him, he'd been absolutely lovely.

"And a great lay," Nancy had added when they'd been debating what to do. Annie had made retching noises.

So, they would stay in America, but where? They looked at maps with the children and finally decided on somewhere that ticked their boxes.

Jack went upstairs and threw the toys into Harry's toybox and caught the view of Peak 8 of the Tenmile Range through the window. Yes, Breckenridge, Colorado, ticked all their boxes. It offered the kids a clean, outdoorsy lifestyle, access to skiing, hiking and climbing, an amazing school in nearby Frisco, and it wasn't *too* far from a decent airport. Finally, it had two features they had all agreed were essential: it was over six thousand feet above sea level and the nearest ocean was seven hundred miles away.

THE END.

Afterword

Please review this book!

Reviews make a huge difference to the success of a book, so if you enjoyed The Bermuda Covenant, please consider leaving a review on Amazon or your favourite book review site. I'd very much appreciate it.

If you want to see what I'm up to, then you can find me on Facebook

I try to keep news about what I'm having for lunch (with pictures) to an absolute minimum, but if I'm having something incredible, I do reserve the right to post it.

Or, if Facebook isn't your scene, you could throw yourself into the abyss of chaos that is my website VJNash.com

There, if you are brave enough, you can sign up for my newsletter with exclusive info on what's coming up and access to the occasional short story.

Made in United States
North Haven, CT
08 June 2024

53365867R00275